INSURRECTION
AT 1600 PENNSYLVANIA AVE

Best Wishes!
Rob Taney
July '19

INSURRECTION
AT 1600 PENNSYLVANIA AVE

ROB TENERY, MD

BROWN BOOKS
PUBLISHING GROUP

© 2017 Rob Tenery, MD

All rights reserved. No part of this book may be used or reproduced in any manner without written permission except in the case of brief quotations embodied in critical articles or reviews.

This is a work of fiction. Any similarity to real persons, living or dead, is coincidental and not intended by the author.

Insurrection at 1600 Pennsylvania Avenue

Brown Books Publishing Group
16250 Knoll Trail Drive, Suite 205
Dallas, Texas 75248
www.BrownBooks.com
(972) 381-0009
A New Era in Publishing®

ISBN 978-1-61254-946-0
LCCN 2016953359

Printed in the United States
10 9 8 7 6 5 4 3 2 1

For more information or to contact the author, please go to www.RobTeneryMD.com.

I want to dedicate my book to my wife, Janet Forrest J. Tenery, and to my editor who taught me how to tell my stories, David Groff.

*My appreciation to Milli Brown and her team,
who helped me turn my dreams into reality.*

PROLOGUE

AT 8:10 P.M. A GARBLED MESSAGE came through to the emergency room's front desk. The message mentioned a cardiac arrest, a female in her late fifties. The rest of the information would arrive with the ambulance.

"Doctor Russell, probable Code Blue en route!" the triage nurse spat out over the intercom that piped vital information to every nook and cranny of the emergency department. Dan Russell's pulse quickened at the message. The emergency-room physician had begun his shift at three o'clock; he was due off at eleven. He put the finishing touches on the torn lip of a very nervous fourteen-year-old who had tried to separate her poodle puppy and a Dalmatian that had found a way out of its yard down the street. He patted the child on the head. "Within two weeks, you'll look as good as new," he said. "Next time, don't try to play referee."

Insurrection at 1600 Pennsylvania Avenue

Russell had moved toward the front to complete the discharge papers on his young patient when the emergency-room doors flung open, shattering the relative calm and startling the staff. Outside lights streamed in from all directions. Surprisingly the first people through the doors were not the paramedics with a patient on a stretcher, but the police. Except for the time he attended the funeral of a policeman who had died in the line of duty when Russell was back in medical school in Tucson, Russell had never seen so many officers together at one time.

These officers seemed almost frantic. Guns drawn, they fanned out, spilling into all areas of the emergency room. Russell put up his hand to stop one of the red-faced officers from entering the small cubicle where the young girl and her mother were gathering their belongings. His effort was to no avail as the surly cop pushed him aside.

In less than ninety seconds, the all clear went out. It came from the police lieutenant, who had placed himself squarely in front of the entry door. As Russell stepped aside, four men armed with automatic military weapons sprang through the door. "Who's the doctor in charge?" the first man shouted, his temples pulsating as his squinted eyes surveyed the area. Russell's mouth went dry.

Russell realized that these four were not police officers, at least not in the conventional sense. Similar in size and build, each wore a dark gray suit and tie with a white shirt, and each man sported a clear cord that exited one ear and then curled down the neck before disappearing under his coat collar.

Russell, aware he was no longer in control of the emergency room, reluctantly stepped forward. "I am," he answered, trying to mask the tremor in his voice. The man who had barked the question moved toward him. Russell had the urge to move back but stood his ground. "I'm in charge. Do you think you might let me in on what's coming down here?" He forced out the words in an attempt to assert his authority.

As the man grew close, Russell had a better look at him. He was shocked to see that the man seemed as frightened as he was. He could tell it from his eyes, which contained a look he had seen in patients thousands of times. But like Russell, he appeared to be trying desperately conceal his fear.

"Listen, Doctor, I have a very sick patient out there. A wreck closed the freeway to Parkland Hospital, so they diverted us here. I need your help to try to save her. Now!" It seemed as if the man in the suit was doing all he could to keep control of his emotions, which made Russell nervous since the man was holding a large automatic weapon under his arm.

Russell motioned to the trauma room. "Take the patient in there. I'll see what we can do." The tightness still tugged at his chest and he felt his pulse drop a notch or two. "I can do a lot more if you could just give me some type of history."

The man in the suit either did not hear Russell's request or did not want to. He whirled around and motioned to the police officer still standing by the front entrance. "In there," he said, stabbing his finger toward the trauma room.

By this time the uniformed police officers had placed themselves strategically throughout the emergency room as if they were standing guard. The few patients who happened to be at this wrong place at the wrong time remained huddled where they were. The men in suits raced into the trauma room and took up positions in each corner. Along with the continual moan of the incoming sirens, Russell thought he could hear the whirring of a helicopter somewhere off in the distance.

The paramedics swept through the entrance. There were three of them. They were almost sprinting as they shoved the gurney loaded with the patient into the trauma room. One was carrying what appeared to be a toolbox. Although the cool night air had dropped the temperature into the upper forties, Russell could tell the paramedics were sweating profusely, as were the men in the suits.

Without saying a word, they flung loose the two straps that held the patient safely on the stretcher. The paramedics were barely in position when they grabbed the woman and lifted her onto the emergency-room table. The nurse flicked on the overhead operating lights, which illuminated the patient's head and upper torso.

Russell rushed to the bedside and began to examine the patient. An external defibrillator was already attached to her chest. The device was one of the newer automatic models, doing the job of propelling the blood out of the heart and to the vital organs since the patient's own heart was apparently unable to perform this necessary function on its own. He remembered that when the device was first introduced it had been controversial, but numerous studies since had demonstrated its improved efficiency over the conventional hands-on method. The machine was now standard on all emergency vehicles and even on most commercial airplanes.

Putting the stethoscope first on one side and then the other of the patient's chest, Russell next checked to make sure the endotracheal tube coming out of the patient's mouth was in the proper position. He nodded, then removed the stethoscope from his ears. The paramedics had done their job well. He glanced at the Ambu bag, which one of the paramedics compressed at regular intervals—the device forced lifesaving oxygen into the patient's lungs. The IV inserted in her right forearm was barely running. Russell signaled to the emergency nurse, and she took the saline-filled plastic bag from the paramedic's shoulder and hung it up higher on the portable stand.

"We did everything we could, Doc," the frustrated paramedic said, looking at Russell as they moved around the table.

Russell had spent his entire professional career learning how to assess rapidly a patient's condition, even without having the benefit of a good history. It was the one ability that separated a great emergency-room physician from a good one.

Although you would not expect this level of expertise in a small, relatively quiet emergency room such as Irving Central, Russell was a great one, a natural. And he knew it. Even in his early days as a resident, he had an uncanny ability to glean out the most critical problems so they could be treated first.

"Can you tell me anything about her?" Russell asked, glancing at one of the paramedics. He did not wait for the answer, noting the patient was small to medium build, probably about one hundred ten pounds, and Russell guessed in her late fifties, as reported earlier.

A sudden gasp of air clogged his throat. He had seen that face before . . .

1

His smudged fingernails, grotesquely long and unkempt, tapped nervously on the remote control as the television blinked from channel to channel. Almost the same story showed up on every channel. "Do they think all the audience cares about is him?" the man asked, his thick accent laced with coarseness from his continuous smoking habit.

The man's sound, muffled only by the volume control of his tuner, deafened the two men watching the television in the Manhattan apartment that night. In the background on the screen, almost drowned out by the roar of the immense crowd with their blaring air horns, the band played "The Star-Spangled Banner." Thousands of multicolored balloons had just been released from giant nets suspended above the raucous delegates. Coupled with the streamers and countless bags of confetti, they created an awesome sight. In political circles, they referred to the extravaganza as "controlled chaos." The behind-the-scenes operatives had spent months of careful planning to make it look spontaneous. Television cameras throughout the mammoth Denver Convention Center honed in as the president, standing atop the platform, raised both arms in victory. Watching in their darkened room, the two viewers could plainly see the crowd loved him. The delegates' hero, the man who would carry their banner, had just been nominated by their party for a second term as the most powerful political leader in the world.

"His election won't be automatic," the man, nestled in his smoky haze, said with a snort as he flicked his ashes in the direction of the overfilled ashtray that balanced precariously on the edge of the sofa beside him. "But I hear in your Las Vegas there're only a few poor souls taking bets against him." Exhaling a plume of smoke above his head, he turned to the oversize figure seated on the sofa beside him just as he caught a fleeting glimpse of the vice president and her husband, slightly left of center stage. They would not be featured in the picture, for this was President Raymond Winslet's moment.

Two hard-fought campaigns and almost four years of one-hundred-hour workweeks had earned him that spot of honor atop the speaker's platform. The unprecedented national coalition that had fallen in behind former President George W. Bush after terrorists obliterated the sanctity of American soil had finally evaporated, as the country's insatiable appetite for economic comfort began once again to trump the concern for safety. Although many considered Bush's crusade against the nomads of fear to be a success, America's lingering fiscal constraints eroded public sympathy and left the country's silent majority searching for new hope.

Searching for a close-up picture of the vice president, the man in the Manhattan apartment roamed the channels as President Winslet turned to his wife, Sharon, who was standing just behind him with their two children, and kissed her. The man knew the president's curriculum vitae by heart.

Insurrection at 1600 Pennsylvania Avenue

Five years ago, when Winslet, then a representative from Colorado, had announced his run for the presidency only a few gave him much of a chance. But the nation was still languishing in the funk of September 11, 2001, and wanted to move in a different direction. Eight years of Barack Obama's administration and four more under Donald Trump failed to restore the nation's confidence to the level that prevailed prior to the destruction of New York City's Twin Towers.

The renewal turned out to be young Congressman Winslet. After narrow defeats in the first two primaries, he never lost another election. Tonight would most likely propel him into a second term and alongside the great presidents of history. But only if the plan failed. The plan, carefully mapped out by those whom President George W. Bush had exiled into the anonymity of darkness, would not fail. The man in the Manhattan apartment and his fellow operatives would see to that.

The occupants of the darkened room held their collective breath as the president looked to his left in the direction of Vice President Rosalyn Delstrotto. Their briefing on her had been more extensive than on the president. The daughter of a leader in the underground opposition who sneaked his family out of Communist Poland in the early 1950s to avoid reprisals, Delstrotto had served her president and the country well over the preceding four years. She had earned her place at the table. A brilliant negotiator, she thought better on her feet than anyone else who surrounded the president. And if the successes of the next term came even close to the preceding one, Rosalyn Delstrotto, affectionately called Rosie by her friends, had a real chance of becoming the first woman president of the United States.

Jabbing at his remote, the man with the cigarette finally locked the picture on the shot he had been waiting for, a full-body view of the vice president. Given the forced smile painted across her face, only the trained eye could have detected a problem as she took her place alongside the president. Leaning heavily on her husband, Delstrotto made the final steps, almost groping her way to the center of the platform. Barring that one station, the television cameras continued to focus most of their attention on the president and his family.

But two thousand miles away from the Denver convention site, in the high-rise apartment overlooking downtown Manhattan, the unkempt foreigner and his obese accomplice did take notice. "It's working," he said, his tobacco-stained teeth barely visible in the subdued light.

The two sat mesmerized by the events unfolding on the television in front of them. They fixed their attention on the screen, watching as the two first families stood together, united in purpose.

"Did they say how long it would take?" the rotund figure asked, chewing a date thoughtfully.

"Patience, my friend," the other man answered, pulling a drag from his ever-present cigarette. "Our day will come."

. . .

The president's chief of staff blew a thin stream of smoke out the small crack he had opened in his window. Chad Madden glanced nervously toward the closed door to his outer office. He had tried to quit smoking on numerous occasions, but each time he failed, going back to his old habit with yet another promise to try again at some future date. He felt like a five-year-old child, afraid his mother would catch him, as he hastily drew another drag off his cigarette. Only this time it was the president of the United States who had laid down the law: no smoking in the White House as long as he was in office. Not willing to pass up the greatest opportunity of his career, Madden reluctantly agreed . . . well, almost.

"Mr. Madden," the operator said over the intercom. "Jason Clark is on line four, calling from *Air Force Two*. He said it's an emergency."

"Put a hold on any other calls and tell the Joint Chiefs of Staff that I will be with them in a few minutes." Madden snuffed his cigarette, sliding the makeshift ashtray back to its usual spot at the far corner of his top drawer, and punched in line four, reserved for those people who had a special relationship with the first assistant to the most powerful political figure in the world.

"Jason, I thought you and the vice president were on the way to the West Coast?" For a moment Madden thought Clark had dropped the telephone. He could hear yelling and what sounded like utter chaos in the background. It chilled him.

"Chad, I can barely hear you. All hell has broken loose here." Clark's speech was rushed, agitated.

Madden cupped his hand over his other ear, trying to make sense out of the ragged words coming through the line over the airplane's roar.

"She may be dead," Clark cried.

Madden shuddered as visions of a blood-spattered airplane flashed before his eyes. Had terrorism once again pierced the nation? Was Clark talking about the vice president?

"Jason, what in the hell are you telling me? Are you talking about Delstrotto?" An alarm was going off in the background on the plane. He pulled open the center drawer of his desk. At the back was a set of buttons attached to recording devices hooked up to all the lines that went through the Oval Office as well as to the chief of staff. They had first been installed by President Truman in the late 1940s. The equipment had been updated and replaced several times since then, but the purpose remained the same—to record any telephone conversation that the listener wanted. What made the system different from most was the lack of beeping that was usually present on recorded calls. The underhandedness may have been a violation of the caller's privacy rights, but this was the White House, and often its occupants made their own set of rules. This was the way it had been done for over eighty years and it was not about to change with President Winslet's administration.

Static crackled through the telephone as Madden pushed the fourth button and closed the drawer. He covered the receiver with his palm and hit the intercom button with the other. Jason was yelling, or crying, to someone.

"Get me the president, stat! I don't care what he's doing," Madden snapped to his assistant. "Jason, try to calm down and tell me what's going on. I'll get to the president as soon as we hang up."

"I'm not sure," Clark answered. "The vice president had some kind of convulsion and . . . well, you know she's been acting sort of strange for the last week or so. I told you about it the other day."

Madden was embarrassed he did not remember, but he was not about to tell that to his colleague. "Sure," Madden answered. "Go on."

"Well, about fifteen minutes ago, she just fell out of her seat and started having a seizure. I was just across the aisle from her. I want to tell you it scared the hell out of me! Fortunately, the paramedic was right there." Remembering Vice President Cheney's heart condition, Madden had suggested years earlier that someone with medical knowledge travel with Delstrotto.

Madden was getting more and more agitated. "What in the hell is going on, now?" he demanded.

"She wasn't breathing, so the EMT put a tube in her throat. Then he strapped this machine on her that automatically pressed on her chest to keep her heart pumping. He's also got an IV going and has given her a lot of medicines, but so far nothing."

"Jason, what do you mean, nothing?"

Jason's voice was trembling. "From what I can tell, and I'm no doctor, she hasn't responded. I tell you, this thing makes me sick to my stomach. Fortunately the EMT has been talked through the procedure by an emergency-room doctor from Parkland—the big county hospital in Dallas. If he wasn't here, they'd have to give *me* cardiac resuscitation instead."

"Why Parkland?" Madden asked.

"Because it's the closest major medical center. It's where they took Kennedy, you know. We're being given special clearance to land at Dallas/Fort Worth International Airport and should be on the ground within ten minutes. There's an ambulance standing by to evacuate the vice president to the hospital. I think they should have taken her in by helicopter, but evidently one was pulled out of duty because of some sort of mechanical problem and the other two were already out on other emergencies. They tell me the only ones left belong to the Dallas police or the local media types and they're too small to transport patients. That's not worth a shit, if you ask me, for a city of this size. If I had my way, I'd kick someone else out and come get the vice president."

"I'll talk to the president immediately. The Joint Chiefs of Staff are waiting. I'm sure this will give them something to grumble over. They're always looking for a new conspiracy." Madden clicked off the recording device. "I want an immediate update as soon as you know anything else. What about her husband, Ben, and the rest of the Delstrotto family?"

"In all the commotion, I forgot. I haven't contacted them."

"Keep it that way. Get Rosie to Parkland before you alert anybody else."

Feeling an ache deep in his chest for the lady who had taken on the role of the nation's mother, Madden laid down the telephone. He could only hope that his friend was overreacting about the vice president's condition. Somehow he doubted it.

Jason Clark and Chad Madden went back a long way. Madden's degree was in international business, Clark's in political science. Madden had served a brief stint with General Motors' European division but quickly decided he felt more comfortable helping craft legislation than finding ways to get around it. Washington, DC, was his logical destination.

Still intoxicated with the ideals of ivory-tower liberalism, Clark also made a beeline to the nation's capitol. From opposite ends of the country, the two men arrived on the doorstep of the conservative senator from California almost simultaneously. But changing sides was politics, where the lines between the political ideologies blurred on both sides of the aisle on Capitol Hill.

Those days were long behind them. After the next election cycle and a failed marriage for each of them, they were now seasoned Capitol veterans. Their careers had taken different paths, however. Madden next worked for a still wet-behind-the-ears congressman from Colorado—the very same congressman who, to the surprise of Washington's prognosticators, was elected president on the wave of national discontent over the war on terrorism. When it came time for the new president to pick a chief of staff, Madden's name was at the top of the list.

Meanwhile Clark took an unexpected and unexplained leave of absence from the Washington scene. When he returned six months later, claiming he had needed to find himself by living alone in the Sierra Nevadas, Clark pressured Madden to place a few calls on his behalf. Madden never fully accepted Clark's explanation of his time away, but, as with so many other issues in the nation's capital, knew there were some things better left alone. In his new position, Madden was able to get his old friend taken on as a personal adviser to Vice President Delstrotto. The rest was history.

Madden snapped to his feet, putting his own anguish aside. The door to Madden's office closed as he headed to the conference room across the hall from the Oval Office. The Joint Chiefs of Staff were waiting.

. . .

A familiar ring went off. It was the ten-year-old iPhone that the senator always carried in his coat pocket, his constant connection to the outside world. Even though communication technology had leapfrogged, the senator had not. He claimed a vague connection to tradition, as if the phone was like an old smoking jacket. The truth was that he was mechanically challenged.

"Yes," the senator answered abruptly.

"Our sources have confirmed that *Air Force Two* was diverted to Dallas/Fort Worth International Airport. Someone was taken off on a stretcher to a waiting ambulance. We can't be a hundred percent about this because we have not been able to confirm with our person on the inside, but more than likely it was the vice president."

The senator leaned back in his rocker. A smile came to his lips. The view was spectacular from his back porch, which looked out over Chesapeake Bay. That night the water was dotted with lights as the most dedicated sailors undertook the finishing touches for the next day's regatta.

"Call me when you find out more," the senator said. "Let's keep these conversations to less than thirty seconds." He pushed the red *end* button, and the portable telephone went silent. A small green light flashed across the top left corner of the screen every two seconds. The telephone was ready when the next message came through.

So was the senator.

2

"IS THIS THE VICE . . . ?" Dr. Dan Russell called out to the Secret Service officer who stood by the door to the trauma room.

The man in the dark suit nodded. "I'm afraid it is," he answered, his eyes begging for help.

As the son of a very successful pediatrician in Dayton, Ohio, Russell had planned to follow in his father's footsteps when he graduated from medical school. But he was a risk taker. So when the opportunity to go into emergency medicine came along, it seemed like a perfect fit, preferable to the endless snotty noses and crouping babies of his father's practice.

That was twenty years and five hospitals ago. He drifted to the Dallas area when a position at Irving Central opened up. It had not been his first choice, since Russell enjoyed the action of a busier emergency room. That was over two years ago. During that time, three positions had been vacated at other, busier hospitals, but Russell turned them all down. Even though his boss was something of a prick, he felt comfortable where he was. The emergency room staff was like his extended family. He was reluctant to move back into the fast lane.

Tonight he would not have a choice.

Russell spun back to the patient. Seeing her lying in front of him with a seemingly lifeless stare called up agonizing memories of his dying mother. He had fought the flashbacks most of his life, but so far he had not been able to clear the indelible pictures from his mind.

Russell had been barely sixteen when his mother agreed to drive with him one afternoon. He had only a beginner's license, and the unexpected downpour was more than he could handle. After he struggled to make it to the shoulder of the busy freeway, his mother dashed around the front of the car to take over, only to be met head-on by a hydroplaning pickup. A horrified Dan watched as his mother was hurled twenty feet onto the side of the road.

In hysterics he had dashed out into the storm, pulling his mother's broken body from the flooded culvert, just in time to watch her gasp her last breath in his muddy arms. Why hadn't he come around to the passenger side instead? The question would haunt him forever. Without his realizing it at the time, that day decided that his life's work would be to save lives. As for the driver who sped away on that stormy afternoon . . . Russell would never give up the hope of trying to right that injustice.

Russell shuddered and pushed those haunting memories to the back of his mind. His evaluation continued unabated. He saw no signs of bleeding or obvious trauma. Vice President Delstrotto was cyanotic without spontaneous movements. He noted she was nude from the waist up, probably done in order to attach the defibrillator and start the IV.

Russell pulled out his penlight and shined it into her eyes. Her pupils were equal and did not respond to bright light. They were also constricted. He turned to the emergency nurse who was trying to put the electrocardiogram leads on the patient's chest. The nurse was having a very difficult time as the defibrillator banged away.

"Let's get this thing off so we can see what's going on." He turned off the pump as one of the paramedics loosened the straps that held it on the patient's chest. One of the men in the dark suits moved to stop him, but he was waved off by the man Russell had first addressed.

Besides being anxious over his dying patient while having to contend with all of these strangers in his emergency room, Russell was also becoming angry. He once again turned to the paramedic who had traveled with the vice president. "I asked you, what in the hell can you tell me about the vice . . . patient?"

A nurse hooked the electrocardiogram up to the wall monitor. At the same time a laboratory technician struggled to draw blood from the patient's other arm into several Vacutainer tubes with different colored rubber stoppers.

With a line of sweat rimming his collar, the paramedic spoke. "Not much more than you see, sir. I was with her on the airplane. She was like this when I was first called up to see her. No pulse. No respiration. The people around her said it looked like a seizure. It's a miracle I could even get the IV started."

By that time, the wall monitor had come on but showed no signs of spontaneous cardiac activity. "Get me the adrenalin and give her two ampules of bicarbonate," Russell blurted out. He raised his fist and then brought it crashing down directly in the middle of her exposed chest.

The technician jumped. As Russell watched, one of the partially filled vials of blood rolled out of her hand and tumbled to the floor below. He started performing external cardiac massage and looked at the wall monitor for any signs of response. When there were none, he picked up the external massage again, while he waited for the intracardiac epinephrine. He glanced at the agent standing by the trauma-room door in the dark suit. "Did she say or do anything just before she passed out, anything that might help me here?"

The Secret Service agent shook his head. "Not that I remember." Then he paused. "She did cry out 'Ben,' her husband's name, just before she tumbled from her seat. But that was all."

By that time, the nurse was ready. Grabbing the syringe, Russell plunged the long needle through his patient's chest wall and into her heart and injected the adrenaline.

Simultaneously the nurse injected the two ampules of bicarbonate into the IV tubing.

Everyone in the room watched the monitor. There was still no response. Russell signaled to one of the paramedics. "Take over for me, will you?" The paramedic moved into position.

Russell walked over to the man in the dark suit. In addition to his weapon, the stranger had a satchel under his arm. "Look, I don't know what's going on, but if you want me to help her, I need some information here," Russell hissed.

The man holstered his gun. He laid the satchel on a stool by the door, opened it, and pulled out a file. The stamp on the front of the file caught Russell's eye. *Top Secret* was stamped across the front and above it was the very official round seal of the vice president.

The man broke open the seal and handed Russell one of the sheets of paper from inside. It was a summary of Rosalyn Deltrotto's medical records. He was struck that there was no name identifying the record, only a number. He scanned the one-page document: Allergic to penicillin. Only medications were an estrogen replacement and a new medication for osteoporosis. Two children by natural childbirth. Cholecystectomy (removal of the gallbladder) by laparoscopy about two years ago. The record was clean. No help here.

Russell moved to the unresponsive patient and took up his position. By then the crash cart had been rolled up beside the table. Russell waved off the technician who was applying external massage. He picked up the paddles of the electric defibrillator and placed them on the patient's exposed chest.

As he applied the first jolt of electricity, all eyes in the trauma room fixed on the wall monitor attached to the electrocardiogram leads. The first jolt failed to bring her dying heart back to life.

"Turn it up another notch!" Russell barked. Again there was no response.

He tried three more times, each time sending a higher blast of electricity through the patient's ashen body, but to no avail.

"Get me the chest set, stat!" Russell snapped.

The nurse sprinted to the cabinet and pulled out a pair of size seven-and-a-half sterile gloves but dropped them on the floor in her haste. Nervously she grabbed for another. Russell did not wait. He scooped up the first pair, ripped off their protective wrapper, and slapped them on as the nurse tore open the sterile set of instruments for the surgical procedure. Grabbing the scalpel, he made a deep horizontal incision along the left wall of the chest for about eight inches. Blood oozed from the wound—only a small amount and very dark, a sign it was carrying almost no oxygen.

Russell reached into the vice president's chest and grabbed her heart in his hand.

He began to squeeze it rhythmically at about one per second. The monitor began to reflect what he was doing.

"Hook her up to one hundred percent oxygen and give her two more ampules of bicarbonate," Russell shouted, increasingly flustered by his inability to reverse her situation. He had done this same procedure hundreds of times before. This time, it was different. He was not sure why or even how she had ended up here. And if anyone else in the room knew any more, they were not about to tell him.

Russell looked up to see Dr. Carver Whipple, his supervisor. Eight minutes had passed since Dan cracked her chest, and still no response. Whipple's eyes widened as he took in all of the uninvited guests positioned throughout his emergency room. With a quick, uneasy look at the monitor, he moved over to the patient. "Do you need an extra pair of hands?" he asked.

"It would be appreciated," Russell responded without looking up. "Do me a big favor. Just check her over to see if I'm missing anything."

"Get me some gloves," Whipple ordered the nurse. He took out his penlight and shined it in the patient's eyes. Reaching over, he lifted the otoscope off the wall and peeked in each of her ears. In all the confusion, Russell had forgotten to check for blood behind the eardrums, the first thing to do in ruling out an intracranial fracture. He was glad when Whipple gave him the clear sign.

"I don't see anything you've missed. You're in charge on this shift, but if you want my opinion, I think it's over." Whipple said, heading for the door. "You did all you could."

Russell felt like a blown-out tire, but he knew his boss was right. He just wanted to hear it from another physician before he called off the resuscitation. He pulled his hand out of Rosalyn Delstrotto's lifeless chest, and the monitor on the wall went to a straight line.

"You can shut it down," Russell said, almost in a whisper. "Would you get me a sheet to cover the *vice president*?"

Whipple stopped in midstep, his eyes widened in shock as silence fell over the room. Almost simultaneously, the wall monitor turned to black. A mist of grief flooded the room, especially among the Secret Service agents. Russell looked up to see tears in their eyes. He scanned the room to see that all were near weeping except for the one in the far back corner, who had stayed severely dry-eyed.

Russell's boss, his hand on the door, stopped and turned around. "I hope you drew a toxicology screen," he said, his voice sounding almost like a threat.

Russell nodded as he begrudgingly removed his bloodstained gloves. They had just been thrust together, he and the vice president, but in those few moments Russell had felt a connection with her, a woman who had done much and who deserved to live longer to do more. He looked above the milling crowd, fighting back his own emotions. Had he done everything he could to save the second most powerful person in the free world? He knew that question would stay with him for the rest of his life.

"Dan, it's strange. The vice pre . . ." Whipple choked on the words. "She's gone, but her pupils are still constricted. You may have seen that before, but I haven't." Whipple departed without waiting for a response.

Russell acted as if he had not heard the last remark. Yes, he had noticed, but he also did not know what to make of the patient's reaction either. There were so many questions and not enough answers. Was the vice president on some sort of medication that would cause those effects? Did she have a silent tumor, somewhere deep in the brain? He would have to leave those questions for the pathologists to answer. Right now all he knew was that he had lost her.

3

DEMORALIZED, Russell opened the trauma room door to leave, but not before scooping up the patient's chart and heading for the nurses' station. He had ahead of him a good thirty minutes of forms to fill out. He would get to it at the end of his shift. The only thing worse than the paperwork was that his patient had not made it. Russell had not quite reached the desk when one of the Secret Service agents stepped in front of him.

"Doc, I'm going to do you a big favor." The man in the dark gray suit grabbed at the clipboard with the patient's records and jerked it out of Russell's hand.

Russell tried vainly to resist. "What're you doing? I've got to fill out all those forms."

He motioned for Russell to be quiet. "Can we talk somewhere in private, Doctor?"

Russell looked around for a moment in bewilderment. What now? He noticed this agent was not wearing one of the ear microphones with the cord that ran down his neck the way the others did. "I guess so. The dictation room over there is probably the best spot."

As they sat down the agent closed the door behind them, but not before Russell caught a glimpse of four more agents slipping into the trauma room where the vice president's body still remained, carrying what appeared to be large black garbage bags.

"Doctor Russell, it would have been better for all concerned if we hadn't had to bring her here, but . . ." The man paused and his jaw tightened. "It *never* happened!" he said, his eyes locked on Russell.

Russell was shocked. He was not sure how to respond. A matter of this importance—and to act as if it had never happened? Impossible!

"Doctor, I'm one of the vice president's personal advisers, and we feel that in the interest of national security you should let us determine the cause of her death . . . if you know what I mean. I must ask that you and all the staff here go along with our instructions."

"The pathologists will determine that, not me or you. For your information, I don't know what the hell killed her," Russell blurted out. "But I resent being told by you what I can or can't say. This is America, and everybody hates a cover-up. So if I don't 'go along,' agent?"

"It's Ken Trainer," the man returned. "And, as I just said, I'm the vice president's personal assistant." He stood directly in Russell's face, anger spreading across his features. They were now less than a foot apart. "You're not one of those conspiracy nuts are you, Doctor?"

Russell shook his head. The whole ordeal was beyond his comprehension. "I didn't think so, Doctor Russell," Trainer continued.

Russell looked away, knowing that to take the conversation further might bring consequences he was not equipped to handle.

"Now, Doctor, I would suggest that you and your staff get back to taking care of the rest of the patients here and let us do our work. We should be out of your way in a few minutes."

The man left the dictation room. Russell's pulse raced as he sat in silence, staring at the wall for what felt an eternity. He was scared. Why couldn't they just tell the truth?

Whatever the situation was, they had taken it out of his hands. Maybe the vice president's assistant was right to ask that they forget this ever happened. Maybe it was a matter of national security. Maybe it was supposed to work this way. What had happened after Kennedy died at Parkland?

Within minutes they were gone. He watched silently as the vice president's body was rolled out on the stretcher in a body bag. What perplexed Russell were the five to six other large black plastic garbage bags they carried out with her.

Numb, he somehow finished the last two hours of his shift. It was a strange few hours. No one talked about what they had just been through. He wondered if the agents had also approached Whipple before they left. The personnel acted as if the incident had never happened. Had the man in the dark suit spoken to them too?

He turned over the remaining patients to the physician who had drawn the night shift. There were only two left: one who was waiting for a cardiology consult regarding a possible myocardial infarction, the other an elderly gentleman with a bad cough and a spiking fever.

Russell thought he probably had bronchitis, but he was not going to release him out without a chest X-ray in case it turned out to be pneumonia. He had called for the technician and she was supposedly on her way.

Taking off his white coat and putting on his jacket, he headed for the back entrance to the doctors' parking lot. But once the cold air of the blackened night hit him, he stopped. He was not sure why, but he wanted to go back to where Rosalyn Delstrotto had died, just one more time.

The door to the trauma room was closed and had been since the last Secret Service agent left, over an hour and a half ago. Russell pushed it open. The room was dark. He was overwhelmed by the odor, however, so strong it almost burned his nose. He recognized the smell of chlorine, most likely bleach.

He flicked on the overhead lights. Except for the smell, Russell did not notice anything different. The room looked the same as it did every time he came on shift, only a little neater.

That was it. The place looked too neat. The table had been stripped of its sheet.

The two trash receptacles were empty and the red plastic bags that lined them were gone. Even the red plastic sharps container for needles and syringes, usually kept on a shelf at the far end of the room, was gone. Everything. The room had been swept clean of all traces of the vice president's brief visit. To top it off, they had probably wiped down the floor and the table with bleach to destroy any remaining specks of her blood, Russell thought.

Why all this? What were they not telling him? He turned to leave when a small glimmer of a reflection caught his eye. It came from under the examination table. Russell walked back over and bent down on one knee to get a better look. He reached under the table and brought out a small vial of blood. It was the one he had seen roll out of the technician's hand in the midst of all the bedlam. He fingered the vial, intending to dispose of it before he left. He started to deposit the tube of the vice president's blood in the red container on the wall used for contaminated medical supplies, but they had taken that also. The Secret Service agents had missed the vial, not thinking to look so far under the table. He slipped the sealed vial into his pocket and turned off the light. The answers to a lot of his questions might now lie in his pocket.

The cool night air felt refreshing as he walked out the employees' entrance of Irving Central. Russell always enjoyed coming home after work where Cindy, his girlfriend of late, would be waiting with a hot cup of coffee and a sympathetic ear. Tonight would be different. For her own good, he would not tell her everything.

His commute was a full thirty-minute ride even in light traffic. Russell had wanted to stay away from the congestion of a city, so he had to settle on a house far out in the suburbs. He turned on the local news radio station that was his usual diversion, giving him time to catch up on world events and reflect on his own day at the same time.

Even though Russell had the radio on, his mind was miles away, back at the emergency room, rehashing the unforgettable events of the last several hours, when he caught the name "Delstrotto" on the radio program. The mention of her was not even the lead story. Russell did not catch it all. The announcer said something about how the vice president had taken ill and was canceling a political campaign trip to the West Coast.

That was it? Russell shouted to himself. *The vice president dies in my emergency room and a canceled trip is all the country is told?* He pulled off the highway and gazed straight ahead, numbed by the events that were unfolding around him. A light mist spotted the windshield. He felt overwhelmed. How good a doctor was he? He had not saved his dying mother, and today he could not bring the vice president of the United States back to life.

Off in the distance Russell could see five, maybe six, airplanes circling Dallas/Fort Worth International Airport, preparing to land. Several hours earlier one of them had belonged to the second most powerful political leader in the nation.

Something was terribly wrong.

. . .

The television screen flickered brightly in the Manhattan high-rise apartment. The red numbers in the LED box on top read *64*. Seconds later they moved on to another channel as the man with the grotesque fingernails kept punching the remote.

"Do you think it's over?" the rotund figure beside him on the couch asked.

"No," he answered with a broad, nicotine-stained smile. "I think it has just begun."

4

RAYMOND WINSLET was with Chad Madden in his private study just off his bedroom when the second call came through from Jason Clark. The president had been upstairs having a quiet dinner with his family, something that had become a rarity. Madden had called with an urgent request to meet him in the Oval Office, but after his fifteen-hour workday Winslet decided to tell his chief of staff to come to him. Winslet had already heard from Madden about Vice President Delstrotto's dire situation when the phone rang.

"Jason, the president and I are here together. What do you have new to tell us?" Madden asked.

"She didn't make it."

The president looked at Madden in disbelief. Tightness clutched at his chest.

Clark continued, "I'm in the car with the Secret Service. The vice president's body is in the ambulance behind us. We're on the way to the airport. They have *Air Force Two* refueled. We should be back in Washington in about two and a half hours."

"Damn it, man! What in the hell happened to her?" The president could feel the blood drain from his face. He clenched his fists in frustration. He had been close to his vice president. Over the course of their first term in office, they had become almost like sister and brother. He, the older sibling, protecting his sister but often turning to her for advice and counsel. Now she was gone.

"I just don't understand," he said, embarrassed at how plaintive he sounded.

The president never had cared much for Jason Clark in the first place. He did not trust anyone he could not read, and Clark was one of those people. But the vice president trusted him, and so did Madden, his own chief of staff, and therefore the president had accepted him.

"Well, sir, we never made it to Parkland, the major emergency hospital here. Some sort of traffic accident shut down the freeway from the airport. We diverted to a small hospital, close to the airport."

The president felt distraught beyond words. Madden appeared to notice and took over the conversation. "Jason, did you get her to a doctor?"

"I didn't see what happened when they took her into the hospital," Clark replied, and then paused. "Oh, I remember now, the hospital was called Irving Central Medical Center. Trainer said the Secret Service thought it was better if I stayed in the car. The emergency room had a doctor. In fact, according to the Secret Service, there was another doctor who also came down to help from somewhere else in the hospital. Evidently they even opened the vice president's chest and tried to get her heart started."

"Jason, what did the doctors say was wrong?" Madden asked. "From what the agents are telling me, they didn't know."

"What do you mean, they didn't know?" Winslet burst out. "Hell, they're doctors, aren't they? Jason, let me talk to the agent in charge who was with her. Maybe he can tell me what's going on down there, since obviously you can't."

"That would be Ken Trainer, Rosie's adviser." Clark managed to keep his voice steady even as the president lashed out at him. "He just took over after she got sick. He's in the ambulance with the vice president's body. He decided we should bring everything back with Rosie, I guess so that we could sort all of this out in Washington."

Winslet saw a puzzled look cross Madden's face. "What do you mean by that?" Madden snapped.

"He told them to load it all up, and they did. The Secret Service left nothing behind. They took the sheets, the syringes, everything. I assume Trainer thought that if there were any questions as to why she died, it was better to have all the equipment used on her in one place." Clark sounded hesitant.

The president was not so sure about the decision, but they could hardly go back now. "What about the hospital employees and the other people in Dallas who were involved?" His mind reeled with possibilities.

"Trainer took care of that too," Clark answered. "Hopefully the hospital employees will keep it quiet until morning. That might buy us three hours, maybe four at the most. Fortunately most of the country will still be asleep while we try to figure out what to do next. But still the word will leak out pretty fast."

The president could not swallow his frustration. "Why in the hell are we trying to keep this quiet? Then the media really will think something is going on."

"They might be right," Madden interjected. "That's if—and I mean a big *if*—there's a problem determining her cause of death. At least when you break the news to the media, we can excuse the delay as a matter of respect for the family. We haven't even told Ben yet, so he doesn't know his wife is dead unless he heard from some other source."

"Jason, call us when you know your estimated time of arrival. I'll have someone there to meet you." The president clicked off the speakerphone and turned to his chief of staff. "Do you think it's possible?" His voice was full of doubt. "That she was . . . killed?" A wave of nausea welled up in his throat at the thought of foul play.

Madden just shrugged. Winslet knew that, as disconcerting as this was, Rosie had probably died a natural, if abrupt, death. But he would not, could not, disregard the possibility of conspiracy. The president sat on the sofa in a daze. He had just lost his number one ally. The nation had also lost someone who would have probably been the first female president of the United States. His mind raced with too many thoughts, too many possibilities. It was a cruel world, but was it that cruel?

"I hope the pathologists will give us that answer, but now, Mr. President, we need to contact Rosie's husband. He should be at their home on the grounds of the Naval Observatory," Madden said, breaking their brief silence. When Madden and President Winslet were alone, Madden always referred to the vice president by her first name, Rosie. It was not disrespectful, since she had been a mother figure to Madden. "Would you mind seeing if you could get through to Ben while I arrange for Rosie's return to Washington?" The president nodded, rose from the sofa, and headed down to the Oval Office. He needed some time alone.

He heard Madden pick up the telephone and punch in a number. "Find Davenport and tell her to get over here now. Then locate General Clayton Spivy at Andrews Air Force Base. I don't care where he is or what he's doing. Just get him!"

. . .

Just after one-thirty in the morning, the converted Boeing 727 set down. The landing had been relegated to runway 6-L, which was used rarely and set apart from the regular traffic at Andrews Air Force Base. As the aircraft rolled to a stop, an army ambulance and six unmarked black Ford Explorers pulled up alongside.

Within five minutes, a rectangular box, measuring two feet by six, slid from the cargo hold into the waiting ambulance. The only light around the airplane came from the headlights of the Explorers, which revealed that the box was draped in an American flag.

Several passengers descended the aircraft steps and disappeared into one of the waiting vehicles. Just as suddenly as they appeared, seemingly out of nowhere, the ambulance and two of the unmarked Explorers headed off into the darkness. Noticeably absent was the sound of a siren or flashing lights.

. . .

Two hundred yards away in an auxiliary tower used only as a training area for air traffic controllers stood two men looking out of the darkened windows in the direction of the recent arrival on 6-L. One of the occupants held a pair of electronic Nikon auto-zoom binoculars, the latest in Japanese technology, top secret and touted to able to spot a gnat on a fly's ear at one hundred yards even in the dead of night. Supposedly the United States military had an exclusive contract with the manufacturer.

The only sound in the room was a whirring as the binoculars focused on the aircraft at the end of 6-L. "It's got to be her. It can't be anyone else. That was Ken Trainer and Jason Clark who just left with the ambulance."

The other occupant pulled his cellular telephone from the carrying case attached to his belt and dialed a familiar number. "She's back in Washington," he said. "Her plane landed about fifteen minutes ago. They took her off in an army ambulance about five minutes ago."

"Where were they headed?" the voice at the other end of the line inquired. "Can't tell. It looked like the east exit."

He smiled and then hung up the telephone. It was now time to call it a night.

The man from the other end of the line felt a chill from the cold air blowing up from the blackened water in front of his property. He needed a good night's sleep. It might be the last he would get for a long time.

. . .

"Ben, I can't tell you how terrible we all feel." The president choked up. "You know what she meant to all of us around here."

Winslet could hear Benjamin Delstrotto sigh. "Thank you, Mr. President. Serving under your leadership was the greatest honor of Rosie's life. We both. . ." Delstrotto broke off the conversation and the line went painfully silent.

Winslet continued, "I wanted you to hear it before the rest of the nation did.

We've scheduled a news conference in the morning. Marty, my press secretary, will hold a briefing with the White House press corps at eight o'clock. The details will be scanty, other than to say foul play was not a consideration. Hopefully we can release more specific information as it becomes available and will satisfy the ravenous appetites of the media." There was a long, uncomfortable pause as Winslet fought emotion. "They've taken her body to Walter Reed. Her plane arrived about one thirty this morning, so she should be there by now. Do you want me to send someone over to the Naval Observatory to pick you up?"

"No, I'll be all right, Mr. President. I'll need to call the kids. It's better they hear it from me than on television tomorrow morning. Thanks anyway. I need some time by myself."

Rosie, the president knew, had been the strong one in the family. Ben was the supportive helpmate, content to be in the background. They would have been married thirty-five years in June—quite an accomplishment in this day and time, especially for one of the power couples on the Washington scene.

The president recalled Rosie telling him how she first met her husband-to-be when she was clerking for a prestigious law firm in the DC area where Ben, twelve years her senior, had just been made a partner. The firm had been hired to take on the tobacco lobbyists making efforts to suppress the growing body of evidence pointing out tobacco's harmful side effects. That was in the late 1970s, when smoking was still socially acceptable and it seemed no one wanted to acknowledge the truth, including Congress.

Ben Delstrotto, acting as the lead attorney on the case, was soundly defeated on the issue but in the process won her heart.

According to Rosie, the experience soured her to the system, not so much because the representatives of the tobacco industry had been able to suppress the facts but rather because the legislators allowed themselves to be blinded to the truth, appearing to support only those issues that assured their position in the food chain. The legal system was not at fault—they were just doing their job. It was the electoral system. The elected officials came to Washington with lofty ideas about right and wrong but sold them out for votes in the next election.

Rosie felt the system had to change but that she would not be able to change it if she was a practicing attorney. To make a difference, she would have to become part of the system, working from within. Therefore when she graduated from law school, she refused any offer to join a DC firm. Needing stable employment, she applied at the State Department and was hired. She had not planned to make it a career, but she never found a good reason to leave.

Winslet first met Rosie during the senior Bush administration. She had been plucked from the State Department and eventually advanced to third in command under Secretary of State James Baker. An articulate woman who never seemed to lose her cool under fire, she found herself in more and more confrontational situations as she rose to prominence. The secretary and his first assistant, Rosie's immediate supervisor, were afraid that if they appeared in high-profile, no-win situations, such as confrontations with various Middle East militants, the result would hurt their long-term careers. So instead they sent Delstrotto. In the end, this plan backfired. Delstrotto moved up and the secretary of state and his first assistant were gone when President George H. W. Bush failed to win a second term.

During the Clinton administration she was appointed assistant chief of the Drug Enforcement Agency but quickly earned her way into the White House during his second term, when many of his closest aides abandoned him. Rosie came in as an adviser to shore up the president's image, which also placed her own reputation on the line. Many thought her presence was an attempt to encourage the Republicans to back off a little, though no one was quite sure since the beleaguered president sought support anywhere he could find it.

When George W. Bush came into office, she stayed over as an adviser to the president, serving as a sort of envoy from the previous administration. After that tragic day in September 2001 exploded the myth of America as a safe harbor, Rosie was asked to join Secretary of State Colin Powell as he crisscrossed the globe, drumming up support for the fight against world terrorism.

Even though Rosie was well respected among the Washington insiders, outside of the capital no one had ever heard of her. Winslet's invitation to join him on the presidential ticket took the nation and his own party by surprise. Though a longtime Washington official, she was on no one's radar. Never having run for office before, she had no preformed base. But her acceptance speech changed all that. When she was on the podium, she seemed to come to life. In the span of fifteen minutes, she went from a no-name to having the audience on its feet, chanting her name and supporting her as the next vice president of the United States.

The remainder of the campaign was considered anticlimactic by comparison. Although by no means a shoo-in, Winslet and Delstrotto won the November election, carrying seventy percent of the electoral votes. Not bad for two relative unknowns. The rest was history. Growing public dissatisfaction had swept the slate clean.

Over the last four years, the president had paid little attention as Ben Delstrotto's career appeared to take a backseat to his wife's. Since moving into Number One Observatory Circle, Delstrotto stayed out of the political fracas in which his wife thrived. He acted more as a senior statesman, advising those special interests that failed to generate enough public support or funding to barter their way through the halls of Congress.

"Mr. President, where in Walter Reed do they have her?" Delstrotto asked, his voice trembling.

"Wait a minute, Ben. Let me find out." The president muffled the receiver as he punched through to Madden's office to get the answer. Within a minute, he was back on the line. "Ben, they've taken her to the pathology department. Just go to the rear entrance by the emergency room, and we'll have someone meet you."

"Thank you, Mr. President."

5

"Mr. President, I don't see that we have any choice but do an autopsy," said General Laura Briggs, chief medical officer of Walter Reed National Military Center in Bethesda, Maryland. "Unfortunately there's nothing in the vice president's past medical history that is of help in determining her cause of death. From a clinical point of view, my guess would be she suffered a stroke or had an arrhythmia. But unless we perform an autopsy, we'll never know."

Winslet peeked over his horn-rimmed glasses as he thumbed through the recommendations Briggs had assembled for their meeting. "General," Winslet said, laying down the papers, "from your report and the accounts by the eyewitnesses, no foul play is suspected. So as you already know, we can't just order one. Rosie was a public figure, but her family maintains the right to refuse."

"But this case is different, Mr. President," General Briggs insisted, frustration evident in her voice. "I think we need to know. What's more important, the American public needs to know. I would bet the media and the conspiracy nuts—who always flock to these kind of tragedies—won't let it rest. Even then, a definitive autopsy may not be enough. Look at the Kennedy assassination—that debate is still going on." The general's voice was urgent but still respectful.

Madden, who stood behind the president, knew she was right. If the public had even a whiff of the possibility of foul play or a hint that an attempt to suppress information took place, it would upend the impending fall campaign and send the entire nation into an uproar. And Madden would be caught in the middle, because the brunt of all the problems that confronted his president fell first on his shoulders. Already the country was in shock at the death of the vice president. Within minutes, literally, they would be asking questions. The only way to stop the debate before it started was to perform an autopsy, find the cause of death, and release the results.

"General, if we are able to get permission from the vice president's family, how would you suggest we proceed?" Madden asked.

"We have an excellent team here at Walter Reed," Briggs said, beaming now that the argument seemed to be turning her way. "Lieutenant Colonel Weldon West, who studied at the Stanford program, heads up our pathology department. He assures me that he would perform the autopsy himself."

"I'm afraid that won't be good enough, General," the president interjected. "You mentioned the Kennedy assassination and the public doubt that lingers even today. Well, if we are going to push for the autopsy, it can't appear to be an inside job."

General Briggs visibly bristled. "I can assure you, Mr. President, that we will take utmost care to insure..."

Winslet held up his hand, cutting her off in mid-sentence. "I'm not saying that your Colonel...West shouldn't be in charge," he said carefully, as if trying to find just the right words. "I'm saying only that to remove any thought of collusion we need to bring in an outside civilian expert. As I recall, they did the same thing after President Kennedy's death, and it did seem to make a difference—at least to the reasonable part of the population."

Madden let out a slow sigh of relief. "Mr. President, we still need to get the family's permission. Respectfully, sir, that's where you come in. You and Ben go back a long way." Madden hoped Delstrotto would see the situation the same way they did and let them go through with the autopsy.

The president nodded. The responsibility to convince Rosie's husband fell on him. "Enough said. I'll call Ben immediately. You two have made your point. I think he'll understand. You know, it's ironic how much we expect of those who are in the public view. Even in death, we demand more."

. . .

"I would feel the same way, Ben," the president said into the telephone. The whole encounter made him uncomfortable. The vice president was his closest ally and confidant, and here he was, insisting that she be the subject of an invasive postmortem investigation. "It all has to do with the nation's best interest."

"What about Rosie's best interest?" Delstrotto asked. Winslet could hear the anger seething through his voice. "What about me—knowing that my wife's body would be permanently disfigured so that a bunch of reporters and conspiracy freaks who have nothing better to do with their decrepit lives can have closure? Everyone says that she probably died of an arrhythmia. Isn't that enough? "

The president shot a frustrated look at Madden and shook his head. "Ben, this is really important. With the election just weeks away, the party, not to mention the entire nation Rosie loved, could be in real trouble if the inevitable questions are not laid to rest," Winslet said, feeling guilty that he was pushing so hard. "I believe that Rosie would understand. It's for the good of our country."

Delstrotto grunted into the phone. "I just don't know. I would almost rather see her cremated than gutted like an animal."

Winslet was taken aback by his analogy. "Ben, cremation could certainly be arranged," the president offered. "After the autopsy, we could have her ashes placed anywhere you would like from Arlington National Cemetery to her hometown."

There was a long, uncomfortable pause on the other end of the line. "You win, Mr. President," Ben Delstrotto said, sighing deeply. "Rosie has suffered enough. What we don't need is some fanatical group trying to dig up her remains years from now. The American public, at least, owes her that dignity."

The president felt the bitter taste of success catch in his throat. "Ben, I thank you. The nation owes you a deep debt of gratitude for doing what Rosie would have—"

"That means they cremate everything, Mr. President," Ben Delstrotto interrupted. "I don't want her organs on display in some laboratory jar, stuck away as an exhibition for some gawking high-school kid."

. . .

The chairman of the Department of Pathology at Georgetown University agreed to assist the team from Walter Reed. They scheduled the autopsy for seven o'clock the next morning. Already concerned voices from across the nation, still recovering from their shock at the abrupt death of the country's most powerful—and most beloved—woman, were starting to ask questions about why she had died and who would succeed her.

. . .

Dr. Carver Whipple confronted Dan Russell as soon as the emergency-room physician entered the doctors' lounge. His hands thrust in his pockets, he paced back and forth. "What in the hell went on yesterday?" he barked, his voice taut. "That Secret Service agent threatened me if I said anything about—"

Russell raised his hand, cutting Whipple off. "I don't know any more than you," he said, his voice barely above a whisper as he shut the door. "They were as scared as we were. I could see it in their eyes."

It had promised to be a particularly difficult shift for Dan Russell even before Whipple's haranguing. Not only was he still trying to shake off the memories of the previous day's horrifying experience, but he had already run into several difficult patients. One woman had an acute psychotic breakdown and nearly tore up the emergency room. It took Russell along with the help of two oversize orderlies to bring her under control until she could be transferred to the psychiatric ward at Parkland. Then there was the young boy with a fish bone lodged in his throat. Fortunately the ENT specialist arrived just in time to keep Russell from having to perform an emergency tracheotomy. All through these events, the staff had looked with awe and fear at Russell, clearly afraid even to mention what had happened in the ER just hours before. The news about the vice president's death had broken, but no report had mentioned where she had died. Russell had thought about calling the staff together, but decided against it—the less said, the better.

"Scared of what?" Whipple retorted. "That they screwed up and let the vice president die?" He drew in a deep breath, the vessels on his temples pulsating. "Then they try to intimidate me. I'll be damned if they're going to come into my hospital and talk to me that way."

"Carver," Russell answered evenly, trying to cut through Whipple's posturing. "That guy who claimed to be the vice president's personal adviser said he was doing us a favor by taking the matter out of our hands. For now, I think we should follow his advice." But even as he calmed down his boss, Dan Russell felt something was very wrong.

. . .

Chad Madden hung back from the group as they moved down the long corridor that led to the basement autopsy room of Walter Reed. He was not happy about being there in the first place. The whole idea of an autopsy gave him the creeps, but the president had insisted—he wanted his chief of staff there to personally make sure there were no foul-ups.

Madden tried to ignore the numerous military police who dotted the hallway and the pungent smell of formaldehyde that began to irritate his nose. He glanced down at his watch. It was straight-up seven o'clock when he and General Laura Briggs, MD, and the team of two pathologists—one from Walter Reed and the other, Dr. Clayton Thomas, the chairman of the Pathology Department at Georgetown—pushed through the door into the autopsy room.

Lingering by the door, Madden gulped hard at the sight. It was as if he had been transported back to the 1950s. Green tile, floor to ceiling. The only light came from four giant, open-faced fluorescent lamps, each of which hung suspended over one of the four autopsy tables. Today all four sets of lights were on even though all the tables save one were empty. Two portable operating-room lights on movable stands were positioned at the top and bottom of that table, while a black plastic sheet lay draped over the body in the far right corner. The laboratory was empty except for an older black man dressed in a white T-shirt and army fatigue trousers covered by a large apron. He was filling specimen jars with clear liquid from a large bottle that rested on top of the cabinet adjacent to one of the sinks. Madden felt claustrophobic in the eerie surroundings.

"Good morning, Colonel. I see you have company with you today," the man looked around as he addressed Lieutenant Colonel Weldon West, Walter Reed's chief pathologist. "A sad occasion, sir."

Colonel West nodded. "Yes, Sam, very sad," he said. The team of pathologists moved over to the table where Delstrotto's body was resting under the cover. Madden elected to stay against the wall, figuring as long as he was in the room he was carrying out the president's wishes. He had no desire to encounter the lifeless body of the woman with whom he had worked for four years and so admired, even loved. General Briggs whispered a few words of encouragement to West and Thomas, and then came alongside Madden.

Madden watched as Sam carefully pulled off the sheet, neatly folded it, and placed it on a shelf under the autopsy table. General Briggs leaned over toward Madden. "Sam Gunn has been a fixture at Walter Reed for as long as any of us can remember.

"He's not actually in the military," she said, her voice low. "But like many other people throughout the country, he has a civilian position in a military institution. Sam has run our autopsy room since long before I arrived. He knows everybody and everybody knows him." She smiled. "He's just as comfortable talking to me as he is to the privates around here. If Sam has a fault, it's that he's too meticulous. Every detail has to be just so. As far as Sam is concerned, if there's going to be a mistake, it's not going to be on his watch."

Allowing himself his first sigh of relief, Madden realized that with Sam Gunn around he didn't have to bear all the responsibility. An ordinary citizen would help insure that justice was done for Rosie Delstrotto. Looking over, he saw the pathologists had divided themselves into examining two areas of the body, Clayton Thomas taking the head and neck and Colonel West concentrating on the torso and extremities.

Thomas was a world-renowned expert in neuropathology, so it all made sense. Around the pathologists' necks hung small microphones into which they dictated their observations.

It had been less than two minutes when Thomas stopped and signaled to Colonel West. Both men peered into her open eyes. Madden straightened up to get a better look, but did not attempt to leave his secure position as West reached up and adjusted the operating light so it shown directly into Delstrotto's face. The two doctors were talking to each other, but since he was so far away, Madden could not hear what they were saying. Colonel West motioned for Sam to bring over a copy of the vice president's medical record, which was lying on the table next to the specimen bottles. After a quick review of the first page, Colonel West shook his head at Thomas, and they both returned to what they had been doing before.

"Do you mind telling the rest of us what you found?" Madden called out.

West looked up as Thomas went back to work. "We were just looking at her constricted pupils," the colonel answered crisply. "Not sure what to make of it yet. Maybe Doctor Thomas will come up with something when he cracks her skull—or we'll see something when we get the results back from the drug screen." With that, West buried the sharp pointed saw blade into the vice president's chest and began to lay it open.

A wave of nausea welled up in Madden's throat, forcing him to look away from West's incision, which extended all the way from the vice president's sternum to the top of her pelvic bone. Sweat rimmed his collar, but the nausea gradually started to subside. By the time Madden was able to look back again, the colonel was already probing around the giant cavity he had just created. Madden watched in shock as the colonel began to remove Delstrotto's vital organs one by one, handing them to Sam, who carefully weighed each one on a scale that hung from a stand next to the autopsy table. Then he deposited each of them into one of the bottles he had been filling when the group first entered the room. Even though Madden had positioned himself all the way across the room, he caught the smell of death now emanating from the body. The foul odor brought on another surge of nausea, but somehow he fought it off. He could only imagine what it was like standing right next to the corpse.

"Nothing here that I can tell so far," Colonel West said in General Briggs's direction as Thomas started the incision on the back of Delstrotto's head. "I guess we're going to have to wait for the toxicology screen and the micro on this one, unless Doctor Thomas can come up with something."

Dr. Thomas just nodded without looking up, now deeply engrossed in his own area of dissection. After he had finished making a large flap that extended almost from ear to ear, he carefully began to peel away the back of the vice president's scalp, bringing it forward until it essentially covered her ashen face, exposing her bare skull.

The ghastly sight nearly rocked Madden off his feet. He slammed back against the wall. General Briggs whirled around at the sound. "Are you OK?" she asked.

"Yeah," Madden managed. "I even had trouble in high-school biology when we had to cut up the frogs." Embarrassed, Madden waved her off, determined he would see it through.

Sam handed a saw to Dr. Thomas. Madden remembered reading in Thomas's dossier that he was a stickler for detail. A type-A—for "anal"—personality, he wanted to do everything himself. That way, if something was missed, he knew he was the only one to blame. According to the background material, Thomas did not accept blame easily.

That dedication had allowed him to work his way up to his position at Georgetown, where he served as the youngest department chairman of pathology of a major university in the country.

Madden glanced up at the clock on the wall. It had taken Thomas less than five minutes to remove the top portion of Delstrotto's skull and lay it on the instrument tray adjacent to the table. Now, almost fully recovered from the shock, Madden strained to see. The outer coverings that protected the vice president's brain lay exposed, glistening under the glare of the bright lights.

After gently running his finger over every nook and crevice of exposed tissue, Thomas mumbled a few words into the small microphone that hung from his neck. Madden could not hear what he was saying but was reluctant to ask any more questions.

Thomas picked up the scalpel that Sam had carefully laid out and made a large incision across the thick outer covering that had protected Delstrotto's brain for her fifty-plus years. "He's cutting through the dura," General Briggs offered to Madden. "This guy has made the study of the brain his life's work. He knows every contour and convolution better than you and I know the layout of our own homes. Personally I'd rather work on them with their skin on. That's why I chose internal medicine."

There, exposed, lay the physical engine that had fueled the character of the woman whose body lay silently before him.

"General," Thomas said, looking over at Briggs across the room, "at first glance, the subject's brain seems normal. There are no obvious contusions, nor is there any sign of a hematoma or tumor." Thomas stopped and gently ran his fingers over the contours once again, and then shook his head. Madden watched as Thomas delicately inserted a scalpel into the narrow space between the brain and the skull and pushed the tissue aside with his fingers.

"He's going to cut the brain away from the spinal cord so he can take it out and get a better look," the general whispered in Madden's ear. "I'll bet he could do it in his sleep."

Sort of an odd talent, Madden thought, being able to remove someone's brain while in REM state.

"Damn it! What the hell are you doing?" Dr. Thomas barked.

Madden strained to see. Colonel West, absorbed in removing the final organs from the chest, had inadvertently bumped into Thomas. Something that happens when too many people are involved, Chad realized.

"At most autopsies, only one pathologist is present," the general muttered under her breath. "But this is what the president wanted. These guys get accustomed to moving around freely, and I guess West just forgot."

Thomas continued the dissection, severing the brain just below its base. He carefully lifted it from the cranium, making sure not to disturb any of the delicate surrounding anatomy. As he held the specimen up to the light, Thomas suddenly flushed. It was then that Madden noted bright red blood dripping onto Delstrotto's covered face. For a moment, Thomas just blinked as if stunned. What was happening? Madden knew enough to know the vice president's blood had long ago clotted. Then he realized the horrible truth. The blood belonged to Dr. Thomas.

Thomas quickly placed the specimen in a jar of preservative Sam held, and then looked at his hand. Madden could see it from across the room. Thomas's blood filled one of the fingers of the glove covering his left hand. He knew the blood must be coming from a small laceration at the top of the bloodied finger. "He must have cut himself when he and West collided," Madden muttered to the general.

Briggs looked over at him. "Those scalpels are so sharp that Thomas probably didn't even notice. A stupid slipup."

The result of having not one but two pathologists doing the dissection in order to soothe the media and the conspiracy-theory fanatics was maybe having one doctor too many.

Madden wondered if the president had made a mistake. Thomas must have been nicked many times before. Though with AIDS a persistent epidemic worldwide, nobody took chances. But Thomas would be OK. After all, this autopsy was for the vice president of the United States.

"Sam!" Thomas called out. "Make sure you test for her hepatitis and HIV and get back to me as soon as possible." The technician nodded as he carried the jar with Delstrotto's brain over to the shelf on the wall.

West turned around, appearing to notice Thomas's bloody glove for the first time. "What happened?" he inquired.

"Cut myself, probably when you bumped me," Thomas answered, his agitation showing in his terse reply. "It's no problem. I'm sure she's safe. The tests should be back within twenty-four hours."

"Doctor Thomas, I'm sorry," West said quickly. "Forget it. It's happened to all of us."

Thomas stripped off his gloves and gown and threw them toward the large trash container in the corner. Madden watched as they fell short, landing on the floor. Thomas walked over to the sink and began to wash the blood off his hand. "Colonel West, you can carry on from here," he said.

West nodded, taking up where he had left off, peering inside Delstrotto's empty chest and abdominal cavity. "I'm just going to take one more look around before closing her up."

Sam leaned over and picked up Thomas's discarded gown and gloves.

"Do you think you might have a Band-Aid for my finger?" Thomas barked as he slipped his jacket on.

Madden cut a slight grin when he saw that Sam already had one out. He pointed to it on the instrument tray next to the autopsy table. Thomas grabbed it. "Don't forget to call me about her HIV status and the hepatitis screen as soon as they come in."

Thomas exited the autopsy room, barely acknowledging Briggs and Madden. Madden let out a slow sigh of relief. General Briggs moved toward the autopsy table. "Colonel, what do you think?"

"So far, nothing," he answered. "I guess we will have to wait for the micro. One thing, General. I can't explain her pupils. They're not dilated; they're constricted. Maybe she was on medicine for glaucoma, but it doesn't say so on the record. It probably means nothing, but I'll check it out."

"What about the toxicology screen, Colonel?" Briggs asked.

"We have several vials of blood that were drawn from her at the hospital in Texas," West said. "And I plan to send the lab some of her fluids from here. My guess is we won't get a final report back until the end of the week."

General Briggs smiled. Madden knew she didn't want a screwup either, especially here at Walter Reed. It seemed they had covered all their bases. All they needed now, as far as he could tell, were the results from the microscopic examination of the vice president's tissues and from the toxicology screen. After that a final report could be drafted for the president. Hopefully then they could bury Rosie Delstrotto, mourn her properly, and move on to the upcoming election.

6

RAYMOND WINSLET awoke with a jolt, covered in sweat. The events of the last two days had been almost too much for him. Delstrotto was not only his vice president but also one of his closest confidants; she had become part of his family, as he had of hers. The president would miss her, more than most people would realize.

The illuminated dial on the clock beside his bed read 2:45 a.m. Winslet tried to go back to sleep, but it seemed the harder he tried, the more his brain came to life. After another fifteen minutes, he gave up. He would just start his day three hours earlier than usual. He slipped out of bed, trying not to disturb Sharon. That did not work.

"Where are you going, Raymond?" she asked, still mostly asleep.

"Everything's all right," the president told her. "I just can't sleep. Maybe I'll try some hot milk."

Sharon Winslet seemed pacified as she rolled over, drifting off into her own slumber once again. The president often wished he could shut out the world and sleep like his wife. She had an amazing ability to compartmentalize her life; unlike the president, she did not take problems from one part of it to another. Sometimes he felt Sharon had a more presidential temperament.

After brewing a cup of hot milk in the microwave in the small alcove adjacent to his study in the living quarters of the White House, the president settled down in his overstuffed chair. This was his one place of refuge, away from the public and, except for special occasions, away from his staff. Here he could really be alone with his thoughts.

He could only imagine what important decisions in American history had been made in this room. Maybe Nixon finally decided to resign in this very room, or Kennedy failed to back the Bay of Pigs invasion in Cuba. Winslet would never know. That was what made this room so special for him.

The vice president's funeral was scheduled for noon. At Winslet's request, Rosalyn Delstrotto would be awarded presidential honors. Her ashes would be placed in a ceremonial casket and carried by a horse-drawn carriage down Pennsylvania Avenue to Arlington Memorial Cemetery. Winslet could never forget the image of young John Kennedy saluting his father's casket as it passed by the reviewing stand. Rosie stirred a different kind of ardor, and he knew it would be a day of fervent feeling, not just for Ben Delstrotto and their children but also for the millions of Americans who had admired the former vice president. The latest word from General Briggs seemed to confirm the suspected diagnosis of a cardiac arrhythmia, reinforcing how precious and fleeting life was even for the anointed few.

One urgent question kept recurring to the president: Who would take Delstrotto's place on the ticket? The election was now only three weeks away. A vice presidential candidate would have to be selected—and fast. The public loved Rosalyn

Delstrotto, but now she was gone, and the public did not love uncertainty. Failure to select her replacement quickly could be interpreted as weakness. On the other hand, too quick a choice might be construed as disrespect for her memory. The president's insomnia resulted from this concern more than anything else. One thing was certain. Winslet would have to select someone who would have had Rosie's approval. Such a choice would insure support for those loyal to Rosie, and in a very personal way he felt he owed it to the vice president.

The president ran his finger around the rim of his steaming cup and then scribbled a few names on the notepad in his lap. He needed to talk to Chad Madden. He glanced at the clock on the mantle across the room. Twelve minutes after three in the morning—still too early. Even the president's chief of staff has to sleep sometime. He knew Madden would be up by 4:30 a.m. The president would go it alone until then.

Although Raymond Winslet felt almost assured of a victory for a second term, he knew the one thing he could not do was pick a running mate who brought controversy to the final weeks of the campaign. George McGovern, some five decades earlier, had ruined his chance for victory by picking Thomas Eagleton as his running mate, a man whose psychiatric treatments jettisoned him from the serious contention of the nation.

Walter Mondale had been plagued by questions on Geraldine Ferraro's finances. If George H. W. Bush had picked Dan Quayle under these circumstances, it could have cost him the election. There just was not enough time before the election to work through significant negatives any candidate might bring. Winslet's selection had to be squeaky clean and noncontroversial—a tall order given the nature of the challenge, since almost everyone in public life had a few skeletons neatly tucked away in the back of their closet.

Winslet felt slightly chilled in the early morning air and wrapped his hand around the hot cup. Although he would never admit it, the president felt oddly vulnerable. He had no constitutional backup other than the Speaker of the House and those next in the list of succession, many of whom did not share his views on the future of the country.

September 11, 2001, had changed everything, especially in the executive branch of government, where there was now a designated substitute for every key position, ready to take over at a moment's notice. That was—except at the top. Winslet sighed and looked back down at his notepad.

The president's best choice would be someone from the Senate or House leadership. They had proven track records, and the public had already viewed most of their skeletons. Winslet also included three names from state lower houses on his short list. They were all considered slightly on the conservative side, but only one, David Truitt of Illinois, had ever been tested in a major statewide election. This is where Chad Madden would need to do some homework, undertaking the "closet check," as the inner circles of Washington referred to it. They had to explore all potential secrets or problems. By now it was now almost four o'clock. The president had only thirty minutes to wait.

. . .

"We need to get something out there that sets the tone," Chad Madden said, holding a copy of the *Washington Post*. He felt utterly drained by the prospect of the vice president's funeral. "These guys will do anything to sell more papers, especially if they think there's a story. What we give them is pabulum. We have to hope the report from the autopsy backs us up."

"I'll just play off her physician's comments," Marty Davenport, the White House press secretary, answered, pulling out her notepad. "Brief and to the point. Rosalyn Delstrotto's cause of death was a cardiac arrest. The experts think it was probably due to an underlying cardiac arrhythmia—something that is also frequently seen in otherwise healthy young athletes. Then I'll add that at the request of the president and with the family's permission, an autopsy was performed and the results will be released when they become available."

Madden turned to leave as Davenport scribbled down the last sentence of her press release. "Never tell them more than they need to know," he said, smiling as he closed the door to her office behind him. After all, he was just doing his job.

. . .

"The Battle Hymn of the Republic" emanated from Dan Russell's television as he brewed more coffee. He glanced into the living room to see tears filling Cindy French's eyes. On the screen dignitaries from all over the world walked slowly behind the vice president's flower-covered casket. There was President Winslet, looking grim, beside the First Lady, and beside them was the vice president's widower, his face a mask of grief. Security officers nearly obscured the cameras' view of them.

"Aren't you going to watch this?" asked Dan Russell's girlfriend and possible future mate, her gaze fixed on the picture of the vice president's casket glistening in the midmorning sun.

"The gloomy weather that hung over Washington for the last several days appears to have cleared for the occasion, probably out of respect for Delstrotto," drawled the television commentator in the background. "There have been rumors that today's event might not take place because assembling so many of the world's leaders in one place increases the threat of terrorist activities. But with the cooperative efforts of numerous law-enforcement agencies and the support of the Maryland National Guard, officials were able to . . ."

"It's a sad time when they have to go to all that trouble just because some deranged group of extremists wants to inflict their pain on the rest of the world," observed Dan Russell. He cast his eyes back to the newspaper, scrutinizing the special section in the *New York Times* devoted to Rosalyn Delstrotto. He had been reading everything about her sudden demise that he could get his hands on and conducting regular scans of the Internet, but so far he had uncovered nothing unusual. The official statement from the vice president's personal physician claimed she had died of natural causes, most likely a cardiac malfunction. White House officials promised a full report after the results of the autopsy were finalized, a process Russell knew should take at least a week.

"It's part of history," Cindy answered, never looking away from the television as the screen filled with the image of the carriage drawn by six perfectly matched black horses. She stuffed another pillow behind her back, bringing her legs up underneath her. "Come on over here. You might learn something."

"Usually a ceremony of this kind is reserved for the head of state," the commentator continued. "But Rosalyn Delstrotto was the country's mother figure, so no one quibbled openly over the formalities, especially since the president issued a special order for the arrangements." A large wreath of white roses on top of the casket flashed on the screen.

Dan watched Cindy sniffle in sorrow as the casket made its way into Arlington National Cemetery. The route was jammed by the grief-stricken throngs. The respect that Delstrotto had earned from both parties was truly unique. She had never allowed herself to be mired in the public mudslinging that every politician claims to detest—but always found a way to justify. In the last two years of Winslet's term, the vice president had gained such public adoration that many referred to the highest office in the executive branch as a co-presidency. Today was Delstrotto's day, and Cindy French was captured by every moment of it. Dan knew how much the success of Rosalyn

Delstrotto meant to a young woman like Cindy who was still trying to figure out her place and her power in the world.

Cindy peeked over at Russell. "Is there something you're not telling me?" she asked, rearranging the pillow behind her back.

Russell shook his head, glancing toward the screen that was now focused at the gravesite, where Ben Delstrotto and President Winslet stood side by side on the front row. Then Dan saw him. He caught only a passing glance before the camera zoomed in on the president's tear-stained eyes, but it was enough. Russell jumped up and moved over next to his girlfriend.

"I see you've decided to join us in the real world," she said, patting his knee.

"No," Russell answered, his eyes never breaking contact with the television. "I just thought I saw someone I met once."

Cindy shifted toward Russell. "And who might that be?"

"I . . . I think it was the congressman from my home district," Dan said, trying to make his answer sound convincing. But he was lying. He only hoped Cindy did not catch on to his thin charade. There were things he was not willing to share with her, at least not yet. Why, Russell was not sure. Maybe because he had been sworn to secrecy by the very man he thought he had just seen on the screen, standing just behind Ben Delstrotto.

Maybe he was afraid if he did tell Cindy that something tragic would happen to her, and then she would appear in his nightmares. He was confused. All Russell knew at this point was that the vice president did not die of an unprovoked arrhythmia, not with those pinpoint pupils he had seen.

The camera focused in once again, this time as the president wrapped both his arms around the late vice president's husband in a moment of consolation. They exchanged a few words, the president nodding in agreement at something the widower said. Russell sat transfixed just as the camera panned back, barely catching the man who had claimed to be Rosalyn Delstrotto's personal adviser.

"Speculation is already floating around the capital as to who will join President Raymond Winslet on the ticket. The names of . . ." the reporter continued on as the screen flashed with a close-up shot of the vice president's flower-covered casket being placed on the frame atop the grave.

Cindy's eyes welled up with tears once again at the sight. "They're like a bunch of wolves. She's not even in the ground and they're already talking about who's going to replace her."

Russell looked over at her, forcing a weak smile. "It's a cruel world out there," he said, hoping when all the facts were known it would be as simple as that.

. . .

The majority of the viewing audience would not have noticed. Most of the commentators were now doing their final wrap-up, the pictures of the gravesite serving only a backdrop, and they would not have noticed either. However, in the high-rise Manhattan apartment overlooking Central Park, the man with a partially spent cigarette clasped tightly between his yellowed lips watched a video playback of the vice president's burial. He had noticed.

"I think the contact was made," he said. "Come in here and I'll run it back." He pushed on the remote and the picture rushed in reverse to the point when all the dignitaries at the vice president's gravesite paid their condolences one by one to the Delstrotto family.

Cuddling a half-eaten bowl of potato chips, the obese man plopped down on the sofa as they replayed the scene five or six times. "Looks like it to me. We'll know soon enough," he said, his fingers plunging back in the bowl.

An eerie smile crept across the face of the man holding the remote. Someday soon he would be the next secretary of defense.

. . .

"Hell, it's like everybody and their mother has an idea about who should be on the ticket," Winslet said, letting his jacket fall onto the Oval Office sofa. He looked at his watch. It was close to 1:30 p.m. when their motorcade arrived at the White House. "We just buried Rosie, and all the Washington ghouls can talk about is who's going to take her place."

"It's been that way since day one," Madden said. He popped two Advil he had just retrieved from his coat pocket into his mouth and threw his head back to help them go down. "You should see the calls I've already screened," he answered, palming his temples. "Although they say they're not, Butler and Spears are already campaigning for the spot. They were both on talk shows this morning. And Ivy—all he does is flash his ugly face in front of the camera. Did you notice how long he mugged in front of Rosie's casket? I thought we were going to have to get one of the Secret Service to push him out of the way. I told Davenport to tell the press corps we would release your suggestion in two or three days at the most. That's not a lot of time, but I figure that's all we've got until the voters begin to have doubts." Madden paused, hoping he had sparked a response in Winslet. Seeing none, he continued. "I've arranged a meeting. Since all the governors are in town for Rosie's funeral, it wasn't too difficult."

"Four o'clock, right?" Winslet asked listlessly, glancing at the scribbled note in the margin of his schedule.

"Four o'clock."

Winslet pulled out a crumpled piece of paper from his suit jacket pocket and tossed it on the sofa. "Chad, early this morning I jotted down some possibilities. I included both Ivy and Butler."

Madden picked up the list: six names, two from the Senate, two from the House, and two who were sitting governors. The usual suspects.

"Respectfully, sir, two of these guys have opposed just about every damn policy initiative you've put forth. I honestly don't think you could work with them. And Ivy—we just saw further evidence he won't have an easy time being number two." The chief of staff looked up from the list. "I'm sounding like the protective father now, aren't I? Judging everybody against Rosie?"

The president nodded. "Any other suggestions?"

Madden grimaced. Winslet's list did not include all of the safe, likely candidates. "Not for now. Six is probably enough for a start. I'll get Roberts and Lopez on it right away and tell them I'll cut their throats if they leak anything. There shouldn't be many skeletons with this group. But you never know. I should have a preliminary report on each of these guys by late tomorrow."

"The sooner the better," the president replied. "Oh, Chad, Ben Delstrotto wants to talk to me about something he says Rosie would have wanted. I had this strange feeling about it when he asked me at the funeral."

"What do you mean, Mr. President?"

"I can't put my finger on it, Chad. Just a hunch. I told him to get in touch with you so we can set up a call sometime tomorrow. It shouldn't take more than five to ten minutes."

"That's something you don't have, Mr. President—an extra five to ten minutes. You have to do that rally in Philly at noon, which we felt we couldn't cancel. The campaign has to start up again sooner or later. OK, somehow we'll make it work. I'll give him a call and set it up for you."

"Thanks, Chad."

"Are you ready to take up where you left off?" Madden questioned. The president's face looked drawn from the sobering events of the day and his lack of sleep the previous night.

"First will be a meeting with the steel executives who are trying to get you to waive the tariffs. Then about ten vital diplomatic condolence calls. The briefing files should be right there on your desk. I'll give you a couple of minutes to review them before they start coming in." As Madden headed toward the door, he looked back at the glum president. "I know you've heard it from everybody else, Mr. President. But if it means anything, I miss her too."

. . .

The senator had been at Delstrotto's funeral. Although he was barely noticed by the television cameras, the remorse painted on his public face was real. But it was overshadowed by his conviction that the role he was about to play was worth the sacrifice. He did not see himself as a traitor. That term might apply to those who led the change. He thought of himself more as an opportunist, the man in the position to lead after the change occurred—a very important distinction, which followed in the footsteps of many great leaders throughout history.

The senator was convinced if they had not picked him it would have been someone else. A new world order was in the wind, and he was just playing his part. He had heard rumors of a top-level meeting of his party's leadership at the White House later that afternoon, but so far he had not been invited. All that would change. Soon he would be the one the cameras would focus on. He would be included in all top level meetings at the White House. One day he would be the one who would call them. But for now he had to bide his time.

With the burial of the vice president, the day marked the end of an era. For the senator, it signaled a new start, though most observers, except for maybe his office staff, would not have noticed the changes in his appearance. The suit he wore to the funeral was custom-cut, the stripes smaller and more widely spaced. His shirt tapered, with his monogram barely visible on the cuff. He had even stopped by the Capitol barbershop for a shoeshine. If he were going to play the role, he had to look the part.

He had always been concerned with his outward appearance, tending to overdress for an occasion—anything to draw attention away from the ten or so extra pounds he had carried around his waist ever since his days of collegiate binge drinking. All that was about to change. He had turned in his brightly-colored paisley ties for the more sophisticated muted tones of solid silver and gold. He would assume the character of a statesman, knowledgeable, but without the nerdy, bland appearance of the technocrat. The change would be gradual so as to not arouse much notice. When the time came, as the senator was certain it would, he would be ready.

The senator's arrival back at his office barely turned heads from his staff. They had a job to do, and he knew to them their activity was nothing more than a job. He just happened to be their current employer. They were loyal only to the paychecks that arrived every other Friday. The senator knew this, and down deep he loathed all of them. But he had been elected to do a job, and he could not do it without them.

That would all change too. In his new position, he would not need them. He would be surrounded by people who would listen to him properly and obey.

"Welcome back, senator. Is that a new tie?" Ms. Levin asked, barely looking up from her desk as the senator walked by.

"I believe it is," he responded, knowing full well it had not been out of its box until this morning. "I thought a new one would be appropriate for the vice president's funeral. Any messages while I was gone?"

"A few, but nothing really earth-shattering. I left them on your desk along with the completed forms on Senator Barton's bill, the one he's asked you to cosponsor," Levin answered, her tone abrupt.

He went blank. "What bill?"

"Senator, we went over this several times last week. You pat Barton's back on this, and we get the munitions plant," she said, letting out a low sigh. "Now, sir, if you'll just sign the papers, I'll do the rest."

The senator ignored her and went on into his inner office to see if one of the messages was from the White House, requesting his appearance at the top-level meeting later that afternoon. He closed the door to allow both himself and Ms. Levin more privacy.

A quick glance at the six or seven pink message sheets revealed nothing from the White House. He was not really surprised. The senator had that number memorized. He was just about to walk away and hang up his jacket when he saw the final message. It was set apart from the others and he had missed it the first time. He froze. Quickly he picked it up and stuffed the note into his pants pocket so no one else could see, even if Andrea Levin already had.

The senator's respiration became shallow and rapid. He started to pace, not knowing what to do. *They must not know,* he thought to himself. He had given strict orders that the instigators of the "change" were not to call him at his home or office.

The senator never took off his jacket that afternoon. He left his office just as he found it, the other messages and the unsigned papers on the Barton bill still on his desk.

"Ms. Levin, I'll be back later." She reached for another file and never looked up as the senator bolted out the door.

. . .

"It's really your call, Mr. President," Derek Stanton said, lining up the stack of papers in front of him. "We've already talked about it. When you've made your choice, the party committee board will conduct a voice vote by conference call to make it official."

The president scanned the group in the small conference room just down the hall from the Oval Office. The room filled with the party leadership from both the House and Senate along with Stanton and two other key members of the Republican National Committee. His arrival at the meeting had been delayed by a call from the State Department.

Just before Rosie's memorial service one of the diplomats from Argentina had been found with a concealed handgun. The man claimed it was for self-protection from members of his own government. Since he had made no attempt to use the weapon, it was decided to send him quietly on his way home on the next plane. The president would send a courtesy letter through the diplomatic corps, but if there were lingering problems he hoped to mend them during the Argentine president's upcoming visit. One thing Winslet did not need right now was an international incident.

"As each of you knows, the choice of who joins me on the ticket is critical. Time is against us," the president declared. "Whoever we choose must not, I repeat, *must not* create controversy. With the media starved for any bit of crap they can dig up, we would not have enough time to recover." Winslet cast his eyes in the direction of his press secretary, who was tucked away in the far corner of the room, and then read aloud his list of potential candidates. "All of us in this room need to be together on this decision."

To no one's surprise, two of the men whose names were on the president's list sat at the conference table. Those mentioned did, however, seem to tighten visibly at their inclusion on the president's list.

"I have asked Chad Madden to investigate each of these candidates to make sure there will be no unforeseen problems if anyone included on this list appears on the ticket. Standard procedure. And besides, nobody in Washington ever has anything to hide—right?" the president asked with a slight chuckle.

Everyone joined the president in mild laughter except for the two potential candidates at the table, who, Winslet noticed, tried to put on a smile. It was obviously an uncomfortable situation. The president continued, "I would be honored to have any of these individuals serve with me." He looked across the table at the two possible candidates who were present.

"Thank you, Mr. President," said Congressman Jim Rolands of North Dakota. "I'm sure I speak for Senator Tate as well when I tell you that we are honored to be on your list."

Majority leader Harrison Tate nodded but did not attempt to reply. The president went on, "I would also ask you to suggest any other names I might have left out. Since you might feel uncomfortable doing that here and now, you can call Chad Madden with your suggestions as long as you make them by noon tomorrow. And, of course, I would be happy to hear your opinion of any and all candidates. Whatever we do, let's make Rosie proud of us." He then nodded, signaling an end to the formal order of business, and stood up.

Winslet felt good about how his presentation had gone, even though he did most of the talking. As the attendees began to file out of the room, the president stood by the door and thanked each one personally for being there. When he turned around he saw only Madden and Senator Tate still seated at the table.

"Harrison, I didn't hear much from you at the meeting. Is there anything wrong?" the president said, moving closer to him.

"No, not really, Mr. President. I just wanted to talk to you—alone," Tate said, almost in a growl. The strained look on his face and his mussed hair were out of character for the usually impeccable senior statesman.

The president signaled to Madden, who gave him a quizzical look but closed the door to the conference room as he left.

"Harry, what's going on?"

Winslet and Tate went back a long way. When Winslet first arrived in Washington as a wet-behind-the-ears representative, Senator Tate took him under his wing. Winslet replaced Tate when his mentor ran for and won a place as a senator from Colorado. Although they did not always see eye to eye on issues, they held a deep respect for each other. Thus the president saw Tate as logical match to join him on the ticket.

"Mr. President," the senator said with a sigh, "It won't work, you and I on the same ticket."

"What?" Winslet questioned, pulling up a chair.

"Hell, I'm ten years your senior. I wouldn't do well as number two, even under you. Besides, it may not even be constitutional. We're both from the same state," he said, stuffing down the contents of his half-smoked pipe.

The president gazed blankly at the now empty conference room. "You're right. I guess it was just wishful thinking. I'll tell Chad to stop the background check on you. All your secrets are safe." The president chuckled.

Tate adjusted himself in the chair. He looked uncomfortable but determined. "Mr. President, there is one name that was not on your list that you might want to consider—Jonathan Savage."

Winslet leaned back. "Savage. Hmm. Harry, I don't know much about Senator Savage, but I guess that shouldn't matter. Why him?"

Savage, currently in his third term, was the senior senator from Maryland. His politics were just to the right of the middle of the road. He had never given Winslet any problems, and his less than conservative state consistently sent him back to Washington.

"For one, he's been a supporter on numerous legislative efforts and cosponsored more bills than anyone I can think of." Tate's response seemed faint praise. The president followed Tate's eyes.

"I can't remember that he ever authored any of that legislation himself—a rarity for someone with such tenure in Washington." Tate shifted uneasily at the president's stare.

"He is vice chairman of the Senate Armed Services Committee and has been so for the last seven years."

"What do you know about him outside of Washington political circles?" Winslet asked, deciding to see how deep Tate's convictions ran.

"I am told the senator's nonpolitical life centers around his family's wholesale grocery business on the Maryland shore. Savage's father started Greater Market Foods on a shoestring after he arrived from Ireland on a cargo ship. At first the old man sold produce out of a wagon to the local retailers. But with a lot of luck and a great deal of ingenuity, he parlayed the family business into a reasonably large corporation. Then in the 1980s Savage inherited the business and grew it into the state's second largest wholesale grocer." Tate laid down his pipe. "Jonathan Savage has grown up in the business. He knows people and how to get things done. He'll be a good fit, Mr. President. And maybe, since he has not led the floor fight on many issues, Savage doesn't have a lot of enemies here in Washington either."

Winslet narrowed his eyes and regarded Tate clearly. The whole conversation seemed rehearsed. He had a strange sense that he was being hustled, but that did not make sense coming from Tate. "I can't remember any issue where this senator has taken the lead, Harry."

"As you said, time is critical," Tate answered. "We can't afford any bad publicity over your choice. Savage is a neutral. He may not get many rave reviews, but I doubt if he'll get much bad press either. And the ticket would be stronger on the East Coast."

"Sort of a sad commentary on our political system, don't you think?" the president asked. "But I'll ask Chad to check him out with the others, mostly as a favor to you, Harry."

"Thank you, Mr. President," Tate replied. "I think you'll be pleasantly surprised."

7

"Mr. President," Chad Madden called out, barely avoiding the secretary of agriculture and her entourage, who had just finished their meeting with Winslet. "Ben Delstrotto is holding on line three, and Davenport wants an update. The press is trying to pin her to the wall about the timing for the VP selection—they want to know when they'll hear."

Winslet held up his hand as he scribbled on a notepad and then tore the page off. "Here, add this name to your list," the president said, handing Madden the folded piece of paper.

"Senator Jonathan Savage. I don't understand," Madden mumbled in low tones. Why would the president consider this mediocre legislator as one of his potential running mates?

"I'm doing an old friend a favor." The president then picked up a folder embossed with the DOA seal. "While you're at it, run this through OMB to see what it would cost. The drought in California is sending the price of vegetables through the roof, and the secretary has this idea to let our importers barter with our excess soy and dairy products. It just might be enough to get the farmers through the season without having to dip into our commodity budget. Not a bad move to announce right before the election either." He smiled. "Now, Davenport and who are on hold?"

"Rosie's husband is on three," Madden said. "I think we should tell Davenport you need four days for the selection process."

"Why four? Why am I supposed to take that long?"

"With background checks you'll need that much time."

"We're in the middle of a campaign. Tell her to say I'll announce my choice by the day after tomorrow."

. . .

The president reached for the telephone in his top desk drawer. "Ben, sorry it took so long. As you may know it's been more frantic than usual, sadly."

"I understand, Mr. President. Thank you for taking the time to talk to me." Delstrotto sounded distant, flat.

"What's on your mind?" Winslet asked. His eyes scanned his massive desk for the paperwork he had filed with the National Archives to establish a memorial for Rosie.

Then he remembered that he had been told it would take a week for them to develop an appropriate response. He had hoped to keep the idea a surprise for Ben until he had a solid proposal, but if the memorial was the topic of Ben's call, the president could tell him it was in the works.

"It's about Rosie's replacement."

This caught the president off guard. Delstrotto had always been careful not to stray from his own DC activities into the center of the political arena.

"What about it, Ben?" the president asked warily. "Do you have any suggestions?"

"As you know, I'm mostly a behind-the-scene player. That's why Rosie and I made a good team." Delstrotto's voice broke with emotion.

The president could only imagine the pain Delstrotto felt. "Ben, we're all still so devastated..."

"No, no, let me go on," Delstrotto cut in. "I'll be OK. Over the years, I have come in contact with a great many people here in the capital. If nothing else, I would say that I have become a an excellent judge of character—recognizing both the good and the not so good. That's why I feel compelled to suggest you consider asking Senator Jonathan Savage to be Rosie's replacement on the ticket."

The president was rocked by Delstrotto's suggestion. His fist tightened around the receiver. "Why Savage?" he asked, trying to conceal his surprise. For the second time in less than an hour, people whom the president respected had mentioned Savage's name.

"Rosie and I held him in great esteem. He's someone like me, you might say—he has accomplished a great deal, but he lets others take the credit. Savage works best behind the scenes while others bask in the spotlight. In fact, Mr. President, Rosie once told me that if anything ever happened to her, she hoped the senator would fill in for her. I guess it was a premonition or something."

Winslet was puzzled. He had never heard the vice president mention Savage's name, not even in the context of legislative vote counting. If Rosie and Savage were so close, the president thought, he should have known. Still, he did not know everything about Rosie's affections and alliances.

"Well, Ben, thank you for the suggestion. We will add him to the list of possible candidates," the president said, nervously tapping his fingers on the desk. "Oh, by the way, I put in a request to the National Archives about a proper memorial for Rosie. They said they would get back to me in about a week. We'll have a long discussion then."

"Thank you, Mr. President. I hope you know how much Rosie and I cared about you," Delstrotto said softly. "Just because Rosie's gone—that doesn't mean I'm not around if you ever need anything."

Winslet did not have long to reflect on Delstrotto's suggestion and offer. As soon as the line went dead, his administrative assistant paraded twelve Boy Scouts and their chaperones through the door of the Oval Office.

. . .

The telephone rang seven or eight times before someone answered. The man with long, unkempt fingernails pulled a slow drag from his ever-present cigarette. "Yes," he answered, gazing out of the large picture window that overlooked downtown Manhattan, twenty-eight stories above the street below.

"Don't ever call me at my office! Are you a fool?" the caller yelled into his mobile telephone.

"Senator, I have some information I thought you needed to know," the man said, spitting a bit of tobacco from his tongue.

"What?" Savage barked.

"We've heard from Tate. He's carried out his end of the bargain. It's now up to you and your people," the man, surrounded by a cloud of smoke, responded evenly.

"Have you made the corrections?" Savage asked.

"Funny you should ask. That's just what I was about to do."

Snuffing out his half-smoked cigarette, the man laid the receiver back in its cradle and pressed a button. The curtain over the picture window closed, blocking out the picturesque view of Central Park. With a whirring sound, the panel on the far wall moved away to expose a bank of computer screens.

Within minutes the occupant of the apartment had hacked into his intended connection. Seven familiar names appeared on the screen to the left. Two were senate leaders from the president's party. Two were from the House of Representatives, and two were leaders in the state houses. The final name, listed a line below the rest, was Senator Jonathan Savage.

Projected on the central screen was an access page labeled Federal Bureau of Investigation. The man seated at the terminal typed in a series of five-digit numerical codes. Within fifteen seconds, the words "Clearance Confirmed" appeared on the screen. He typed in a name: Congressman James L. Rolands.

Within two minutes, all the information was downloaded and began to appear on the screen. Name. Date of birth. Education. Family history. Hobbies. The observer scrolled the screen down to the text that dealt with Rolands's military career: "US Army commissioned: First Lieutenant, 2 April 1964. Stationed: Frankfurt, Germany, 30 June 1964–13 May 1966. Intelligence Division: Section leader. Honorable discharge: 18 May 1966, Fort Bragg, North Carolina."

The occupant of the apartment clicked on the mouse and began typing on the screen, inserting an additional sentence after the words "Section Leader." The entry now read: "Section leader. Letter of reprimand issued for security violation, 12 May 1966. Honorable discharge." The man in front of the bank of computers smiled to himself, clicked "Send," and reached for another cigarette.

Over the next thirty minutes he repeated the process five more times with each of the other names on the screen to the left. Each time he made slightly different additions to their records, except when it came to Senator Jonathan Savage. In Savage's case, the operator pulled down the information on the screen just as he had done with the others.

But instead of adding information to the file, he deleted two paragraphs.

After he was finished, the man pushed away from the screens, which disappeared into the smoke-filled darkness as the panel closed in front of him.

. . .

It was barely past 6:30 a.m. when Chad Madden appeared in the president's private dining room, coffee in hand. Winslet was already scanning the morning edition of the *New York Times*. The chief of staff had a package of folders tucked under his left arm. Usually Madden tried to suppress a bad mood, but today was different. He could not hide the concern on his face.

"Your usual, Chad?" the president asked.

"That would be fine, sir," Madden told him.

Winslet pushed a button beside the table. Almost instantly a young man appeared from the First Family's private kitchen.

"Bill, bring Mr. Madden some grapefruit juice, two pieces of whole wheat toast, and a refill on his coffee."

The young man nodded. "Yes, Mr. President."

"Chad, you look troubled. What's going on?" Winslet asked.

Madden sat down in his usual place to the president's right and placed the files on the table. He picked up the top file, labeled "Top Secret," and handed it to the president.

"This is the background information you requested for your six suggestions for vice president, plus Savage." Madden pointed to the files. "Look at the parts I've highlighted in yellow, Mr. President. The party committee guys ran their usual cross-check and essentially came up with nothing the public hasn't already seen. But in order to make sure there were no skeletons that might come back to bite us on the butt, I went to the top for one final check," he continued, his stomach churning over what he was about to reveal to the president. "I realize I bent a few rules, including bribing an old buddy over at the FBI with a fifth of Chivas. But he was able to pull these out for us."

"If you had told me that you felt we weren't getting the whole story, I probably could have called the FBI director and requested these files," the president said, a little uncomfortable with Madden's questionable tactics.

"It's not that simple, even for you, Mr. President. Since this is still a political matter—until whoever we select takes office—it's not usually something the FBI will agree to be involved with," Madden answered, feeling a little frustrated with the whole process. "It all goes back to J. Edgar Hoover's day. No one sees the files unless it's a matter of national security—except, that was, for Hoover."

Winslet gave him a look and then thumbed through the seven files. The file on Congressman James Rolands was on top. Madden watched the president's eyes grow wide as he read the part outlined in yellow: "Letter of reprimand issued for security violation, 12 May 1966."

"Something is wrong with almost all of them, Mr. President," Madden said. "One of our favorite governors bought his girlfriend off with an abortion. The other congressman on your list has been on probation for driving under the influence, not once but twice. Who knew? These issues never surfaced during their campaigns. Their problems are all different. But most of your potential candidates have a secret that stinks enough to bring this ticket down."

"What do you make of this, Chad?" the president asked, frowning.

"I guess what they say was true: J. Edgar Hoover had something on everyone in Washington," the chief of staff answered. "Looks like folks over there continue in his grand tradition."

The president continued to examine the papers one by one. "I just don't understand. All the likely choices." He stopped when he came to Jonathan Savage. "Chad, did they find anything wrong with Savage?"

"There's nothing serious in the FBI files, Mr. President. Just some fraternity thing. Harmless."

Winslet nervously thumped the table as he looked over the FBI files of the seven candidates. By that time, Madden's breakfast arrived.

"Chad, I have this strange feeling. First Tate withdraws and instead suggests Savage. Next Ben Delstrotto delivers Rosie's message from beyond the grave—did I tell you? He thinks—and says Rosie thought—that Savage is the great secret treasure of Capitol Hill. And now this."

"Do you think we should look for any more possible candidates, sir?"

The president took a sip of his now cold coffee. His hand trembled slightly as he set the cup back down. Picking up the FBI file on Savage, he went over it carefully once again. "No, I don't think so. That will just make me look indecisive," Winslet said, his voice breaking slightly. "We're down to two and a half weeks until the election. I do recall seeing Savage present a check on one of those Jerry Lewis telethons a few years ago. Chad, see if the senator can join me for lunch."

. . .

"Code Blue in 409! Code Blue in 409!" The voice of the page operator repeated the same alarm over the communication system at Irving Central. Dan Russell, bent over the old man on the stretcher with his stethoscope in his ears, jerked back as a nurse tapped on his shoulder.

"What?"

"Cardiac arrest in room 409," the nurse blurted out. "We've already sent the crash cart over."

As the emergency-room physician on duty, Russell was also responsible for all unexpected medical emergencies throughout the hospital if the patient's doctor was not around.

He broke into almost a dead run as he headed toward the stairs to the fourth floor. The exertion and anticipation set his heart racing. By the time he arrived at the patient's room, he was gasping for air.

"Tell me what's going on," he demanded, pushing his way past the various medical personnel collected around the bed.

"Thanks anyway," Dr. Peter Lippus said, ripping off his gloves and tossing them into the red plastic receptacle beside the bed. "I was already on the floor when she arrested, but we were both too late."

Russell stopped, suppressing his panting as his pulse eased back to normal. "What happened?"

"More than likely a pulmonary embolus. She was admitted with a diagnosis of thrombophlebitis and had just started anticoagulants." Lippus passed through the door and out into the hall. "I guess we'll have to wait for the autopsy to find out for sure—that is, if they get one."

A sudden feeling of déjà vu gripped Russell as the memory of the tragic events of days before came flowing back to him. Feeling compelled to do something, he looked down at the newly deceased patient. He pulled the penlight out of his pocket and shined it into her eyes, hoping against hope there might still be a chance. But like all the other patients Russell had encountered over the years who had died of natural causes, her pupils were fixed and dilated. Rosalyn Delstrotto had been the only exception.

. . .

"Mr. Madden, I know who you are. What can I do for you?" Savage asked.

Chad Madden had tracked down the senator without difficulty. Time was at a premium. "The president would like you to join him for lunch at the White House."

"I would be honored," Savage answered without hesitation. "What day?"

"Today," Madden answered quickly.

"Kind of short notice, isn't it, Mr. Madden?"

"He'll tell you more if you can join him," the president's chief of staff responded. "It will take some rearranging, but I'll be there. What time does the president want me?"

"In his private quarters at 12:30. Just check in with security. They will take you up. See you then, senator."

Chad Madden had a lot to do before the luncheon meeting. If the president decided to choose Savage as his running mate, Madden wanted to have run the decision by the party leadership. He would start with the party chairman.

. . .

This time the telephone in the Manhattan apartment rang only two times before someone picked up. The call came from an unlisted mobile telephone.

"I'm having lunch with Number One. Maybe you should update Central, just in case there's any change in plans."

"There won't be any," the occupant of the Manhattan apartment replied.

"Look here," Savage exclaimed. "My ass is on the line. If there's a screwup, it is *me* they will be giving last rites. So I want to make damn sure everything is covered."

"Calm down, senator. I'll give them an update and see if they have anything to say. Keep your line clear for the next thirty minutes." The senator clicked off without another comment.

The smoking man pushed the button and the panel at the far end of the apartment rose again to expose the bank of computers. This time only the central screen turned on. The occupant of the apartment logged on to the Internet and typed in an international prefix and telephone number. Within sixty seconds the connection was made, untraceably, via Hamburg, Minsk, and Ankara, to a telephone in Baghdad.

. . .

"The tax code is something that every administration since I came to Washington has vowed to correct." Savage paused, squinting as he searched for just the right words. "But, as you know better than I, Mr. President, every solution proposed just adds another volume to the stack. No, I'm in total agreement with you, a flat tax with modifiers at the top and bottom is ultimately the only answer. And to be totally forthright with you—and maybe a little forward," he chuckled nervously, "such a proposal just might have a shot at passing in Congress if you have a vice president with legislative experience and a lot of friends on the Hill."

Savage felt he was speechifying under pressure. Winslet's questions had been direct and to the point. So far the president appeared pleased with the senator's performance. Although the president had not intended their get-together to be a dissertation on Savage's legislative knowledge, it had worked out that way. In preparation Savage had rehearsed his part until he could do it in his sleep. When the president finally popped the momentous question over coffee and sorbet, Savage acted both surprised and honored that Winslet would consider including him on the ticket.

"This is a wonderful compliment," Savage said with restraint. "May I have a few hours to think it over before I give you a final answer?" Although his ultimate response was clear, the plan was that he not seem too eager.

"How long would you need?" Winslet asked bluntly. Savage could tell the president was a little put off by his indecisiveness, but he knew he was the man's only choice. "Never mind.

That will be fine, senator. Though keep in mind that we need to assemble our team quickly in order to keep the public's confidence."

"I'll let you know first thing in the morning, Mr. President." Sensing their meeting had come to an end, Savage stood to leave. "I hope Rosie would be pleased," he added. Savage smiled as he excused himself and headed for the elevator that would take him back to reality. He had passed the test, but it was only the first of many yet to come.

. . .

As the senator was escorted out of the president's private quarters, he passed a painting of Barbara Bush that hung in the hallway near the elevator. The smiling maternal portrait brought a wave of sadness over Savage. So much was about to happen, but he had no one to share it with. Savage's wife, childless by choice, had died from multiple sclerosis just over four years ago. Savage had no bloodline to protect, only a terrible feeling of loneliness. Her premature death had also changed the senator's outlook on life. He was now a realist, his idealism left behind in earlier years. He was no longer concerned with right over wrong; his concern was now about the strong versus the weak. Dominance was fluid among the world's civilizations, rising and ebbing. For close to a century the United States has been the dominant force in the world. In their own way Russia, Germany, and Japan had contested that role, but each had failed. Throughout history the pattern had always been the same, first the rise, then the fall. The time had come for the United States to move over. Barack Obama had been the first to push his global agenda.

Now Savage would play a pivotal role in making America part of a new global system. Bearing an untraceable, hefty check to fill his campaign's coffers, they had come to him over two years ago. At first they made simple mentions about changing the way the United States conducted business with the world community in order to be more effective. Initially he was put off, but as time passed Savage realized those who looked ahead would be the winners. The senator did not consider himself an evil or unpatriotic man; he was more of an opportunist, someone who was smart enough to ride the edge of the next wave. History would remember him as a man who led his country into a fresh and invigorating world, where the so-called superpowers no longer dominated but rather interacted with others nations who held similar interests. He was committed. He had no doubts. If he did, he could not turn back now.

Savage sucked in a deep breath and headed out alone from the West Wing gate up toward Pennsylvania Avenue. If all went as planned, this would be one of the last times he would leave the White House without a contingent of Secret Service agents surrounding him.

. . .

Savage accepted the president's offer. A news conference was called for two o'clock that afternoon to announce the new ticket. With Savage at his side, Winslet outlined a glowing dossier on the senator, though it was scanty in places. He painted Savage as a true American hero, a leader involved in many important pieces of legislation. "The senator has influenced much of what has gone on in Congress since I have been in Washington." Winslet failed to mention that Savage was always a cosponsor of new bills and never the original author, a point he hoped the media would overlook.

Within minutes of Winslet's announcement, operatives in the opposing party were busy trying to dig up smut on Winslet's new running mate. They were not alone. Every reporter with even the most remote tie to the presidential campaign joined the hunt. If there was any dirt out there on Senator Savage that could change the course of this election, they were going to find it. Or at least that was their plan.

But except for a run-in with the local authorities over hazing practices when he was rush captain of his college fraternity, Savage's record was clean. There were several unsubstantiated stories about questionable business practices told by former associates, but all that was so long ago no one could remember the details. When the time came to put these stories in print, the witnesses all backed out. The White House and the campaign staff heaved a collective sigh of relief. As far as the public was concerned, Senator Savage was as pure as the newly fallen snow—but more boring. The man in the Manhattan apartment had done his job, blotting away any questionable events.

Fortunately he would be paid well for his labors.

. . .

"Glad you could make it," said Britt Barkley, Irving Central's chief executive officer, ushering Dr. Dan Russell through the door and into the penthouse suite of the Anatole Hotel. "As I recall, this is the first of these fundraisers I've ever seen you attend."

Russell scanned the large central room filled with suits and cocktail dresses. "Politics isn't usually my thing," he said. This was a campaign reception Barkley had organized for the person the local Republican Party had hoped would be—as now was—on the ticket to be the next vice president of the United States. "But let's just say I had a special interest in this one."

Maybe it was just curiosity; he was not sure why he was there. But Russell felt compelled to see up close the person chosen to take the place of the lady who haunted his emergency room. Barkley appeared to tighten at Russell's reference to the unreported incident that took place in his emergency room barely a week before. Everybody at Irving Central knew about the incident, but they were reluctant to discuss it, at least publicly.

"Well, yes," Barkley mumbled, but recovered quickly. "Now, where's your price of admission?"

Reaching in his breast pocket, Russell took out the folded check made out to the state party committee and handed it over reluctantly. "What do we do now?"

"Mingle," Barkley answered, his response curt as he turned to greet the next set of guests. "The senator has several stops to make, visiting city officials and the local polls before he comes here."

Amid the unknown party loyals, Russell drifted over to the long serving table set up in the middle of the room and began to fill his undersized plate. Soon a low rumble filtered through the room. Looking back toward the door, he recognized Jonathan Savage surrounded by an entourage. Russell also spotted the mayor of Washington, DC, and someone else he thought was a local congressmen, but he was somewhat naive regarding local politics and was not positive who was who.

Britt Barkley walked to the center of the now crowded room and held up his hands. "Ladies and gentlemen, it's an honor to introduce to you the next vice president of the United States."

A polite murmur of applause spread through the room. Russell stood by a far window and watched as Savage turned toward the crowd. After making a few unmemorable remarks—thanking everyone for coming, expressing sadness at the death of Rosalyn Delstrotto, urging everyone to vote for the Winslet-Savage team—the vice presidential hopeful began a slow trek around the room, shaking hands as he went.

Russell decided that if he wanted to meet the senator he was better off staying put and letting Savage come to him. Suddenly Russell caught a glimpse of a face buried in the crowd of political groupies swirling around Savage. It was a face he knew he had seen before. He continued to pick at the collection of half-eaten morsels on his plate, watching the crowd, trying to get another glimpse of that face. Close to twenty minutes passed, but Russell's wait finally paid off as Rosalyn Delstrotto's replacement moved toward him.

"Thank you for coming," Senator Savage recited, thrusting out his hand in Russell's direction.

"Nice to meet you, sir," Russell answered, the hair on his neck bristling. "I'm Doctor Dan Ru—" His voice stopped in mid-sentence as his eyes locked onto those of the man glaring at him from just behind Savage's right shoulder. Russell's heart raced when he recognized the face he had encountered in the emergency room on that fateful night. It was the face of Ken Trainer, now serving as Savage's aide.

Suddenly Trainer stepped between them, forcing his stale breath through pursed lips not twelve inches away from Russell's face, stinging his nose. "Excuse us, *Doctor*." Trainer's tone became threatening as he raised his hand to move Savage on down the line of guests. "The senator has other obligations."

. . .

"Johnny Walker straight up," Chad Madden told the server, glancing down at his watch. Jason Clark was already ten minutes late for their meeting, a meeting Clark had requested. He claimed it had to do with synchronizing his new boss's campaign schedule with that of the president. No one knew why, but Senator Jonathan Savage had picked Clark as his first assistant almost immediately.

As it turned out, Savage had not brought any of his Senate employees into the White House with him. It was as if he wanted to start over with a clean slate. Rosie's people had already departed. Except for Ken Trainer and Jason Clark, the rest of Savage's new staff were unknown to Madden. As far as Madden could tell, they were all outsiders, none of them having worked previously in Washington. He would have to use Clark as his liaison as he worked to insure that Savage stayed a team player.

Just then Clark slipped into the booth across from him.

"Make that two." Madden signaled to the server, remembering that he and Clark shared the same taste in spirits. "What can I do you for?" he asked directly.

"The senator just wanted me to coordinate Election Day victory speeches with you and your boss."

"Shouldn't be a problem—if we win." Madden chuckled. "If the opposition's concession happens by eleven o'clock, the president can declare victory from the White House by eleven-thirty. He wants as big an audience as he can get."

"But what about Savage? Does the president want him at the White House?"

"I think it would be a nice touch, although I haven't asked Winslet."

"Just let me know so I can get the word to Savage. I think he's staying in Chicago tonight," Clark answered.

Madden was puzzled by Clark's uncertainty. "Don't you know exactly what his schedule is?"

"Yes and no," Clark stammered. "That's where they told me he would stay, but I haven't talked to him directly."

Suddenly Madden had plenty of questions. "Jason, who are 'they'? Don't you talk to the senator directly? After all, you're his first assistant."

"*They* are the new people Savage hired, Chad. Except for Trainer, I don't know any of them really," Clark answered. His drink arrived and he swallowed half of it. "I know their names and what they're supposed to do. But that's it. And, no, I almost never talk to Savage directly, just receive information through Trainer or Gerald Lynn, one of the new guys."

Madden had a million other things he should be doing with the election just two days away. But his interest had been piqued. "Do you think there's a problem the president should know about?"

"I don't think so," Clark replied. "You know, any time changes occur there's a period of adjustment. It'll probably smooth out. I guess we're all just a little on edge with the election so close. Just forget I said anything for now. I simply want to make sure Savage stays on board."

"Well, that's your job, Jason. I'll give you a call once I talk to the president about the election night plans." Madden held up his glass. "Here's to a new start," he declared.

Their meeting ended after they made plans to get together for a round of eighteen holes once the election madness died down, but as he hurried back to the White House, the president's chief of staff could not quite forget what Jason Clark had said. As a man, if not as a politician, Senator Savage was virtually unknown to almost everyone on the president's team except Rosalyn Delstrotto. Unfortunately she was not around to shed any light on his character or motives. For now, Madden would have to let this bit of strangeness go. The election was less than forty-eight hours away.

. . .

At first Dr. Clayton Thomas passed it off as clumsiness. Because he was a natural athlete, he had never had a problem navigating around the multiple obstacles strewn throughout the pathology department at Georgetown. But in the last two days alone he had fallen three times, twice at work. The first fall took place at work when he tripped over a stool in the middle of the aisle between work areas. The second time, at his home, he had tripped over his own vacuum cleaner. In both cases he simply had not seen what stood in his path.

Now the third instance occurred when, in the privacy of his office, he had stumbled over his own feet and slammed into a wall. Thomas checked himself over. No pain. Just some bad bruises and a scraped elbow. But what alarmed him was his loss of peripheral vision. When he held his fingers to either side of his face, he could not see them. A quick look in the mirror revealed nothing different except that his pupils were so small they looked like no-name dots on a road map—a strange reminder of something he had noticed about the vice president during her autopsy at Walter Reed. He needed to get to Dr. Albert Hayes, his ophthalmologist, fast.

Thomas placed the call to the ophthalmology department during the noon hour. The recording on the other end of the line said the office would be reopen at 1:30 p.m. There was an emergency number listed, but Clayton decided it could wait. He hoped that Hayes would let him drop by at the end of his regular schedule since normally he was booked up for weeks in advance. Thomas often wondered if ophthalmology might have been a better choice for him even though he loved the challenge of surgery. He had long ago rejected ophthalmology since he deplored the thought of fitting glasses for the rest of his life. But with the income and the hours it offered, it was still a very attractive specialty.

His afternoon was especially busy. Dr. Thomas first met with the dean, since he had been selected as head of the search committee for the new chairman of Georgetown's biochemistry department. Then it was off to the residents' reading room to review the day's pathology specimens. By the time he finished, his vision still off and his balance delicate, it was close to 5:30 p.m. Clayton tried the main number to the ophthalmology department again, but the phone was back on the recording. He knew Dr. Hayes fairly well, but not well enough to drop by unannounced. He called one more time in hopes of catching Hayes. As luck would have it, Hayes answered. He said he would see Thomas first thing in the morning.

It was past dusk by the time Dr. Thomas headed for the parking lot. The overhead lights had just come on, but unfortunately for Thomas there were only two of them. Most of the parking area still lay in shadow as the doctor, half blind in the evening dark, groped his way to his car.

Thomas fumbled with his key, stabbing at the door lock until he managed to insert the key on the third try. Inside the car he felt secure—until he began the drive home. His condominium was just eight blocks away from the university, but if Thomas had not known the route by heart he would not have made it. He was alternately blinded by the bright lights from the oncoming cars or feeling his way along the darkened road. Either way, he could not see anything. Though it was less than a mile, it was the worst trip of his life. He had a pounding headache by the time he pulled into the covered parking area below his building. He hoped two Advil and a shot of scotch would solve that. The last thing Clayton Thomas remembered was opening the car door.

. . .

When Clayton failed to show up for dinner, Sharon Remmers, his current lady friend, made a call to his office. Her kids were hungry and could not wait any longer to eat. She began to worry when no one answered at the office. Out of instinct she walked down to the parking area.

At first she was relieved when she saw Clayton's car. The door was partially open and she could see him sitting behind the wheel. Sharon called to him, but Clayton did not respond. Sudden dread overwhelmed her.

Sharon rushed to the car. The paramedics arrived within eight minutes of her call.

They put Clayton on a ventilator and gave him external cardiac massage in hopes that something could be done for him at the hospital, but to no avail. Thomas was pronounced DOA in the emergency room and never even taken off the cart.

Insurrection at 1600 Pennsylvania Ave.

. . .

He stepped to the side with his head aslant, agitated that his solitude had been broken by the constant flow of human traffic in and out of his Manhattan apartment.

"Move," he barked at one of the new associates, who had been brought in by his employer to man the bank of computers that filled what had once been his second bedroom. "I can't see." With his free hand he grabbed for another cigarette from his pocket, lighting it off the unspent butt that had clung to his lips just moments before.

"As far as elections go, this one is a landslide," the television commentator declared. "Now that the final totals are in from the two remaining contested states, the ticket of Winslet and Savage has taken 61 percent of the popular vote. On the coattails of their win comes a majority in both the House and Senate. Another big winner, we are told, is the representative from North Dakota, Jim Rolands, who won a one-sided victory in his home state. According to our sources on Capitol Hill, Rolands is the odds-on favorite to assume the prestigious and powerful position as speaker of the House of Representatives. We will confirm . . ."

The man pulled a long drag from his cigarette. Without his efforts none of this would have come to pass. The operation in the high-rise apartment overlooking Central Park had changed to keep pace with its new role. Hours after the polls closed, his small bank of computer screens had been replaced. Most of the old furniture, as well as his own bed, had been either pushed to the side or taken away as the four-room apartment converted into a furiously humming command center. The curtains shrouded each room in a darkness broken only by the low lights of the assorted terminals, printers, copiers, and fax machines that lined the walls.

The stream of blue smoke spun upward from his nose, disappearing into the acrid cloud created by the additional occupants that arrived with Savage's sudden rise to power. The fumes stung his eyes as he flicked off the television screen and made his way back into the kitchen.

"Shit!" he muttered under his breath as he tried to extract the last drop of coffee from the battered drip pot tucked into the corner of the littered countertop. The new recruits, as he called them, were not pulling their load as far as the non technical duties were concerned. Sometimes he felt like a dorm mother, chaperoning the three shifts that came and went. If he had not been promised a place of prominence in the new administration, he probably would have cashed in his IOUs and moved on.

"Don't you bastards know how to make coffee?" he bellowed as one of the other occupants thrust the still-warm copy into his outstretched hand. "What the hell is this?"

"It is from headquarters," came the reply in heavily accented English.

Leaning back against the counter, he eyed the contents of the communication. The only identification on the unsigned memorandum was the three-digit numerical prefix that appeared just before the sender's number. It was the unique number assigned to the city of Baghdad, Iraq.

8

THE LAME-DUCK CONGRESS decided to forgo the usual formalities and act on the president's request, passing legislation that allowed Jonathan Savage to assume his position prior to the official inauguration date in January. Congressman Rolands, hoping to assume the role as Speaker of the House, led the move on Capitol Hill. The action also relieved the current Speaker of the possibility of temporarily assuming the role of president should something happen to Winslet.

By his second week in office Vice President Savage had proved himself to be a valuable member of the president's team. Winslet now included him in all top White House meetings. Savage swallowed his discomfort in his new role and soon found his footing, settling into his new quarters down the hall from the Oval Office. Though only Ken Trainer and Jason Clark were veterans of the Washington scene, the rest of

Savage's staff quickly became familiar faces on the first floor of the West Wing at the White House.

. . .

Jason Clark reached over and rearranged the files laid out on his desk. He knew the action amounted to busywork, but since he had come on board as the vice president's first assistant, busywork was about all he had been allowed to do. He was almost never included in the vice president's private meetings and functioned more as a press secretary to Savage than as a trusted adviser. What little information he was privy to almost never came directly from the vice president himself, but rather filtered through Trainer or one of the new assistants. The situation was considerably different to what Clark had been accustomed to when worked alongside Rosalyn Delstrotto.

Clark picked up the file labeled "Daily Schedule" and punched in the two-digit code on the intercom to connect to the vice president's assistant. "Has Savage gotten back yet?"

"No," came the curt reply, no other explanation offered.

"He was supposed to . . ." Clark sputtered, his frustration evident. "What the hell." He cut off the intercom and tossed the file back on his desk.

. . .

Most of the White House staff was too busy with the constant demands on their time to notice how Savage's team, other than Clark, usually kept to themselves. Chad Madden noticed. In spite of all the demands on his time, very little went on at the White House that Madden did not know about. That was his job. Madden could sense when something was not right.

He needed some time alone with his old friend, Jason Clark. His chance came when both the president and vice president were out of town at the same time. Winslet had been asked to attend a fund-raiser for a close political ally in the Senate from Oregon. Even though his friend and supporter had won his campaign, it had been costly—close to three million dollars more than the campaign had taken in, according to the local press.

Now it was payback time, and no one could raise contributions like the president.

According to sources in the White House, the vice president said he needed some time off, citing the stresses of the campaign, which Madden thought strange since he had been involved only for the last two and a half weeks before the election.

But even though the day was cold and blustery, the slow Thursday afternoon offered an opportunity to get in eighteen holes with his old friend, and Madden took it. He waited until the tenth hole to broach the subject. The back nine was farther away from listening ears.

"Where did they say the vice president was going?" Madden asked Clark, although he already knew the answer since he had Savage's exact itinerary from the Secret Service contingency plan that accompanied him everywhere.

"Some fund-raiser in Ft. Lauderdale, I think," Clark replied.

That was all the opening Madden needed. "What do you mean, you *think*? Hell, especially with the president out of the White House, it's my job to know where Savage is at all times, and so should you. You're Savage's first assistant! You're supposed to know where he is every minute of the day. After all, he's only 'a heartbeat away' from the presidency."

Madden stopped the golf cart halfway down the fairway. Fortunately the cold weather of late fall had discouraged many of the old-timers from coming out that day. The next twosome was still a hole back.

"You tell him that," Clark retorted, frustrated by Chad Madden's comments. "It's not that I haven't tried. With Rosie,

I was in on everything. Not now. I hear only what they want me to."

"Who do you mean by 'they'?"

"Trainer, along with the new guys, Rafer Peters and Gerald Lynn. Savage's inner circle." Clark shifted uncomfortably in the cart.

"What about Savage?"

"What do you mean?" Clark asked.

"Don't you talk to him?" Madden already suspected the answer.

"Sure," Clark said almost reflexively. "No, that's not quite the truth. I talk to the vice president, but not about anything important. It's not like it was with Delstrotto. It seems more like I'm around for looks—to be the familiar face on the Washington scene. Window dressing for everyone else to see. Sometimes it scares me."

Madden glared at Clark. "Do you want to explain that comment?"

Clark looked nervous, as if he had gone too far. Although he was confiding in his old friend, a lot had happened since those days when they had spent more time together. "Forget I said anything," Clark continued. "I think I just feel a little paranoid about not being included in the vice president's inner circle. But I shouldn't expect him to treat me the way Rosie did. It'll all work out."

They could hear the voices of the next twosome in the background. Madden started up the cart. Their attention turned back toward the green and the little white balls that lay forty yards ahead. But Madden knew he had a lot to ponder.

. . .

"Carver," Russell said as he shut the doctors' lounge door behind him. This was the first opportunity Russell had found to be alone with his superior since the vice presidential candidate had visited their city. "I'm telling you, something doesn't add up. Why was that guy Trainer hovering around Savage when he came to Barkley's fund-raiser?"

Carver Whipple folded his arms and stepped back. "Dan, a lot of things go on in Washington that the public doesn't know about. It's done that way in the interest of national security. With all those sickos trying to buy their way into the history books, I can imagine plenty happens that we don't understand."

"After the way that pompous ass glared at me, I'm even more convinced he never wanted to see me again," Russell said. "Carver, I don't think the vice president of the United States died of natural causes. Not with constricted pupils."

. . .

The voices of the golfers in the background stopped when Madden's cart moved on. As one of the players came off the tenth tee, he stopped and pulled a cell phone from his golf bag. The connection was made in less than thirty seconds.

"I couldn't tell what they were saying," the caller whispered. "But whatever they were talking about, Clark looked uncomfortable. Maybe we should close the loop."

"Not now," responded the man in the Manhattan apartment on the other end of the line. "We still need him. We just have to control what he says. That's Trainer's job."

The line went dead. The twosome behind Madden and Clark approached their second shot.

9

Dan Russell waited patiently for just the right moment. Suddenly he sprang from the safety of his sidewalk, dashed across the wet grass, and swept up his newspaper just in time to miss the next pass of the errant water sprinkler. It was a routine Russell had gone through all too often since his next-door neighbor gave up on his automatic system and started hand watering, claiming that he saved on his water bill and was also more in touch with nature. Russell was not sure about either of these claims, since much of the neighbor's water ended up in his yard and dragging a hose around the yard did not seem like much of a communion with nature. Why bother when you could just push a button? As far as Russell was concerned, modern technology had certain advantages and automatic sprinklers ranked right up there with the best of them.

Mumbling a few choice comments, Russell shook off the damp paper and headed back up the walk to his door. He loved the solitude of his surroundings in the cool, crisp Texas mornings. The only sound on the street was an occasional passing car. He had settled in this area because it was away from the big-city hustle and bustle—yet not so far that a quick jaunt in the car would get him where he needed. His girlfriend, Cindy, wanted him to live closer to where the action was. But this was his home, and—at least for now—she stayed over only on weekends.

One of the advantages of his three-to-eleven shift was having the morning to himself. If Russell wanted to sleep in, he could. The morning was his time to do whatever he wanted. He was a man of routine, however, and part of his routine was reading the morning paper.

Russell reached for his cup of coffee and tossed the newspaper onto the counter. His adrenalin must have been pumping from his dash across the yard, he thought, since the paper skidded across the counter and fell to the floor. Reaching down to collect the scattered pages, Russell paused when the byline "Noted Pathologist Dies" caught his eye. He picked up the section, plopped down at the counter, and opened the paper to the referenced page:

Clayton B. Thomas, MD, who led the team of pathologists that performed the autopsy on former Vice President Rosalyn Delstrotto, died unexpectedly of viral encephalitis on Friday. He is survived by his former wife of fourteen years and . . .

Russell set the paper down. "There just might be . . ." he muttered under his breath, his mind swimming with possibilities. Russell had continued to read everything he could find about the vice president's untimely death. The pathology report—at least the one released to the media—stated that Delstrotto died of cardiac arrest. *But ultimately, almost everyone dies of cardiac arrest,* Russell thought. *The real question is what causes the heart to stop beating.* He continued to grow more convinced that the public was not hearing the whole story, especially given the odd lack of reporting about her eyes. And then there was Ken Trainer's intimidating presence in the emergency room. The whole situation was strangely akin to the unusual reports resulting from the John F. Kennedy assassination and autopsy—it was decades after his death, and there were still questions.

Until now Russell had never been one to give much credibility to those who believed in conspiracies. But the vice president died unexpectedly and mysteriously. Weeks later so did her pathologist. It was a reach, but there could be a connection. What had killed Delstrotto could have killed—or murdered—Dr. Clayton Thomas.

. . .

"How could I forget the guy who was always willing to do the dirty work while I supervised?" said Dr. Lowell McCarty, a member of the faculty at Georgetown University, when Dan called him. They were old friends, but it had been at least ten years since they had talked. They had been lab partners when they dissected their cadaver in medical school. "I guess keeping my hands clean was why I chose internal medicine instead of surgery. You're one of those emergency-room docs, as I recall—eight o'clock to five and then pack it in."

"More like three to eleven, but at least I have my mornings free," Russell acknowledged. "And you, still married the daughter of some big-shot Washington lawyer?"

"Going on twenty-two years. Three daughters and that sailboat I always wanted," McCarty answered. "I'm stuck at second in the pecking order here at Georgetown's School of Medicine. I decided early on there are more important things in life than going to meetings and trying to make the budget. Are you still trying to rekindle your youth on the tennis court?"

"As much as I can. And I bet you're still trying to drown yourself in the Chesapeake Bay."

They both laughed. Then Dan felt he could get to the point. "Lowell, I read in the paper this morning about Clayton Thomas."

"Yeah, it took us all by surprise around here," McCarty replied sadly. "What happened?" Russell asked.

"Don't really know," Lowell answered. "His girlfriend found him in his car just a hundred feet from his townhouse. Nothing suspicious. They coded his death out as viral encephalopathy, but that's what they call everything neurological when they don't know the cause. If you don't mind my asking, why are you interested?"

Suddenly sweat broke under his collar. The icy stare of the vice president's special assistant flashed before him, telling Russell to forget anything that happened on the night of Rosalyn Delstrotto's death. He felt it was safer to tell McCarty a little white lie, at least for now.

"Thomas dated a friend of mine in residency, and well . . . I was just wondering," Russell said, his voice measured. He paused to see if Lowell bought his response.

"Must have been a good friend," McCarty returned.

"She was," Russell answered, somewhat relieved. "Did you know him well?"

"Yes and no," McCarty answered. "We sailed together—competitively, I mean. We almost never saw each other except from afar. Unfortunately it was almost always Thomas looking back at me as he crossed the finish line. He was very competitive, hated to lose, and usually never did."

"How was his health?"

"No problems anyone knew of. He was always very fit, an athlete." McCarty paused. "Now that you mention it, I remember one of the residents saying something about Thomas running into him in the hall."

"What's so strange about that?"

"I mean that Thomas literally ran into him and almost knocked him down, as if he didn't even see the guy. It's awful hectic around here sometimes, but the resident seemed to think this was different, as if Thomas acted like he was half blind."

"Did he have a drinking problem?" Russell was searching for anything.

"The resident? No idea. If you mean Thomas, the answer is no. That's one thing I know for sure. Other than the occasional scotch, he was famous around here for being against drinking, smoking, and drugs. He was even chairman of the faculty rehabilitation committee here at Georgetown, counseling professors and staff with alcohol or drug problems."

Dan did not want to act too interested, but he wanted to know more about Thomas's behavior. "Maybe he just forgot his glasses."

"Never saw him wear any. Strange that you should bring that up, old buddy," McCarty said. "Evidently he tried to see one of our ophthalmologists the day before his death, but never made it."

"How do you know that?"

"You know how people like to talk. Especially since Thomas was famous, you might say—he had lots of attention after the vice president's autopsy. Everyone wants to tell their story about Thomas. One of the assistants in ophthalmology said he called one evening to see Dr. Hayes, but it was too late in the day. Said she saw it on the caller ID. It was the night he died."

Russell knew he had more questions than McCarty had answers, and if he went too far his colleague would get suspicious.

But he had to try. "How about doing your one-time anatomy partner a big favor?" Russell asked.

"What?"

"Get me a copy of Thomas's autopsy report." Russell knew he had crossed the line and felt very uncomfortable. "Let's just say my friend needs to know. Please trust me on this."

"I'll have to break the rules," McCarty warned.

Russell kept silent as he waited to see if his ex-classmate would agree. "You'll owe me one for this, Dan," McCarty finally said. "Mostly I'll be interested to hear a good explanation. Let me have your fax number. I'll take Thomas's name off the top, but I'm sure you'll recognize the document."

Russell gave McCarty the information and hung up the telephone. Then he opened the top left drawer of his desk and picked up the vial of Rosalyn Delstrotto's blood, which he had hidden under a stack of letters. He walked over to the window and held the red cylinder up to the light.

. . .

Three bronzed gentlemen were seated at the far end of the long table in the Cabinet room down the hall from the Oval Office. Each was swathed in a long tunic held in place only by the black cords tied around their foreheads and waists. They were deep in a heated conversation. Just above and behind them, like birds of prey, stood three more individuals who held black satchels and only intermittently joined in the debate. Vice President Savage leaned forward slightly but was still unable to make out what was being said.

Suddenly the central figure seated at the table broke from the group and turned back toward Savage and the others.

"Mr. President?" Ambassador Rasheed called out as he folded his hands in front of him.

Savage stiffened as the president, deep in his own conversation with his secretary of state, appeared caught off guard by the response of the ambassador from Kuwait.

"Ah . . . yes, Mr. Ambassador," Winslet answered.

"I'm afraid we cannot accept your proposal. Militarily speaking, ours is a weak country. Despite the efforts of your country, we are not free from the tyrants to the north. If given the opportunity, these radical elements—who you failed to eliminate—will climb out of their subterranean corridors and try to take over our precious oil reserves once again."

The president appeared ruffled and stared at the representative from Kuwait.

Savage could only guess what had gone through the diplomat's mind after the president unexpectedly laid out his plan to reduce the size of the American military presence in the area.

"Then, Mr. Ambassador, I believe we are at an impasse," Winslet said, his face drawn as a result of the grueling negotiations.

Secretary of State Thornhill, who was seated on the other side of the president, leaned forward. "Maybe I could clarify our position for our friends from Kuwait, Mr. President?" he asked.

Winslet nodded and leaned back in his chair to give Thornhill the floor. Savage knew the secretary was a skilled negotiator. In fact, he was the only high-ranking official who remained from the George H. W. Bush administration of the early 1990s. If anyone in Washington had thorough grasp of the world situation, it was Thornhill. From what Savage could tell, Thornhill had become so successful at negotiating that, even though he abided by the president's foreign affairs policies, he was his own boss. Maybe, the vice president thought, he could find a place for Thornhill in his administration.

"Mr. Ambassador, we receive nominal help from our allies, and we cannot be the world's peacekeeper all by ourselves. The war against terrorism continues to require a large part of our military's attention," Thornhill continued, his delivery forceful but not aggressive. "We have no intention of abandoning your country. But you must stand up and take over some greater responsibility for yourselves."

Savage could understand why the representatives from Kuwait were alarmed by this sudden change in United States policy. Iraq had attacked them before. Now Iran would hunger for their oil. Many members of Saddam Hussein's tyrannical regime avoided annihilation when the United States led the Iraqi Freedom campaign. They went underground only to reawaken as ISIS. They formed a caliphate state, whose sole purpose was death to all non-believing infidels. Fortunately Donald Trump made good on his promise to wipe out ISIS, but Iran was still problematic, stronger and more determined than ever to spread its power across the globe.

"We are prepared to pay your country to defend our interests," the ambassador declared, wrapping his hands into a tight ball. "But we need your manpower in our territory, not as a part of some larger, remote force."

"We are not for hire like mercenaries," the secretary replied sharply. "You're talking about putting the lives of our people on the line, people who are willing to shed their blood alongside yours to protect the freedom of your precious country."

Savage was surprised by Thornhill's sudden change in demeanor. Then he remembered that Thornhill was particularly sensitive on this issue since his son had been killed in the former Yugoslavia, representing the United States under the NATO command. Evidently the ambassador from Kuwait knew this too.

"I'm sorry, Mr. Secretary," Rasheed said, his voice apologetic. "That is not what I meant. Defending my part of the world from tyranny is in the best interest of both of our countries."

The president and Thornhill stayed silent. They appeared to be waiting to see what the ambassador from Kuwait would say next. Vice President Savage did not utter a sound. He knew his place was as an observer for now.

"Can you imagine what would happen to your massive industrial infrastructure if the oil reserves in our part of the world fell into the wrong hands? Until you can develop alternative energy sources, your country has no other choice other than to guard your own interests. We have the petroleum. It's as simple as that." The ambassador sat back in his chair.

"You cannot use that as a threat," the president said, his jaw visibly tight in frustration.

"Mr. President, I'm just pointing out reality," Rasheed said, his response almost defiant. "You need our oil; we need your protection."

The ambassador was right, and the vice president, torn between the philosophies of his current and future roles, knew it. Savage wondered if the president agreed. Without direct American protection, it was only a matter of time until that oil-rich area fell under the rule of those in control of Iran.

Secretary Thornhill motioned to the president to let him speak again. "Mr. Ambassador, the people of America say that they want us to stop spending American money and risking American lives in order to save the entire world. We need other nations to do their part to safeguard themselves from terrorism and international instability. That means a commitment not just of money but also of manpower."

"We cannot defend ourselves alone," Rasheed said. "History has shown that Kuwaitis don't make very good soldiers."

The secretary looked at Rasheed hard, and then leaned over to the president and whispered something inaudible to the others in the room. Winslet turned around to speak to one of the individuals standing behind him. The three conferred privately as Savage, feeling conspicuously alone, sat silently at the president's other side.

Secretary Thornhill turned back to readdress the representatives from Kuwait. "I have a proposal that might fulfill both of our needs. We haven't had an opportunity to run this by all the leadership on Capitol Hill, but if we have your support, they will acquiesce, I believe." Thornhill shifted in his chair. "What I suggest is that . . . we pull out, but then again we don't."

Rasheed was puzzled. So was the vice president.

"Our ground troops leave. We move the two aircraft carriers we have there back into the Mediterranean." There was a long pause as the secretary thought carefully about what he was going to say next. "In their place, we station so-called oil field technicians, who will be there to service our petroleum interests. The United States petroleum industry spent almost four billion dollars putting out the fires and reinstalling equipment damaged by the Iraqis in the Kuwait War. And the amount of money we continue to pour into insuring the religious fanatics in your part of the world don't start a global war—well, it's incalculable."

Savage could tell the ambassador and his entourage still seemed somewhat puzzled by the secretary's proposal. One of the men in black suits kept bending over to whisper in Rasheed's ear. Savage could not help but wonder why no one had informed him about this scenario earlier.

Thornhill rested his elbows on the table and continued. "I realize your country paid for part of the damages and has been supportive in our efforts to suppress the subversive activities of the Islamic jihad, but the United States has still lost a great deal of money. My country does not want the same thing to happen again. These so-called oil field technicians I mentioned would really be support personnel for the underground missile batteries we would build—with your permission, obviously, Mr. Ambassador—throughout the oil fields."

The ambassador withdrew from the conversation and conferred with his entourage. Savage could tell the secretary's proposal had taken them by surprise. He also knew they were not authorized to make decisions of such major importance on their own. They would have to confer with the Kuwaiti royal family.

The ambassador turned back toward the president. "I cannot speak for the royal family, but your proposal sounds attractive," Rasheed said.

"There are certain stipulations that would have to be met first," Thornhill hurried to say. "The equipment would be leased by your country, and the technicians who operated it would be paid by you also."

Rasheed nodded slowly. "As long as my superiors approve the plan, the financial questions should not be a problem."

"There is one more thing, Mr. Ambassador," President Winslet interrupted. "We retain total control as to if, when, and how these missiles are used. We do not even promise to consult with you about deployment of this weaponry."

The president's comment stopped Rasheed cold. "You cannot expect us to pay you and rent the equipment from you and let you run it without our having any say as to how and against whom these weapons would be used. That is almost as if we are captives, not of Iraq this time but of the United States." His voice was angry.

Savage felt his chest constrict as the president responded to the ambassador from Kuwait and moved closer to the conference table. "Let us say we are once again at an impasse." Winslet's eyes fixed on the representative from Kuwait. "That is our offer, Mr. Ambassador. An absolutely secret and very powerful weapons installation, funded by Kuwait, under the control of the United States. Take it or leave it."

In the heat of this exchange, the vice president had been forgotten. It was almost as if he was not there. In some ways Savage was glad to be ignored. If they had paid attention they would have seen the band of sweat that had broken out on his collar and the trembling hands hidden in his lap. Here he was, the highest-placed mole in the history of his country.

The meeting broke up after the president's final comment. There was nothing more to say. The next move was up to the leadership in Kuwait.

Savage headed toward his office just down the hall, eager to get away as quickly as he could. "I'll be tied up for about fifteen minutes," he said to his assistant as he closed the door to his inner office.

Savage picked up the telephone on his desk and dialed his home number. Then he set down the receiver to the side and took from his breast pocket his iPhone with the unlisted number provided by his other employer. Savage never trusted that the telephone lines out of the White House were fully secure.

"The boss has changed the rules," Savage whispered, cupping his hand around the small portable telephone.

The voice on the other end of the line waited, apparently to see if Savage was finished speaking, and then replied. "Trainer will brief you at six o'clock."

"Where?" Savage questioned.

"The usual place," the man responded in heavily accented English.

Savage punched off his phone and put it back in his breast pocket. With his other hand he hung up the receiver that lay lifeless on the desk.

10

From: Jed Willerson, medproff@airmail.net

To: Dan Russell, emergencydoc@zianet.com

Subject: PATHOLOGY REPORT—Doe, Jane

Toxicology screen: *Negative*

Infectious disease screen: *Positive*

Diagnosis: *Transmissible Spongiform Encephalopathy—Probable Kuru*

DAN RUSSELL'S lips moved silently as he read the cryptic report off the e-mail message relayed to him by Jed Willerson, his contact in the toxicology department at Southwestern Medical School. Now he understood why it had taken so long for him to receive these results. Russell had never seen anything like this before in his medical training. A layer of green fluid had formed in the tube of the vice president's blood, between the milky plasma on the top and the larger layer of red cells on the bottom.

His friend at the school had analyzed the sample as a favor to Russell and his request for anonymity had been honored. Since computers don't think that way, they had substituted the name Jane Doe for Delstrotto's. Russell had a hunch. If he was right, well . . . he would think about that option later. If he was wrong, he would let the vice president rest in peace. But as he stared at the message before him on the screen he thought, *mad cow disease*. In England and a few other Western European countries, all infected livestock had been slaughtered to prevent the spread of this disease to humans and other animals. But had it spread to humans? A bolt of fear shot up his spine.

He typed his diagnosis into the search engine and pushed "Enter." The search took almost three minutes. When it was completed over three hundred entries on the obscure diseases were listed before him. He clicked on the ones that looked the most medically sound as well as descriptive.

According to the laboratory report on the blood sample, the vice president had been infected by one of a family of diseases that were at one time called slow viruses, of which mad cow disease was just one variety. Was that why she died? Russell could not be sure. The new theory, according to the articles, held that the infecting agent was a *prion*, something with which Dan was totally unfamiliar. These organisms were composed of infectious protein that specifically affected the nerve cells of the brain. They were extremely resistant to the usual methods of sterilization such as heat, which is why the threat of mad cow disease had been taken so seriously. One of the first scientists to study these types of diseases had been awarded the Nobel Prize in medicine recently.

The most common route of transmission was by ingestion of contaminated animal products—such as the infected English cattle. The brain and spinal cord were the parts of the animal most likely to spread the disease, but even the other cuts of meat were possible sources of infection since all tissues contain nerves. In most cases a long time, often many years, passed between exposure and development of symptoms. But one of the articles referred to reports of more virulent strains of prions, ones that resulted in relatively rapid onset of symptoms. Somehow that fact worried Dan even more.

Most experts felt these diseases were really not an issue anymore. Since the mass destruction of infected animals in the 1990s, only sporadic cases had been reported for almost a decade. Legislation passed in the late 1990s prohibited the earlier practice of feeding leftover slaughtered beef products back to livestock cattle—an odd type of forced cannibalism that had contributed to the spread of mad cow disease.

Maybe, Russell thought, the vice president had contracted the disease on a trip to England years earlier, before they had slaughtered the majority of their infected livestock.

There was probably nothing sinister about Rosalyn Delstrotto's death. His initial suspicions appeared unfounded. At the same he could not get the thought of a potential epidemic of this kind of disease out of his mind. He hoped he was not turning into one of those conspiracy nuts he so often complained about.

Nevertheless, why had this real diagnosis not been made on the vice president?

Had it seemed too embarrassing, or was there a political downside to announcing it? Had the pathologists at Walter Reed missed it? Russell knew he would probably never know.

Russell reached for the copy of the autopsy report on Dr. Clayton Thomas from Lowell McCarty, which had come in the day before. He ran his finger down the page to where the diagnosis had been coded out—viral encephalitis. He blinked: encephalitis . . . encephalopathy.

His mind raced at the possibility.

At that moment he would have taken a bet that Thomas's blood had not been screened for one of the transmissible spongiform encephalopathies. He had to find out more. Maybe he was just being inquisitive. Or maybe he was entering a nightmare.

. . .

Arriving late, Vice President Savage and Ken Trainer slid into a couple of chairs near the side of the conference room as Chad Madden briefed the president and the other members of the National Security Council. Madden looked over at the vice president, barely acknowledging his presence, and then continued. "As we had hoped, the Kuwaiti royal family has accepted the president's proposal, though reluctantly."

Savage knew that the royal family had no other option apart from a continued overwhelming American presence in Kuwait. Otherwise it would only be a matter of time until their precious oil reserves fell victim to one of the tyrannical regimes that kept that area of the world in a constant state of turmoil.

"We are determined that this project, code-named 'Mother Lode' by the Army Corps of Engineers, will not turn into another Cuban missile situation. That would be more than just a diplomatic disaster. Therefore the president and the Joint Chiefs have decided to keep the whole operation quiet, even to the United States' closest allies. That includes Saudi Arabia, which would be furious at what they would call a destabilizing and permanent intrusion in the region. Obviously we believe it to be otherwise." Madden paused and picked up a folder from the table. "It is estimated that construction will take twelve to fourteen months. The majority of the work can be done in the secrecy of the missile plants here in the United States."

As Madden continued his top secret briefing, Savage leaned back against the wall, trying to absorb as many of the particulars as possible without appearing too obviously attentive. The final analysis planned for the construction of forty-four missile sites. Each would have the capability of delivering up to twelve nuclear-tipped missiles to a predetermined location in Iran, each location carefully mapped out by American reconnaissance satellites. They would be more than enough to render the dictatorship powerless to launch a major offensive against the small, supposedly defenseless monarchy of Kuwait.

American military forces would remain in the country until construction of the sites was complete. Their presence would act as a perfect cover for the operation. Since the infamous war of the early 1990s security in the oilfields had been a top priority. To the outside observer nothing would change as the missiles were introduced. The weapons would be housed inconspicuously below ground. The only visible sign of their presence would be the scattered buildings designed to look like the typical structures that housed oil field equipment.

"What will keep the Russian spy satellites from noticing our Mother Lode secret?" Savage asked. He thought this question would impress the president.

"Construction of the sites will be done mostly at night," Madden said, looking over at the vice president and his almost constant companion, Trainer. "Large tents resembling the desert terrain will be erected directly over the sites to block satellite observation. As an added precaution, a newly developed liquid acrylic will be sprayed on the underside surface of the tent material to block infrared and radar penetration. The substance is Monsanto's latest contribution to the world of intrigue."

Winslet seemed pleased enough with Savage's query and appeared satisfied with the plan. He broke into a reserved smile as Madden closed the folder and continued. "Once construction is completed, United States forces will be withdrawn quietly from the area, leaving only the Kuwaiti-paid technicians. The withdrawal will not be formally announced. If we are challenged on it, we'll emphasize that in case of a real emergency, the two carriers in the Mediterranean can be moved into position within twenty-four hours—and in the worst scenario, the big bombers stationed in Germany could be over the area in four hours. Though we did not consider using the awesome power of the nuclear submarine force, it does at least afford the president some measure of reassurance in case the Russians or the Chinese decided to get involved, or if Iran or even Syria actually pulled out their small arsenal of nuclear weapons."

"We're getting the final approval on the site selection from the royal family," the secretary of state interjected. "To us it may seem like a formality, but the defense ministry officials over there don't make a move without their approval. If the prince says no, the deal is off."

President Winslet looked surprised. "I thought they already had their approval," he said. "Should I get involved?"

Thornhill shook his head. "No, not yet, Mr. President. The royal family has more to lose than we do."

Savage suppressed a grin, knowing that if all went as planned the president's camouflaged missile sites would actually be turned against the very parties they were meant to protect.

. . .

Chad Madden stood somewhat apart from the group, mostly observing. He noticed that Vice President Savage looked on quietly as well, not adding much to the conversation. Savage seemed more interested in the plans of the missile sites, studying them as if there would be a quiz after they were taken away. Trainer, who had eased his way forward until he was positioned directly over the drawings, did the same.

Glancing around the room, Chad wondered why the vice president's chief of staff, Jason Clark, was never at these closed-door meetings. Although Trainer was competent enough and had received his security clearance with no problem—his dossier was one most Explorer Scouts would envy—Madden felt that something was not right. There was something he could not put his finger on. He wanted to raise his concerns to the president, but he had nothing to mention except a vague sense of unease.

Suddenly a flash of light caught Madden's eye—a reflection off Trainer's coat sleeve. Madden flicked his head around, but by then the reflection was gone. Even if he had seen it for only an instant, he knew something was different about one of the vice president's adviser's buttons. Madden had also noticed that Trainer had been holding his arm strangely as he was hunched over the plans. It could not be anything sinister, could it? Madden wrestled with himself. No, not here in the Cabinet room. This job was making him a little too paranoid.

. . .

He tapped his ashes toward the empty Coke can at the far end of his worktable. It had taken him almost four hours, but with the aid of the vast array of technological support positioned around his Manhattan apartment, he had been able to reconstruct an almost exact copy of the proposed top secret missile site locations in the Kuwaiti oil fields. In a matter of minutes, a duplicate would be hanging on the wall of the war room in Tehran.

He sent a plume of smoke into the stale air, a tribute to his tireless dedication. The job of extracting the data from Trainer's infinitesimal camera and converting it into an understandable copy of the oilfield plan had been surprisingly difficult. But his efforts had been worth it. The Iranians would now have in their possession the exact location of the weapons that threatened them. They also had something else: A direct link to the most powerful political figure in the world. The man in the Manhattan apartment knew the first step to power was knowledge and access. But it was only the first step.

. . .

Chad Madden fidgeted with the telephone cord as he waited for the call to go through. His thoughts went to J. Edgar Hoover, the man who knew everything. During his decades of tenure the director of the FBI had been the most powerful figure in Washington. Even without the miracle of computers, Hoover accumulated and stored such extensive information in the Bureau's files that he could control the lives of many of the so-called power players on the political scene. Although people complained privately about his abuse of privileged information, they were never willing to confront him publicly, fearing that he would turn the tables on them. Presidents had abused that information. So had their staffs. Was Madden about to abuse it now?

"Jennifer, it's Chad. Can I take you to lunch?" Madden tried to suppress any hint of strain in his voice.

"When?" asked Jennifer Smitts. She sounded caught off guard. Madden's invitation had come out of the blue.

"Now," Chad said. "Today."

He had decided to venture out on his own and not bother the president with his petty suspicions. He would start with an old friend in the Federal Bureau of Investigation's information services—if in fact "old friend" was the right term for a former girlfriend who might not even want to see him. Although their relationship had never developed to the point where they considered marriage, they had shared some very good times together. Both had been too preoccupied with their careers, however.

Jennifer Smitt had joined the FBI directly out of college, at a time when the Bureau was making a push to recruit more women. She was part of a group of two hundred women who were all hired around the same time, all with visions of defending this nation against crime and terrorism complete with guns drawn and hidden microphones. The reality had been different, of course—they spent hours on the telephone and computer and days following endless blind leads, either on screen or by pounding the pavement. Jennifer had told Madden she had been a member of the force for twelve years and never once found it necessary to draw her gun. After ten years in the field, mostly putting the heat on small-time drug traffickers, she opted for a position in the Washington, DC, office.

According to Jennifer, she thought initially that her desk job would be boring since she was accustomed to the hustle and bustle out in the field. But to her surprise she found her new assignment as information specialist fascinating. Information was power, and she had access to the largest store of confidential data in the Western Hemisphere, which was just exactly what Madden needed.

"It sounds important," Jennifer said warily.

"It is. Or maybe it's not. That's what I need to know. I'll meet you in the FBI cafeteria around 12:15." He did not wait for her reply. No one turned down the chief of staff of the most powerful person in the Western Hemisphere, not even an old girlfriend.

. . .

"Do you realize that what you're asking me to do, even for someone as important as you, violates three, maybe four FBI clearance policies?" Jennifer Smitt tapped nervously on the table, her sandwich so far untouched.

Madden looked around to see if someone was paying attention. "Keep it down," he said in a low voice. "Eat up."

He pointed toward her food. "The president wants to know more about Ken Trainer and put me in charge of checking him out."

"Then why in the hell don't you just ask him? He has the same background check and the same security clearance as you," she lashed out, glaring at Madden. "And don't tell me when to eat. You gave up that right the last time we were together. When was that . . . over a year ago now?"

Madden forced a grin. She was right. "Look, it wasn't my fault," he said, feeling himself cringe. "It's this damn job. It takes you over . . . I don't—"

Jennifer cut him off. "I've heard those excuses before. What I haven't heard is why I, or anyone else in the FBI, should bend the rules." She picked the napkin up off her lap and tossed it on the table. "I've lost my appetite. You're not turning into an H. R. Haldeman over there, are you? Or are you?" Her question hung in the air.

Madden had wondered that too. He kept his voice even and quiet. "Since Vice President Savage joined the team, he's brought Trainer with him everywhere." Madden paused again to look around. "Even to the briefings of the National Security Council. It's like they're joined at the hip."

Jennifer looked up, and her icy stare melted slightly with the warmth of her professional courtesy. "Many of our elected leaders do that all the time."

"Maybe I'm just becoming more cynical in my old age," Madden answered, sensing a change in her demeanor. "It's just that he was never included like this when he worked for Rosie, and now he's everywhere—even though Jason Clark is still, in theory, the VP's main guy."

Jennifer shot him a quizzical look. She picked up her sandwich, began wrapping it in her napkin, and then scanned the room one more time. "I'll see what I can do. I should have some information for you in twenty-four hours."

"The President has requested that we keep the matter between the two of us. It's not that he doesn't trust the vice president's assistant. It's just that he wants to know more about the people who are part of his inner circle."

She stood up, taking her lunch with her, and looked back at Madden, who was still fumbling with the tip. "In case you haven't noticed, that's how I make my living—collecting everyone else's secrets and then storing them away until just the right opportunity."

He forced a weak grin, the guilt washing over him as he watched her disappear into the growing crowd of diners. Even though Madden felt he had made a valiant effort at maintaining their relationship, Washington was a rough place for privileged, career-minded individuals. Personal relationships frequently took second place to professional goals. The place was crawling with paramours and adulterers, some bound by genuine affection or desire, others possessed of the urge only to climb up one more rung on the ladder. Madden had never thought of his relationship with Jennifer in that way, but he was not sure the chemistry was mutual. Just then, he felt his beeper vibrate at his side. He looked at the LED readout on the top.

Winslet. Madden needed to find somewhere private to return his call. He would try to redeem himself with Jennifer later.

. . .

The president had summoned Madden back to the White House because the Kuwaiti royal family was out of sorts over their lack of control about when and if the missiles were used. They had threatened to cancel their agreement to the plan. Furthermore, a source close to the Kuwaiti leadership had leaked something to the press about a disagreement with the United States government, the terms of which were, fortunately for both sides, not disclosed. The intent of the leak appeared to be to pressure the White House into acquiescing to the royal family's demands rather than to expose the Mother Lode project. Regardless, Marty Davenport had spent her lunch hour fending off the press inquiries. The Kuwaiti ambassador was already at the Oval Office by the time the president's chief of staff arrived.

The president turned to Madden. "It seems our secretary of state is unavoidably occupied—something to do with that economic summit in Tokyo next week. Chad, the royal family of Kuwait is concerned about a few of the details of our new plan. I would like you to take the ambassador down to your office to see if you can work out the particulars."

Madden and the ambassador started to leave but the president pulled Madden aside. "I owe you on this one," Winslet said softly as he handed Madden the top secret file on the Kuwaiti proposal. "If you can work something out, shoot a statement over to Davenport so she can get the press to stop digging around and threatening to blow our cover."

. . .

"Got a minute?" Dan Russell asked as he grabbed at his boss's jacket. Carver Whipple was making his usual run through the emergency room before he headed over to his office to complete whatever administrative responsibilities came with his position.

Dr. Whipple flashed Russell his usual I-would-rather-be-anywhere-else look and then acquiesced to follow Russell to the doctors' lounge. "I've got to be in a board of directors meeting by eight-fifteen."

"What do you know about prion diseases?" Russell asked, topping off his cup of coffee as Whipple let the door close behind them.

Whipple stiffened slightly at Russell's question. "All I know is that prions cause mad cow disease." His eyes searched Russell's. "Why do you ask?"

"That's probably what the vice president died of," Russell answered. "At least a variant of the disease."

Russell's boss moved closer. "I haven't read anything about that. How do you know?"

"Let's just say I have an inside source in Washington." Russell was not prepared to tell Whipple the truth about how he came by his information. "The important thing is that no one else seems to know either. Or if they do, they're not telling."

"Is that why her pupils were constricted?"

"I don't know," Russell answered, taking a sip of his steaming cup. "All I know is that one of the pathologists who performed the autopsy on her just died as well, supposedly of some unexplained encephalopathy."

Whipple stepped back in shock. "You're not saying . . . ?"

Russell took one last gulp of coffee and tossed the cup in the wastebasket. "After that night in the emergency room, I don't know what to think."

. . .

Two hours of intense negotiations took place between the Kuwaitis and the White House administration before they struck a deal. Everything had to be relayed back to representatives of the royal family and to the president before final approval could be given. In the end, the Kuwait prince acquiesced and the president got his way, though with several face-saving stipulations. Only the royal family members were allowed access to the installations. And only at predetermined times. It was a compromise, Madden knew, that did not breach the security of the project. The chief of staff had done his job.

And after the press secretary silver-tongued the White House press corps, they were none the wiser.

. . .

Madden always arrived early at the White House. The following day was no different. He arrived just after 5:30 a.m. He allotted himself time to put together a briefing on the previous night's activity for President Winslet, which usually took about an hour. Then he went to join the president for breakfast in his private quarters, where they strategized for the day and for weeks ahead. When he returned to his desk, he found a note saying that Jennifer Smitt had called. It was just after ten o'clock when Madden found time to call her back. Jennifer picked up Madden's call on the second ring.

"It's Chad."

"I have your information," she said, her voice distant, low.

"Great! Can you courier it over to me this morning?"

"I'd rather not," she responded, her tone solemn. "If you can find the time in your busy schedule, there are some items that I want to show you personally."

"I'll make the time," Madden answered, deflecting the patent hostility in her voice. "How about lunch in that deli down the street? I think the president can do without me for that long."

"Maybe somewhere more private. I think you'll understand why."

Madden had long since learned that Jennifer had an uncanny ability to judge the truth of a situation. When he had stumbled into a one-night stand while out of town on presidential business, she had picked up on it instantly. He was not sure whether her ability was due to her woman's intuition or the skills she had developed working for the FBI for twelve years. But he was not about to question her this time, not on matters of this importance.

"How about Tyson's Corner?" he asked, recalling the small pub where they had first dined, tucked away in a remote corner of the shopping mall in Alexandria. "Say about 12:30, at the taxpayers' expense, of course."

Jennifer did not laugh. "Yes," she said tersely and hung up.

. . .

"Did our message get through?" Savage flipped nervously through a stack of papers on his desk. He hated briefing reports. They were always too long.

Ken Trainer looked up from his magazine and nodded, his expression void of emotion. He then buried his face back in the article he was reading.

"Taking that camera in there could have put us on death row if you'd been caught," Savage badgered. "I don't want you to do that again." The vice president's contempt for his associate was growing by the day. Not only was Trainer brazen to the point of lunacy, but the man also did not show Savage the respect he felt he deserved.

Trainer laid the magazine in his lap, his eyes burning into Savage. "Listen, you sorry son of a bitch." Trainer's muted voice seethed with annoyance. "In here, it's just you and me. Your job is to stand around and try to act intelligent. I'll take care of the rest. Do you understand?"

Savage looked back down at the papers. Yes, he understood. He also understood that in the new administration, Trainer would be one of the first to go.

. . .

Chad Madden glanced at his watch as he slid into the booth in the far corner of the dimly lit restaurant. He had made his appointment with two minutes to spare. The president was addressing the broadcasters' association, which should keep him occupied until after two-thirty. That was plenty of time for the chief of staff to get the information he needed and be back before the president realized he had been gone.

Jennifer must have been right behind him. She brushed past, depositing a large manila envelope on the table in front of him. Then she sat down across from him with another envelope, identical from what Madden could tell, tucked tightly under her arm.

"I know you've gone out on a limb for me over this," he began. "But this is legitimate business."

"Don't start with that bullshit," she said, her tone unsympathetic. "It's always going to be business with you, isn't it? That's why we're just friends."

Sheepishly Madden opened the folder and began perusing the copy of a two-page FBI file on Kenneth B. Trainer. "Graduate of the University of Arkansas School of Business. Masters degree from New York University. Married. No children," Madden mouthed the words. "Grew up in Cleveland, where his father managed a Ford dealership. Pretty routine. I guess my suspicions were off base."

Jennifer watched patiently as Madden reviewed the document. Then she opened the envelope she had held under her arm and removed a stack of files similar to the one Madden was reviewing. "Check out the date of birth on Trainer's file," she said.

"July 2, 1961." He looked over at Jennifer, still not sure where all this was leading.

Jennifer handed him another file from the stack she was holding in her lap. The name at the top of the file read Chad R. Madden.

Madden was surprised. "I see you're investigating me." Jennifer did not laugh. "Read your date of birth," she said.

"October 10, 1960," Madden responded impatiently.

"No, read it the way it is written on your file."

"10/10/60," he answered, still puzzled. "Why?"

"The FBI has very strict coding rules for their files." The stern look on her face never broke. "It goes back to the days when we first put all this information on computers. No exceptions. Look again at your birth date entry and Trainer's."

Madden picked up both files and examined the two entries.

"Your entry is the way all FBI files are formatted," Jennifer continued. "Trainer's is not."

"What are you saying?" Madden asked, puzzled, as his eyes danced between the two files.

"I'm not sure," Jennifer said, her voice hesitant. "Trainer's file might have been altered. I'm not in a position to say why or how, but I think that's a real possibility."

Madden was not convinced. "Maybe the coder was having a bad day when he opened the file on Trainer."

"Possible, but unlikely," Jennifer answered. "I took the liberty of looking up a couple of other names."

Jennifer reached over and handed Madden the two other files that were tucked away in the folder she had kept. The names on the top of each read Rafer Peters and Gerald Lynn, the other members of Vice President Savage's inner circle. "Peters was top in his class in law school. Lynn got the Medal of Freedom. The way these files read, these guys are saints."

Madden's eyes grew wide as he reviewed each entry for date of birth. They were formatted the same as Trainer's. He looked up at Jennifer. "Why would anyone want to change his date of birth?" he asked, holding up one of the files.

"They may have not actually changed the date," Jennifer said. "We have a crazy software package at the FBI. Most of us don't like it, but it was installed for security reasons. The program is set up so that you can't just change one entry in any given file. All the information has to be taken out and then reformatted back in."

"How does that apply here?"

"If some hacker was able to get into our system and wanted to alter an entry, he or she would have to delete everything in a particular file and start the file over," Jennifer continued. "They probably would not know all of the FBI's formatting rules, thus we have a possible reason for the differences. It is a laborious process, but it helps to keep our files accurate and secure."

In wanting to satisfy himself about Trainer's past, Madden had uncovered more than he expected. He was no longer sure what to do next. His heart racing, he stuffed all the files Jennifer had brought back into the envelope and then placed it on the seat beside him. "For now, let's keep this between us," Madden said, reaching for the menu as he tried to suppress the tremor these new revelations had brought.

Jennifer hunched over the table, her nose flaring as she looked in Madden's direction. "I'm beginning to feel like one of those misguided souls I used to chase down when I was out in the field," she declared, her voice breaking slightly. "The last time I counted, you've asked me to break five FBI policies. I could get fired for this . . . or worse."

"Thanks! I need time to think this out. This could be nothing—or it could be a hell of a lot more than either of us is prepared to handle. Either way, we'll get our butts burned if we don't play this right."

The server arrived to take their order. She waved him off and turned back to Madden. "You have forty-eight hours. After that, I don't have a choice except to report what could be a crime if these files have been hacked the way I think they have." She scanned the lunch specials and pushed the menu away. "It seems you always make me lose my appetite."

Madden strained to put on a grin and then leaned back against his seat. "As long as you are willing to give me forty-eight hours, I need one more big favor." He looked over at Jennifer, hoping his direct gaze, which had been so successful for him in their earlier relationship, would break down her glare.

"What?" Jennifer asked, a look of disgust spread across her face.

Madden reached in his pocket, took out his fountain pen, and began scribbling on his napkin. He folded it and handed it over to Jennifer. She opened it up immediately.

Her lips moved silently as she read the seven names of prominent political figures: two from the House of Representatives, two currently serving in the Senate, two sitting governors, and a final name—that of the Jonathan Savage, vice president of the United States. "What you're asking me to do drove Nixon and his whole administration out of office." Her voice was barely above a whisper.

Madden did not have to say another word. He could tell Jennifer knew what he needed.

. . .

The next morning Senator Harrison Tate woke with a cry and sat up in bed. He had not slept well lately, and a vague but furious nightmare had awakened him. He stared blankly at the dying flower arrangement the maid had brought over to dress up his condominium the week before.

Most people would say he did not look his seventy-two years. In his younger days he stood over six-feet two inches. Today he measured only slightly over six feet. But he still cut an impressive figure, and he was still considered one of the patriarchs of the Washington scene. He was also a close friend and confidant of the president. Tate had considered himself above reproach, essentially independent of the special interests that festered among his constituency and in the nation's capital. He had never been beholden to anyone. Until recently. His public support of Jonathan Savage for vice president was his first and only exception.

His hands wrestled each other in his lap as he thought back to the invitation to join Leonard Palmer, an old acquaintance and campaign supporter, on a weekend hunting trip in the desolate outback of the Colorado Rockies. This trip was the only time Tate could ever get away, really away, from his obligations as a United States senator. As it turned out, the senator was not the only guest. A so-called investor from the East Coast also joined the excursion. Tate did not understand the connection between this man and Palmer, but initially did not think much about it.

The weekend had started out innocently enough. Palmer and his guest had met him at the Denver airport as planned. His camping attire allowed him to blend easily into the crowd of busy travelers. As the trio worked their way through the airport, only an occasional passerby even gave Tate a second glance. Tate was relieved, however, when they were finally free of the airport and on their way to the mountain retreat.

"Harrison, you and Stanford Melton have something in common," Leonard Palmer remarked.

"Jonathan Savage and I are old business associates," Melton told him.

"Small world," Tate replied flatly, not particularly interested in their relationship.

Neither had he been particularly impressed by Savage's performance in the Senate. "We've worked together on several issues."

The conversation turned back to the events of upcoming weekend as their four-wheel-drive Range Rover turned off the interstate.

Leonard Palmer had been an ardent supporter of Tate since he first entered politics. Philosophically they were like twins—or at least Tate had thought so. Palmer had owned three car dealerships in the Denver area, finally selling them for more money than Tate could have earned in ten lifetimes. Many times during Tate's tenure in Washington he had turned to

Palmer for both emotional and financial support. Palmer had never asked for anything in return.

Like almost everyone else in Washington, Harrison Tate had one deep, dark secret. Although he had been happily married for more than thirty years, the senator from Colorado had become romantically involved with a young extern from Boulder who spent the summer in the senator's office. One late July evening, Tate confronted her and told her that the relationship would have to end.

The extern reacted with tears and fury. The next morning when she failed to report to work, Tate rushed to her apartment to find that the volatile young woman had committed suicide with an overdose of drugs and booze. Tate panicked and turned to Palmer, afraid to notify anyone in Washington. Using his own contacts in the DC area, Palmer resolved the matter without entangling Tate at all. Although Tate and Palmer never talked about the incident after it was over, neither could ever forget it.

Tate never had been an avid hunter. He took his greatest shots with his Canon 420 Zoom. Instead of stuffed trophies mounted on his wall, Tate had an album of photographs showing off some of the greatest specimens on the North American continent. He was proud that both parties walked away from their mountain encounter and lived to talk about it.

Although Palmer and Melton brought rifles, neither got a clear shot at a kill the whole weekend. Except for a few pictures that Tate took, there would be no souvenirs. The trip was not a loss, however. The senator appreciated having time away from the demands of public office. He was also treated to a steak dinner cooked over an open pit Palmer built just outside the cabin. It was one of the best meals Tate could remember having. Palmer claimed he had the steaks cut specially and saved the largest one for the senator. Tate wondered why he had not taken weekends like this more often.

On the drive back to Denver, the conversation turned once again to Jonathan Savage. Melton said nothing specific, just made comments about all the legislation the Maryland senator had sponsored. Tate knew Savage was only the cosponsor of these bills, having initiated nothing on his own, but he was not about to argue with Melton.

Then Melton went off into space. "I see Senator Savage taking over the leadership of this country in the future," he said. Tate could not believe what he was hearing. He knew nothing about Savage's private life, but as far as the senator's public life was concerned, it in no way qualified him to be president.

Tate responded evenly to Melton's suggestion. "I have a great deal of respect for Senator Savage. He has cosponsored a large amount of important legislation. But I don't feel he would be the best choice for president."

Tate, who sat alone in the backseat of the Range Rover, thought he had given a reasonably tactful response. Evidently not. The demeanor of the occupants in the front seat changed suddenly. Palmer accelerated abruptly. Melton, his face flushed, twisted around to glare back at Tate, almost in a rage. "What in the hell do you know?" he screamed.

Tate was taken aback by Melton's almost irrational behavior. He started to respond when Leonard Palmer reached over and put his hand on Melton's shoulder as if to restrain him. "Slow down, Stanford," Palmer replied, his voice calm. "The good senator knows who his real friends are when he needs them."

Tate was speechless. He knew what Palmer meant. But what the senator did not know was where all this was leading. Was the whole weekend a setup to gain Tate's help? And for what purpose?

They spent the remainder of the ride to the Denver airport in silence. Tate was afraid to make another comment. He wanted out of there and ached for the safety of Washington.

He would wait until later to sort out the implications of what had transpired.

Palmer pulled the car up to the United terminal. He did not even turn around as he made his final comments before the senator's exit. "Harrison, Stanford will be asking for your support on a very critical issue in the near future," Palmer spoke softly. "Please don't disappoint me. It could be very embarrassing for both of us."

The senator exited Palmer's car without uttering a word. He felt a chill course through his body. Unfortunately it wasn't from the outside air.

As Leonard Palmer predicted, the Senator Tate received a call from Stanford Melton with a special request.

The day after Rosalyn Delstrotto died.

11

THE OLDER GENTLEMAN'S piercing blue eyes scanned the encrypted message he had just downloaded, sent from the man in the Manhattan apartment. According to Ken Trainer's information, the president had cleared the final hurdle, convincing the Kuwaiti royal family to agree to the Mother Lode project. Since the president and the leaders on Capitol Hill were still in the honeymoon period after the election, funding for the project, which would be hidden deep within the overall military budget, was virtually a given. No one in Congress—not even the chairman and ranking members of the Armed Services or the Intelligence committees—needed to know about it. The president had insisted. There had been too many leaks in the past, and this agreement was too vital to America's strategic interests.

According to the message, the so-called oil field advisers would be assigned civilian status so they could accept their salaries from the Kuwaiti government. Even the participants in the US military would remain on a need-to-know basis. The clandestine operation, revealed to a handful of Washington insiders only, appeared poised for success.

The older gentleman hit the delete button on his keyboard. In the world in which he now operated, he held only one absolute: *Hold on to nothing for it can only slow you down.* Pushing back from his desk, he let a smile play across his lips. He knew that the so-called top secret Mother Lode project was common knowledge to the Iranian high command. There were now almost daily briefings for the senior Iraqi staff in Iran on the progress of the covert Kuwaiti operation. The Iraqis knew their sources were reliable because the information came directly from the highest echelon of the United States government.

He had lived the lie for so long that it now seemed almost true. Disillusioned with American society and its values while still in college, he disappeared into the Middle East during a summer sabbatical, only to return even more convinced that the self-fulfillment of Western culture was not conducive to man's ultimate good. Back in the United States, he took up where he left off, now guided by those whose thoughts were similar to his. He set his course on effecting change—not by confrontation, but from within. He sought positions that would put him in direct contact with those who made the critical decisions of leadership. When the time was right, he would take over.

The older gentleman had watched patiently as what was left of Saddam Hussein's ill-fated regime worked tirelessly under the cloak of darkened corridors and undiscovered bunkers buried deep below Iran's capital, where they developed a massive network of counterintelligence agents throughout the Middle East. After the humiliating defeat of the regime by the American-led coalition forces, this was the only alternative for Saddam Hussein's followers if they were to take their rightful place as the descendents of Nebuchadnezzar and Hammurabi and dominate that area of the world.

After having been blinded by their leader's insatiable appetite for power, Hussein's cohorts watched in pain as their common dream vaporized under the constant barrage of America's laser-guided weapons. Hussein's heirs had learned their lessons, both good and bad, from their master, and would not make the same mistakes again. The Mother Lode project was only a small step toward their goal to control the land on top of the world's richest source of energy. Then the true loyalty of Israel's allies in the West would be put to the test.

It was only a matter of time until the supposed leaders of the free world would be at their feet, willing to pay any price for the black gold that kept their respective countries running. And after the establishment of a unified Palestinian state . . . well, the balance of power would be totally shifted. The older gentleman had waited half a lifetime to play this deciding role.

. . .

"Can't this wait?" Chad Madden demanded. "I've got ten things going right now."

"No, sir," the aide from the National Security Council said, thrusting out the envelope stamped top secret. "I think the president should see this immediately."

Madden, who had been cleared for all top-level security matters, grabbed the document. "What's so damned important that we have to interrupt the president?" Madden asked, tearing open the envelope.

"It's a memo from the Central Intelligence Agency, sir. Evidently a United States spy satellite picked up a coded telephone message coming out of Tehran."

"That happens every day."

"Apparently this is more serious than most, sir."

"That will be fine." The aide made his departure. As Madden started to scan the document, one word stopped him cold. He dropped into his desk chair, his legs weak beneath him.

"Mother Lode," he muttered. The word had been used not once but twice in the course of the conversation. Flushed, Madden arched in his chair, going over the two-page document carefully a second time. When he finished, the chief of staff, his hands trembling, threw the document on his desk. "How could they know?" he asked aloud.

"Mr. Madden," his assistant piped up. "Davenport is on line two. The press corps want to know when news about the president's initiative on auto emissions will be out."

Who gives a shit, thought Madden, far more concerned about other things than the crap that was spilling out of America's tailpipes. "Tell her to tell them two weeks. If they don't like that, drop it to one. We're bound to come up with something by then."

Madden clicked off the intercom. There it was, all laid out in black and white, the whole top secret plan, known only to a select few in the United States and Kuwait—and now apparently to all of the Iranian high command.

Madden's first thought was for President Winslet. It had been Winslet's idea to hide the funds for the project in the military budget, not telling even his closest supporters in Congress. He felt the fewer who knew about the operation the better. Already that was clearly a major mistake. Now the president would pay the price. His post-election honeymoon with the other end of Pennsylvania Avenue would be over. The news, if it got out, would reverberate hugely, just as it had in the Iran-Contra affair. If Ronald Reagan had not been so popular, that controversy could have cost him the presidency.

. . .

"Get this copy of my speech down to Davenport, Mrs. Sims." Winslet sighed. "Then hold everything for about five minutes."

Madden handed Winslet the envelope with top secret stenciled across the front. "It was picked up by one of our satellites over the Middle East late last night."

The president sat down at his massive desk in the Oval Office and opened up the document. Madden saw his eyes transfixed on the same word as Madden's had been—Mother Lode.

"How?" he asked, almost in a rage.

"I don't know, Mr. President," Madden answered. "Obviously there's a rat somewhere."

"Bastards!" Winslet roared as he slammed his fist on the desk. "You can never trust those Kuwaitis, even when it is for their own good."

Madden jumped back at the president's outburst. Then he moved over behind the president and pointed at the open document lying before them. "That was my first thought too," Madden answered. "But I don't think so."

"What do you mean?" Winslet asked, his face contorted in confusion.

"If you look here," Madden pointed to the bottom paragraph of the first page, "you'll see that the Iranians' informant knows the exact location of where we're going to put the missile batteries. It's almost as if they have a copy of our map, the one you looked at the other day. The Kuwaitis have never seen it. They don't know the exact location yet. It was part of the deal I worked out."

The two men stopped and stared at each other. A look of disbelief came over Winslet's face. "You're saying it's one of us?"

"I'm afraid so, sir."

The president dropped back into his chair. "Well . . . we have to do something about it." Winslet spoke in a barely audible voice. His frown registered his devastation at finding out that one of his closest confidants had betrayed him—as well as the security of the United States.

"I'm already working on it, sir," Madden answered. "By tomorrow I'll have a list of everyone who could have possibly seen the map. Then we can decide what to do next. For now, that part of the problem should be between just the two of us."

Winslet nodded.

"We have another problem, Mr. President." Madden moved back around to one of the chairs across from the president's desk.

"What now?" Winslet asked, an almost helpless expression breaking across his face.

"It's Congress. Although we didn't exactly lie to them, we didn't tell them the whole truth either. Since we hid the costs for the Mother Lode in the military appropriations budget, this is not going to play well with them if it gets out," Madden said uneasily. "If the members read about the proposed operation for the first time in the *New York Times*, your final term could be shorter than we anticipated. At the very least, it would be a miserable four years."

"Reminds me of Reagan's Iran-Contra fiasco." The president sighed and looked over at his chief of staff. "What do you suggest we do?"

"I think you have to tell them yourself, before the Iranian high command does—if it does."

"You're right," Winslet answered. "Can you arrange a meeting with the leadership of both the House and the Senate and the Armed Services and Intelligence committee leaders? But I swear I'm going to make them sign in their own blood to keep this as secret as it can be."

"I've already put it on your books as a breakfast meeting tomorrow," Madden replied. He smiled slightly, glad he had anticipated the president's request. "I hope that was all right."

The president did not even look up as he continued to review the top secret document lying before him. The meeting was on. Madden turned to leave.

"Chad, call Harrison Tate for me, and see if he can come over for dinner tonight in the private quarters. Tell him it is important. I need to test this out on someone up there on the Hill I can trust."

. . .

Dan Russell's girlfriend, Cindy, had prodded him to tell her why he seemed so preoccupied. Russell was reluctant to say anything, although he was not sure if he was afraid of getting her involved or scared of the possibility of embarrassment if his suspicions turned out to be baseless. In either case, he was not prepared to let her in on his secret, at least not until he was able to find out more about the pathologist's cause of death.

The evening shift at Irving Central usually had a short lull around suppertime.

Russell went in the doctors' dictating room and placed a call to Lowell McCarty, hoping to catch him before he headed home.

"I hope that answered any unresolved questions," McCarty said as soon as he recognized his former anatomy partner's voice.

"Well . . . almost," Russell said hesitantly.

McCarty should not have been surprised. Even in the days when they had been anatomy partners in medical school, he had known Dan would never give up until he had all the answers. McCarty once told him that Russell's dogged determination almost drove him crazy at first, but he finally came to accept that was just the way his friend was.

"What do you mean by 'almost'?" he questioned.

"The report on Thomas said he died of viral encephalitis," Russell said. "We all know that's a wastebasket term used by doctors for a lot of different viral disorders that affect the central nervous system. I was wondering, did they made any attempt to culture for viruses or do any serotyping?"

"I looked over Thomas's report. There was nothing I recall to say they did," McCarty told him. "My guess is they didn't, since there was little question about the cause of death. Why?"

"I don't know. Just a hunch." Russell didn't want to tell his old friend too much for fear of being thought of as a conspiracy theorist. "I guess since he'd become semi-famous, I thought there might be a little more interest in exactly why he died."

"Oh, you mean because he was part of the team that worked on the vice president," McCarty said. "Around here that never got much press. We get used to working on the so-called dignitaries. It's all in a day's work."

Someone knocked on the door of the doctors' dictating room. "Yes?" he barked out.

"Doctor Russell, we have a patient in the trauma room in pretty bad pain," the emergency-room nurse said through the closed door.

"I'll be right there," he called before returning his attention to the phone. "Lowell, do me a really big favor if you can. See if you can run down a sample of Clayton Thomas's blood and send it to me. I promise you, if it's what I think it is, I'll tell you everything. If not, chalk it up to your old crazy medical school friend turning into one of those conspiracy nuts."

. . .

"I told you I'd get back to you as soon as I was through." Harrison Tate punched off his cellular telephone and thrust it into his breast pocket. The calls from Stanford Melton were now a regular occurrence. "How much do I have to give to pay off an old debt?" he muttered to himself as he pushed open the door to the guardhouse at the east entrance to the White House.

"I'm here to see the president," he said, flashing his security clearance card to the guard. Tate felt like an old dog tethered to a choke collar—his neck jerked at their whim, the air blocked from his lungs as he was forced to do their bidding. If they did not back off soon, he would tell the president everything, no matter the consequences. Then he would see what Savage and his goons thought about that. He grinned to himself.

"The president is waiting for you," the guard said, hanging up the phone. "You know the way, senator."

As Tate bent over to pick up his briefcase, blackness closed in around him. He quickly straightened up, blinking off the fogginess. This was not the first time he had experienced these strange sensations. Over the last several days his vision had playing tricks on him, going in and out like a lightbulb that was about to burn out.

"You all right, sir?"

Tate nodded and pushed open the door. "Just too many things on my plate." But he told himself that if his symptoms did not clear, he would give old Doc Ramey a call in a day or two. First he had an appointment with the president.

. . .

"Let's wait in the study," Sharon Winslet said as she headed down the hall after greeting Tate at the door to the private quarters on the second floor of the White House. "Raymond promised he wouldn't be too long. But you know how that is."

They had not made it more than halfway down the hall when Tate felt the darkness close in around him once again. This time he could not shake it off, and he thrust out his arm to try to break his fall. But it was too late. He lunged forward, his hand striking soft flesh before he fell out of control into the blackness that opened up in front of him.

At first he saw only a faint light off in the distance. Tate blinked repeatedly as the long hall slowly came back into focus. The First Lady's coughing urged him back to reality. He struggled to a sitting position as the darkness faded. Sharon Winslet was sprawled out on the floor before him. "I'm sorry," he choked out. "I must have tripped on the carpet and brought you down with me." Embarrassed, Tate fought to make sense out of what had happened. "I hope I didn't hurt you."

"I'm just more startled than anything," Sharon answered as she righted herself to her knees. "Let me help you." She stood up and then reached out to help Tate to his feet. "Nasty scrape you've got there," she said, noticing the cut on the top of his head.

"Yes, another embarrassing moment, I'm afraid." Tate's answer was weak. "I think it happened yesterday. Lately my memory has been playing tricks on me."

"What the hell?" Winslet barked as he appeared at the master bedroom door. "Never mind, I just thought I heard—Good evening, Senator," the president said as he held out his hand. "I hope Sharon has taken care of you."

"Quite the opposite. I almost took care of her. Good to see you, Mr. President."

The threesome proceeded into the private dining area, Winslet totally unaware of what had just occurred. Tate knew Sharon would relate the whole story to her husband after he had gone.

The meal was without incident as they made mostly small talk about happenings back in Colorado and their families. As the dessert was cleared from the table, Sharon excused herself. Tate stumbled to get up but once again he felt a wave of darkness come over him, pushing him back into his chair.

"Senator, all you need is a good woman to take care of you," Sharon said as she turned to leave. It had been two years since Tate's wife died. To most of the Washington establishment, Tate had been a model husband. Only the senator himself—and Palmer, Melton, and a dead young woman—knew otherwise. The First Lady was just one of many who wanted to fix up the senator with one of Washington's numerous widows. So far, Tate had resisted.

"Maybe one of these days I'll take you up on your offer," Tate answered, trying to be gracious as he waited anxiously for his vision to clear.

"Harrison, I have a real problem," the president said once Sharon had left. He stood up from the table and moved over to the caddy against the far wall. "I need your advice and, I hope, support." He signaled to Tate to select an after-dinner drink.

"How about a Kahlúa?" Tate pointed. "Takes care of the coffee and liquor all in one."

The president poured one for Tate and one for himself. Then he returned to the table with the drinks. "The code name is Mother Lode."

The president laid out the particulars of the project as Tate sat motionless in his chair, not sure what his response should be. The more the president told him, the more Tate felt boxed in. What pushed him over the edge was when the president mentioned a possible spy in his inner circle. A feeling of suffocation filled his throat and he reached for a sip of water.

"Watch out," the president said, leaning forward. But Tate's arm lurched, knocking over the glass and spilling the dark brown, sticky liquid onto the antique white tablecloth to his right. Tate squinted. Something had happened, but he couldn't make sense of it.

"Harrison, are you OK?"

"I have been a little under the weather." Tate forced out the words, hoping the president had not picked up on his edginess. "Mr. President, you just caught me off guard."

"The whole thing has me pretty upset too," Winslet said. "That's why I need your help. Don't worry. I'll get someone to clean up the mess."

"Clean up what?" Tate looked around and realized what he had done. "I'm sorry. I didn't even see it."

"Harrison, let me get you another one."

Tate held up his hand as he pushed himself up from the table. "Mr. President, I know who . . ." He stopped cold, not able to get the words out. One part of him wanted to scream the name of the White House informant; the other responded to the choke collar tight around his neck. "I know that I will give you my full support. But if you'll excuse me, I need to see if I can get in touch with an old doctor friend of mine. I've got a headache that just won't quit."

. . .

"Seems like we did this just yesterday," Chad Madden said, slipping off his jacket and hanging it on the hook next to their dimly lit booth in Tyson's Corner. "I'm sorry I'm late, but you know how that is."

He threw her a weak grin, hoping the forty-five–minute delay wouldn't put a damper on the evening. Although he had a lot on his plate, their previous meeting at the remote pub had rekindled some of his old feelings. After their business was out of the way . . . well, Madden was never one to pass up an opportunity if it presented itself. That was, if the Iranians did not attack Kuwait and ignite a war in the meantime.

The message from Jennifer Smitt had been on his desk when he arrived after a luncheon briefing with the president: "Tyson's Corner at 6:45. I'll make the reservations." In the aftermath of the death of Rosalyn Delstrotto, the election, and the new tasks of helping organize Winslet's administration, Madden was tired. Four years of mostly eighteen-hour days were taking their toll. Were it not for the occasional outings with Jason Clark, he would have had no social life at all. And even Clark had been preoccupied. Being chief of staff had become Madden's entire life. He ate, drank, and slept it. Madden could not blame anyone but himself. But maybe tonight, if business went well and Jennifer had found evidence that would blast away the worst of his suspicions, he could have some private pleasure.

"I quit counting after the first fifteen minutes," she answered, sliding over to make room. "I already ordered the first round." Jennifer nodded toward the second glass of wine already sitting on the table.

Madden scooted in beside her, his pulse up a notch in anticipation. "Did you already order us dinner too?" he said, trying to take the edge off.

"No. It's been so long, I wasn't sure what you would want," Jennifer answered without a smile. She slid an envelope out from under her plate and put it under Madden's.

"The files are in there, including the last name on your list," Jennifer said quietly. "The birth dates on all of the files were entered the same wrong way as Trainer's. But there's even more."

Madden took a sip of his wine and then scanned the small restaurant to see if anyone was looking at them. As far as he could tell, everybody else seemed to be doing their own thing. Only he knew what was happening between himself and Jennifer, although it could affect the future security of this country. The thought left him burdened and lonely.

"You said there was more?" Madden set his glass down.

"Yes, I decided to go through one file and check it out completely. I looked at Congressman Rolands for anything out of the ordinary. The one thing that struck me was the letter of reprimand he received for a security violation before his discharge from the army. He was caught fraternizing with a known East German sympathizer." She paused. Her hand trembled slightly as she fingered a breadstick from the basket on the table. "The matter seemed out of character based on the rest of his career. He was an Explorer in the Boy Scouts, ROTC in college, and volunteered for the military. The accusation just didn't fit his profile."

"It shocked me too when we found it in his file," Madden said, hoping once again he was not turning into one of those crazy conspiracy theorists. "That was the reason Winslet took Rolands' name out of consideration. I have no doubt he's a good man, but we just couldn't afford to take the chance so close to the election."

"Well, I checked out his military record," Jennifer said, the breadstick now in crumbs. "With my clearance, I can get into all the US intelligence information files. So I looked up Congressman Rolands' name in the US Army file. There was nothing about a letter of reprimand. Just the opposite. He received a letter of commendation upon discharge."

Madden was more puzzled than ever as he fumbled with the file under his plate. "Maybe the army just wanted to do him a favor and leave it out since it wasn't serious enough to get him court-martialed."

"I thought of that. But it would be against US Army policy," Jennifer continued. "And even if that was what they did, there would still have to be a record somewhere. He was stationed in Frankfurt, Germany, so I pulled up the proceedings of all hearings that took place when Rolands was stationed there. As far as I can tell, the incident didn't occur."

Dumbfounded, Madden stared at Jennifer. Had the same thing happened to the other five candidates, or was someone out to discredit Rolands in particular? He had to know more.

"What about the last name on the list?" Madden asked anxiously as he glanced around the low-lighted pub once again.

"I'm not sure," Jennifer answered. Her eyes fell from his.

"What do you mean, dammit?" he asked.

"First, nothing in Savage's file really stood out the way it did with Rolands," Jennifer answered, her voice low. "In fact, that's what bothered me."

Madden stared at Jennifer, not quite sure what she meant.

"Look at the length of the other files, such as Rolands or Senator Jarratt." Jennifer went on. "Their files are much longer, and they haven't been around Washington half as long as the vice president. It's almost as if something was missing."

"Did you check anywhere else?"

"I was afraid to," Jennifer retorted. "My job is already in jeopardy because of your hunches. I don't need to add to the problem by getting caught snooping into other security areas where I'm not supposed to be."

Madden knew he was pushing too hard. She was doing him a favor in the first place, especially given the casual way he had treated her in the past. "I understand," he said softly. "But the whole thing makes me wonder. In fact, it scares the hell out of me."

Jennifer did not look up. Her hands trembled as she popped a few pieces of what was left of the crumbled breadstick into her mouth.

Madden continued. "Listen. Something's going on here. I'm not sure what. Right now I don't even know who to go to. You've done enough." He looked over at Jennifer, recognizing the fear in her eyes. "Getting in trouble with your boss at the FBI over a few files could be a slap on the wrist, though, compared to the magnitude of what might be happening. But I have to ask you—beg you—to keep this private. You need to give me time to figure out what's going on."

Jennifer nodded, patting his knee. Madden slipped the envelope out from under his tray and placed it in the briefcase.

"Now," he said, picking up the menu. "What was that you used to get on your pizza?"

"Artichokes," she replied with a forced smile. "They say it's supposed to be an aphrodisiac, but I wouldn't know." She glanced down at her watch. "Because it looks as though I'm going to have to take a rain check."

"We just got started," Madden said, sensing his opportunity slipping away.

"Maybe you did, but I never mix business with pleasure," she answered, her voice turning stern once again. She gently nudged him in the side to let her out. "If you want a real date, you've got my number."

. . .

"Just be patient," the man in the Manhattan high-rise repeated, the swirl of smoke surrounding him like a cloud. "If Harrison Tate follows the same course as the others, he should no longer be a problem in a couple of days."

Stanford Melton's voice was troubled. "I'm telling you, the son of a bitch is going to spill his story—if he hasn't already," he said. "When he called after meeting with the president, he told me that if I didn't get off his back it was going to be over for all of us. He's threatened it before, but I think he means it this time. Then he mumbled something about a doctor and hung up."

The man tapped his smudged nails against his keyboard. "I know. We've been monitoring Tate's calls. After he hung up with you, he tried to get in touch with his doctor." He waved the thick smoke from around his face. "Right now, it looks as if the senator is more concerned with the personal matters on his mind than intrigue . . . that is, whatever mind he has left."

. . .

"Follow her," Gerald Lynn said at a table not more than ten feet away from where Madden and Jennifer had been seated. The other occupant at Lynn's table got up and followed Jennifer out of the restaurant. He was careful to maintain his distance so as not to be noticed.

Gerald Lynn, Jonathan Savage's chief of domestic policy, had just arrived. He noticed Madden and the young lady in the far corner as he was looking around for the person he was supposed to meet. At first Lynn was going to go up and say hello.

Savage's staff had been given orders to "get to know" all the president's people. It was a way of building trust. But when he saw the girl slide some papers slid under Madden's plate, Lynn decided to back off.

Lynn could sense when something was not right. Madden fidgeted in his chair, constantly looking around. So far, neither the president's chief of staff nor the girl had had anything to eat. And now she was leaving. It was not a lover's quarrel. Through his long years as an espionage agent, Lynn had learned a great deal about people by just watching them. He was trained to spot a fake at fifty yards, anything that was not what it appeared to be. His life had depended on it. Right now, Madden and the girl were the fake.

. . .

Chad Madden stood up to leave, tucking his briefcase under his arm. As he turned, he recognized Gerald Lynn seated at a table near the front door. Madden thought about just leaving, as if he had not seen him, but it was too late. Madden drew in a deep breath and walked up to Lynn, extending his hand.

"What brings you here, out to the wilds of suburban Virginia?" Madden asked.

"You know the vice president," Lynn answered quickly. "He has us running all over Washington. What about you?"

Madden had to think fast; he could not claim it was for business. "Just a little R&R," he responded. "She's an old flame and needed a little fatherly advice from her former boyfriend. I'm told women do that a lot—move their ex from being a lover to a father." Madden could not tell if Lynn bought the story. It sounded good, and to a certain extent it was true, which was good in case Lynn had her checked out. "I'm headed back to the White House to finish up some correspondence. Are you just leaving? Do you want a ride?" he asked, hoping Lynn would not take him up on the offer.

"No, thanks," Lynn answered. "I have a few more things to do while I'm out here."

Suddenly Madden's iPhone started vibrating at his side. He punched the readout.

It was Winslet's assistant's private number. "Got to run. The president calls."

Lynn nodded without saying a word as Madden walked away. Once Madden reached the door, he cut a quick look back over his shoulder, only to see Lynn still looking at him. There was an odd smile on Lynn's face. Madden would have paid a million bucks to know why.

. . .

Gerald Lynn glanced down at his watch. He had planned to make this trip to the FBI library the evening before. The chance meeting with Madden had set him behind. If he was going to get the information he needed, he needed to move fast. Trainer and Savage would be waiting. He grabbed his Samsung smartphone and stuffed it into his pocket.

Then he headed to the part of the building that contained the archives of all historical events that affected the security of the United States in any way.

Lynn weaved his way through the maze of open display cases containing documents and photographs from past FBI investigations until he arrived at the rear desk. He was not interested in the part of the library that was open to the public. After presenting his credentials to the guard on duty, he opened his briefcase for inspection and stepped through the metal detector.

Once he cleared security, the guard pushed a button below his desk. Two metal doors on the rear wall opened before him. Lynn entered the second room and walked up to the desk in the center. This part of the library was much different from the first. There were no display cases or pictures. The room, easily as large as the first Lynn entered, was lined with boxes from floor to ceiling, like a bank for documents. This was where the FBI kept all classified documents from previous investigations. Much went on within the organization that the public would never know of even if the investigations had long since ceased.

"I believe the vice president informed you that I would be coming," he declared, handing the attendant his identification card with his photo and thumbprint on it.

"Thank you, Mr. . . . Lynn," she replied, checking to see that his face matched the one on his ID card. "Would you put your thumb on the scanner?" She pointed to a black pad with a small green light in the center that lay on the counter.

Lynn did so as the attendant slipped his card into a scanner box located in front of her. Within ten seconds the screen lit up with the word "Accepted." She handed Lynn his ID card.

"Yes, sir, he did. And I believe we have the items the vice president requested." She handed him three files, each about two inches thick. "And this one I believe you requested. We had to get the director's approval first." She pulled up a fourth file with "Top Secret" branded across the front and pushed it in Lynn's direction. "Don't forget this," she said, holding out a key with the number sixteen imprinted on it. "Do you know how it works around here?"

Lynn nodded, scooped up the key, and headed off in the direction of the individual cubicles that were used for private viewing of the confidential documents. Before he disappeared into the booth, he looked up at the four security cameras that loomed above him. Tucking the folders under his arm, he grinned to himself, knowing how blind they were to what really went on behind the locked doors.

He had an hour until he returned the files to the attendant. That was enough time, however, to get the information he wanted. Closing the door behind him, he looked down at the printing on the front labels as he set the files down on the small table. The first two words on all of the files were the same: Transition Period. The last were all different: Roosevelt–Truman, Kennedy–Johnson, and Nixon–Ford. The last file, the one with no label, was on a different subject altogether. Lynn's heart raced as he untied the cord and pulled out the papers. This file was coded "Iranian Bioterrorism Agents."

12

AS THEY FILED into the Cabinet room, Madden made mental notes about the character, typical reactions, and political loyalties of each legislator. By 8:30 a.m., they had all arrived, all but one—Harrison Tate. The leadership of both parties and the ranking members of the appropriate committees assembled around the conference table, not more than fifty feet away from the Oval Office. To a casual observer, they might have seemed part of an old fraternity, friends to the end, not bitter rivals, as Madden knew they were, whose stances on the critical issues of the times were so polarized that without a legislative outlet for their contention, many of their disagreements would have been settled with dueling pistols. But not this morning. With the latest election cycle finally over, it was time to repair old relationships and commit to the work for which they had been elected, pretending to set aside politics in favor of policy.

All heads turned when President Winslet entered the room. The participants, including Madden, stood in unison, not only to honor the presidency but also because they esteemed

Winslet, the man. He had brought the parties together on many critical issues during his first term in office, earning a great deal of personal respect on Capitol Hill. Madden knew history might not judge Winslet as one of the greatest US presidents, but he would easily make the top third, and part of the reason was the content of his character.

"Where's Harrison?" Winslet whispered in Madden's ear after he had made his way around the room, shaking hands with each of the leadership in attendance.

"I don't know, Mr. President. I talked to him yesterday and he said he would be here. He did sound a little different, however."

"What do you mean?" Winslet inquired.

"I'm not sure," Madden answered, in a low tone so as not to be overheard by the other participants. "Not like his usual self. He seemed really uptight, said there was something I ought to know about your decision. But when I tried to probe him further, he cut me off."

"What decision?" The president asked, confused. "Chad, as soon as we finish here, check on him and let me know." He then turned to the group who were eating their breakfasts and pushed back his untouched plate. "I know you must be wondering why I have asked you here," Winslet began uneasily.

The conversations stopped. The president came right to the point.

"Several months ago, in an effort to moderate our role as the policeman of the entire world, I asked our military leaders to bring to me proposals that could allow us to better allocate our military and defense resources. This was a policy that everyone in this room has advocated since we all came to Washington. My first priority was to keep from compromising our own national security. Additionally we needed to protect this country's financial interests abroad, if at all possible. The third requirement was to avoid allowing the security of our allies to be threatened as we reappraised our commitments. A fairly tall order but, according to our military leaders, doable at least in some areas."

Madden watched, wondering how the president would present his administration's unilateral defense decision in Kuwait.

"In order to protect the security of the countries involved, my administration decided to keep certain of these plans secret until they had reached a more formal stage. As it turns out, the plans were closer to going into effect than we anticipated. Not informing the Congressional leadership may have been a mistake, for which I am totally to blame."

When Ken Trainer, who was seated behind the vice president, edged back against the wall, his movement caught Madden's eye. At first Madden had objected to Trainer's being invited, but he felt that openly protesting could only lead to questions from the president he could not have answered. He would let it be, at least for now. Trying not to look obvious, Madden continued to watch as Trainer slowly slipped his hand inside his jacket pocket and then pulled it back out again quickly.

"The first of these projects was to take place in Kuwait, but something went wrong," Winslet said. "The Iranians found out about our scheme. We don't know how, but it has been confirmed through our sources."

Madden knew the president did not want to share any more information about United States intelligence activity than necessary, especially since there had already been a leak somewhere in his inner circle. But in an intractable position, he had no other choice. Now he painstakingly laid out the proposed plans of the Mother Lode project.

"With all due respect, Mr. President," the Senate minority leader interrupted, his tone harsh. "It sounds like you've gotten your ass in a crack and you want us to help bail you out."

Madden expected that reaction from the opposing party. But as long as they could keep the anger secret, confined to this room, and not let their differences spill over into the halls of Congress and to the media, he and the president would consider they had achieved a partial victory.

"Joe, you and I go back a long way," the president replied. He fixed his stare on the senator from Florida. "As I recall, we have had presidents from both sides of the aisle who have led this country into questionable conflicts. Let me remind you of two such instances in my own party: Eisenhower's funding of the Bay of Pigs invasion and Reagan's support of the Contra affair. Kennedy's mistakes belong to your party. Some of these missteps were made with the blessing of the Congress and, unfortunately, some without. These leaders supported ill-fated causes because they thought they were in the best interest of their country. As commander and chief, I must live with that responsibility."

The senator shuffled in his chair. "I was only saying . . ."

"I know what you were saying," Winslet fired back without giving him a chance to finish. "My unfortunate misjudgment aside, the issue is: Are we going to abandon perhaps the world's most important energy supply or are we, as the elected leadership in this country, going to come together to protect it?" Winslet leaned away from the table. "Joe, it's your call."

The senator sunk back in his seat. Madden watched as all those in attendance responded to the president's every word, save one—the vice president. His eyes darted around the room. Beads of sweat glistened on Savage's forehead. Suddenly his and Madden's glances met. Savage forced a weak smile, and then looked away.

"Mr. President, does that mean you aren't going to go through with the project, now that the Iranians know?" the new speaker of the House of Representatives, Congressman Rolands asked.

"I'm not sure at this point, Jim," Winslet answered. "That's part of the reason I asked all of you here, to seek your advice. To ask for your pledge of secrecy at this point. And . . . to acknowledge that I should have been more open with the congressional leadership from the start."

Madden knew that because the president had admitted his mistake in keeping the project from them, there was not much the leadership on either side of the aisle could do, especially since the plan had not even gone into effect. Everyone would agree that national security required further secrecy. He let out a slow sigh of relief as the congressional anger was tempered by Winslet's conciliatory comments. His boss had almost four more years in office left. It was time to build bridges, not tear them down.

Given their continued silence, Madden assumed that those in attendance would stand at the president's side on this issue. Everyone agreed that the United States could no longer be the world's policeman. At the same time, the country had to protect its own interests and those of its allies. America had to look carefully at the alternatives to direct military muscle, especially in the Persian Gulf. An uncomfortable hush fell across the room; everyone seemed to be waiting for someone else to continue the debate. The new Speaker of the House began. "Mr. President, my recommendation would be to continue as planned."

The president appeared concerned. "Don't you think we've lost our element of surprise, since the Iranians already know?"

"Yes and no," Rolands answered. "They know about our plans now. What they don't know is that we might change them. Evidently the Iranians have the exact location of each of our planned missile batteries. Let's double that number—but move the other half to different locations." Rolands stopped for a moment, appearing to collect his thoughts. "The initial sites could be dummies with fake missiles."

The Speaker's plan made sense to Madden. A perfect distraction with the knowledge of the real deterrent known only to a handful of technicians and the president's chosen few.

"If the Iranians decide to attack, they would waste their energy on the dummy sites, leaving the real locations to inflict their damage," Rolands went on. "All the while, the whole project is at least partially funded by the Kuwaitis themselves. Even they wouldn't need to know that half of the sites weren't real."

"Jim, you are a genius," Winslet said, smiling. Madden wondered if the president was thinking to himself that it was Rolands he should have selected as his running mate instead of Savage.

The president turned to the rest of the group around the table, wanting to see their response. To a person, they all nodded. "I hope I can take your agreement to mean you will support the additional allocations, which we will slip into the defense budget." Winslet's voice cracked with what sounded like relief.

After the meeting adjourned, Madden and the president returned to the Oval Office, where Winslet's administrative assistant, Leta Sims, pointed to her wristwatch. "You know we're already fifteen minutes behind schedule, sir."

"Leta, we're always behind," he told her with a slight grin. "It's only a matter of how much. Now close the door. Another couple of minutes more won't be much worse." Winslet turned to Madden. "I want to put you and Savage in charge of this project."

"What do you mean?" Madden asked, feeling his chest constrict at the thought of his new assignment with the vice president. "Why?"

"The leaks," the president replied. "We have to stop the leaks. The only way to do this is either find out who the spy is or, if that's not possible, cut down on the number of people who know."

Madden moved over to the president's desk. "Why me?" he questioned. "Why Savage?"

"Why not?" the president snapped back. "Chad, as you just said, there are only two ways to deal with people who can't be trusted—you either cut them out, or you do something to bring them out. Both of you are supposed to be my closest allies. If only the two of you and a handful of military advisers know the exact location of the second set of missile batteries, then there shouldn't be a problem—should there?"

Madden was not sure if the president's last remark was a statement or a question.

Until the chief of staff could find out more about the leaks—and those suspicious FBI files—he would act as if it were the former.

. . .

The call came in to the president's assistant around three o'clock that afternoon. Harrison Tate had been rushed to Georgetown Medical Center's emergency room. No other information was available except that he was listed in critical condition. Madden had tried to call earlier, but was not able to get through to the senator's office.

"Mr. President, I told them who I was," Madden said. "They said it didn't matter, that it would matter even if I were you. The only information they would give out was that Tate was critical."

"Shit! First Rosie and now Harrison." Winslet looked over at Madden, his face painted with anguish. "Just go on over there and see what's going on. I'll put in a call to the hospital administrator's office to clear the way."

Madden had turned to leave when the president called out, "Chad, we need to know what Harrison meant about my 'decision.'"

. . .

"Mr. Madden, the senator is in room 816," the guard said as they stepped off the elevator at Georgetown Medical Center. "Just follow the hall and turn to the left."

Madden made his way down the dimly lit corridor. There were no doors on the rooms, just curtains he assumed could be drawn for privacy. He could hear muted conversations and an occasional moan, often drowned out by the whirring sounds of the respirators and the beeping of the monitors. The place gave Madden the creeps. He avoided looking at the patients, most of whom lay half conscious, kept alive by modern technology until their own bodies could take over again, if their bodies ever could. It seemed like forever until Madden found 816.

Madden pushed back the half-drawn curtain and stepped uneasily into Tate's cubicle. The senator was barely recognizable in the darkened room. The monitor mounted on the far wall cast an eerie green hue across the senator's motionless body. Madden looked up at the flashing numbers and squiggles that danced across the screen. A tube of life-saving oxygen wrapped around his face, while fluids rushed into his body through the IV that clung to the back of his right hand.

Madden approached the senator carefully, not wanting to disturb him. Suddenly Tate opened his eyes. For a moment, Madden was startled. "Good evening, sir. The president sent me over here to make sure they were taking good care of you."

The senator smiled when he recognized the familiar face. Then his smile quickly turned to a frown. "Whatever this is, Madden, it's taken . . ."

His voice cut off abruptly as he thrust his arm in Madden's direction. Madden felt a blow to his groin, which caused him to jump back and almost knock over the IV stand beside the senator's bed. At first he thought the senator was having a seizure.

"Senator, are you all right?" Madden asked, still trying to recover from the surprise.

"Yes... I think so," Tate replied vaguely. "Please forgive me. I just didn't see you. Come around to the foot of the bed."

Madden realized that Tate must have had a stroke, since he appeared to be blind to the side. Tears began to cloud Tate's eyes.

"Chad, I'm scared," the senator sobbed. "I don't know what the hell is going on. I can't see. I'm falling all over the place. Now they tell me I had a seizure."

Madden didn't know what else to do. He was no doctor. So he did his best. He tried to comfort Tate. "They tell me you're going to be fine," Madden said, knowing it was a lie.

"Bullshit," the senator shot back angrily. "You don't know that. It's probably a... brain tumor."

The senator appeared to stop in mid-sentence. Madden was not sure what would come next. Then Tate held out his hand.

"Come over here," he said, almost in a whisper.

Madden walked around from the foot of Tate's bed to where he had stood before and held out his hand. The senator motioned to Madden to bend down as he began to whisper. "Do you remember when I told you about the president's decision?"

Madden nodded as he bent closer. "Yes, sir, about the Mother Lode project."

"No! It's about the information leak in the White House." Tate's eyes flashed.

"Whatever happens, I need you to tell the president something for me." The senator drew in a deep breath and then raised his eyes to meet Madden's. "Tell him I misled him about the *recommendation*. He'll know what I mean."

. . .

Cindy French's car was parked in his driveway when Dan Russell nudged open his back door. "Smells like I'm in for a treat," he called out as the aroma of Cindy's famous spaghetti sauce tickled his nose.

Russell had taken the day shift to fill in for one of his fellow doctors who had gone on a brief vacation. The day shift was usually not too bad. The patients were mostly a procession of minor injuries or snotty-nosed kids whose parents did not have insurance and so had nowhere else to bring them. In some ways, Russell felt sorry for them, because they had no choice. The real tragedy was that at least half of the patients who presented to the Irving Central emergency room could afford health insurance premiums but chose to spend their money elsewhere. Now they would pay the price for their choice. Russell did not set the rates charged by the hospital, but he knew the patients paid at least double, sometimes even more, than they would pay a regular physician, because the emergency room had to get its cut too.

"I hope you worked up an appetite," Cindy answered, peeking her head around the cabinet door.

Today had been unusually hectic for Russell. There had been an outbreak of dysentery at the local high school. Unable to handle all the cases, the local physicians had triaged their sickest patients to the emergency room for intravenous fluids. Fortunately for most, all they needed were IVs and medications to stem the tide of their uncontrollable diarrhea. But about ten of the sickest patients had to be admitted for observation and systemic antibiotics. He had made it through the shift. The pace, however, had left him exhausted and hungry. Cindy's offer to cook dinner was very inviting.

Since he was paying more attention to what his girlfriend was cooking than to the mail, Russell nearly missed the small package tucked under the stack of unsolicited junk mail that arrived at his home each day. All of his important correspondence came to the billing office at the hospital, but as he picked up the assortment of brightly colored pamphlets and envelopes, a brown package measuring approximately one inch wide by four inches in length dropped to the floor.

Thinking it was just another drug sample from one of the numerous pharmaceutical companies that constantly solicited physicians, he tossed the small box on top of the pile and laid the stack next to his answering machine on the kitchen counter.

Russell grabbed a beer from the refrigerator and turned to Cindy. "When's the first course?"

"Not so fast," she said, barely looking up from her position at the hot stove. "We need to talk before we eat. You've been somewhere else recently, mentally and emotionally, that is."

Russell sighed. It had been a long day. "Well, I've been working hard, but—"

"That's not what I mean," she interrupted. "Something is going on that you're not telling me." Her face was long, troubled.

"It's that I'm . . . the vice president's death," he forced out. "Well, it wasn't by natural causes, the way the press has said."

She laid down the spoon and rolled her eyes. "That's why you spend hours scouring the newspaper and staring into the computer screen." She cut him a doubtful look. "You're not turning into one of those conspiracy—"

"Nuts!" He stopped her. "I hope not." Now he was even more convinced that, for now at least, she did not need to know what little it was he knew. "It's that I'm . . . let's say . . . intrigued. It's my medical duty."

She turned back to the stove and picked up the spoon. "There are just a lot of other things in this world I'd rather spend my time on," she muttered.

Frustrated by Cindy's dismissal, Russell cut his eyes back to the stack of unopened mail. "Well, I'll be damned," he blurted out, recognizing the return address.

Suddenly the travails of the day and Cindy's brush-off vanished as Russell snatched the small package off the top of the pile and grabbed a paring knife from the counter. His pulse quickened as he cut open the end, shaking the contents out onto the counter—cotton padding surrounding a vial of blood. Also included was a folded piece of paper. Russell opened it up and read silently to himself.

Dan,
You owe me one. Most of Thomas's blood was already clotted when they brought him in. But this was left over from the toxicology screen. You were in luck. They were just about to throw it out because all the tests had come back negative. I had to twist a few arms. They have this strict protocol. I told them it was for a research project. Even then, it cost me a lobster dinner.
—Lowell

"What's that?" Cindy asked, looking back over her shoulder.

Russell shot her a glance. "Just a drug sample." Stuffing the vial and the note into his shirt pocket, he picked up his beer. "The pharmaceutical companies never seem to give up." His mind raced as he thought about the possibilities. Frustrated, he realized it was too late in the day to contact his friend at the medical school. He would have to wait until the morning. For now he would have to suspend his curiosity and resign himself to focusing on Cindy's home-cooked meal. He reached into the cabinet and pulled out two wine glasses. "How about I make myself useful and set the table?"

. . .

"Why in the hell did I have to hear about it over the damned television?" Leonard Palmer yelled into the telephone. His clenched fist clung to the receiver as he fought to control his anger. He would never have claimed to be the most ethical businessman in the community, but he had never done anything like this before. To make things worse, he had betrayed a friend. He had sold his soul to the devil to make good on some pressing debts. As far as he was concerned, the least the son of a bitch could do was keep him informed about what was going on.

"Calm down," Stanford Melton answered, his tone even, almost condescending. "You're going to give yourself a heart attack. He isn't dead yet. At least, not that we know, and my contact at the hospital is pretty reliable."

"Listen, Stanford, my ass is on the line and—"

"Just shut up!" Melton dictated. "You never know who might be listening."

"Has he talked?"

"I don't know. The president's chief of staff came over and they spoke a few minutes. We couldn't get close enough to hear what was being said."

Palmer's guilt was getting the best of him, and he knew it was beginning to show. If he had it to do again, he would have turned down the offer. He just wanted this to be over. Then maybe he could go on with his life.

"Your friend should be out of his misery in the next day or two," Melton said, his voice icy. "If not, we know someone who might help him along."

. . .

As President Winslet's administrative assistant, Leta Sims, ushered the ambassador from Paraguay out the door, Winslet leaned in to hear Madden's words.

"Tate said you would know what he meant."

The senator's remark literally shook the president. Winslet reached out and grabbed the edge of the desk for support. "Did he say anything else?"

"No, not really," Madden answered. "He did complain about not being able to see."

"Was he blind?"

"Not exactly. He said something about falling and maybe having a seizure. I have a bruise in my groin to prove it."

"What about the doctors? What did they say?"

"Are you ready for the gentlemen from the NAACP, Mr. President?" Mrs. Sims interrupted as she poked her head back through the doorway.

"No, Leta," the president said over his shoulder as he fought to make sense of Tate's message. "Give me and Chad a few minutes."

"I never saw a doctor," Madden answered, "just Tate's nurse, and she wasn't sure what his problem was. According to the information she had, the most likely diagnosis was a stroke."

Winslet grew more and more disturbed at the news. Not only was one of his closest confidants probably dying in a hospital halfway across town, Tate's whispered and inexplicable retraction of his recommendation suggested that the president may have made a disastrous blunder in choosing Savage as his vice president. But how had this happened, and why?

"I have to see him!" the president blurted out.

"Let me look at your schedule for tomorrow and see what we can arrange."

"Not tomorrow. Now!" Winslet's voice reverberated through the Oval Office as he reached for the interoffice telephone. "I'll see the NAACP lobbyists while you put it together." Winslet had to know exactly what his close confidant was trying to tell him. "Mrs. Sims, please bring in our friends." He rose from his chair, prepared to greet his guests.

. . .

As he looked out across the Washington landscape, the older gentleman fingered the drawstring on the window shade. He squinted at the bright light that flooded into his apartment—a harsh harbinger of the spotlight that would soon fall on him. The capital had always been his city. In the past he had operated out of the shadows, which is where he would like to have remained, but all that was about to change. This time his voice would be the one they would follow in the silent war to change the direction of the United States from within.

Some would say he had betrayed the values of his country. History, however, was on his side, as it showed how leader after leader throughout the ages had been able to command a country to his cause—to capture hearts and minds that were committed to an opposite set of beliefs and to make them his own through his power and persuasiveness. What seemed impossible now would soon be more likely than anyone could imagine.

A thin grin spread across his mouth at the news from his contact in the Manhattan apartment. With the senator's impending demise another loop in the circle would be closed. They had been friends once, but, like the others, Tate would give his life, however unwillingly, to a greater cause.

13

"**Code Blue!** Intensive care unit! Code Blue! Intensive care unit!"

The alarm emanated from every speaker at Georgetown Medical Center. Code Blue was the signal for a cardiac arrest. Although there was a team assigned to cover such emergencies throughout the hospital, it was still the obligation of any physician in proximity to respond to the call for help until the team arrived. Lowell McCarty just happened to be in the ICU, making final rounds on one of his own patients, when the alarms in Tate's cubicle went off.

"He's in 816," the nurse sputtered as she pointed anxiously down the hallway. "Can you tell me anything about him?" McCarty asked as he hurried off in the direction of 816.

"Senator Harrison Tate," the nurse called back, somewhat out of breath, almost running as she tried to keep up with McCarty. "The admitting diagnosis is cerebral vascular accident, but it could be an aneurysm or even viral encephalopathy at this point. None of the tests are back yet. More were supposed to be done in the morning."

Apart from the nurse assigned to Tate, McCarty and the head nurse were the first to arrive. The senator lay motionless. McCarty glanced at the pattern on the cardiac monitor on the wall above Tate's bed. He was in ventricular tachycardia, and McCarty recognized it immediately.

"Get me 100 milligrams of Xylocaine—*stat!*" he shouted.

Just then the resuscitation team arrived with the crash cart. Within sixty seconds McCarty was pushing the life-saving medication into the senator's veins through the IV in his right arm. Almost simultaneously the resuscitation team assumed their positions in case the Xylocaine did not work. McCarty stepped back, the empty syringe still clasped in his hand.

All eyes were fixed on the cardiac monitor, waiting for the tracing to return to normal. It always made a strange picture, McCarty thought, when no one was looking at the patient. All the complex machines did the looking for them.

As quickly as the problem had started, the senator's tracing returned to a normal sinus rhythm. The team held their positions for a full five minutes. No change. He added more Xylocaine to the IV bottle to maintain cardiac stability as the team began to pack up their equipment.

"Who is he?" the leader of the resuscitation team asked.

"Harrison Tate, the Colorado senator, I'm told," McCarty replied, relieved that he did not have to see another patient die today. "The nurses said the preliminary diagnosis was a stroke, but that's all I know. I was just on the floor when the monitors started going crazy." He turned to the nurse. "Who's his regular doctor?"

"Doctor Arnold Stone admitted him, but I think they have also called in a neurologist," she answered.

McCarty pointed to the telephone on the desk at the nurses' station. "You'd better notify Doctor Stone. From the looks of what is going on here, I don't think the senator is going to make it through the night."

The nurse put in a call to Stone's answering service. McCarty could sense her frustration as she watched the resuscitation team packing up to leave.

"I've known Arnold Stone for years," McCarty said, walking over to the nurse as she waited on the telephone for some response. "I don't think he would mind if I helped out until he can get here."

The nurse seemed relieved as McCarty moved back into the senator's cubicle. He picked up the senator's chart at the foot of the bed and began thumbing through it for pertinent information. There was nothing other than vital signs and a brief admitting note. Stone had dictated the history and physical, but because the senator had just been admitted that day it was not yet on the chart. Since the patient now appeared comatose, he could offer no information. McCarty would have to revert to the very first lesson he learned in medical school: When all else fails, check the patient.

McCarty pulled out his stethoscope and listened to the senator's heart and lungs. There was nothing remarkable there. He palpated his abdomen for any pathology. The numbers on the monitor were all back in the normal range.

"Get me an ophthalmoscope," McCarty told the nurse as he put the stethoscope back in his pocket. She hurried off to fulfill his request. McCarty looked over the senator's extremities for any incriminating signs, also with no result. When the nurse returned, McCarty took the instrument from her.

"Close the curtain for me," he ordered. The room needed to be dark for him to look inside the senator's eyes.

He could see nothing! McCarty blinked and shined the light into the palm of his hand to see if it was working properly. It was. He looked again, this time with no better results. McCarty stepped away from the senator's bed and handed the ophthalmoscope back to the nurse. He pulled a small penlight from his pocket and shined it into the senator's eyes. Surprised,

McCarty looked up at the nurse. "His pupils are pinpoint. No wonder I couldn't see in. What medicines is he on?"

"None," the nurse answered, looking at Tate's chart. "At least not that I know of, except the Xylocaine you gave him."

"That wouldn't make his pupils practically disappear," McCarty snapped. "Call the lab and see if they have anything back on him yet."

The nurse turned to leave but stopped dead in her tracks. Coming toward her were two Georgetown campus police officers, followed by three or four other men in dark suits. "What the . . .?" She never got to finish her oath as the security guards rushed past her and down toward the other end of the hall.

"It's OK, ma'am," one of the men said. He wore a dark suit. "Your patient has a visitor and we just need to prepare."

McCarty started to leave the senator's room.

"Doctor, if you would please just stay here," the man stated firmly. "The president may want to talk to you about the senator's condition."

"What!" McCarty exclaimed. He wanted to tell them that Tate was really not his patient, but it was too late. The man in the dark suit stepped aside as a gray-haired gentleman walked into the room and stopped at the foot of Tate's bed.

"Doctor, what can you tell me about the senator's condition?" asked the distinguished-looking man, his steel-blue eyes fixed on McCarty.

McCarty was speechless. He could not remember when he had been so nervous. Here he was, a board-certified internist and vice chairman of the department, but McCarty did not know anything about Tate apart from his arrhythmia problem. And he had to tell that to the president of the United States.

. . .

The man in the Manhattan apartment answered on the third ring, long enough for the display to identify that the caller was his contact at the Georgetown hospital. The senator had survived the last episode of cardiac arrhythmia.

"He's a tough old bird," he said through a stream of blue smoke. "With the president and his people hovering over him, we can't take any more chances that he'll talk—that is, if he hasn't already. It appears the time has come for you to help him along."

. . .

The president stayed around for about ten minutes longer, trying to get more information on the condition of his old friend, but his wait was to no avail. The staff present had virtually no history and a paucity of results back from Tate's workup. With the senator's status temporarily stable, Lowell McCarty excused himself to finish up his rounds and try to calm his nerves. He made one last swing by the ICU to check on Tate before he headed home. Since the neurologist was on the way in to take over Tate's care, McCarty felt he was no longer needed. The president could wait no longer either. Still feeling a little guilty, McCarty requested for Tate's nurse to have the neurologist relay any new information on the senator's condition to the White House.

Although the diagnosis of viral encephalopathy was just one on a laundry list of possibilities the nurse had named, Lowell McCarty found himself nagged by this coincidence with Thomas's cause of death. He fought the urge to tie the two cases together, fearing that the paranoia of Dan Russell, his old anatomy partner, was beginning to rub off on him. Drained from a full day of his regular responsibilities in addition to his run-in with the president, McCarty drove home. As he pulled into his driveway, he started to push the garage door opener but held off and reached for his cellular telephone instead. McCarty scrolled down to Dan Russell's number and punched it. When his call transferred to the voicemail on the fourth ring, he hung up without leaving a message.

The last thing he wanted to be was labeled a conspiracy nut.

. . .

"Chad, the message you gave me from Tate?" Winslet's face revealed his troubled mind as they walked through the wintry Rose Garden after his return from Georgetown.

"Yes, Mr. President?"

"Well, he was talking about Jonathan Savage." The president spoke in a very low tone, as if the rose bushes held microphones. "I'm sure of it."

Madden walked alongside. He did not know what to say.

"Tate was asking you to tell me that he made a mistake when he suggested that I include Savage on the ticket," the president went on, his eyes looking blankly at the naked tree branches. "I don't know if he was just trying to say there was a better choice on the list, or . . ." His voice trailed off.

His escalating suspicions crying for attention, Madden could hold back no longer.

He has kept his concerns from the president long enough, wanting to wait until he had more time and more evidence. He had even considered using another source, not associated with the FBI, to double check Jennifer Smitt's fact-finding. But he could put if off no longer.

"Mr. President, I think their records were altered," Madden said softly.

"What records?" Winslet asked, his eyes hard.

"The files from the background checks. The files I pulled up for you on Rolands and all the others," Madden answered, his hands jammed in his pockets.

The president put his finger to his lips, a signal for Madden to lower his voice.

Just above a whisper, the chief of staff laid out the discrepancies that Jennifer had found in the files of Winslet's proposed vice presidential candidates. He also added his concerns over the brevity of Savage's dossier. Madden left out the part about Trainer's role in the Oval Office. For now that was just too big a reach.

Winslet leaned forward and rested his hands on his knees. "Chad, this could be some pretty heavy stuff, if your contact at the FBI is right."

Madden nodded quietly, feeling the president's pain. He had nothing else to say.

"Any suggestions?" Winslet inquired.

Madden stared back blankly. He did not have any. They walked on silently, caught in their separate thoughts. After several minutes of quiet, Chad Madden looked over at Winslet. "I do have one suggestion, Mr. President. Pray for Harrison Tate to wake up."

. . .

Savage sucked in a deep gasp as he opened the door to his inner office. The sight of Kenneth Trainer seated behind his desk caught him totally by surprise. "What the hell?" the vice president blurted out.

Trainer gave him a penetrating stare and leaned over to the telephone on Savage's desk, lifting up the receiver. "Shut up, Mr. Vice President!" the aide muttered. Then he punched in Savage's assistant's extension. "The vice president has asked me to tell you to hold all his calls," Trainer told her, his voice brusque.

Savage looked at Trainer in disbelief. Here he was, the vice president of the United States. Trainer had no right to talk to him like that, much less take over his office. "I demand a little respect. What would the president think if he heard you talking to me like that?"

"You don't demand anything from me," Trainer replied, barely above a whisper. "We're both in this together. The only difference is that your role has a little more visibility. Any respect I show you is for the good of the project. To me you are one step up from a maggot, feeding off the flesh of dead animals, off society, aching for a longer bio in the history books."

The vice president stepped back, shocked. Trainer was nothing more than a mercenary, a hired gun in a three-piece suit. He had figured out enough about Trainer to know that he had lost two older brothers in Vietnam, fighting a war that should never have been. Not only had the United States lost the war in Asia, they had lost Trainer's loyalty as well. As far as Trainer was concerned, it was every man for himself. Savage knew the only loyalty Trainer had was to the American dollar. Whoever paid the most had him on their side.

Yet Savage resented Trainer's insinuations. Fame and monetary gain had never been what motivated the vice president; he wanted only to lead his country into a new world order where black gold was the currency of choice, which was good for everybody.

Savage's chest constricted as he sat down in the chair in front of his desk and waited for Trainer to continue. His aide leaned forward, his arms outward. Savage, uncomfortable, arched backward slightly.

"Savage, I had the girl followed. The one I told you about who met Madden. She's the one who works for the FBI. So far, nothing has turned up," he said, his face absent of expression. "I can tell you though, something's not right. She passed him an envelope that they didn't want to be made public."

"You're just looking for trouble," Savage answered with confidence he did not feel.

"That's my job!" Trainer retorted. "If it wasn't for guys like me who do the dirty work, your ass would have been gone a long time ago."

Savage did not understand why Trainer was so hostile, but he was not about to ask. The less he knew about the seamy side of the operation, the better. The vice president did, however, consider himself to be a man of moral conviction, even if Trainer did not think so. The vice president was just more of a realist than the rest of his peers on Capitol Hill. Change was inevitable; Savage was convinced of that. History had proven him right again and again. The vice president wanted to be at the front of the next change. "What about Tate?" Savage asked.

"So far he's still around," Trainer said. "Madden came to visit and we couldn't tell what Tate might have said to him. By the time the president arrived, Tate was unconscious." Trainer stopped, looked at his wristwatch, and smiled. "If all goes as planned, by the time you wake up tomorrow he will no longer be a problem."

"Are you sure that's the way it has to be?" the vice president said, feeling a hint of remorse. "After all, it was Tate who helped guarantee my spot on the ticket."

"You can pay your respects to him later," Trainer answered.

The very thought sent a shiver to every part of Jonathan Savage's well manicured, chubby body. "What did you come in here to talk about?"

"It's about the envelope," Trainer whispered, glancing at the door. "What envelope?"

"The one the girl gave Madden, you idiot!"

Savage stiffened in his chair. Trainer's mood was so unpredictable. When Savage became president, Trainer would have to go. They would, at least, have to grant him that after all his efforts.

"I assume you want to know what's in it," the vice president said.

Trainer nodded. "Maybe it's really nothing. Or maybe it's something Madden doesn't want the president to know about. Or maybe it's . . ." Trainer's voice trailed off. "In any case, we have to know."

"How do you plan to find out?"

"I don't plan to do anything." Trainer leaned over so that he was an arm's reach away from Savage's sweaty face. "You will."

"Me?" Savage stammered. "Are you crazy? What if they caught me snooping around in Madden's office—snooping, the vice president of the United States?"

In less than a blink of an eye, Trainer's fist shot out across the desk and grabbed Savage by the collar. His eyes burned into Savage. "Well, Mr. Vice President, let's just hope you don't get caught."

. . .

There were two messages on Lowell McCarty's answering machine at home. Both were from Dan Russell. He needed to talk to McCarty, no matter how late it was. Russell would be at the Irving Central until eleven o'clock. Then he would be home by eleven- forty five. He left telephone numbers for both places.

. . .

Russell could hear the telephone going off as he approached his back door. Though he struggled with the lock, he was able to pick up McCarty's call by the fourth ring.

"Lowell, we have a problem!" he opened, having recognized his friend's number on the caller ID before McCarty had a chance to say anything.

"What do you mean?"

"I just found out that your pathologist died of a variant of mad cow disease, not viral encephalitis," Russell answered, out of breath. "And I guess he got it in some way from the vice president."

There was a long pause on McCarty's end of the line. "I'm . . . not sure if I understand," he muttered, his shock evident.

Russell could barely contain himself, having waited all day to tell his friend the startling results. "It's a long story and the results aren't final, since they still have to do the serotyping. I would say it's a ninety-nine percent certainty. The vice president tested positive for a rare organism in the prion family similar to what has been called kuru disease—but evidently she was infected with a much more virulent strain."

McCarty listened as Dan carefully laid out the whole story, telling him everything from the time the vice president arrived at the Irving emergency room until Thomas's blood sample tested positive for a variant of kuru disease.

"I'm embarrassed to say I don't know much about prion diseases," McCarty confessed. "As I recall, most of the cases have been in England and Africa. There hasn't been much interest in this country. I do remember they were called *slow viruses* in our medical school days. The only doctors who had any interest in them were the neurologists and neurosurgeons. Even then, since the cases were so rare, they usually ended up as the focus of a grand rounds at some academic medical center."

"I looked it up on the Internet," Russell told him. "The whole family of organisms are a kind of infectious protein. The problem is that they are so resistant, so nothing is very effective at killing them. That is why they had to shoot all those cattle in England in the late 1990s. Even cooking the meat didn't seem to kill all the virus. I was told if the patients test positive for the organism after a neurosurgical procedure, they now throw out the whole set of instruments."

"Maybe Thomas got his somewhere else?" McCarty asked.

"It's possible. The serotyping should answer that for us. If the two match, the odds that it wasn't a cross-contamination are remote."

"Dan, the only thing I remember off the top of my head is that the slow viruses had incubation times of years before the symptoms began to show up."

"Good memory," Russell said. "Some of the new strains reported in Central Africa have a much more rapid onset, with symptoms showing up in several weeks."

"Pretty scary."

"That's why I asked you to call tonight. We don't want to create a panic, but there's a possibility that everyone who came in contact with the vice president could be affected if the strains match—even me." Russell took a deep breath to steady himself. "From what little I've been able to dig up, with these new variants they haven't worked out all the transmission routes yet."

"What about you?"

"That's a good question, especially since I cracked her chest. Fortunately I had on gloves." Russell answered, trying to suppress his own fears. "I've got an appointment with my contact at the medical school for a brain scan and blood tests in the morning. Except for the three of us, nobody else knows."

"If you didn't get a break in your gloves, you're probably okay."

"Thanks, I needed to hear that." Russell sighed, glad to finally be able to confide in somebody. "I guess we'll know in a couple of days. Right now we need to make sure nobody else gets exposed."

"Don't you think we should wait for the serotyping to come back before we put up the red flag?" McCarty asked.

"Probably. I just thought that with all your connections in Washington, you could help pursue this if there turns out to be a match. The results should be back in forty-eight hours."

"Let me see what I can do, Dan. Call me as soon as you know anything."

"I'm sorry to bring you in on this," Russell said. He realized he did not want to get off the phone and face his fears in solitude. "But I didn't know who else to go to. I needed to talk to someone."

There was a pause on the line. "You're not the only one. It just comes with the territory," McCarty said.

"Want to tell me about it?"

"No big deal. Except for saving the life of a United States senator and flashing my ass to the president of the United States, my day was pretty routine."

"So you're a hero?" Russell said.

"Not exactly. I was just in the wrong place at the right time." McCarty told Russell his story about being in the intensive care unit when Tate's heart went awry. "Fortunately he turned around, at least temporarily. The worst part was having to tell President Winslet that I really didn't know what was wrong with the senator."

"I don't know what else you could have said under the circumstances," Russell said.

"You're right, but still, it was embarrassing," McCarty said. "I did try. I checked him out head to toe, but nothing turned up." He was quiet for a second, and Dan waited for him to continue. "Well . . . I'm almost ashamed to mention it. Dan, it reminded me of Thomas's tentative diagnosis of viral encephalopathy. When I responded to the Code Blue, the nurse mentioned that same condition as a possible diagnosis for Tate."

"You're kidding." Dan felt cold.

"Well, I tried to check in his eyes to see if the senator had increased intracranial pressure and couldn't," McCarty said.

"Couldn't what?"

"See anything. His pupils were pinpoint. Probably a medication or drug effect, but according to the nurse he wasn't on any drugs that would cause it."

"Did you say *pinpoint?*" Russell snapped back.

"Ah . . . yes. Why?"

Russell felt a wave of panic wash up his throat. "Lowell, so were the vice president's!"

. . .

"Jim, thank you for standing by me on this," the president said warmly as he signaled for Speaker Rolands to join him on the sofa.

It was a typical wintery Saturday in Washington, DC. The last snow from earlier in the week was melting slowly in the noonday sun. Except for a few of the key players on Winslet's team, most of the staff used the weekend as a chance to recover from the grind of the week's eighteen-hour workdays. Congress was trying to clear out the final items on the agenda before the long winter break. Led by Rolands, Winslet's allies on both sides of the aisle had stood firm and silent on the Kuwait issue. In doing so, they helped the president avoid a potentially very embarrassing situation.

Speaker Rolands had agreed to carry the water on the Mother Lode plan on Capitol Hill. It was decided that even though the Iranians seemed to be fully informed, the fewer who knew of its existence the better. That way if more leaks did occur there were fewer people to suspect. With his help, the original funds along with the additional monies for the extra sites were neatly camouflaged in the military budget. Kuwait was going to shoulder much of the financial responsibility once the project was up and running. The allocation equivalent of one less Stealth bomber would be barely noticed.

Since Rolands had not been privy to the original plan, he was not considered a suspect for the leak. The president felt he could be open with him. "Jim," Winslet continued. "Harrison Tate is a good friend and confidant."

"He was a good friend of mine too, Mr. President." Rolands paused. "I should say he *is*."

"What I am leading up to, Jim, is that when I was deciding on a running mate I had a list with six names on it. And as you know, yours was included."

"I was honored, Mr. President."

"Well, Jim, it was Harrison Tate who threw Savage's name in the ring. So did Benjamin Delstrotto."

"He suggested Rosie's husband?" Rolands asked, surprised.

"No, Jim," the president answered. "I meant to say that Delstrotto also suggested Savage as a running mate. He said something about that's what Rosie would have wanted."

"I wasn't aware that any of them were that close to Savage," Rolands said.

"Neither was I. But after the reports came back," the president replied uneasily, "I had no other choice."

Rolands looked up. "What reports, Mr. President?"

The president had always prided himself in never having to lie. He would stretch the truth a little, maybe. That was politics. Every so often you had to carry the truth to the edge. As long as it was for the public good, Winslet rationalized that it was right. But now only the truth would do.

"Jim, I had an FBI background check done on everyone on my list," Winslet said, his tone meek. "Standard procedure. With only a couple of weeks left before the election, we had to work fast."

"And?" Rolands asked, his eyes now firmly fixed on the president. Winslet felt trapped. "Savage came out on top," the president said simply.

Rolands continued to look at the president. "I don't think you are telling me everything, sir."

The president got up from the sofa and walked over to the window near his desk, which overlooked the White House lawn. Without turning around, he started to speak. "Jim, you're right. Maybe I should have said that, according to the file, Savage was the only one with a perfect record. But that's the other part of this problem I was just made aware of. According to Chad Madden's contact at the FBI, the files I used to make that decision may have been altered."

There was a long pause in the conversation. Winslet turned, facing Rolands. "So I picked him. I had no other choice."

"What about me?" Rolands's mouth fell open. "What did you find wrong in my file?"

"Nothing major," the president said as evenly as he could. "There was something about a misunderstanding in the army just before your discharge."

"A what?" Rolands exclaimed, his face flushed. "Why didn't you just ask me without assuming? My military career was flawless!"

"In retrospect, it was a mistake." The president hung his head. "We should have gone to you about it."

Rolands stood up and moved over to the president's desk. "Mr. President, I want to see my file," he asked, his voice raised. "I believe I have that right."

Winslet nodded and walked back to his desk. He opened the top drawer to the left and picked up the telephone receiver. "Chad, bring in Speaker Rolands's file. The one I asked you to keep in a special place."

Madden protested loudly on the other end of the line. Fortunately Rolands was not able to hear Madden's response. Almost instantly the president's chief of staff appeared at the door of the Oval Office. Under his arm were several large manila folders. Madden handed over one of the envelopes to the president, who immediately sat down at his desk, opened it, drew out a file, looked it over, and then abruptly turned to Madden.

"This is a file on you. What's it doing in here?" the president queried.

"Oh, that was just a cross check, sir," Madden stuttered, reaching for the file and handing the president the other envelope. "That was just to see if the test was working. They used me as a guinea pig."

The president gave him a hard look and pulled out the files from the other folder. "Here it is, Jim," the president said as he handed the file over to Rolands.

The congressman sat down and started going over his dossier. The president glanced toward his chief of staff, who was just now getting his breath back.

"What the hell is this?" Rolands barked, pointing to the entry in his file that read *Section leader. Letter of reprimand issued for security violation, 12 May 1996. Honorable discharge.*

"That never happened!" Not able to control his anger, Rolands threw the file onto the president's desk. "It's a lie!"

"I was hoping you would say that, Jim," Winslet said, caught between wanting to know the truth and unsure what he would do with it.

"He's right, Mr. President. As we discussed earlier, my contact at the FBI specifically tried to confirm the contents of that document," Madden stated in a somber tone. "There is no record of such a reprimand anywhere. Not in the army files. Not in the court records at the army base in Frankfurt, Germany. Nowhere, that is, except in this FBI file."

They faced each other as a deafening silence fell across the room. The president's telephone rang on his desk, but no one turned around to answer it.

14

BEWILDERED, Madden returned to his office. The president wanted a thorough explanation about what was going on, but that would have to wait until later, when they had more time to be alone. Madden pulled open the bottom drawer of his desk and slid the envelopes that the president had requested back under the pile. Just as he was about to lock the drawer, the president's administrative assistant appeared at his door.

"Seems the boss wasn't through with you after all," Mrs. Sims said. "He wants you back in there. He said something about tomorrow's luncheon meeting with the Army Corps of Engineers. And Davenport's still waiting for an update on Senator Tate."

Madden nodded and waved her off. "Tell her Tate's doctors are still evaluating him, but they promised to keep the president informed. And ask her to notify Tate's office about what we're saying." With the distraction, Madden slipped the key back in his pocket without locking the drawer and picked up the top secret file labeled Mother Lode. As he was about to leave, he scanned the pink message notes strewn over his desk. One name caught his eye: Jennifer Smitt. He picked up the piece of paper and stuffed it into his jacket pocket.

. . .

"You still know how to charm them," Jennifer said.

Madden smiled as he pushed open the door for her to enter the small, family-owned German restaurant tucked in the heart of Georgetown. They had agreed to meet for dinner. He was not sure what to make of their last meeting. The pat on his knee, the gentle nudge—were they more than just friendly gestures? He wanted to find out.

With her raven black hair, green eyes, and a half-cocked smile, Jennifer had always been attractive to Chad. But it was more than just her looks. Maybe it was her tenacity to uncover the truth, even though she might be putting her career on the line for him. No matter the reason, the feelings he once had for her were beginning to resurface. Madden was determined not to let it show. The last thing he needed was another responsibility.

"I hope so," Madden answered as she passed by him and into the restaurant. "One never wants to miss an opportunity." This time their encounter would be more like a real date. Madden had arranged for a small table in the back corner. Since the establishment lighting could be called subdued at best, the location afforded them a reasonable chance at privacy.

"Opportunity for what?" Jennifer asked, masking a slight smile.

He decided not to follow up on his comment, at least not until he had dispensed with more important matters. As they sat down, Madden ordered two glasses of port. He would try to relax and enjoy himself, even if his pleasures proved only temporary.

Jennifer opened her briefcase and removed two sheets of paper, handing them to Madden. "I did more checking," she said softly. "If I'm in this far, I thought I might as well go all the way."

"Did you find out anything else?" he asked, taking a gulp of his wine. Jennifer shot a look at Madden. He could sense fear in her eyes.

"I think so," she answered, her voice breaking slightly. "I talked to one of my friends in the Entry Department. She's basically just a programmer, subcontracted by the FBI to make changes on entries into the FBI's master file."

"And?"

Jennifer flicked a nervous look around the small restaurant She then moved closer to Madden and pointed to the entries on the first piece of paper. He had to smile at the move. She acted as if she did not notice.

"Look at this first entry. See the little pi marks at the bottom? That's the code of the person who entered the data."

"What does that tell us?"

"Two things," Jennifer said. "First, it says which employee made the entry, since each person making changes in the system has a different code. And second, it tells us that someone who understands FBI protocol rules was involved."

Madden sat back, fearing he knew the answer to his next question before he asked. "This other sheet, what is it?"

"It's the last part of the file on the vice president," Jennifer whispered.

Madden looked closely at the page, sliding it over by the candle. He squinted in the dim light as he concentrated on the bottom right corner.

"There's no mark," Jennifer said under her breath, pointing to the page. "There's not even an entry code on any of the files I pulled up for you, except yours."

"You're saying this means that—?" Madden began.

"Yes. It was no accident. These entries on your seven people were made by someone outside the FBI."

"How?" Madden gulped the rest of his first glass of wine.

"I don't know, Chad. Someone has the FBI's top secret access code but doesn't know the Bureau's protocol. It doesn't make sense."

Madden felt a sense of panic come over him as he remembered the files in his office and the drawer he now realized he had forgotten to lock. His priorities for the evening suddenly changed. He took the paper, folded it, and stuffed it in his pocket. He had to get back to the White House. Fighting off the rush from the wine, he mumbled, "Jennifer, I left the drawer unlocked. I've got to get . . ."

Jennifer's eyes widened in the candlelight as she drew back. Madden knew he did not need to say anything more. It was obvious from her response that she realized he had to take action.

"Next time, I promise," he said, reaching over and placing his hand on her knee. Jennifer moved away and his hand fell off.

"I won't hold you to it."

He picked up the check and left Jennifer to finish her port.

. . .

Jennifer stayed for about ten minutes, her hand wrapped around her half empty glass of port, before she left the restaurant. Just as when she came in, she did not leave alone, although this time she was not accompanied by Madden. The man who threw a ten-dollar bill on the table and followed her out of the restaurant thirty seconds later was the same man who had followed her out of Tyson's Corner.

. . .

Vice President Savage told his staff he had a lot of reports to finish reading. The first floor of the West Wing of the White House can, at times, be tumultuous, since many of the most important decisions in America are made there. Tonight though the whole place was deserted except for a few guards, a few tired aides, and the cleaning crew. To give the appearance that he was deeply engrossed in whatever he was doing, the vice president had his dinner brought in from the White House kitchen. It was one of his special privileges: gourmet food twenty-four hours a day, all at the taxpayers' expense.

Savage left his door open so he could see who was still around. When the last aide decided to call it a day and passed by the door to his outer office, he looked down at his watch. It was just past eleven fifteen. Off in the distance he could hear the sound of a vacuum cleaner as it swept its way through the most important offices in the United States. Savage knew the routine by heart. The only areas that were off limits to him were the Oval Office and the president's private study. The rest were open to anyone who was allowed access to the first floor of the West Wing. Two guards were stationed at both its entries. An additional guard was placed at the door to the Oval Office.

In a throwback to his days on the campaign trail, the vice president had made it a point to learn the names of all security personnel by heart. They turned over every four hours to avoid inattention from fatigue. The guard positioned in front of the door to the Oval Office came on at eight o'clock and was well known to Savage. Lucky Brown was known to everyone, having been around since the Nixon era. Savage was told he was one of the best during his prime. But that was several administrations ago.

The vice president knew Brown should have retired several years ago, but no one wanted to tell him so. Last summer he had been relegated to the night staff of the Oval Office, who stood guard when the president was seldom around. There was very little chance any intruder would get that far, especially since there was a SWAT crew of sixteen Special Forces agents stationed on the White House roof and throughout the grounds.

Yet from his demeanor, Savage could tell Lucky Brown still thought he was irreplaceable. His perfectly starched uniform did not show one wrinkle even though he usually slept in it over half of the time he was on duty. Savage had even heard reports that the cleaning crew had to roll his chair away from the door with Lucky still asleep in it when they needed to clean the president's office. Savage did not really believe the story, but it made for good conversation.

The vice president hoped to use Brown's sleeping habits to his advantage. The longer Lucky slept, the less he would be able to keep track of the time Savage spent in Madden's office. Savage did not know how long it would take him since he was not really sure what he was looking for in the first place. Most likely whatever it was would be in the envelope that Trainer had seen. Savage felt he had fifteen minutes at the outside before Brown would get suspicious.

"That sorry son of a bitch." Savage cussed under his breath at Trainer for turning him into a two-bit larcenist. He popped a yellow Valium in hopes of calming his nerves. Savage did not consider himself a criminal. In his life he may have condoned some practices that were not always on the up and up, but that was business. All this intrigue was new to him.

Moving slowly past the entrance to the Oval Office suite, Savage called out, "Good book you're reading, Lucky?" He suspected the White House veteran had not turned a page in ten minutes.

Brown appeared to tense a little, aroused out of his half-sleep. He was good, however. Only a trained eye could have told the difference. "Ah . . . yes, it is Mr. Vice President," the guard said. "I see you're burning the midnight oil."

"Yeah. The president has me working on a special project," Savage answered, getting to the point. He needed to move on, but not before establishing his alibi. "You know how the president is. The job never stops."

Brown nodded as Savage headed off in the other direction.

"I have to get something out of Chad Madden's office," Savage replied, looking back. Lucky had already turned his attention back to his book.

If he were true to form, in two minutes Lucky Brown would be asleep again with his book balanced precariously in his lap. From still off in the distance down the hall, but getting closer and louder, came the noise of the vacuum cleaner. As expected, Lucky Brown, positioned in front of the door to the Oval Office, did not seem to notice.

. . .

He looked at his watch. The time was approaching twelve minutes. So far Savage had come up with nothing. First he had examined the open files on the shelves behind Madden's desk for anything remotely suspicious. Then Savage settled down at Madden's desk, laboriously rifling through the stacked folders and papers laid out before him. Next he started going through all the drawers.

The bottom drawer on the left was the only one with a lock on it. Savage fully expected not to be able to open it. Should he break it somehow? He let out a sigh of relief when he pulled on it and opened.

Fourteen minutes had passed. Beads of sweat trickled under his collar. He was almost out of time. Savage's hands shook as he rustled through the large stack of papers in the drawer. At first all he could see were files labeled top secret; most he recognized from briefing sessions in the weeks before. Additionally there were a few expired schedules and various pieces of correspondence addressed to the president.

Savage blinked. The corner of a file stood out a little apart from the rest, as if it had been inserted in a hurry. Savage pulled the manila envelope out from underneath the pile, but in his haste he caught the edge on the lip of the drawer. To his shock, the envelope flipped out of his hand, spinning to the floor. In the distance, he could hear voices coming from the other end of the hall in the direction of the Oval Office. One was the voice of Lucky Brown. He dropped to his knees and scooped up the errant file, and then stood back up quickly.

Suddenly he froze. He heard the voice of Chad Madden. What excuse could Savage give for being in his office at this time of the night? His mind raced.

Almost in a panic, knowing his time had run out, Savage forced open the envelope. His sweaty hands trembled as he pulled out the contents. His eyes scanned what seemed to be copies of FBI files, held together by a paper clip and a pink memo cover sheet. He read the imprint on the memo sheet: *From the Desk of Jennifer Smitt*. All the names were familiar to Savage: Tate, Rolands, Savage himself, Madden. They must have been the files the president pulled up on his potential running mates. But why was Madden among them, and why did he have them?

Madden's voice grew louder. Savage trembled as he stuffed the files into the envelope and then shoved the file back into the pile where he had found it. He swallowed hard when Madden's questioning face appeared at the door of his office. Their eyes locked. Savage could not tell which one of them was the most shocked. Out of Madden's line of sight, Savage slowly raised his left leg, gently nudging the drawer closed.

"What are you doing here, Mr. Vice President?" If there was an unevenness in Madden's voice, Savage was too nervous to notice it.

"I was going to ask you the same thing," Savage stated, deciding a positive approach was his only chance.

"This is my office," Madden sputtered, his eyes sweeping the room in disbelief. Savage paused and then walked out from behind Madden's desk.

"The Mother Lode project," he answered, trying to appear as if he were in a hurry. "You know the president put it on our shoulders. I thought you might have the file, so I thought I would begin reviewing it while I had some time without interruptions."

Madden's mouth dropped open at the vice president's response. "No... ah... I don't," Madden said, looking confused. "Since the leak the president has kept all that under lock and key. I can't get to it without Winslet's permission."

"Well, that's unfortunate. Since I was already here," Savage said, his hands still trembling at his side, "I thought I would use the opportunity to check it out. Just let me know when you want to get together on it."

The vice president slid by Madden, who had not moved since entering his office, and headed down the hall. Having gone a safe distance, Savage stopped and turned around, a ring of perspiration rimming his collar. "Chad, you never told me why you came back."

Madden, still standing in the door to his office, did not respond to the vice president's question.

. . .

"Lowell, it's a match!" Russell barked into the receiver. "Both the vice president and Clayton Thomas died of the same disease, some variant of kuru. In fact, I'll take it one step further. They both died of the same organism. Their serotypes are identical."

"He must have contracted it at the autopsy," McCarty answered. "That would be my guess."

"I did some checking since we last talked. Clayton Thomas had not been farther east than Long Island for the last five years. From the contacts I've talked to, it sounds like he only went to the British Isles two times. The last time was ten or eleven years ago. And he's never been to Africa," McCarty said. "You haven't mentioned your own test results."

"They said unless something else shows up, I'm good for another forty years, but they're going to repeat another set in a month." Russell tried to mask his relief. "Lowell, this makes it pretty clear that there is, at least, the potential for an epidemic," He fingered his copy of the report that lay before him on his kitchen counter.

"I'm going to contact the Centers for Disease Control and Prevention and let them run with it," McCarty said.

"I wouldn't do that. At least, not right now," he warned, shifting the receiver to his other shoulder.

"Why?"

"Because, old friend, I think you may have a third case on your hands in Senator Tate. My bet is he's dying of the same thing," Russell responded. "If he hasn't already."

"Dan, where are you coming from? Why would you think that?"

"The eyes," Russell blurted out. "The vice president had pinpoint pupils, even after she died. I saw them myself. Thomas's pathology report also mentions the same thing."

"You think Tate has the same disease because his pupils were so constricted?" McCarty asked. "I'll bet my career that he had a stroke or has a tumor, maybe in the pineal area."

"Don't plan on retiring soon. Just do me a favor," Russell answered. "Get a blood test on your senator and ask them to check for the prion diseases. If it's positive, you may have an epidemic on your hands. Then we're going to need more than the CDC!"

. . .

"That will be all, ladies and gentlemen," Savage said, a signal that the regular morning briefing with his staff was over. Jason Clark and the others headed for the door. Only Ken Trainer stayed behind. Savage went to the door and looked at his assistant, who was pulling the protective cover off her monitor.

"Hold all calls for a few minutes," the vice president requested and closed the door behind him. He moved back to the conference table where Trainer remained seated.

"Well?" Trainer asked, his voice flat. "What did you find out?"

"Is that all you can say?" Savage snapped. "I could go to prison for this. Maybe even be convicted as a spy, and you know what happens to spies."

Trainer did not appear to be moved. Savage knew that to him all this intrigue was just a job. The vice president would do his part—or else. Trainer waited.

"I almost got caught," the flustered vice president exclaimed.

"By whom?"

"By Madden himself! He walked right in. Fortunately I heard him talking to the guard, so I was able to cover."

"Does he suspect anything?"

The vice president shook his head, walked around the conference table, and sat down next to his aide. "I don't think so, but I just don't know," Savage answered.

Uncertainty gnawed at his insides. "I told him I was looking for the Mother Lode file. I think he bought it."

"Dammit, man, did you find out anything or not?" Trainer asked again, his face puffed with irritation.

"At first, I thought I did," Savage said. "I found an envelope like you described, stuck under a bunch of other stuff in the bottom drawer of his desk. Actually I found two envelopes. I was able to look at only one."

"And?"

"It turned out to be the FBI files Madden must have pulled out for the president when he was selecting his vice president. The ones our people had *improved*, as you say."

"Whose files were they?" Trainer inquired. He leaned over closer to the vice president.

"The list. Like I told you, everyone on the list. There was also a memo attached with nothing on it except for the name of FBI agent Jennifer Smitt," Savage answered, his breathing rapid. "I was lucky just to get a look. Madden was all over me by the time I found the envelope. So I only took a quick scan and saw me, Rolands, Madden . . . and Tate, as I recall."

Trainer sat quietly, his face frozen in contemplation. Without warning, he sat up, his finger pointing at Savage. "You said Madden . . . Chad Madden?" Trainer snapped. "Are you positive?"

"Yes." Savage nodded, not sure what Trainer was thinking.

"Madden wasn't on the president's list of candidates," Trainer said. The vessels in his neck were taut. "His file in that group doesn't make sense, unless . . . they're on to something."

The vice president sat motionless. By now there was no turning back, but there was no way out either. "I don't know what else to do without tipping our hand," the vice president replied meekly. "And it's too early for that."

"You're right about that part. Central has a lot more they have to do until we are ready to take over," Trainer said, his tone even. "There's one person, however, who might know the answer as to why they would pull up Madden's file along with the rest."

"Who?" Savage asked.

"The less you know about that part of the operation, the better, Mr. Vice President." Trainer looked up, a smile on his lips. "Let's just say that the major downside will be getting the FBI involved."

. . .

It was close to midnight when a man in his early forties entered the intensive care unit. He carried a clipboard under his right arm. With his left hand he pushed a portable ventilator. He stopped at the nurses' station and examined the list of the patients written on the board next to a row of cardiac monitors. He scribbled a few notes on his clipboard and headed across the hall to room 816.

"You must be the technician from respiratory therapy. Can I help you?" Senator Tate's nurse asked.

The young man glanced up, his look stern. "No," he replied. "I don't think so." He proceeded into Tate's cubicle, pushing the ventilator ahead of him.

"Wait," Tate's nurse called, her voice emphatic. "What are you doing?"

"What does it look like?" he retorted. "I'm going to give this patient a breathing treatment."

The nurse retreated to Tate's chart, which lay on the table just outside the cubicle, and scanned the order sheet. "I don't see any order for it here."

The young man stopped and turned toward the nurse. His eyes stared through her. "I can't help that," he said. "It says right here, Doctor Arnold Stone ordered the treatment to be given every six hours. As busy as he is, Stone probably called the order in directly to my boss over in respiratory therapy and forgot to tell you."

The young man pointed to an entry on the sheet of paper attached to his clipboard.

The nurse did not question him as she moved away into the adjacent cubicle.

The young technician hooked the ventilator up to the wall oxygen and turned on the machine. A rhythmic swishing sound began as the oxygen circled through the complex instrument's internal parts and then into the patient. The technician glanced over toward where Tate's nurse had disappeared. Following the normal routine, he removed a circular plastic cylinder from his pocket, attached the apparatus to a long tube extending from the ventilator, and inserted it into the senator's mouth. Tate barely responded as the machine attempted to push oxygen into his failing lungs. Unfortunately, owing to Tate's debilitated state, most of the life-saving gas was lost as it leaked out around the plastic tube that hung limply from his lips.

The technician did not seem to care. He was not even paying attention to see if the machine was doing its job. He had come to visit the senator for another reason. He glanced again toward the hall. Tate's nurse had disappeared into the adjacent cubicle with her other patient. From his other pocket, the technician removed a syringe that was filled with about ten milliliters of a clear liquid. He moved over to the bag of intravenous fluid that hung on the pole above the senator's head. After checking one more time to ensure that he was out of sight of Tate's nurse, the technician used the injector port to push the contents of the syringe into the bag of fluids.

A smile escaped his lips as he put the empty syringe back into his jacket pocket. He removed the plastic apparatus from the senator's mouth and unhooked the ventilator from the wall oxygen. By the time Tate's nurse made it back to the senator's side, he would be gone. There would be no sign that he had ever been there. He retraced his steps toward the intensive care unit's exit, quickening his pace noticeably. Just as he arrived at the door, he heard the emergency alarm go off in the direction of the senator's room. As he slipped out he saw Tate's nurse dash back into the room of her famous patient.

Her efforts would be too late. The cardiac-arrest team made repeated attempts to revive him, but to no avail. The young resident who led the team even injected epinephrine into the senator's failing heart, trying to reverse Tate's downward spiral.

After fifteen minutes they halted, when the consensus around the room was that the good senator from Colorado had gone through enough.

. . .

Room 816 now sat empty. The senator's body had been taken to the morgue about twenty minutes before. All that remained were the dangling wires and tubes that had been connected to the senator's failing body. An orderly who had been called up from housekeeping entered the cubicle and flicked on the overhead light. He had done this same task thousands of times before—preparing the bed for another tragic situation.

With one hand he pushed a mop bucket and with the other a large trash bin.

Within ten minutes, Tate's cubicle was ready for the next occupant. The attendant flicked off the light as he turned to leave. Out of habit, he looked back for one final check. His instincts were right. The half-empty bag of IV fluids that had gone into the senator's body was still hanging on a pole above the bed.

The orderly walked back into the room. He removed the bag from the pole and tossed it into the trash bin. The last traces of evidence would soon be gone, consumed by the flames of the hospital incinerator.

15

JASON **C**LARK said a brief hello to a passing intern as he moved toward his office in the West Wing, which was located directly across the hall from his boss. Having had trouble sleeping the night before, he was forty-five minutes early for his usual seven-thirty arrival. In passing, he glanced over at Savage's inner office and caught a quick glimpse of light streaming out from under the door. Had the vice president changed his usual schedule? Clark reversed direction and walked directly into Savage's office without thinking or knocking.

"What the hell?" Trainer blurted out. Trainer, Savage, Lynn, and Peters were huddled around the vice president's desk. They turned in unison toward Clark.

"Good morning, gentlemen. I hope I haven't disturbed anything," Clark said.

"No," the vice president answered, his shoulders still stiff after Clark's unexpected entrance. "We were, ah, just going over the speech I'll give to the AFL-CIO tomorrow."

Lynn and Peters nodded in agreement. Trainer, however, turned back around as if Clark were not even present.

"Isn't it sort of early to get started?" Clark wondered aloud. Why had he been excluded from their predawn get-together?

"I was about to say the same thing to you," Savage told him.

Clark shuffled his feet in the doorway and readjusted the unopened *Washington Post* tucked under his arm. "The truth is, I couldn't sleep," he answered. "Too much caffeine last night, I guess. Also, since I know you have such a busy schedule over the next couple of days, I thought it wouldn't hurt to get a head start."

Savage's eyes darted to the men seated around his desk and then back to Clark. "Do you want to meet me back here . . . say in thirty minutes, to go through the schedule?"

"That would be fine," Clark answered. He turned around and headed back across the hall to his own office.

After punching buttons on the automatic coffeemaker that his assistant had set up the day before, Clark plopped down at his desk to wait for the coffee to brew. He scooped up his copy of the *Post* for a quick run-through. As he scanned the front page, an item in the bottom right corner caught his eye:

HARRISON TATE, COLORADO SENATOR AND WINSLET MENTOR, DIES AT 68

Harrison B. Tate, the four-term Republican senator from Colorado and longtime confidant and proponent of fellow Coloradan Raymond Winslet, whose rise to the presidency he fostered, died shortly before midnight from complications of a recent stroke at Georgetown Medical Center. He was 68. A full obituary will appear in tomorrow's newspaper.

There was no other information about the senator's death. Clark guessed it was probably because the death occurred so close to the paper's deadline that this was all they could pull together. A pang of sorrow swept over Clark. Winslet had now lost another good friend and an adviser he trusted.

Fifteen minutes later, Clark picked up his scheduling book and headed back across the hall, but not before retrieving a mug of his freshly brewed coffee. This time Clark decided to knock.

"Come on in," the vice president replied in a muffled voice.

Clark opened the door and saw no one. The door to an adjacent bathroom stood slightly ajar.

"Jason, is that you?" Savage called out from the direction of the bathroom. "I'll be right there."

Jason Clark moved over to Savage's desk and sat down. He could hear the vice president flushing the toilet in the background. He leaned forward to place his scheduling book on the vice president's desk. Several memos and copies of e-mail lay scattered in front of him. Among them was Savage's cell phone, its face side up. Most of the time, Jason tried not to pry into matters that were not his business—it was a lesson he had learned from Rosalyn Delstrotto. Life was easier that way. But the off-angle LED screen, its message still visible, caught his eye. He tried not to look, but the temptation was too much. Jason nudged the telephone around slightly so he could get a better look. A quick glance was all he saw, but it was enough. *The Colorado connection was confirmed interrupted at 11:50 p.m.*

Just then Savage entered his office. Clark jumped up, hoping the vice president had not see him looking around the desk.

"Are you ready to get started?" Savage asked, grabbing his phone before jamming it into his breast pocket.

Jason Clark, chilled to the core, nodded without saying a word.

. . .

Although common sense had told him it was coming, Tate's death hit Madden hard. Close to 1:00 a.m., after he had been awakened by the chief of administration at Georgetown Medical Center, Madden knew he must be the one to break the news to Winslet. By the time he had contacted the president and they had finalized all the arrangements for Tate's body, over an hour had passed. He tried to go back to sleep, but instead lay wide-eyed until the numbers on his alarm clock blinked to straight up five o'clock.

He had grown accustomed to working on empty. Madden gulped down a giant swig of hot coffee, hoping to pacify his throbbing headache. He had just tucked a pile of folders under one arm and scooped up his steaming cup so that could head down to the Oval Office when the light for the private line on his telephone lit up.

"Chad," Jason Clark said, his voice strained. "I need to talk to you."

Madden could hear his urgency, but he had so much to do that he just did not have the time, and the lack of sleep put on him edge. "How about later on, noontime or this evening?" he asked, massaging his temples.

"No!" Clark barked. "I don't think it can wait. It's has to do with what we talked about on the golf course."

Madden placed the folders back on his desk and glanced at his watch. "How about now?"

. . .

"Mr. Madden, the president wants you to work up a statement for Davenport to give to the press about Tate," his assistant called from her desk in the outer office. Madden nodded, accustomed to her informality, as Jason Clark brushed passed her and closed the door to Madden's office without giving the assistant a second look. He plopped down in the chair across from his longtime friend and pulled out a torn bit of newspaper. It was the brief front-page item from the *Post* about Tate's death.

"I heard at one o'clock this morning," the chief of staff said. "Winslet is pretty torn up over it. They went back a long way. First Rosie, now the senator. I really feel for him. The job is lonely enough even when you have friends you can trust."

Clark nodded, reaching in his pocket. He pulled out a sheet of paper and handed it to Madden.

"What's this?"

"A text message I copied off Savage's cell phone. I wrote it down as close as I can remember."

"How did you see it?"

"His phone was open on his desk early this morning," Clark said, his tone hesitant.

Madden picked it up, still perplexed. "I don't understand."

"Look at the time," Clark insisted.

"11:50 p.m."

Clark pointed to the newspaper article. "Now look at the time in the clipping from the *Post*."

Madden's eyes scanned the note from the paper. "Shortly before midnight."

He carefully laid down the clipping and looked up at Clark. Then he picked up both pieces of paper to compare. "What are you trying to say?"

"I really don't know," Clark answered, his breathing labored. "As I told you before, it may be just my imagination, but I think something strange is going on. I arrived here this morning before seven o'clock and they were all here."

"Who?" Madden put down the papers and looked over at his friend inquisitively.

"The vice president, Peters, Lynn, and Trainer. The four of them were huddled around Savage's desk when I interrupted."

"You interrupted them? Hell, you're his chief of staff!" Madden exclaimed.

"We don't need to go over that again," Clark retorted, glaring at Madden. "I already told you—they tell me only what they want me to know. Mostly Trainer is in charge."

"What about the message?" Madden asked, a feeling of urgency building up inside him.

"When I came back about twenty minutes later for a meeting with the vice president," Clark answered, "I saw Savage's cell phone sitting out on his desk."

"Did he see you?" Madden asked, sensing Clark's uneasiness.

"I don't think so. He was just coming out of the bathroom."

The piece from the *Post* and the text message on Savage's phone were probably a coincidence, the chief of staff thought. But given the other information Madden had learned from Jennifer Smitt, and with Tate's final message . . . Madden did not think he would sleep tonight either.

Jason Clark had been a close friend and confidant of his, but Madden no longer knew how much to trust his sense or his sanity. He had never been completely satisfied with Clark's explanation of the six-month hiatus he had taken early in their Washington careers. For now Madden decided to keep his growing doubts to himself. "You and Rosie had a special bond," Madden said, moving the papers to the side. "No matter how hard you try, your relationship with Savage will never be the same."

"What does that have to do with this message?" Clark asked, his tone guarded.

"The vice president is not going to confide in you the way Rosie did. Is it possible you haven't given Savage a chance?" Madden stepped back from his desk. "Don't push—just take what he gives you for now. He's new on this job too. My guess is that the next time he holds one of his early morning briefing sessions, you'll be at the table."

"I don't think so," Clark answered softly, but Madden could tell he had made him question his own judgment. Madden hated to mislead his friend, but he had to buy time, and he wanted to keep Clark as a source of information without letting him in on the whole story.

"Let's keep this between us." Madden stood up and grabbed a folder off the top of his desk. "I've got to get this over to Davenport." Heading for the door, Madden stopped, his hand resting on the doorknob, and looked back at Clark. "And, Jason, when things have settled down a bit, let's try to get in eighteen holes."

. . .

Jennifer Smitt finished her work at the Bureau close to her usual time, which was one of the perks about working at the headquarters in Washington. Unless there was a crisis situation, which did not happen very often, she had regular hours, which allowed her time to get back on her exercise program and even enjoy an occasional round of tennis with a neighbor from down the hall. Such leisure was relatively unheard of in the field.

The sun was just setting as she headed out the employees' entrance for the two-block walk to the Metro. Even though she was a trained agent, she had found walking alone a little unnerving when she first came to Washington, though before long her uncertainty passed.

She was engrossed in her own thoughts, considering both the files and the impossible character of Chad Madden when she noticed a dark blue van pull out of a parking space across the street. Before she could react, two men in dark coveralls jumped out of the van and dashed toward her. She recoiled as one of the assailants grabbed her around the shoulders while the other threw something dark over her head. Jennifer lashed out in desperation, but it was no good. The men were much stronger, and her flailing kicks made no contact. A sharp, piercing pain radiated from the base of her skull down her spine, and then darkness engulfed her.

When Jennifer awoke a short time later, she found herself lying prostrate in the back of a vehicle, probably the blue van. Her head was still covered and her hands were tied in front of her. She was tossed from side to side as the vehicle jerked through what she supposed were the narrow streets of Washington, DC.

She tried to sit up, but a hand grabbed her shoulders and forced her back down.

She had been trained by the Bureau not to panic, but she could not help herself. She uttered a muffled cry for help.

"Shut up," came a voice from above her.

"What are you doing to me?" Jennifer pleaded through the thick cloth. Her head pounded. For a moment there was silence as the vehicle continued to rumble toward its unknown destination. Jennifer waited anxiously for someone to say something.

"We know you work for the FBI," said the raspy voice in accented English. "Just a little information. Then we let you go."

"I only work in the typing pool," she tried. "I don't know..."

"Shut up, bitch," the unknown abductor blustered. "Shut up, Agent Jennifer Smitt."

The sound of her own name sent a wave of fear coursing throughout her body.

Jennifer knew that once an abduction victim had been isolated, chances of survival were slim. She had to get away before her abductors reached their final destination. At least on the streets of Washington, if that was where she was still, she could attract attention, maybe even help.

Jennifer fought to get air under the hood that blocked her view. She knew she had to put the panic behind her and call on her years of experience as a field agent. *Calculate*, she told herself. *Plan*. She was fairly certain there were only the two abductors who first accosted her, one driving and the one watching her. If there were a third, her plan probably would not work. With her eyes of no help, she would have to rely on her hearing to locate the abductor who was being jostled around the back of the van with her.

"Tell me what you want to know," she choked out. She hoped the question would start him talking so she could get a bead on where he was positioned.

"I think we should wait until we can talk to you properly." An almost sadistic tone ran through his voice, but his words were enough to tell her that he was just to the left of her, about waist high. Jennifer waited until the vehicle came to a halt. She assumed the van was at a stoplight because she could hear the sound of crossing traffic in front of her.

"Please, tell me!" she screamed and struggled to sit up. As she had hoped, the hands of the abductor grasped her shoulders to pin her back toward the floor. Using the force of her momentum, she tightened her stomach muscles and kicked up directly over her head with all the force she had left in her body. Her pointed toe found its mark. She felt her foot come into contact with the soft tissues of the abductor's face.

"Ahhh!" he screamed out in pain.

She reached up and jerked the hood off her face with her bound hands. Her eyes squinted in the dark. She could see she was in a cluttered van. To her left the abductor writhed on the carpet, his hand clasped over his eye. Through the shards of light that streamed in the rear window she could see blood oozing between his fingers.

For the moment the abductor was not aware that Jennifer had removed her mask.

He was more concerned about his own situation. The driver of the van shouted something, but for one precious instant he hesitated, torn between driving and lunging into the back to tackle her.

Jennifer wasted no time. She dove for the back door of the van and hit the release button on the first try. It flew open, and Jennifer rolled out onto the busy street, her hands still bound in front of her, her shoulder slamming onto the pavement. The startled driver behind her began to honk his horn. Jennifer tried to get her feet under her and run amid a growing chorus of horns. Car doors in all directions flew open. She looked up to see her bleeding abductor crawl to the back door. Suddenly the driver of the van slammed the vehicle forward, almost throwing his accomplice out the back as the van lurched forward through the red light. The only reason the man did not join Jennifer on the pavement was that the other rear door was still latched.

Jennifer picked herself up to her knees. Her abductor, hanging precariously out of the van with blood streaming down his face, screamed profanities in a foreign language as the van hurtled down the twilit street. Exhausted, Jennifer fell back onto the pavement and lapsed into darkness.

. . .

"The president would like you to sit with him at Senator Tate's funeral," Chad Madden said, fingering the list of Washington elite who would be invited to join Winslet at the somber occasion. The president had asked Chad to make the most significant calls himself.

"You know I haven't felt like going out much since Rosie died," Ben Delstrotto answered, his voice distant through the receiver. "Now it seems that when I do, it's to attend funerals."

Madden decided not to follow up on the sad comment. "I know the senator held you and Rosie both in high regard." The truth was that he had no idea what Tate thought about Ben Delstrotto, since the man had pursued his causes behind the scenes while his wife took the spotlight. But Madden was not about to quibble with particulars at such a sad time. The point was that he and the president wanted Delstrotto at the funeral. It was as much a show of respect for Delstrotto's deceased wife as it was for the senator.

In death, Rosie would be remembered for her accomplishments and nurtured in the annals of history for generations to come. But it was her husband who, like Jacqueline Kennedy, would be shouldered with her legacy, which he could carry either as a banner or a cross. There are some who would call it a burden, others a golden opportunity. The choice was Delstrotto's.

"Chad." Delstrotto hesitated and then spoke. "Tell the president I would consider it an honor."

. . .

The vice president was on the telephone when Kenneth Trainer barged into the study at his official residence. Startled, Savage looked up as Trainer made the cutoff sign, slicing his hand across his neck.

"Mr. Ambassador," the vice president said hastily into the mouthpiece. "I will talk to President Winslet personally about your concerns. We can probably have an answer for you by early Thursday."

Savage managed to appease the ambassador from Paraguay, who was still angry that the administration had not allocated more foreign aid to his country in the upcoming budget. Hurried, Savage hung up the telephone.

"Can't you at least knock?" he barked, perturbed by Trainer's unexpected entrance. "What would the staff think if they saw the way you come bursting in here trying to take over?"

Trainer moved over to the music tuner buried in the shelves on the wall behind Savage's desk. The device was piping out a low level of elevator music. He turned up the volume. He was in no mood to take harassment from the vice president.

"That girl from the FBI, Jennifer Smitt, got away," Trainer told him. "I hate incompetent people."

"What do you mean?"

"Just what I said. They had her in the van, and she kicked one of the men in the face. Then she jumped out the back. He's at the hospital now. He lost an eye."

Savage cringed. "Can't your goons take care of one little female?" he snapped. "Did she talk?"

"She was gone before our people had a chance to talk to her," Trainer replied, keeping his voice low. "At least I don't think she can point a finger at anyone. The van was unmarked, and she was blindfolded most of the time."

"You're not dealing with idiots, you know," Savage said. "They'll have all of the FBI out looking for that van."

"It's already scrap metal."

"What about your employee with the eye?"

"He checked out of the hospital, sooner than he wanted. He has a reservation on an oil tanker out of Richmond early this morning."

Savage sat back in his chair. Trainer had covered all the angles, but this was all so risky. "Why in the hell did you come storming in here?"

A broad smile spread over Trainer's face. "There has been a change in plans. It seems that Central feels you're going to have to take over sooner than we had anticipated."

Savage gasped. "When?" he sputtered. He grabbed for the cup of cooled-off coffee on his desk.

"Soon, Mr. Vice President, soon," Kenneth Trainer said calmly. Savage saw he had kept his mouth close to the speaker near his head.

Savage felt a wave of panic suffuse him. He nervously set down his cup and tried to stand, but his knees buckled under him and he reached for the desk to keep from falling.

"Mr. Vice President, you're going to have to do better than that," Trainer remarked as his eyes turned to slits. "I believe it's time for you to earn your keep."

. . .

Dan Russell laid out his copy of the morning paper on the breakfast room table. This was one of the luxuries of keeping his relationship with Cindy French to weekends only; he had all the space he needed to spread out and read the paper. He had drifted halfway through the first section when the article caught his eye: NATIONAL GUARD CALLED IN TO SLAUGHTER 10,000 DEER IN COLORADO. Russell took a gulp of orange juice, bit off a piece of his toast, and read on.

According to the article, an epidemic caused by a variant of Creutzfeldt-Jacob disease had broken out in the deer population in an isolated area of Colorado. This offshoot of one of the prion diseases had not been reported yet in humans, but the authorities did not want to take any chances.

The article went on to say that isolated cases of C-J disease had been reported for years in the deer population, but only recently had epidemics become a problem. Experts said that with the growing intrusions made into the deer's shrinking habitat, such epidemics of communicable diseases were as inevitable as with mad cow disease had been in the commercial cattle operations. Something clicked deep in Russell's mind when he remembered that the late Senator Harrison Tate was from Colorado.

"Contaminated venison," he whispered to himself. He sat back in his chair, his mind racing. *Maybe,* he thought, *instead of looking halfway around the world, we need to look for the source of the problem in our own back yard.* Bothered that he could not keep his thoughts from turning in the direction of conspiracy, he moved on to the next page.

He could only do so much with his suspicions. McCarty's suggestion of turning the matter over to the CDC was the logical next step.

. . .

Chad Madden had not seen so many dignitaries from throughout the world in one place at the same time since Rosie Delstrotto died. During Senator Tate's long tenure he had connected with many important political figure in both hemispheres.

A teary Winslet fell into his seat next to the former vice president's husband after eulogizing his friend and close confidant. After the funeral at the National Cathedral, Tate was to be buried in Arlington National Cemetery not fifty yards from where the president's other confidant, Rosalyn Delstrotto, had been laid to rest.

"I'm exhausted," Winslet sighed as he turned toward Madden after the formal proceedings were complete. "Cancel out the rest of the day for me." That request was a first for the president.

Back at the White House, as Winslet napped in his study off the Oval Office, Madden decided to use the respite to call to Jennifer Smitt. He wanted to know if she had found any new information, but mostly he wanted to hear her voice.

"I'm sorry, but she's unavailable," said the person on the other end of the line at the FBI headquarters. "Can I take your name and have her return your call?"

Madden was about to say no but changed his mind. "Yes. I'm Chad Madden, the president's chief of staff. Ms. Smitt already has my number."

There was a pause on the other end of the line. "Could you hold on for a minute, Mr. Madden?" the person at the FBI asked. "Ms. Smitt's supervisor would like to talk to you."

Within two minutes Madden heard a deep voice. "Mr. Madden," the man began. Instantly Madden recognized the voice of the deputy director at the FBI. "Mr. Madden, this is Sterling Padgett. Ms. Smitt is . . . ah, well, let's say she is indisposed. Would you mind if I asked the nature of your call?"

Madden was taken aback. He decided not to answer Padgett's question fully. "She's an old acquaintance. Is there any problem?"

"I'd rather not discuss it over the telephone," Padgett responded, his tone guarded. "Jennifer was involved in a potentially serious incident."

"Is she hurt?" Madden stiffened in his chair as his heart jumped to his throat.

"Not seriously, Mr. Madden. She's basically OK. But for now we have decided to take her out of circulation."

Madden was puzzled. What did "out of circulation" mean? "I have to see her!" he blurted.

"Normally we would say no," Padgett told him. "This is a matter for the FBI to handle. But, considering who you are, I think we can make an exception."

"When?" the chief of staff demanded. "Now, if possible. And you have to tell me what happened. It's a matter of vital official business that I know." He did not particularly like people who tried to pull rank, but in this case he would make an exception for himself.

"Let me check and call you back," Padgett said evenly. "I know where to reach you."

. . .

Padgett called him back in less than fifteen minutes. Jennifer wanted to see Madden. The deputy director had no objections, but his directions were specific. "Come to the underground parking lot below the FBI headquarters. From there, you'll have to put your trust in the hands of the Bureau. It's policy." They made no exceptions to such policy, not even for the chief of staff of the president of the United States.

Madden stopped by his assistant's desk on his way out, and then rushed on, hoping to avoid any meaningful contact with the numerous faces and figures who crowded the halls of the West Wing on a daily basis. In case anything important came along, he had his iPhone on vibrate. If the president could have an afternoon to himself, Madden could as well. Besides, he had a bad feeling that he would be seeing Agent Smitt on official—and dangerous—business.

. . .

The guard at the entrance of the underground parking lot instructed him to go to area B, where he was transferred to an unmarked Suburban. An agent assigned by Padgett would take him to Jennifer's location. As they exited the building, Madden was struck by how darkly tinted the back and side windows were. "I don't see how you could pass code with this," he said, knowing that many state laws prohibited excessive window tinting for reasons of safety.

"Oh, Mr. Madden," the driver answered. "I think the authorities make exceptions when it comes to national security. You must know by now that everyone doesn't have to play by the same rules."

Somehow the words chilled Madden, although he had realized this when he first became involved with the political scene. Nowhere else was this more apparent than in the nation's capital. There was one set of rules for private citizens, and one set for the elected leadership, and yet another set for the foreign diplomats who came here on behalf of their countries.

Such rules and how they worked—or how they ought to work—had been a touchy subject for Madden ever since a close friend's daughter had been paralyzed permanently in an automobile accident. A diplomat from one of the Eastern European countries struck her car when he was driving under the influence and ran a stop sign. Initially he was charged with a DWI, but the charges were dropped when his country filed a protest with the local authorities. The girl's parents tried unsuccessfully to seek restitution for their daughter, but received nothing other than an official letter of apology from the country's ambassador and the relocation of the diplomat to another country.

For a short time this incident cast a pall over Washington. Congress even talked about drafting legislation to deal with such issues. But, as it happened with so many other controversies over right and wrong in the nation's capital, the greater power won. There was no real contest between the compromised life of one girl and America's relationship with an entire country. Madden hated the exigencies of power even when he resorted to those exigencies himself.

As the Suburban sped through the busy streets of Washington, Madden noted it was becoming progressively more difficult to see out of the windows in the back seat.

"What's going on?" he asked.

"It's new technology from Kodak," the driver responded. "Time for you to go dark, Mr. Madden."

A black panel began to rise, totally blocking Madden's view to the front seat. He could only imagine what clandestine operations had been propagated in this very car.

Alone, his thoughts shifted to Jennifer and what he might find when he saw her. She chose a life in the FBI knowing she could be harmed. But if whatever happened to her had anything to do with what she had done for him... Madden shoved the disturbing thought from his mind.

Madden's moment of contemplation was broken when the driver blared over the intercom. "This is the Bureau's latest acquisition. It sure beats the hell out of a blindfold, don't you think?"

Since he was isolated completely from the outside, the president's chief of staff was not sure the situation was any better than a blindfold. He helped run the government, and it bothered him that there were things he was not supposed to know, even on behalf of America.

. . .

After thirty minutes, the agent opened the rear door. They were in another underground parking lot. He thought to himself that it would be just like the FBI to bring him back to the place where he started.

"Just follow me, sir," the agent stated.

He led Madden through a long doorless corridor. At the end was an elevator.

Madden noticed several surveillance cameras overhead. Once they were in the elevator, the agent inserted his ID card into a slot and punched in a code on the panel to the left of the door. Madden was unable to see because the agent blocked his view. Probably deliberate, Madden thought. After a short ride, they exited into a long hall. A guard was seated by the elevator door.

"Good morning, Mr. Mason," the guard said.

"Good morning, John," the agent replied. "Is our guest home?"

"I don't think she's gone out shopping." The guard chuckled.

Madden and the agent walked about halfway down the hall to the fourth door on the left.

"This is where I leave you. John and I have some catching up to do. When you are through, I'll be down there." The agent pointed back to the elevator.

"Thanks." Madden thought this type of duty must be boring for the agent. He knocked, his heart pounding in anticipation.

Almost instantly the door swung open to reveal Jennifer's smile not twelve inches away.

. . .

"They're a bunch of imbeciles," the older gentleman spat into his cellular telephone. "Trainer put the whole operation in jeopardy with that stunt."

The man in the Manhattan apartment sounded almost apologetic as he fielded the caller's caustic remarks. "We tried to warn him, but he felt he had to know."

"From now on nothing happens out in the field without first going through me," he bellowed and adjusted his coat collar against the cold breeze that swirled up off the Potomac. "Nothing!"

. . .

Her kiss caught him completely off guard as he stumbled through the doorway. "Maybe I should visit your undisclosed location more often," he mumbled.

"That would be nice," Jennifer answered, drawing back from him. "At least here you can't run away."

Madden stepped back and saw that Jennifer had a large bruise under her left eye.

Otherwise, from what he could tell, she appeared unharmed.

"Why all this?" His mind brewed with a million questions, but as long as she was safe, he would let her answer them at her own pace.

"Come in." Jennifer closed and locked the door and lead him over to a sofa. The place was a one-bedroom efficiency, comfortably furnished, nothing fancy. What struck Madden was that there were no windows.

"Let me get you some coffee first," Jennifer said. "Cream, no sugar?"

Madden nodded and slid onto the far end of the sofa to wait. This was so bizarre. Jennifer handed Madden his coffee and sat down at the other end of the couch.

"They grabbed me while I was walking to the Metro. It really scared the hell out of me."

"A girl is just not safe on the streets anymore," Madden said weakly. "I guess they didn't know they were fooling with an agent of the FBI."

"It wasn't that way," Jennifer answered, her voice quavery. "They not only knew I worked at the Bureau. They knew who I was."

Madden was shocked and filled with emotion. He wanted to grab her and hold her in his arms, though he was not sure if he wanted to protect her or make love to her. He placed his cup of coffee on the small table and moved closer. "Did they try to . . . ?" His voice trailed off.

"No!" Her eyes flashed at Madden's approach. "Anyway, I didn't give them a chance." Jennifer did not retreat. "As far as the Bureau is concerned, the most important part of it all was what my abductor said—something about wanting information from me. He told me they would let me go after I told them what they wanted to know."

"What did he want to know?" Madden slipped his arm gently over her shoulders.

"They wouldn't say. They said they wanted to take me somewhere else to get their answers." Jennifer tensed up but then relaxed under his protective arm.

"Anything else?" His eyes locked on hers.

"No," Jennifer said, returning his stare. "That's what my bosses keep asking. There's nothing else except that the man had an accent."

"What kind?" asked Madden, drawing her close beside him.

"Probably Middle Eastern. The Bureau thinks the incident is related to something I'm working on," Jennifer continued. "But right now the only cases I'm directly involved with are drug smuggling out of Mexico. And that accent was definitely not Hispanic. I know that much."

Madden stiffened at her revelation, concerned that he was the reason for her kidnapping. "Any leads on the van or the abductors?"

"Not to speak of, so far," Jennifer said. "They have an all-points bulletin out on the van. The driver of the car that was behind the van when I jumped out got the license number, but according to the plates, the van was stolen."

"What about the guy you injured?" he asked urgently.

"The Bureau is checking out all the hospitals and emergency clinics and . . ." Jennifer paused. "There was a patient at one of the outlying hospitals who could have been the one. He had a bad eye injury. He was even scheduled for surgery."

"What do you mean, 'was'?"

"He checked out against medical advice and vanished. He's a suspect because he signed in under an assumed name."

"How do they know that?"

"According to the person in admitting, he wasn't from this country, at least originally," Jennifer said. "He had no ID or insurance. He paid his hospital deposit with cash."

"Anything else?" Madden asked, his pulse speeding up.

"The hospital employees who were interviewed guessed he was originally from Iran, Iraq, or Kuwait. In that area somewhere."

Madden pulled back from Jennifer as visions of the Mother Lode project flashed before his eyes. Was Jennifer's attempted abduction because of him? Too many things came at him at once. "Look," he said, fighting back his anger. "I can't explain yet, but I think I almost got you killed."

Jennifer's eyes widened. "We're both thinking the same thing, aren't we?"

Madden reached up and put his fingers over her mouth. "I'm not sure what's going on right now," he said, his lips quivering. "Whatever it is, it's scaring the hell out of me. I just don't want you hurt." He bent over and kissed her forehead and then moved down until his lips surrounded hers.

. . .

Later as she closed the door behind him, Madden drew in a deep breath and wondered why he had been so foolish the first time around. The memory of her tender but frightened lips reverberated through his mind.

He left the way he came. The ride back in the seclusion of the Suburban gave Madden time to stitch his suspicions together. He scratched some notes on a piece of paper. The Middle Eastern accent. Trainer's odd behavior. The altered files. Could they all be tied together? For President Winslet's sake and for the future security of this country, Madden hoped not.

16

"D<small>OCTOR</small> R<small>USSELL</small>," the operator paged. "Line two."

Russell whirled around as the sound of his name blared over the intercom throughout the emergency room. "Excuse me," he said, rising from the stool next to the young girl on the gurney. "Let me get that call and I'll be right back."

Russell had given strict orders that he should not be bothered when he was with patients unless it was an emergency. So when the page went out, there was no question about delay.

"Tate died of some type of prion infection," Lowell McCarty blurted over the phone.

Russell's jaw tightened as he looked across the emergency room to the spot where he had first seen the Vice President Delstrotto on the stretcher. "It's an epidemic, probably from infected deer in the Rockies," he said to McCarty. He felt embarrassed. "I think I overreacted."

"You must have read the same article I did," McCarty said. "I checked it out with our people in the infectious disease department here at Georgetown. If the serotypes match—"

"If they do?" Russell interrupted, stunned. "They could have come from the same source."

"Then it's a conspira . . ." Russell's voice trailed off. "I'm . . . I'm coming up there!"

"Are you crazy?" McCarty cried out. "Let the CDC handle it."

Russell gazed into the distance, his eyes blurry, stunned at the revelation of a third case so close to the White House. He cupped his hand around the receiver, trying to avoid being overheard. "The Secret Service told me to stay out of things. Now two other deaths have occurred in Washington. I don't know if we can trust the CDC. I don't know who we can trust."

"My wife's in good with our congressman since she worked on his campaign," McCarty said thoughtfully. "If anyone can get you in to see the president, he can. He's the chairman of the House Foreign Affairs Committee. With all I do for her, tagging along to those fund-raisers, I think the least she could do is give him a call."

Russell reached in his pocket and flipped out his calendar. "I'm off for the next four days after this shift. I'll check with the airport and see what I get out of here late tonight."

"What scares the hell out of me, Dan," McCarty admitted, his voice cracking, "is that you might be right about a conspiracy."

Russell laid down the receiver and fell limp against the wall. The image of Rosalyn Delstrotto's pale face loomed before him, and a slight pulsation began to increase in his temples. Russell pushed himself to an upright position and straightened his white jacket. There was only one way to get rid of his recurring nightmares.

. . .

"Mr. Madden," his assistant called out to him. "Congressman Ferman is on the line. He says he has a doctor friend from Georgetown Medical Center who needs to talk to the president."

"I don't need to deal with Ferman today. Tell him to go to the appointments secretary." Madden continued to stare at the files Jennifer had retrieved for him.

"I did," the assistant said. "But he's really persistent. He said I should remind you about the aid you and the president want for Turkey."

"That blackmailing son of a bitch," Madden muttered. He punched the third line and lifted up the receiver. "Congressman," Madden said pleasantly. "Can I help you?"

"Madden," the congressman barked. "I wouldn't have called personally if I didn't think this was important. This guy who wants to see the president—his wife single-handedly put my campaign war chest in the black, so I hope you understand where I'm coming from. He's a bigwig over at Georgetown Medical."

"Respectfully, sir," Madden answered, "that doesn't give him the right to a private meeting with the president. What does he want?"

"He says he can prove there's a connection between the deaths of the vice president and Senator Harrison Tate—that is, if you're interested."

Madden was stunned. This was a nightmare he would have never imagined. Those isolated facts on the note in his pocket might not be so isolated after all. "I want to talk to him," Madden said.

"No," Ferman said. "He wants Winslet. Listen, if you can't—"

"Wait!" Madden scanned the president's schedule. He would have to move things around, but Madden had no other choice. And he would have to tell the president all he knew. He dreaded it. "Can he call tomorrow afternoon? Say about 3:15."

"He says no calls!" Ferman demanded. "He'll come to you. His name is Doctor Lowell McCarty."

The telephone went dead. "Martha," Madden called over the intercom. "Call the president's administrative assistant and tell her I'm sending over a change in the schedule for tomorrow afternoon."

"Yes, sir," she answered.

"Do me another favor. Call the dean's office at Georgetown Medical Center and find out what you can about this guy Ferman is sending over, Doctor Lowell McCarty."

. . .

He was a small man. He stood at barely five feet and four inches tall and weighed less than one hundred and thirty pounds. But he was strong, or at least his hands and forearms were. His power came from years of kneading dough that later became the bread and pastas served to the rich and powerful.

Alkas Parum's parents, both Bulgarian by birth, had chosen the Muslim faith as well as a new name and immigrated to Iraq several years before the birth of their first child. Always considered special because of his exotic background, Alkas left home at age twelve to attend a special school established by Saddam Hussein himself. There he had been selected over all of his fellow classmates. At first his parents objected, but when the elder Parum was threatened by the Iraqi high command with a transfer to the Northern Province without his family, he acquiesced, and his son disappeared from their lives.

After the US invasion of Iraq, Alkas fled to Iran. It was a lonely life. To instill in him the discipline of solitude and independence, Alkas, like the others at the school, spent most of his time isolated from fellow classmates. He learned the basics of literacy and arithmetic and was taught a trade so that he could survive virtually anywhere in the world. The young Parum also learned perfect English.

Although his skin color and facial features differed from the others who trained with him, he was as convinced as they were that there was no greater honor than to give up his life for his country's cause. By the time he was twenty Alkas Parum was a walking time bomb, prepared to ignite whenever his president, under the direction of Allah, gave the order, regardless of whether it was to inflict pain or destroy property.

Parum had arrived in the United States three years before with a different name.

He received a new set of identification papers each time he moved. He lived in New York City for the first year; the city was a perfect location to practice his American intonations while serving a preceptorship in the kitchens of some of the best restaurants in the country. By the time the year was over, little trace remained of the young man who sneaked into the country on a Saudi oil tanker.

Jim Bilkos, as he was now called, had moved to the Washington, DC, area two years before, where he presented himself as a third-generation Greek Orthodox American from Detroit. Using altered letters of recommendation from two top restaurants in New York City and a remastered graduation certificate from the Culinary Institute of America, Bilkos was hired at Red Sage, a restaurant just a stone's throw from the White House.

Through hard work and basic talent, Bilkos moved up quickly from the position of line cook to assistant sous-chef. When the advertisement appeared for a new line cook at the White House, Bilkos applied.

A White House cook had died mysteriously when his car veered off a bridge one night. There were no witnesses. There were also no signs of foul play, and the screening tests for drugs and alcohol came back negative. Investigators determined the cause of death was a head injury, but no one was sure what led to the wreck in the first place. It was surmised that another vehicle had caused the driver to veer off the road, and that the driver of the surviving vehicle left the scene. Since there was no other evidence, the case was closed. The culprit was probably a late night hit-and-run driver, most likely drunk.

Within two weeks—the time necessary to check out all his credentials (the first "masterpieces" created by the man in the Manhattan apartment)—Bilkos was hired as part of the permanent White House kitchen staff. At first his Greek background had caused some hesitancy among the staff. No matter how hard they tried to ignore it, racial profiling took place when White House staff was entrusted with the final decision as to who would be hired for any position. What made a difference for Bilkos was the letter of recommendation from Vice President Delstrotto and her husband, Ben, which claimed that he was their favorite chef in the capital.

Bilkos's first duty was on the night shift, as backup in case the president or his family wanted a midnight snack. He was quiet, never said much, and for the most part kept to himself. In a large city like Washington there were plenty of people who lived this way—alone. For Bilkos's second line of work, this was better. As long as he did his job well, no one ever asked questions.

. . .

Owing to an unexplained holdup at Dallas/Fort Worth airport, Dan Russell's plane touched down at Washington National an hour behind schedule. By the time he fought his way through the bedlam of the baggage area another forty-five minutes had passed, and Dan was ready to pack it in and head back to his home in the quiet suburbs.

"Damn terrorists," he cursed under his breath, recalling the days prior to 9/11 when airplane passengers were not all treated like criminals.

He noticed a long line of equally frustrated travelers at the taxi stand. Dan slung his carry-on over his shoulder and started to fall in behind them when he felt a tug on his shoulder. "You don't have to wait like all them others, mister," said the man with a thick Eastern European accent. "My brother has a private limousine service."

"I don't know..."

The man shrugged his shoulders and turned away. "It's your choice," he said, looking over at the line of weary travelers all waiting for the few available cabs that trickled up one by one.

"How much will it cost me?" Dan called out after him, his growing impatience showing.

The young man with closely cropped hair cut him a smile. "Depends on how badly do you want to get into the city. He doesn't run no meter, so it's a flat thirty dollars to start."

"That's a little high, isn't it?" Dan asked, knowing he would probably not get a response. Then he remembered that DC was a city where everything came with a price. His arm was beginning to throb from the weight of his carry-on. He cast one last glance at the growing line at the cabstand. "I'll take it."

The young man spun around and signaled. The white Lincoln Town Car pulled up to the curb not twenty feet from where he and Dan stood. "Mister," he said, turning back in Russell's direction and holding out his hand. "I've got to eat too, you know."

. . .

Dan Russell and Lowell McCarty stayed up most of the night reviewing all the possible scenarios. Senator Tate's blood test was positive for the virulent prion infection. Even though the final report on the serotyping would not be back for forty-eight hours, the preliminaries were good enough for Russell.

He was convinced there was a link between the deaths of Vice President Delstrotto and Senator Harrison Tate.

...

"Doctor, I did some checking on you," Madden told McCarty the next afternoon. "It's policy. You would be surprised the kooks who try to get in here."

"I would do the same, if I were in your position," McCarty answered, looking at Russell.

"Not only are your credentials impeccable, you are even listed as the doctor who came to the aid of Senator Tate when he had his first problem in the intensive care unit. I'm afraid I was not able to check on doctor . . ."

"Dan Russell," Russell said. "I'm the doctor who treated the vice president when she was taken to the emergency room in Texas."

"Is that why you're involved?" Madden asked. Russell saw his face go white. "Tell me, did you think—"

"Please don't be offended," Russell interrupted. His eyes locked with Madden's. "But I'm not going to play your game. What I have to say is for the president's ears only."

The intercom clicked on. It was Madden's assistant. "The president is ready for Doctor McCarty and Doctor—Russell."

Dan was less than thirty feet from the Oval Office. He had seen pictures on television and was familiar with fake movie and television sets. But this was the real thing. Then Raymond Winslet emerged into the anteroom, and Russell and McCarty were face-to-face with him. Madden ushered them to one of the two large sofas. Russell's heart raced as he held out his hand to greet the president.

"Mr. President, thank you for seeing us," McCarty mumbled, made visibly anxious by the encounter. "Doctor Russell and I have information that we think is of importance to you."

Winslet nodded. "I'm told that you feel this information could be of importance not just to me, but to our national security?"

"It could be interpreted that way," Russell said. "We need to talk to you in private," he continued, referring to Madden's continued presence.

"I'm afraid that won't be possible," Winslet answered without hesitation. "My chief of staff and I have no secrets from each other. If you have something to say, he hears it too. Otherwise, gentlemen, we're wasting each other's time."

The subject was closed. If Russell wanted to continue his audience with the president, Madden would stay.

"Mr. President," Russell said, beginning carefully. He had to sound persuasive—and sane. The variant of mad cow disease still raged in Colorado's deer population. Russell was not as convinced as McCarty was that there was no connection between the two. But it was his duty to report what he knew to the proper authorities, even when that meant taking the information to the number one authority in the country.

"Doctor McCarty and I have determined that Vice President Delstrotto and Senator Tate died of the same rare infectious prion disease, kuru disease. We believe this is more than just a coincidence. Especially since, according to the Centers for Disease Control and Prevention, there has been reported only one case of kuru disease in the last three years in this country. That case occurred in a laboratory worker who was doing research on the organism. The pathologist who performed the vice president's autopsy also died from being infected by the same organism. That brings our list to three. This is either an epidemic in the early stages or —" he hated to say the words— "a conspiracy."

The president shot a quick glance at Madden and turned back to Russell. His face was stony. "Aren't you being somewhat presumptuous, Doctor? We had some of our best physicians at

Walter Reed and Georgetown Medical involved with these two cases, and they did not uncover such a problem. At least as far as I know." The president leaned back in his chair, confidence spreading across his face. "Why do you think that is, Doctor?"

Dan Russell felt a tightening in his chest at the president's insinuation. "I believe it's because they didn't know to look, sir."

. . .

As he walked down Pennsylvania Avenue, the wind whipping his hair, Dan Russell felt a wave of nausea pass over him. He could only hope that what he had done would quiet those demons inside his head.

He and Lowell McCarty had been asked to join a private meeting tomorrow morning at the Oval Office with Sterling Padgett, assistant director of the FBI, and Joel Cornish, MD, director of the CDC. They had agreed not to mention their suspicions to anyone else. For the present everyone agreed that the fewer who were involved, the better. "We can't risk any leaks—even from within the White House," Madden had told them grimly.

. . .

"Sounds like conspiracy mongering," Padgett, the assistant director of the FBI, responded glibly, turning back to the book on Lincoln he had scooped up off the coffee table. "My people are spread so thin, what with the counterterrorism effort and having to wipe up the messes the folks over at the DEA leave behind. We really have to pick our priorities." He turned to Russell and McCarty, who were planted silently on the sofa while the president and his advisers huddled around Winslet's desk. "Nothing personal. But at the last count, the FBI has received dozens of calls making conspiracy claims about the deaths of both Delstrotto and now Tate—so where are the facts that make this worth the Bureau's time?"

Madden knew his priority was to find Jennifer Smitt's abductors. Dan Russell's convincing argument added gasoline to the flare-up of his own misgivings. Madden did not agree with Padgett. All they needed to undertake was a preliminary investigation. The goal was to see if there was a problem. If Padgett did not agree, so what? He still had a duty. Padgett would comply. He had no other choice.

"Because the cases are so rare, Mr. President, my knowledge of the prion diseases is limited," Joel Cornish began, looking embarrassed. "I've read about kuru disease, but have never actually seen a case myself. Still I can assure you the CDC will get you the answers you need."

To Madden's relief, Cornish seemed genuinely interested. Whether he was motivated by scientific curiosity, political savvy, or a potential threat to national security, his motivation did not matter to Madden as much as his interest did.

"Give me a couple of days," the chief physician at the CDC said. "What I would like to do is get a breakdown of the strains involved and see what develops."

"What do you mean?" Winslet asked.

"Mr. President, by matching strains of the organisms or, as Doctor Russell referred to them, serotypes, we can pretty well nail down the point of origin. We can only hope it holds true with this theory of the kuru organism."

Padgett told the small group that, his own misgivings aside, he would review the hospital records as well as the staff at Georgetown Medical and check for other suspicious cases. Beyond that, he did not have much to go on. For the moment Madden decided not to cloud the picture by mentioning the link to the attempted abduction of Jennifer Smitt. He was afraid it would open their rekindled relationship to unnecessary scrutiny. For now he would protect himself—and Jennifer.

...

"It's all set for the twenty-fourth," Trainer whispered, his eyes dancing to and fro as he looked out from behind the giant podium on the floor of the Senate chamber. This was only the third time Savage had appeared before the august body since he took office, but his presence would be critical given the upcoming razor-thin vote on the president's military budget. "That's the night of the White House reception for the president of Argentina."

"Why then?" the vice president asked, fumbling nervously with the lapel on his jacket.

Trainer cut him a sly grin. "Mr. Vice President, you need to remember we're just soldiers," he whispered. "Too many questions could bring unwanted repercussions."

"Mr. Vice President, we're ready to open the session," the bailiff called down from the dais.

Savage's expression turned into a scowl at Trainer's comment, out of keeping with his call to duty from the Senate. "You may be just a soldier, Mr. Trainer," he mumbled under his breath as he reached for the side rail that would guide him to his place on the dais.

Trainer did not care how Savage valued his worth as long as he did his job. This was business, and that was the way it was going to be.

...

Leonard Palmer landed at Washington National three days prior. Instead of checking into a hotel, he had the taxi take him directly to Tate's funeral at the cathedral, where he arrived just in time to squeeze into the only remaining seat in the back row. Racked by guilt, Palmer thought it was the least he could do.

Palmer was in a state somewhere between frantic and furious since he knew his well-being meant nothing to those who were behind the conspiracy. He had thrown his life away to pay off his debts, and what did they care? His gut ached for freedom from these purveyors of evil. Ignoring the consequences of his plan, he slipped into a small alcove by the mammoth front doors in hopes of contacting someone in the president's party as they left the memorial service. His pulse racing, Palmer pushed forward when he saw them, but he was quickly repelled by the small army of Secret Service agents who blanketed the group as the mourners left the church. The best Palmer could do was catch a distant glimpse through the solemn crowd of onlookers and media types. Sweat still beaded his forehead as he flagged down a cab to the hotel. He decided his best option was a frontal approach on the White House itself.

. . .

"My mother told me to watch out for guys like you," Cindy French railed. "Never willing to settle down. Do you think I believe you're staying in Washington just to help an old friend?"

Dan Russell had called her hoping to soothe her ruffled feathers, but from the direction the conversation headed he could have saved his minutes. "It should be only a couple of more days," he said, deciding to ignore her attempt to grind more information out of him.

"You can't expect me to just sit around," she continued relentlessly.

He slung his jacket over his shoulder and headed for the door of his hotel room, the cell phone balanced precariously between his cheek and shoulder. "Why don't you go visit your mother," he said halfheartedly. "And give her my best."

. . .

"I need to see the president," Palmer told the security guard on duty at the East Gate. "So does everybody else in the country," the guard replied, an indifferent look on his face. "Without an appointment, nobody gets in."

Leonard Palmer knew that he had no chance seeking entrance this way, but he also did not have a choice. His only contact of any importance in Washington had just been killed at Georgetown Medical Center, and he was at the least indirectly responsible. All for a few hundred thousand dollars.

Two years earlier, after the crash of the commodities market, Palmer's investments turned into debts. His debts quickly became obligations. Already stretched to the limit, he did not have the resources to wait it out. They had come to him and offered to repay his debts. As an added bonus, they agreed to set him up with a small nest egg to see him through the remainder of his life. But the deal came with a price that ultimately cost Harrison Tate his life and could possibly bring down the most powerful country in the world. It was too high a price to live with. Racked with self-blame, Palmer had to make amends. He may not save himself from the devil, but he might be able to rescue the country that had given him his chance.

"Tell him it has to do with the death of Senator Harrison Tate," Palmer pleaded to the guard in the small booth at the outer gate.

The guard looked at him hard. "Senator Tate was here last week," he said, and Palmer felt the man truly saw him for the first time. "Would you wait here?" the security guard asked, his eyebrows arched, and pointed to a folding chair parked in the far corner.

Within five minutes, two armed guards appeared at the East Gate office. "Come with us, sir," one of them barked, signaling for Palmer to follow. They led him to the security office in the basement of the White House. After he had been searched from head to toe, Palmer was directed to a small isolation room just down the hall. "Make yourself comfortable," the surly guard ordered, indicating one of the two straight-backed metal chairs that stood around the lone desk in the middle of the small room.

Unable to sit, Palmer paced, wondering if he had made the right decision. After about thirty minutes the door opened again. "Mr. Palmer," the graying officer said. His name tag labeled him as head of White House security. "We've had you checked out. I'm sorry to put you through all of this. But as you can imagine, every crazy person in the country would like to get in here."

"I understand. Now that we've gotten that behind us, I have some important information that the president needs to know about Senator Harrison Tate's death."

"Mr. Palmer, the president is not available, nor is his chief of staff," the senior officer said, his eyes scanning Palmer from head to toe. "So I took the liberty of contacting the office of the vice president."

Palmer interrupted, his throat as dry as cotton, "No! It must be the president."

"Whatever," the officer sighed, his patience growing thin. "The vice president wasn't available either. I did, however, get in touch with his chief of staff. He's on the way down right now."

Palmer reached out and grabbed the back of the chair, smothering in a wave of panic. "You can't—" The door opened, and a handsome, worried-looking man entered. Palmer shrank back, afraid of anyone connected with Vice President Savage. He had already said too much.

"Mr. Palmer, I'm Jason Clark, chief of staff in the vice president's office. Security Chief Buttons said you had information that might be important with respect to the death of Senator Tate." Clark narrowed his eyes at Palmer, who sensed that this aide might have his own reasons for listening to him. Then

Clark picked up Palmer's bag and headed out the door. "Come on up to my office. It will be more private there."

His pulse dropped a notch, and Palmer reluctantly followed the vice president's chief of staff as he tried to figure out his next step. A thousand thoughts ran through his mind as the elevator door closed behind them. The two occupants stood in silence watching the red destination light as the elevator groaned to a stop.

"You're from Colorado, and you were close to Tate for a long time," Clark said. "I checked you out when security called me."

"Tate was my friend, but—"

"This is where we get off," Clark said, pointing to the hallway clogged with personnel jogging back and forth between the offices in front of them. As the two exited the elevator and headed for Clark's office, Palmer froze. He heard a familiar voice from the hallway.

"Jason, I need to—" Kenneth Trainer said. He stopped mid-sentence when he saw Palmer. Palmer's eyes widened. He felt as if he were looking into the face of death. "What the . . . ?"

"You two know each other?" Clark asked.

"No!" Palmer answered, hoping Trainer was not prepared to tip his hand publicly.

He let out a slow sigh when Trainer didn't respond.

"Ken," Clark went on. "Mr. Palmer claims he has some important information relating to the death of Senator Tate."

"Oh?" Trainer said casually.

"It's a good thing I was around," Clark said, breaking into a smile. "Security knew I was close to Tate, so they called me into help. I thought I would take down the information up here. Mr. Palmer was a major fund-raiser for the late senator."

A slow grin crept across Trainer's lips as he realized Palmer had not been able to share his story so far. "Let me join you," he said, heading in the direction of Clark's office.

Panic once again clawed at Palmer's chest. His shaking knees were barely able to carry the weight of his body. He knew if he went inside the office, Trainer and Clark would kill him.

"No!" Palmer screamed out. "No, no, no!" He bolted in the direction of the elevator, almost knocking Clark to the floor.

"Help!" Clark yelled. Palmer saw him reel backward and strike his head against the door frame to his office. Palmer bolted for the stairway, but the guard at the elevator door tackled him and pinned him to the floor. Another guard joined the ruckus and tightened a plastic restraining strap around Palmer's wrists. Although Palmer was not about to let it show, he owed them a debt for pulling him from a certain death.

Palmer looked up from the floor at Kenneth Trainer, who had not moved from the entrance to Clark's office. Trainer's deadly scowl told him all he needed to know. "Take him down to the holding room until the DC police arrive," one of the uniformed officers shouted as they jerked Palmer to an upright position and headed off down the hall with him.

Clark pulled himself to his feet, seriously shaken by the whole incident. He turned around and leaned against the wall for support. Ken Trainer came over to offer assistance.

"You would think with all the security they have around here, something like this couldn't happen," Trainer said. "Luckily the president and Savage weren't around."

Clark nodded, still trying to make sense of the bizarre situation. "I think it's going to take my old ticker a while to get back to normal. What was wrong with that guy? He knew Tate. I checked him out—even got his picture from security. Do you think he really went crazy?"

"We'll probably never know. Now go on in and take a load off," Trainer continued. "I'll make sure the DC police get the full report. If they need more, I'll have them call you. We'll get this mystery solved."

Clark was more than happy to turn the whole matter over to someone else. He rubbed the back of his neck as he realized had been foolish to take Palmer up to his office in the first place. He was painfully aware the mistake could have cost him his life.

Nobody could be trusted.

. . .

Trainer was a seasoned professional, but his heart still raced as he pushed open the door to the holding room in the White House basement. Leonard Palmer shot up from the chair. "Damn, I'm glad you guys got here, I . . ." He stopped midbreath. The color drained from his horrified face as he saw Trainer slip into the room to face him, one on one.

"Sorry to disappoint you," Trainer said, his finger wrapped around the trigger of the sidearm he had just lifted from the now unconscious guard outside the door. "I know you were expecting the DC police, but you'll have to put up with me instead."

Palmer stumbled back. "I wasn't going to tell them about you," he pleaded, his hands extended as if he could ward off Trainer's gun.

Trainer raised his weapon and pointed it at Palmer's chest. "The one thing I hate is a snitch . . . no, make that a lying snitch." He then squeezed the trigger. The sound of the first shot reverberated around the room.

Spatters of bright red blood lit up the far wall. Palmer's mouth fell open as if to scream, but he only gurgled. Three more shots rang out. Trainer wanted to make sure there would be no doubt about the outcome. Palmer recoiled violently and fell back over the chair, his bloodied head slamming against the far wall.

He had taken an unspeakable risk, killing Palmer here in the White House. But he had no choice. The room once again stood in silence. The only sound to be heard as Trainer emerged was the click of the dead bolt and the slow breathing of the unconscious guard on the hallway floor. He walked slowly, his pulse still running at breakneck speed. He replaced the guard's still-smoking gun in his holster, but not before wiping it clean with a paper towel he had picked up on the way down.

. . .

"We're too close to turn back now," Trainer mumbled as he pushed his tray down the cafeteria line in the basement of the Capitol. "We have to hold it together until you take over."

"They know!" Savage babbled, checking up and down the line to make sure no one was close enough to hear their conversation. "I know they know."

Trainer put his finger to his lips and slowed down, moving closer to the vice president. "They may suspect, but they don't know."

"How did Palmer get in the White House?"

"He's no longer a concern," Trainer said with a quick look. "But you're right, it's only a matter of time until they know too much."

"Madden suspects something," the vice president said. He was convinced that he was about to be apprehended at any moment. "I saw the way he looked at me this morning."

Trainer slapped out a twenty-dollar bill as he reached the cashier. "Put both of these on the same ticket," he demanded, pointing to the vice president's tray. "Print me out a receipt. I want everything on the up and up."

"The president is too busy to put all the hints together. Madden and now Clark are the threats," Trainer said under his breath, moving with Savage into a booth in the far corner. "They're no longer necessary to our operation."

Savage looked up, shocked by Trainer's last statement. "You're not talking about killing them too."

"No. Two more deaths would be unacceptable at this time." Trainer brandished his knife, jabbing it into the pat of butter on his tray and spreading it on his roll. "I think we'll be OK if we just keep them apart."

"How do you propose we do that?"

"Didn't you tell me you were supposed to attend the environmental summit in Buenos Aires next week? Maybe you should consider sending Clark in your place."

17

The last thing the White House guard remembered was pain and then darkness from the blow to the base of his skull. He had a large knot on the back of his head to prove it.

. . .

He asked for the president, but the call was routed through the chief of staff. Joel Cornish of the Centers for Disease Control and Prevention called the White House around 10:30 a.m.

"Doctor Cornish, I'm sorry the president is currently unavailable. What can I do for you?" Madden asked. "Does it have to do with the matter we discussed the other day?"

"Yes!"

"And?"

"I don't think I should say any more over the telephone," Cornish continued. "Is there any way I can meet with him?"

Madden went cold.

"Today!" Cornish demanded.

"I can squeeze you in about half an hour. Do I need to bring in Padgett from the FBI, if he's available?"

There was a pause on the other end of the line. "Mr. Madden, not only do you need to call in Mr. Padgett, but I would also suggest you notify the head of the CIA and the Joint Chiefs of Staff."

. . .

"Mr. President," Dr. Joel Cornish said as he fumbled through the copies of reports he had brought with him. "We were able to get complete profiles on the organisms that infected each of the three victims—Vice President Delstrotto, Senator Tate, and Dr. Thomas."

"And?" the president urged.

"They all match," Cornish sighed, a look of disdain across his face.

"What does that mean exactly?" Chad Madden butted in.

"They not only died of a variant of kuru disease, but the particular strains of this infectious protein are identical." Cornish pulled out one of the sheets of paper. "Which means that, in all probability, the organisms came from the same source."

Madden felt a burst of terror. He shot a quick look over at the president to see his response. Winslet's jaw had dropped.

"Just so you know, Mr. President," Madden said. "I've already checked. Rosie and Senator Tate had not taken a trip together, nor had they socialized much with each other as far as I can tell. They were at two fund-raisers at the same time earlier in the fall, but according to my sources they ate the same food as everyone else. No one could remember them even talking to each other except at the podium. In other words, it is virtually impossible that either contracted the disease from the other."

Cornish said, "Let me continue."

"I'm sorry," Winslet replied, "but it sounds as if we could have a small epidemic on our hands, Doctor."

"I'm not so sure, Mr. President."

Now Cornish had the group's full attention. Even Padgett seemed to sit up straighter.

"I ran the serotypes on our master computer," Cornish continued. "At the CDC, we have information stored on virtually every infectious agent that has been reported throughout the world.

"Let me guess," Padgett broke in, getting up from the sofa. "You found a match from some dead monkey deep in the heart of the African jungle."

Cornish shook his head. "No, Mr. Padgett. That's not where we found the match."

"Where then?" Madden asked, expecting that Cornish would then tell them that the match was located in the English countryside, a place where mad cow disease had been reported widely in the mid-1990s.

"Iraq!" the chief of the CDC blurted out. The president blinked but remained silent. "It's the only place we've identified this particular strain. Although we still have some work to do, this organism seems to be an extremely virulent form with a very short incubation period when compared with the other prion organisms we have identified so far."

Madden felt the throb of panic shoot up the back of his neck. "You're not suggesting that this was a terrorist . . . ?"

Padgett burst out, "Like anthrax?" His face flushed as he moved toward the group.

"Worse. At least there is treatment for anthrax poisoning, if it's caught early. Back in the 1990s, Saddam Hussein unleashed some of his biological weapons on the Kurd rebels in the northern province," Cornish continued. "As I'm sure you gentlemen know quite well, our CIA as well as other countries had been supplying the Kurds with arms in hopes they would overthrow Saddam's dictatorship."

Madden remembered it clearly. At the time he had been one of the strong advocates of the operation when he worked on Capitol Hill. After George H. W. Bush had been unable to undermine Saddam Hussein's reign during the war with Kuwait, there had been a move to take him out from within. Unfortunately Hussein had thwarted the American effort and also killed thousands of his own people with the biological weapons.

"How can you be sure that's where the disease originated?" the president asked, his growing concern showing in his grim face.

"Some of our own with Special Ops went in and took samples from the victims. The idea was that we would get all the information we could on Iraq's biological weapons program so we could develop antidotes in case they used them again."

Madden interrupted. "And what did they discover?"

Cornish shook his head. "We were able to collect samples of the organisms, but so far our researchers have not been able to develop a treatment for these particular infectious agents. From what I've learned, infection is certain death."

Sterling Padgett leaned forward and placed his hands on the desk. "Since it appears our military knocked out all their potential to use biological weapons during the last campaign, is there any other way the current Iraqi administration could transmit this disease if they were so inclined?"

"Yes," Cornish answered, looking over at the FBI deputy director. "They could contaminate animal products with it."

"So it would spread the same way mad cow disease did?" Madden interjected. "Exactly," the head of the CDC explained. "I'm not necessarily implying that's what happened here. But it's at least a possibility—say by slipping tainted goods into the food products that this country imports by the hundreds of tons each day. It's important to realize Iraq's supposed weapons of mass destruction—the ones we never found when George W. Bush ordered the invasion—could have been whisked into Iran or stored in a closet in something no larger than a suitcase."

The president moved back in his chair, gesturing with his hand. "Are you saying that instead of blowing up our embassies or sending their brainwashed outcasts over here to take down our major edifices, these zealots of Hussein's defunct regime—now probably working out of Iran—could be selectively poisoning our food with their biological agents in order to take out certain people?"

None of the participants attempted to answer the president as the reality and horror of the situation began to sink in.

Winslet's voice broke the silence. "In retrospect, maybe we went about things all wrong. We spent all our time searching for weapons of mass destruction while the Iraqis were developing and transplanting their deadly biological agents right under our noses. We were looking in their palaces and military facilities while they were breeding them in their barns and meadows."

Suddenly four Secret Service agents burst through the door to the Oval Office, guns drawn. "Don't move, sirs!" one cried as they fanned through the room around the stunned men. Madden nearly yelped in shock.

"We're sorry, Mr. President," one of the out-of-breath agents explained, his eyes flicking around the Oval Office. "But there's been a shooting in the basement and we've been ordered to cover you."

Padgett jerked out his cellular telephone and punched in a set of numbers. He cupped his hand over his other ear and walked over by the wall, spouting questions into the phone as Madden tried to make sense of the situation. Within moments Padgett was back with an answer. "A man—one who evidently caused a great deal of the commotion around here earlier today—was being detained in a holding room in the West Wing basement until he could be turned over to the DC police. He's been shot and killed."

"What?" shouted the president.

"The intruder was not killed by one of your own security," Padgett said, breathing fast. "The intruder's guard says he was struck from behind. When he woke up his prisoner was dead."

"How did the man die?" The president asked, still frozen in his seat. "Our chief of security said he was shot several times."

"Have they apprehended the suspect yet?" Madden wanted to know.

"That's the problem—there is no suspect." Padgett's face was filled with concern. "Mr. President, I think we need to evacuate you to Camp David or maybe back to the bunker until we can get a lead on this. We don't have to make it a big deal—just tell Davenport to leak to the press that you need a couple of days away. I'm sure she can come up with something convincing."

Winslet shook his head. "If our problem came from inside the White House, I don't think I'll be any safer out there." The president slumped back in his chair as a look of despair crept across his face.

. . .

"You're crazy!" Carver Whipple yelled through the receiver. "They told you to keep quiet, and you're up there in Washington to do what?"

"I'm not sure." Dan Russell looked down at the floor in the small alcove off the main corridor of the Federal building. He knew his boss was right. But Russell realized he had made a commitment to his dying mother on that rain-swept highway many years ago when he vowed to right the wrong of her tragic death. As far as Russell was concerned, he had no other choice than to help right the wrongful death of the vice president. "Right now I'm over at the CDC. The director wants to meet with me to discuss what you and I know about the vice president's death," he answered, trying to control the frustration he felt because his boss was so insensitive.

"Me!" Whipple barked. "Don't include me. I just walked in that evening to see if you needed help. I'm not a part of this!"

Russell realized he should have known better than to provide the CDC with Whipple's name as a witness to the events of that night in the emergency room. "I understand," he said. "This is my thing. But I've got two weeks of vacation built up, so I want to take it now."

"They're just going to label you one of those crazies." Whipple grew angrier by the moment. "A conspiracy nut, that's what they'll say. They'll take you off to one of those buildings with padding on the walls and make you regurgitate your whole life story to some asshole psychologist."

"Bullshit!" Russell shot back. Whipple was covering his own ass but also being condescending. "You and I both know there's something going on. Maybe it's an epidemic that the CDC is covering up. That's one of the reasons I agreed to meet with this guy, Cornish. I wanted to see if I could find out where his organization fits in to all this. Just ask yourself—how much money do you think cattle ranchers in this country would pay to keep this quiet?" He felt he had to give Whipple some explanation; that sounded as good as any.

Whipple's tone softened. "I'm talking to you as a friend now—here's a little fatherly advice. If you stay up there and get labeled a nut case, your job may not be waiting for you when you get back." Russell waited, frustrated, for his boss to finish. "Maybe, Dan, I should say *if* you get back."

. . .

Padgett worked with his counterpart over at the Secret Service to put all the agents at the White House on high alert for any suspicious activity. But they were limited in what they could do without tipping their hand to the press.

"Since Jason Clark and Ken Trainer were the last two people to see Leonard Palmer alive, we brought them in for questioning," Padgett said as he perched on the corner of Madden's desk. "Owing to the importance of their positions, we conducted our interrogations in their offices here in the White House rather than dragging them down to the Bureau."

Madden looked up. "My guess is you didn't learn much."

"Both claimed they had never seen or heard of Leonard Palmer before today. The only thing Jason Clark could offer was that Palmer said he had important information about Tate's death. Clark knew Palmer was a friend and fund-raiser for the senator, which is why he let him in without an appointment. But for some reason, which Clark could not explain, when they arrived at his office to discuss the matter Palmer changed his mind and started acting irrationally, running and yelling. Clark said he felt lucky to escape unharmed."

Madden wanted to share with Padgett his concern that all of this could be tied together—Trainer's strange behavior, the vice president's death followed by Tate's, the altered files, and maybe even Jennifer's attempted abduction. However he was the one who had asked Jennifer to cross the line and violate FBI policy. She had put her career in jeopardy for him. Madden was not about to betray her trust, at least not until he had more time to sort out the discrepancies in files she had uncovered.

"Our background check on this Palmer character did reveal that he was indeed a close friend and supporter of Tate as Clark said. We found out they had spent a weekend together at Palmer's retreat in Colorado less than a month before Tate's death." Padgett picked up a pencil off Madden's desk and toyed with it. "So excepting his erratic behavior just outside Clark's office, he would have been considered a credible witness with information about the senator's untimely death."

"I'm told Palmer's death looks like a professional hit."

"He took four bullet wounds, two to the head, one to the heart, and a wild shot to the leg. You do the math. The ballistics matched with the guard's gun. Unfortunately there were no additional fingerprints on the weapon." Padgett rubbed his brow. "In the FBI, we would profile that as someone who's done this kind of thing before."

"For now we might be better off to tell the story that Leonard Palmer was a little crazy. That way we'll be more likely to avoid panic around here. I'll talk to Davenport. She needs to play down the significance of the shooting to the press."

Padgett nodded. "I've spoken to the Secret Service and they're doubling the contingent around the president and vice president. Unfortunately that will mean a lot of new faces around here."

On the surface everything appeared to be business as usual, but Madden knew it was only a matter of time until the White House would explode again.

. . .

Although Leonard Palmer had no record of previous mental issues, the president's press secretary was able to convince the media that the incident did not represent a threat to national security. She cast it as a tragic case of a respectable man gone abruptly berserk who had been allowed into the White House because of his connection with Harrison Tate. He was a potential informant who had for some reason become violent—maybe out of grief or paranoid fantasy about the senator.

Since the truth was not in the public's best interest—as it had not been many times before—the highest authority at the FBI instructed the White House security guard to claim he had shot Palmer in self-defense. He was happy to do so since he did not want to admit he had been ambushed. The story appeared as an item at the bottom of the front page; a couple of days later it had been pushed farther back in the first section. By then Palmer's death was old news to everyone but those at the White House who knew the truth.

. . .

"We've come down a long way," Madden said as he let his two iron rip off the tee. "From eighteen holes in the Maryland countryside to a bucket of balls at a driving range two blocks off Pennsylvania Avenue. Where were you last night?"

"Holed up in my condo," Jason Clark answered after hitting his shot, a topper that dribbled out about fifty yards. "Savage has me going in his place to the environmental summit in Argentina, so he told me to take time off and bone up. If I were the suspicious type, I'd say he was trying to get me out of the White House." He dragged another ball up on the tee and shot Madden a glance. "I really want to know what's happening over there," Clark said, his voice quieter. "I mean regarding the death of Leonard Palmer."

Madden was not sure how to answer Clark. He had been given strict orders to discuss the matter only with the investigators from the FBI and Winslet. He glanced around to see what ears might be listening. "We don't talk much about it." Madden glared at Clark, hoping he would catch on and drop the issue.

Clark did not catch his hint. "Well, it's all so puzzling," he continued. "This Palmer guy acted normal until we got upstairs. Then he just went crazy. It was just after Trainer said something about going in the office with us that the guy went off the deep end." Clark stopped, his face turning red. "I could've been killed, you know!"

"You said Trainer?" Madden interrupted, momentarily forgetting his commitment to secrecy.

"Yeah," Clark answered. "He happened to be there when I brought Palmer up to my office."

Madden had to be very careful. This was not the time or place to discuss any suspicions he had about the vice president's aide. "Do you think this guy knew Trainer?" he asked, barely above a whisper.

"I doubt it." Clark went on. "But he did look a little funny when they first met. In fact, as I recall, so did Trainer. Do you think there's a connection?"

"I don't know," Madden replied, reaching down and setting another ball on the tee. "Let's discuss this again when you get back."

. . .

The cellular telephone in Kenneth Trainer's breast pocket erupted with a familiar ring. Trainer pulled it out and pushed the green SND button. The sound that came in response was a series of beeps. He punched in seven numbers. A recording came on. He listened intently as the two familiar voices of Jason Clark and Chad Madden discussed Leonard Palmer's response when he saw Trainer.

Trainer's knuckles whitened around the phone. These two men were becoming a business risk. The more he heard, the angrier he became. If Jason Clark was not due shortly in South America, Trainer would have killed them both right there on the range. Soon they would have to go.

. . .

Madden grabbed his cell phone and tapped in the number to Jennifer's unlisted line in her FBI hideout. He fought to loosen the tightness in his chest, but his efforts were to no avail. Of all the people in Washington, she was the only one who could understand the ever-growing burden he was carrying. An unfamiliar voice cut in unexpectedly and broke his concentration.

"What number are you calling?" came the curt interruption.

Madden felt a wave of uncertainty well up inside him. He slammed down the phone. Jennifer had done enough. For now he would carry his burden alone.

. . .

Dawn had not yet broken over the eastern horizon. Kenneth Trainer always went out early for his daily three-mile jog. He was usually unaccompanied except for the sanitation trucks and street sweepers. Today would be different. Central had arranged the meeting. Since the new administration would take over soon, Iran had decided it was time for Trainer to meet his new boss—not Jonathan Savage, the next president of the United States, but his real boss.

They were to meet at six o'clock sharp at the bench closest to the west end of the Vietnam Veterans Memorial site. His contact would be wearing a sweat suit with "Notre Dame" stenciled in green letters on his chest. To establish verification, Trainer would open with the words "Washington can be bitter cold in the early morning." Trainer's new boss would reply by saying, "Bradford thought so." Bradford was Trainer's middle name.

When Trainer arrived his contact was already there, wearing his hooded sweatshirt. Short of breath from the run, Trainer could barely gasp his opening line. The older gentleman returned the appropriate reply. They were alone except for the passing cars and an occasional jogger off in the distance. For an instant Trainer did not recognize the man's face, although it was familiar, because it was partially hidden under the hood of his sweatshirt. When he realized who the man was, the vice president's aide was speechless.

"Do you think Savage is ready?" the older gentleman asked, not attempting to identify himself any further. Trainer struggled for words.

"I asked you a question, Mr. Trainer," the older gentleman repeated, made impatient by Trainer's surprise. "I don't want to be out in this cold any longer than absolutely necessary."

"You!" Trainer managed. "How could you?"

"To you and your kind, this is all about money," the man in the sweat suit replied, his voice steeped in disgust. "But for those of us who believe, there is a higher order we must follow no matter what sacrifices we are asked to make. Our rewards will come in another life. As for you, Savage, and the other assistants we hired, well . . ."

Trainer was used to doing whatever needed to be done. But this was more than even he could have managed.

"I'm sorry, sir," Trainer said, still reeling in response to the older gentleman's vehement words. "Yes, I think the . . . ah . . . vice president is as ready as he can be. He really isn't cut out for this type of thing, but he'll have to do."

"They tell me the final process will begin on the twenty-fourth," the older gentleman said as he tugged on the hood of his sweat suit.

"If Winslet responds like the others, Savage will be the acting president within ten days," Trainer answered uncomfortably. "Then the real thing should take place within a week."

A smile crept across the older gentleman's face. Trainer wondered what would happen after that. Until now Trainer's mission had been to place Savage in the presidency. He had not been informed what his role would be in the new administration.

"What will you do, sir?" Trainer asked. "I mean, in the new order of things."

Insurrection at 1600 Pennsylvania Ave.

The older gentleman watched two joggers approach the War Memorial and then head off in the other direction. He stood up, placed his leg on the bench beside Trainer, and started to stretch, as if he were preparing to jog off behind them.

Sensing the conversation was over, Trainer stood up. The older man's eyes locked onto his.

"You haven't heard?" the older gentleman whispered.

Trainer shook his head. The sun, which was just beginning to show over the eastern horizon, cast a sharp glare on the older gentleman's partially hidden face.

"I'm going to be the new chief of staff."

"What will the public think?" Trainer asked, shocked by the older man's revelation.

"A little surprised, at first," the gentleman responded. "But they will get used to it."

"What about Chad Madden?"

"He'll go."

"And Jason Clark?"

The older gentleman snapped a response at Trainer's question. "Mr. Trainer, I believe he's still your problem!"

18

WHEN JOEL CORNISH verified that the organisms from Tate, Thomas, and Delstrotto all came from the same source, Dan Russell was reasonably convinced the CDC was not involved in a massive cover-up. Unfortunately that left him at a dead end as to what to do next. Cornish pressured his agency to track down any and all possible parties who might have access to this virulent strain of disease that had previously been identified only in Iraq.

Madden decided that, with the murderer of Leonard Palmer loose in the White House, it might be better for his health if he temporarily backed off attempting to assemble all the parts of the puzzle and let Sterling Padgett and the FBI do their job. He would still keep a watchful eye on Savage and Trainer, but for now his top priority was ensuring Winslet stayed on an even keel. Given Padgett's interest in the situation, Madden would pick the appropriate time to lay out his concerns.

. . .

The White House dinner for the president of Argentina was only two days away. For everyone except Jim Bilkos the event was routine, the grand kind of evening that presidents hosted for visiting foreign dignitaries. Although the event was not classified as an official state dinner, the staff would roll out the red carpet for their allies from the Southern Hemisphere. The usual lineup of guests from the House and Senate would attend, as would many members of the United States Foreign Service. The president's staff usually invited additional prominent individuals who had personal connections to or business interests with the guest country.

Bilkos exhaled a stream of smoke as he leaned against a corner post and watched the UPS truck back up to the loading dock at the delivery entrance of the White House. It had been scheduled to arrive three hours earlier, but a mix-up in security caused a delay. Though his stomach was still in knots, Bilkos let out a sigh of relief as he flicked his still-lit cigarette off to the side and disappeared back into the kitchen area. He did not want to appear too eager. He knew it would be another twenty minutes or so until the package, labeled "Clearance Red," would be delivered. It had come in on a flight from Houston earlier that morning and would be closely scrutinized before it was cleared by the swarm of inspectors attached to the Secret Service.

. . .

"Want some help?" Bilkos asked, peering at the large Styrofoam container that stood three feet high and had to be carried to the kitchen area on a dolly. Two Secret Service agents were still finishing one final dusting for explosives before they would turn over the cargo to the kitchen staff.

"Sure, Jim," one of the line cooks answered as he eased his way between the ever-present agents who scrutinized every delivery to the prep area. After a casual nod from one of the agents, the cook reached in his pocket and removed a three-inch, steel-gray object. After making a quick 360 with the box cutter, they slid off the top and the cool steam from the dry ice trickled to the floor.

Relief flooding over him, Bilkos waved off the smoky haze and gazed at the still-frozen one hundred and fifty individually wrapped ten-ounce cuts of prime Texas sirloin beef. They looked exactly as he had hoped and expected. "Let's get them in there," he said, pointing to the freezer at the far end of the kitchen. As the agents watched, he and the line cook stacked the steaks in the freezer.

The unloading process complete, Bilkos smiled. He then headed back out to the loading dock for another cigarette. It was a luxury he could afford to indulge. The steaks he had been anticipating were neatly tucked away, awaiting their use at the state dinner on the twenty-fourth.

. . .

A smaller package arrived at the efficiency apartment of Jim Bilkos the next day. Bilkos opened the small Styrofoam container to remove the contents. He dumped the block of dry ice into the sink filled with hot tap water. The layer of cloudy carbon dioxide crept across the floor of his small kitchen.

When the dry ice was gone, the remaining contents of the package became visible: two perfectly matched ten-ounce cuts of sirloin beef. They were virtually indistinguishable from the steaks that had arrived at the White House the day before—except for the plastic covering, which was at least twice as thick.

Before he removed the cuts of meat from the box, Bilkos put on a pair of work gloves that he kept in his toolbox. He then carefully transported the steaks to the freezer section of his refrigerator, where he placed them on top of a plastic plate over on the side, far away from the Lean Cuisine dinners Bilkos ate when he was off duty. Bilkos took the unmarked Styrofoam container and chopped it into tiny pieces before he placed it in the trash chute at the end of the hall of his apartment building.

He was almost ready for the twenty-fourth.

. . .

"Are you sure there's not something you've might have forgotten?" Sterling Padgett said as he clicked off his pocket recorder and set it on the coffee table in Jennifer's efficiency. "If they didn't just pick you up out of the blue, their motive had to be connected to something you are working on."

Jennifer Smitt shook her head. "As you already know, I mostly work on the drug stuff out of Mexico." A thought occurred to her. "Or . . ."

Padgett glanced in her direction. "Or what?" His expression was laced with uncertainty.

"Or . . . maybe it had something to do with an old case from when I was back out in the field." Jennifer edged up off the sofa. "I know one thing. I can't stay cooped up here much longer." She shot him a quick glance, her look edgy. "Want a cup of coffee?"

"No, thanks," he answered and glanced at his watch. "I'm due back for a meeting with the chief."

"OK, sir, but first you need to tell me something," Jennifer said as she moved into her little kitchen area. "What's the latest on the shooting over at the White House?"

"I'm afraid that investigation has been about as productive as asking you who tried to snatch you," he answered, heading for the door. "No one over there seems to be able to give us much to go on either."

Padgett closed the door and headed down the long hall, frustrated that not one but two high-profile investigations had utterly stalled. There was still no trace of the blue van.

The injured suspect had vanished. The FBI had scoured every hospital and emergency clinic but come up with nothing. The sixth sense he honed over his years in law enforcement told him Jennifer Smitt was holding back. And although he was concerned about the nature of the information she withheld, he was even more troubled about why she would keep it from him.

"You don't look too happy, Mr. Padgett," the guard said.

Padgett looked around as he leaned on the elevator button. "It's been one of those days," he answered just as the door slid open. He slipped into the waiting elevator. He and his team of agents had also run aground with respect to the investigation into the death of Leonard Palmer. They had no motive, no evidence, and no witnesses who would admit to anything. Everyone in the White House log had been accounted for. Each of their stories had been checked and rechecked.

Unfortunately since most of what went on in the White House was secret, there was not a great deal of overlap among the staff. Many of the alibis had gone uncorroborated. The consensus, however, was that the killer or killers came from within the building. According to the facts of the case, there was no other explanation.

As time passed the chance of solving either of these cases grew more and more unlikely. Padgett wanted one more interview with Jason Clark, since he had had the most contact with Palmer. Padgett decided he would conduct this interview himself, in case there was anything his people had overlooked the first time.

. . .

After passing through the ever-increasing formalities of White House security, Chad Madden arrived at his desk a little earlier than usual. He had spent a restless night going over what Clark had told him. In addition to his usual preparatory duties for the president, he wanted a little extra time to review the file on Kenneth Trainer and the background information the FBI had assembled on Leonard Palmer. If the killer had come from within the White House, Trainer was at the top of Madden's list. Impulse told him to share his suspicions with Sterling Padgett, though he needed to think it through first. Palmer had information—valuable information—about something, and Trainer was in some way involved. Madden could feel it. Nothing else added up.

Madden read both sets of documents carefully. They offered the usual information: education, vocational experience, special interests, and political activities. There was nothing new that he could find. If the two men were in some way connected, it did not show in their files. But as Madden knew, those files had probably been altered.

According to Jennifer Smitt, at least Trainer's had been changed.

Madden's intercom went off. "Chad?" asked Winslet. "Where in the hell are you? We have a government to run." Time was up. The president was waiting for him.

. . .

"It's chicory, John," Jennifer said, trying to contain her edginess as she set the steaming cup of coffee before him on the small desk at the end of the hall. "An old New Orleans recipe my mother sent me."

The guard was hesitant to take Jennifer up on her offer. "I'm supposed to go light on anything that makes my prostate act up."

"One cup can't hurt," Jennifer pushed. "If you like it, I'll see if she can send me up a can of the decaf."

By the time Jennifer had made it back down the hall, the guard was on his second swallow. She knew it was now only a matter of time until he would have to take a break. To insure that she had slipped into his cup the diuretic she had been saving for her premenstrual fluid retention along with a bolus of caffeine.

Although Padgett was adamant that her remaining in her windowless apartment was for her own safety, Jennifer felt smothered, cooped up while the world went on around her. She was not sure what she would do if she made it out, but she had to try. Jennifer had planned carefully for her offer of a drink to coincide with the time the guard had just come on duty. After the recent personnel cutbacks at the Bureau, she knew his relief would not be around for two hours—far too long for him to hold out without a bathroom break. Jennifer calculated she would need two minutes, three at the outside, if the elevator was in use. Since the john was situated in a little anteroom adjacent to the guard post, she did not have much leeway. She had to be ready.

Once she made it past the guard, Jennifer hoped the rest would be relatively easy. The converted office building in downtown DC was used as a safe house by not only the Federal Bureau of Investigation but also by the Central Intelligence Agency, the Department of Justice, and the Department of Homeland Security. She would make a few distracting comments and flash her ID at the front desk staffed by security, who would have no idea who she was since the different branches of the government were reluctant to share information about who was in the building. And then she should be out the door. After all, everyone in law enforcement knew the intent of a safe house was to keep people from getting in rather than breaking out.

. . .

Chad Madden felt half drugged from his sleepless night as Charlie Sclar, the president's longtime personal aide, led him into the private dining room for his routine morning briefing session with the president,

"Is something wrong?" Winslet asked as he looked up from his steaming cup of coffee.

"No!" Madden said hurriedly, not wanting to burden the president with his growing concerns. Then he changed his mind. This was Winslet's problem too. "Well . . . yes. Could we talk about it in your study?"

The president gestured to Sclar. "Charlie, bring Mr. Madden a muffin and a cup of strong black coffee with cream on the side." He scooped up his cup and what was left of his English muffin and headed to his private study. Madden was ahead of him as they entered the darkened room. He turned on the light and picked up the remote, which he used to flick on the central television screen and turn up the volume.

"Did I miss something last night?" Winslet asked.

"No, sir," Madden answered softly. "It's just that I don't want to be overheard." The president looked surprised—why would his chief of staff assume the Oval Office complex was bugged? But with the pall of uncertainty that had settled over the White House, Madden knew Winslet would understand.

"Mr. President, the man who was killed in the holding room, Leonard Palmer, was not a crackpot," Madden said, his eyes steady on Winslet. "He came here to tell us something important about Tate's death."

"What are you trying to say?" the president demanded.

"Palmer . . ." Madden started to speak but cut off his remarks when Charlie entered the room and set down a tray with his breakfast. "Doesn't he ever knock?" Still flustered, Madden waited for the silently indignant Charlie to leave and then continued.

"Someone snuffed him to keep him from telling us who was behind Senator Tate's death."

"Who do you think is behind it?" the president asked, his voice taut.

"Probably one of us," Madden replied, his gaze fixed firmly on the president.

"Whoever it was is probably also responsible for the Mother Lode leak."

The president physically stiffened, nearly spilling his almost empty cup of coffee. After he had partially recovered, he said, "You'd think that with all the security we have around here, I'd feel safe." The president's hand shook noticeably as he took a gulp of his coffee. "Hell, Chad, I feel like a duck in a shooting gallery."

"Somehow we have to flush them out, Mr. President," Madden said, his own heart aching at the unmanageable threat that besieged the West Wing.

"If it's as you say, I'm a step ahead of you." The fear that had moments before filled the president's eyes was gone as he sat down his cup. "I'm putting the two people I am supposed to trust the most in charge of the classified information on the Mother Lode project," he said, throwing a long look over at Madden. "Then if any of that information falls into the wrong hands, I'll only have two places to look, won't I?"

. . .

The phone at his ear, the tall, dark man pulled out his last cigarette and crumpled the empty pack into a ball before tossing it in the direction of the wastebasket. It was just after 11:00 p.m. when he finally glanced up at the battery-operated clock hanging on the far wall. Even in this city of eternal play and godless ambition, most people were preparing to go to sleep for the night. But in this Manhattan apartment overlooking Central Park, the business of victory never subsided.

He slept when he could, not when he should. He did not care if it was night or day. Although he was not always a perfect follower of his faith, his reward went to his country and Allah. The years of planning and hard work were about to pay off. Within two, maybe three weeks at the most, he and his people would take command of the most powerful country in the world.

He muttered in frustration as he dug through the cluttered drawer of his desk looking for that last pack of cigarettes he had stowed away for emergencies such as tonight. "It's time to get everyone together," he barked into the receiver crammed between his neck and shoulder as he groped for his stash. "We need to make sure that every man has his part down pat before it all starts going down."

"You're right," Stanford Melton answered. "But you know how risky it is to meet face to face. With all his obligations and now the enhanced Secret Service presence, Savage won't be easy to free up."

The tall man in the apartment slammed the drawer shut. "Dammit!" he yelled.

The frustration of dealing with the weaknesses of his American operatives plus the knowledge that he would have to make it through the night on only one pack of cigarettes was almost too much. He could not abandon the phones to make a trip outside; his superiors would be calling from their time zone at dawn, demanding every detail. "Don't complain to me about how difficult it is! Just get them together. I don't care how you do it. I shouldn't have to remind you what the penalty for treason in this country is. That's not going to happen just because we're not prepared!"

"OK, OK. Just calm down," Melton said, his voice distant. "You're going to wake up the neighborhood. The last thing we need is the New York City police knocking on your door."

"You're right," the dark-haired man answered, realizing that Melton, who had adopted Iran and its religious beliefs because it was the homeland of his deceased mother, could do only so much. "It's ironic, that the one we will count on the most is our weakest link. If Savage messes up . . ." He flicked his butane lighter and the flame licked the end of his cigarette. "We won't let that happen, will we, Mr. Melton?"

"We will have your meeting and everyone will be there. No exceptions!"

. . .

"Mr. Clark, if you don't mind, let's review this one more time."

Sterling Padgett had selected Clark's office for the interview, probably for two reasons, Clark thought. First, the interviewee would be more relaxed in the familiar settings. Second, since the location where the incident had taken place was less than ten feet away, it could allow him to recall details he might not otherwise, a trick Clark had seen played out on TV. Clark felt he had already discussed everything he knew with the FBI, yet given the situation and the position he was in, he had no choice but to go along with them. He was not, however, about to engage in conjecture about a matter of this importance.

"You said Leonard Palmer wanted to tell you something about Senator Tate's death," Padgett continued, a small notepad resting on his knee.

Since he had been given break from his office responsibilities, Clark had had a great deal of time to think about the incident with Palmer. He wanted to make sure that his answers were accurate—especially since he was now on the list of suspects who might have killed Palmer. "Yes and no," Clark answered, shifting uneasily in his chair.

Padgett narrowed his eyes. "Go on."

"That's what our head of White House security told me when he called. Palmer really wanted to talk to the president. Since I was the only one available, the call came to me. I was just trying to help out."

"So what did Palmer say to you?" Padgett asked, flicking the pages on his notepad.

"Not much really," Clark said, trying not to make eye contact because it would give Padgett another way into his inner thoughts. "In fact, as I recall, he seemed a little intimidated when I first went in the holding room."

"What do you mean?"

"I don't know, scared maybe. Never gave it much thought. I just wrote it off as White House jitters. We see it all the time. It's the same thing that happens when you meet a movie star."

"So you took him to your office?" Padgett inquired. His eyes veered off toward the door where the incident had taken place.

"As you already know, we never made it this far," Clark answered, growing impatient with the repeated questioning. He strummed the desk top with his fingers. "Just after we got off the elevator we ran into Ken Trainer."

"Did Palmer talk to you on the elevator?" Padgett's eyes locked on Clark's.

"No," Clark said quickly. "After thinking about it, I'd have to say he really didn't say much of anything until he went berserk. He did seem to relax a little when I first saw him—that is, at least until we started to go into my office."

"And?" Padgett pushed, leaning forward in his chair.

"And what? How many times do I have to tell the same damned story to you guys? When are you going to be satisfied?" Clark barked angrily, kicking himself away from his desk in his wheeled chair. "You know the rest. You must have heard the story a hundred times. Palmer started running around, screaming, knocked me down. Luckily the security guy was there within a minute."

"Do you think he meant to hurt you?" Padgett asked, unfazed by Clark's outburst.

"At first I did," Clark answered. He relaxed back in his chair, settling down with Padgett's new line of questioning. "But ever since you first asked me that, I've been wondering. Now I would say no. He just seemed to go off the deep end, reacting in general, not just lashing out at me."

"Do you remember what Palmer screamed?"

Clark remembered it well. In fact, he would never forget. "No, no, no!"

"Was that it?"

"That's all I remember. You might ask Trainer if he remembers anything else."

"We already did. He claims it all happened so quickly he couldn't remember much. Let's go back to just before Palmer 'went off the deep end,' as you said."

"Well, Trainer and I were talking," Clark answered as he looked over at the door to his office where the altercation had taken place. "I said something about taking Palmer into my office, and Trainer wanted to go along. That's all I can recall."

Padgett closed his notepad and looked up. "Do you think Leonard Palmer knew Kenneth Trainer?"

Clark paused, not sure how to respond. Chad Madden had asked him the same question. But this was different. Padgett was the FBI, and anything Clark said was officially on the record. "Mr. Padgett, I have no reason to suspect that. What do you think, since you're the one who's asking the question?"

Padgett did not take the bait. But although the FBI assistant director did not actually say so, Clark knew Kenneth Trainer had now moved to the top of Sterling Padgett's list.

. . .

Savage jumped as his iPhone chirped inside his pocket. Sliding the green answering light to the right, the vice president recognized Trainer's private line on the LED. It was a call he had dreaded and expected at the same time. He glanced nervously at the plastic partition that isolated him in the backseat of his Surburban. "Yes," he mumbled as he checked the intercom button on the display affixed to the door beside him to make sure the conversation was not overheard.

It was all happening so fast. Since he had become vice president, Savage had spent very little time at his Chesapeake retreat. Even though he knew Trainer and the rest considered him a puppet, the vice president did not think of himself that way. Within days he would take over the Oval Office, and that meant something. There would be a lot of important decisions he would have to make.

The stress of what lay ahead was almost unbearable for Savage. He had to get away, even if it was just for a day, to clear his mind and steel himself for the coming days.

A little over an hour before, Savage had thrown a few things in an overnight bag. Then, along with four Secret Service agents, he had sped off to his place in Maryland. Before he left, he told only his assistant where he was going, and told her she was to tell Chad Madden as well. Not that it was a secret. If anyone else wanted to know, all they had to do was ask. Trainer could have asked. Savage was getting sick of Trainer's arrogant attitude. The vice president felt a twang of evil satisfaction, knowing what Trainer would go through when he discovered Savage's unexpected departure. His aide was always so rigid, so all-knowing. This would be good for him.

"You reckless bastard!" Trainer snapped, his anger blaring through the small receiver. "How could you leave at a time like this?"

"Good to hear from you, Kenneth," Savage said evenly for the benefit of the Secret Service agent driving his car, just in case there was a chance of his being overheard. "I'm sorry you're not able to join me for a little R&R. I plan to be back the day after tomorrow."

"You will be back today!" Trainer replied, his voice strained. "You've been asked to be the last-minute presenter at a national meeting of the Boy Scouts of America, so I accepted for you. You'd better be there."

"Based on whose authority?" the vice president asked, so angry that he did not care if he was overheard or not.

"Central's!" Trainer retorted. "They say we need to get together before the big event."

Savage's throat constricted. He realized he was only one intercepted telephone call away from spending the rest of his life in a cell in a maximum-security prison—or worse. He blinked, his head spinning as he braced himself against the car door.

"What time did you say that was again?" he gasped. Savage's telephone went dead. He was not going to get an answer. The vice president's sojourn to his Chesapeake Bay home was over before it started. Once again, Trainer had gotten his way.

"Turn it around," the vice president ordered after he flicked on the intercom button. "We're going back to Washington."

The Secret Service agent behind the wheel shot him a bewildered look through the rearview mirror. "But we're only twenty minutes away, sir."

"No buts," Savage said, still reeling. This was all really happening; the plan was about to go into effect. Somehow he had never believed until now it would occur. "The president needs me."

The vice president's car slowed to a crawl as the befuddled driver flipped on the turn signal. "He got a call from the president," he barked into the speaker phone that dangled from his ear.

"Wait!" Savage interrupted. "Twenty more minutes won't make a difference.

Let's go on to my house. I'll only need a minute there."

The driver of Savage's limousine shook his head, but Secret Service agents never questioned the authority of their superiors. He sped up once again in the direction of the vice president's home on the Bay.

"All clear," he called back to Savage as the car pulled up into his compound fifteen minutes later.

"Keep the car running. I won't be long." Savage bolted out the door and into his house, sweeping past the two guards waiting to greet him. He went directly to his bedroom and closed the door. He reappeared within moments. The sound of a flushing commode could be heard behind him. "I think the president can wait for me to make a pit stop," he announced, grinning, before he ducked back into the car, hoping the agents had not noticed the bulge caused by the .44 Magnum handgun tucked inside of his right breast pocket.

. . .

Dan Russell's frustration grew as he dialed Lowell McCarty's back line. Apparently unaware that Russell was still in Washington, an agent from the local FBI office in Dallas had come by the hospital. Since he was the one who had discovered the real cause of the vice president's death, Russell had hoped his whereabouts would have taken on a higher priority. But because he was still an outsider, he was not surprised he had been sidelined.

"Has anything turned up?" he asked, putting his frustration aside.

"Dan, I've been sworn to secrecy by the president of the United States."

"Listen," Russell cut him off, agitated by McCarty's reluctance to divulge any information. "If it weren't for me..."

"All I know is that the guy from the CDC took over the case after finding out that Senator Tate died of the same disease. I tried to call him directly, but they never would put me through. I left several messages, but he's never returned my calls. You would think a fellow physician would—"

"Have you considered the possibility that *they're* involved? Or maybe they suspect that a problem exists but are afraid to go public with it until they have more proof." Russell's voice was somber as his mind raced with possibilities. "Do you realize the panic that would occur if the public found out that the beef products in this country were possibly contaminated—with a disease that might not show up for several years, has no known treatment, and the CDC is keeping it quiet? I can't just see us sitting back and not at least trying to—"

"Dan, this is how it's done in Washington." Lowell cut him off and then was quiet for a long, thoughtful moment. "Let's just hope we shared your secret with the right people."

19

They were all there—the vice president, Kenneth Trainer, Gerald Lynn, Rafer Peters, Stanford Melton, and the older gentleman Trainer had met at the Vietnam Memorial—huddled in the small room down the hall from the main ballroom of Washington's Renaissance Hotel. Usually the area was reserved for participants of activities in the ballroom to use as they made their final touches. This afternoon it would house Savage's entourage until he had completed his obligations to the Boy Scouts.

Three teams of Secret Service agents were positioned outside of earshot in strategic locations to keep onlookers at a safe distance. The Secret Service had greeted the older gentleman, who was well known to them, warmly upon his arrival at the hotel. They barely noticed the others who filed into the small room, although they were all members of an elite group whose one goal was to replace the existing government while hiding in plain sight.

Rafer Peters, whom the older gentleman had yet to know except by association, stood watch near the door, intermittently peeking out to check the location of Savage's security force. Kenneth Trainer opened the rushed-together meeting of the select six attendees, gathered in a tight circle of folding chairs, who would lead the United States.

"Gentlemen," Trainer said, his eyes darting from one participant to the other. "Our representative is in place in the White House. He tells me the product has arrived and will be ready for the twenty-fourth."

The older gentleman sat patiently listening to Trainer. He knew the twenty-fourth was the culmination of a plan birthed in one of the palatial bunkers fifty feet below the streets of Baghdad in the early days of their disastrous war with Bush's coalition forces. He remembered the plan had been born out of the realization that outright military victory was impossible. The only other way to assume control was a takeover from within. For a brief time, Osama bin Laden and his army of thugs had commanded the world's attention by shining a light on terrorism, but Saddam Hussein and his followers knew these terrorists were doomed from the start.

Bin Laden's people, fanatical in their beliefs, would not listen to the more experienced Iraqi leader who preached that terrorism was meant to be conducted in the shadows, not on bright sunny days such as September 11, 2001. Bin Laden's tactics aggravated the enemy and eventually forced Iraq into a temporary regime change. They tolerated a puppet democracy until the real leaders could regroup in the shadows and once again assume their rightful place atop the world's most important oil reserves.

Now that ISIS's caliphate lay in ruins after Trump recaptured the land stolen in Iraq and Syria, what could be better than to join forces with their neighbor to the east? The older gentleman pondered silently, this time without the patriarch who had taught them to be patient and let the enemy make the mistakes.

If those still loyal to Hussein's doctrine wanted control once again, their only recourse had been to expand their undetected biological weapon's program. They knew the coalition inspectors and American spy satellites could not examine every stalk of wheat and every silo to see what else might be there—these were the locations where they would devote their energy. The older gentleman marveled at his adopted country's ingenuity. Now the team he would head was ready.

Trainer continued to speak as he sat down in one of the chairs. "Until now we have never met the man who will lead us during this difficult time. Now it is time for him to take over. He is well known to all of you, since he played a significant role in the leadership of this country over the last several years. His personal sacrifice on behalf of our cause is extraordinary and will surely be rewarded in the proper time."

The older gentleman could not tell if Trainer was sincere in his praise or just intimidated by him. It did not matter as long as he had Trainer's loyalty. "Thank you," the older gentleman said, rising to his feet slowly, ready to assume the role for which he had spent almost half his life preparing. "Let me ask you a question, Mr. Trainer."

Trainer's head snapped in the older gentleman's direction.

"What makes a country strong?" the new leader of the group asked. He would put his lieutenants to the test. "What makes one country a leader over another?"

"That's easy," Trainer answered quickly. "Military force."

"Yes, in one way, but that is not the answer I was looking for," the older gentleman said. He paused to await responses from the rest of the group, but none were forthcoming.

Stanford Melton reluctantly spoke up. "Information . . . knowledge."

"Also a good choice. But not the right answer either."

Now everyone seemed confused as they waited for an explanation. The older gentleman walked around the small room as if he were pulling them all into his magnetic circle. Suddenly he stopped, his gaze fixed on Trainer. "Energy," he declared. "Mr. Trainer, without it, there would be nothing to move your military forces around. Mr. Melton, without energy the information highways of this world would be paralyzed. That's why we're here. Petroleum products remain the world's number one source of energy."

Vice President Savage wriggled in his chair. "We all know that's been Central's contention from the start, but I don't think you can write off the influence of nuclear power."

"The predominance of nuclear energy is not going to happen," the older gentleman retorted, irritated by Savage's naïveté. "At least not until we run out of other available energy sources. Maybe fifty years from now, but not in our lifetime. It is too costly and difficult to access on a large scale. And the spent fuel is a constant disaster waiting to happen. Petroleum products are here and now, and as long as they are readily available, the world will continue to rely on them. As you already know, the Middle East sits on top of the world's largest proven supply of petroleum products. The country that controls those reserves will lead this world far into the twenty-first century. For many reasons, Iran can't do it alone . . . ."

There was a long pause as the older gentleman circled the room once again. "Mr. Trainer," the older gentleman asked, towering ominously over him. "Following your line of thought, which country is the greatest military power in the world?"

"The United States of course," Trainer said, his voice reeked of confidence, this time sure of his answer.

"Correct," the older gentleman answered. Then he turned immediately to Melton. "And, Mr. Melton, which country is the world leader in information technology?"

"Uh . . . the United States. Maybe Japan."

"You were right the first time," the older gentleman answered. "American technology and ingenuity continue to dominate in this area."

The group sat silently, their faces tense in anticipation.

"Do you get it now? Oil . . . military power . . . technical expertise?" he asked as the group stared back at him. "Us—the people in this room—we are the ones who are being asked to lead the greatest union of the twenty-first century: Iran and the United States."

"I thought we were just going to . . . ?" Savage asked as his remarks stopped short. His mouth dropping open at the implications of the older gentleman's revelation. Even Trainer appeared taken aback.

"Mr. Savage, we will be doing more than just supporting Iran's efforts. As president you're going to use our military forces to take over the vast oil reserves of the Middle East. That means employing whatever force necessary to insure Iran is in control."

"Are you crazy? That wasn't in the deal," the vice president stammered. "Do you really think the rest of the world will stand for that?"

"Yes!" the older gentleman blurted, ready to strangle Savage with his bare hands. "With our Polaris submarines stationed strategically within firing range of the other world powers, they'll have no choice."

"Once the military goals of the United States are accomplished, how will this transfer in power be coordinated with the leadership in Iran?" Stanford Melton questioned, appearing somewhat intimidated, crouched in his chair.

"I'm glad you asked." The older gentleman smiled. "Although the present leadership of Iran would like nothing more than to control all of the Middle Eastern oil resources, they are still puppets of American imperialism and are not willing to make the sacrifices necessary to accomplish those goals.

Unfortunately they have let morality cloud their convictions and prevent their total dominance of their homeland. Those still loyal to Saddam Hussein's philosophy are in place and prepared to take over the government, leading their country into a union with the United States at the appropriate time." The older gentleman paused, his eyes scanning the participants. "As a reward, the United States will be guaranteed an affordable supply of petroleum products not only to feed its gluttonous citizens but to continue to fund its military machine."

"What about the other countries?" Melton continued to question.

"They will have to fend for themselves," the old man answered. "For a price, however, I'm sure the leadership in Iran would be willing to work out a solution."

A strange silence fell over the room. The older gentleman watched as each participant wrestled with his own uncertainties. The initial plan, or so they thought when they first signed on, was to keep the United States on the sidelines while the Iranians systematically incorporated their oil-rich neighbors into their growing kingdom. But to use American military prowess to accomplish this goal—that had been beyond their comprehension.

The reservation he saw painted across their faces was good, the older gentleman thought. It would keep them on edge, make them less likely to make a mistake. Until now, such a union of force—created by the military might and technological leadership of the United States joining with Iran, which would control the majority of the world's oil reserves—had been unthinkable.

Since its inception over two hundred years ago, the United States had been the protector of democracy. The older gentleman knew changing its designation to an aggressor nation would be difficult, if not impossible, even for the president of the United States.

"What if the United States doesn't go along with your plan?" Savage was asking the question the older gentleman anticipated.

"Do you remember the long lines at the gas stations during the Arab oil embargo? Multiply that by tenfold and ask yourself how long it will take to break down the Americans who might attempt to resist our efforts. With no fuel to heat their homes or run their cars, they will come to us on their knees," the older gentleman snapped. "You don't think we're the only group meeting like this, do you?"

Savage stared back at him, his face void of expression.

"Well, Mr. Vice President, we're not. Since shortly after the ill-fated war with Kuwait, our allies in Iran have infiltrated the internal operations of virtually every oil producing country in the Middle East. I am told we have substantial networks in place in Venezuela and Mexico as well. The only areas of significance we have not been able to infiltrate successfully are what is left of the Soviet Union and here in the United States."

"So then, if they already have so much control," Savage persisted, "why do they need the United States?"

"I didn't say our allies had control," the older gentleman retorted, his voice short. "Our operatives have not infiltrated to the point where they could take over the operations, only to the point they could destroy them."

He envisioned smoke from oil fires—hundreds, maybe thousands of times greater than Kuwait—spreading around the world like a blanket. After upwards of seventy percent of the world's oil reserves had been destroyed, there would be a virtual shutdown of the global economy, and all the military force the United States could garner would not be able to preserve it.

A look of disbelief fell across the faces of those who were assembled.

"The ultimate sacrifice," the older gentleman continued, knowing he had made his point. "As you know, I have made mine already. Our operatives are prepared to lay down their lives for our cause by blowing up the facilities where they are located if the leadership in that country does not support Iraq's efforts. Their actions would be akin to the Palestinian suicide-bomber effort against their Jewish landlords, but on a much higher scale." He took a breath as he felt the crushing weight of the responsibility that had been placed on him and the other five individuals gathered together in the small room. "It has taken years to put in place. But I'm told we are ready."

"Ready to put the world on the edge of disaster if our efforts fail," Savage butted in, his reservations showing through.

"We must not let that happen," the older gentleman answered quietly. "And, Mr. Savage..."

"What?" the vice president questioned, his face flushed in panic.

"You might not see another sunrise for the next two years," the older gentleman replied coldly. "And when the world awakes from its sleep without sunlight, there will be no food."

No one spoke. The older gentleman knew he had made his point. "So, Mr. Savage, as you can see, the operation has already started. It is too late to turn back now. If you and I fail to carry out our responsibilities in this effort, this world could go back to where it started. Gentlemen, we shoulder a heavy burden. I hope those of us in this room are up to it."

Suddenly Rafer Peters held up his hand as he moved back from the door. "They're coming," he barked out.

A Secret Service agent thrust his head through the door. "You're on, Mr. Vice President."

. . .

The conversation inside the small hotel room would be relayed to the tall, dark-haired man in the Manhattan apartment. From there, the information would go by scrambled text over the

Internet to the Iranian high command. After consultation with those who would take over if the current leadership failed to follow through, Iranian operations throughout the world would be placed on high alert, waiting for an order they hoped would never come. Surely the most powerful country in the world would see the inevitability of their situation and acquiesce.

. . .

Since almost the day he arrived, Jim Bilkos had worked to build a friendship with Cleve Barber, the senior chef at the White House. It had become a warm, cordial relationship—nothing personal that would have caused Bilkos to socialize with him in their off time. In fact Bilkos loathed the pompous son of a bitch and his foolish devotion to food. But he suppressed his hostility, appearing eager to learn, watching Barber whenever he could as the finicky chef prepared special dishes—especially when he was preparing his favorite beef recipes. So it did not seem strange when Bilkos volunteered to help his new friend cook the main course for the upcoming White House dinner. After all, preparing one hundred and fifty sirloins, each cooked to order, and sending them out at the same time, as was the was the duty of the senior chef, was a difficult task at best.

Barber welcomed Bilkos's help.

During a practice run for the event, Barber had Bilkos prepare some steaks identical to the ones that would be served at the White House dinner. Since President Winslet and his wife ate beef only on special occasions, Bilkos had a chance to taste his own handiwork. It took him three tries to cook the meat to the right degree, sauce it properly, and serve it hot. But after a series of critical remarks, Barber appeared satisfied that Bilkos could help him cook with close supervision. "There can be no foul-ups," he ranted. Bilkos could not have agreed more, but for different reasons.

. . .

"I should have you locked up!" Sterling Padgett bellowed as he pushed through the front door of Jennifer Smitt's condominium. "Obviously you don't seem to agree, but this is for your own protection."

Jennifer edged back but fought to keep her composure after her boss' uninvited intrusion. "I believe that, unless you have grounds to charge me with something, it's my own decision. Besides, I was going stir crazy over there."

Padgett's face was tight with frustration. "The last thing I need is for one of my agents to get murdered right now."

His response angered her. "I was as good as dead in there. What—you just don't want to have to open another file at the Bureau?"

"No, I'm sorry," Padgett answered, calming down as he tossed his jacket in a chair. "It's just that with all these deaths—the vice president, Tate, this guy Palmer—and then a threat to you, I'm not sure of anything."

"Enough said." Since Jennifer did not want him to find out about her illicit activities with Madden, she would not push him too hard. "Do you want some coffee?"

Padgett nodded, the anger gone from his expression. "What the hell difference is another cup going to make." He turned and followed her to the small dining table close to the kitchen.

"I'm not here only to bust you. We have a break of sorts in the investigation on your abductors," Padgett said. "I was hoping you could help me put some of the pieces of the puzzle together."

"I'm not sure what else there is to tell you." She was puzzled since she had already told them everything she could remember at least ten times.

"We found the blue van," Padgett went on. "It was in a scrap-metal yard on the outskirts of Arlington. They had already flattened it down and were about to put what was left in the chopper."

"How did they locate it?"

"An employee recognized the license plate and gave us a call. We don't think anyone working there was in on the deal. It's a place where they buy anything brought to them and don't ask any questions. Ever since the September 11 attacks we've had contacts at places like this. It finally paid off."

"So what have you found out?" Jennifer asked, handing Padgett a cup of coffee. "The blood type in the van matched that of the injured party we had suspected, the man who left the hospital," Padgett said. He stopped to take a sip. "The DNA tests will be back in thirty-six hours to make certain it's a match."

"So how does that help you?"

"It doesn't. But the fingerprint we lifted off the steering wheel does. It matched a man named Salem Mahamad Abdi." Padgett looked over at her, his face drawn. "He's a fairly notorious terrorist who works for the Iranians and is the leading suspect in two of the more recent US embassy bombings in the Middle East and North Africa. Additionally he's never been reported in this country before. His presence must mean something big is about to go down."

"How does that apply to me, since nothing at the Bureau I'm involved with is connected to that area of the world?" Jennifer asked. She suspected that the background checks she had done for Madden were in some way related, but she would remain loyal to Madden and keep quiet about them.

"That's precisely why I'm here. I hoped that maybe ... there was something you had left out." He gave her a weak grin. "Inadvertently of course."

Jennifer looked away as she wrestled with her own uncertainties. "Of course." When she said nothing more, she saw the glimmer of hope on Padgett's face turn cold and flicker out.

"Mr. President, several days ago an agent who works at the Bureau headquarters was abducted on her way home from work," Sterling Padgett said an hour later at the emergency meeting he had demanded with Madden and Winslet. "She was able to get away, but unfortunately so did the abductors. So far, the only major thing we have to go on is a fingerprint we lifted from the vehicle."

"Is that the reason you needed to see me?" Winslet asked tersely.

"Partially," Padgett said. "You see, Mr. President, the fingerprint matches that of one of Iran's top terrorist operatives. Until now he has never been reported in this country. In light of the deaths of Delstrotto and Senator Tate by a disease that has been reported only in Iran, I have to think his presence is more than a coincidence, don't you?"

The president glanced over at his chief of staff to see his take on the revelation, but Madden looked as if he had been struck dumb by Padgett's news. "So you're saying there might be a connection?" The president sat back in his chair as the almost unimaginable reality of what was happening began to sink in.

"And," Padgett continued, "the death of Leonard Palmer?"

"What about that, Mr. Padgett?" Winslet asked, his face contorted in confusion. "Do you feel they are all tied in together?"

"It's possible," the assistant director of the FBI answered, "that he knew something about the death of Harrison Tate, and someone had him killed before he could talk."

"Do you have a suspect?" Chad Madden asked, his voice lower and more grim than Winslet had ever heard it.

Sterling Padgett turned toward the chief of staff. "Yes, I do," he answered reluctantly. "But for now it can't go out of this room."

Both Winslet and Madden nodded in agreement.

"I suspect one of the vice president's aides, Kenneth Trainer," Padgett said softly, his eyes darting between the two men. "The killer or killers had to come from within the White House. After talking to Jason Clark, I'm convinced Trainer was involved in some way. We're checking to see if we can make a connection that will stick, but so far we have nothing. Just as with the case of my abducted agent, we only get so far, and then run into a dead end. Call it what you will, but I am convinced all of this is connected."

"Is that why you came?" the president asked. "To see if we could help you solve this puzzle?"

"Yes and no." Padgett let out a long sigh. "Yes, the FBI will always accept any help it can get with an investigation. But the real reason I came is you, Mr. President."

"Me?" Winslet asked, puzzled by Padgett's last statement.

"Your safety," Padgett continued. "If someone or some group was able kill your former vice president and a senior senator and was able to enter the White House and kills the only potential witness who could shed some light on what is going on, why not take you out next?"

"The risk comes with the job," Winslet said firmly. "Presidents just have to learn to live with that possibility."

"But this is different, Mr. President," Madden interjected. "It's unpredictable, because the potential for harm comes from within. Instead of the White House being a fortress, set up to guard against the dangers from without, it has become your prison, holding you captive to dangers within."

"Don't you think that's a bit melodramatic, Madden?" the president asked.

"No, sir, I don't."

Padgett leaned forward. "In a sense you are trapped, Mr. President. You can't run. You have one of the most recognizable faces in the world. I know you agreed to that kind of vulnerability when you first put your name on the ballot. The frightening reality we face is that any one of those who has been selected to protect you could also end your life in an instant."

A chill shot down Winslet's spine. "So you believe the risk from within is real? Do you have any suggestions, beyond sleeping with both eyes open?" he asked. There was a tremor in his voice that he tried to excuse to himself.

"Respectfully, sir, I think we need to smoke the sons of bitches out," Padgett told him. "I just haven't figured out just how to do that without getting someone else killed. You're no better off than a duck in a pond on the first day of hunting season if we just sit here on our asses waiting for them to make the next move." Padgett paused, his gaze locked on Winslet. "But my instinct from a lifetime in the FBI tells me there's something I'm missing here."

Madden broke in. "Let me see if I can help."

Padgett turned his attention to the chief of staff. So did the president.

"Jennifer Smitt is a former acquaintance of mine," Madden continued. "I had her investigate FBI background files for me on potential candidates for vice president before the election. Granted, we pushed the edge of Bureau policy, but I knew we could not afford to lose the election because we failed to dig up a skeleton in the closet of one of the candidates. If we had not come across the information, the press would have. And—"

"And you never told us this?" Padgett intervened, his tone angry but uncertain.

"No."

"Well," said Padgett, "what did you find out?"

"We found more than we were looking for. Evidently all the FBI files on our potential candidates were altered by someone outside of the Bureau."

"Impossible!" Padgett barked, crossing his arms in defiance.

"I think if you check with Ms. Smitt, she can explain it to you."

It was now the FBI's assistant director who appeared shocked. He stood up and paced around the Oval Office. "What does that have to do with this?" he demanded.

"I'm afraid everything, Mr. Padgett. Don't you see, that's probably why Ms. Smitt was abducted by agents from some Middle Eastern country, most likely Iran. Somehow they're connected to the altering of the files, to the vice president's and Tate's deaths, and to Leonard Palmer. It has something to do with the Mother Lode project." Madden stopped, afraid he had gone too far. He looked hesitantly at the president.

"Tell him, Chad," Winslet said, throwing out his hand. "He needs to know. Everyone else knows anyway, including half the population of the Middle East. No time for secrets now."

As Winslet listened, his own thoughts racing, Madden carefully laid out the circumstances of the Mother Lode project as well as Madden's own suspicions about Trainer as the leak in the White House. Whether Trainer was a killer or not Madden would not speculate.

Padgett agreed to place ten special agents in the White House. The most experienced one would trail only Trainer until they could contrive a plan to try to draw out the conspirators. If there was going to be a break, it would probably come from within, whether someone there made a move or whatever Iran had in the works unfolded further. There was no way to make the White House any more secure without reading the minds of those who worked there.

Padgett was standing to leave when Madden held up his hand. "Mr. Padgett," Madden said, his voice barely above a whisper. "I have one small request."

Sterling Padgett paused and turned back toward the chief of staff.

"Jennifer Smitt," Madden sighed. "She means a lot to me. I hope you take that into consideration."

. . .

"I'm sorry, but I just can't believe you're in Washington for some sort of class reunion." Cindy French seemed more frustrated than angry with her boyfriend. "How come you've never told me about this old friend before? Is she female?"

Russell switched the receiver to his other ear as he dug his toe into the carpet at the hotel where he had spent most of the last week while he searched for answers. Cindy meant a lot to him, he had realized in these last lonely days, and she deserved to know as much as he could tell her safely. "You're right," he admitted, guilty he had kept the whole thing from her. "There's something I've wanted to tell you, but . . ." His voice trailed off. He was still unsure what she would think of his story. She had been the first to call him a conspiracy nut, which was maybe what he had become. "There's no one else for me but you. Something happened at the emergency room over a month ago, and for whatever reason I can't let it go."

"Tell me more," Cindy said.

"I can't," Dan said after a pause. "I'm sorry, but it's too important to risk telling you about."

"Dan, relationships are built on trust," Cindy broke in. "Right now you don't seem to be able to trust me enough to tell me what's made you run off. I called the hospital yesterday to see if they would tell me anything, but even they weren't sure when you were coming back."

Russell's growing guilt was overwhelming. Here he was, putting his job in jeopardy, and now his relationship with his girlfriend. For what? To make amends for the death of his mother by telling the government what it did not want to know? He knew he had his own devils to deal with, but his time was running out. "Let's just say, for now, I'm doing this friend a favor. When I get back, I'll tell you—"

He heard a loud click on the line. Russell stared off across his hotel room. Cindy had heard enough. He could only hope she would give him another chance when he returned home. Right now, he was not giving her much to go on. He couldn't.

20

THE TWENTY-FOURTH.
A dribble of brownish liquid trickled out the side of his mouth and down his cheek as Vice President Savage squinted through puffy eyes into his bathroom mirror. A sad irony, he thought as he continued to swirl the mouthwash behind his pursed lips.

Although his face was recognized throughout the world, in reality, he was just that—a face, a Wizard of Oz with somebody manipulating everything from behind the curtain. "Bastards!" he spat out when he could no longer tolerate the burning sting from the medicinal-tasting mouthwash. For now he would go along with their wishes, for he truly believed a new world order was inevitable. He could see that oil needed to ally with military power and information technology for the world to run smoothly. But one day he would strip off the shackles that controlled him. When that day came, he would lead his country back to her rightful position once again. Only this time, under his leadership, the United States would have it all, including control of the world's oil reserves. The older gentleman was wrong. The country with the strongest military would win because, in the end, they could take what they needed.

. . .

Gusts of wind battered Madden as he rushed to join the small contingent of invitees who waited for the president of Argentina's airplane to taxi to its final destination on the tarmac at Andrews Air Force Base. Today Madden had drawn the short stick, selected as the White House liaison to represent the president on this pointless occasion. With all the tension and sense of imminent ambush he felt at the White House, this was the last place he wanted to be. And he knew the Argentine diplomats would be annoyed at being met by a man who had power but held not even a cabinet position. He grumbled quietly as he glanced at his watch, noting that the plane was already thirty-five minutes past its scheduled arrival time. Off to the side, the military band took up its position. And then Madden caught a glimpse of a familiar face in the small crowd of invitees. "Good to see you, sir," he said, edging over with his hand extended.

Ben Delstrotto looked up as a blast of wind whipped his coat up around his face. "They ought to give you hazardous duty pay for this," he said, pointing to the lose debris flying through the air. "I see Winslet gave you the assignment."

"And you?" Madden asked, nodding at the approaching aircraft.

"President Galvez and I go back a long way," he answered as a look of sadness crossed his eyes. "To back when Rosie and I were . . ." His voice trailed off as he looked away.

Madden decided to change the subject. "Are you coming to the dinner?"

"I've been invited," he answered in a tone that suggested he had reservations about the event.

As the roar of the airplane's engines died down, Madden started to move back up to his position at the foot of the exit ramp but turned around to Delstrotto once again.

"Would you like to join us in the limousine for a ride to the White House?"

"Thank you, Chad," Delstrotto answered, a smile breaking across his face. "Give me a rain check. I brought my car."

Madden looked at him and felt a wave of sadness—they had lost so much in the months since Winslet's triumphant renomination, starting with Rosie.

. . .

Usually Jim Bilkos arrived at the White House a few minutes early for his 2:00 p.m. shift. Today when he clocked in it was just before noon. As was customary, he brought along his lunch box. Today it was to carry his dinner. Even though there was always more than enough extra food for the White House kitchen staff, Bilkos always preferred to bring his own. He claimed it had to do with his food allergies. The lunch box was a bit heavier than usual. Neatly hidden under a carefully folded napkin were two frozen sirloin steaks.

Bilkos placed his usual sandwich and chips on top. White House security, tight as it was, suspected nothing.

Everyone was already so busy that no one noticed that Bilkos kept his gloves on as he began to go about his daily chores. Usually Bilkos worked in the food preparation area, washing and sorting the vegetables for the night meal, assembling the condiments—mundane tasks that were considered an honor to perform for the White House, even for a cook with his experience. Today, because he was working with Cleve Barber on the evening's main course, his regular shift duties had been given to someone else. His first assignment was to take the Texas beef out of the freezer so to begin the slow thawing process before the final preparation later in the evening.

Security kept to the periphery of the action, trying to stay out of the way. The White House kitchen was a busy place. The two additional Secret Service agents who had joined them tonight did not make the crowding any better. The day crew was still finishing the lunch shift, while the night crew had arrived early in order to begin preparing the food for the evening's festivities. In all the commotion, no one paid attention as Bilkos carefully unloaded the one hundred and fifty frozen sirloins from the far freezer onto a portable food cart. If they had, they might have noticed when he slipped the extra steaks, which he secretly removed from the bottom of his lunch box, into position three places up from the bottom of the stack. Once the transfer was complete, it was impossible to spot the extras in the group, which now numbered one hundred and fifty-two. Impossible to everyone except Jim Bilkos.

He stepped back and removed his gloves. Bilkos looked around to see if he was the focus of anyone's attention. He was not. He disposed of his gloves in the trash compactor, and then moved the cart filled with the thawing steaks near the large set of grills that would later turn them into food fit for presidents. If Jim Bilkos did his job as he had been trained to, one of those steaks would be eaten by the president of the United States. He had spent years preparing for this assignment. His country and Allah were depending on him.

. . .

"Welcome to the United States, Mr. President," Winslet said as he escorted his counterpart from Argentina through the side entrance to the White House.

The ceremony was standard protocol. Madden stood off to the side, watching his boss go through the motions. Winslet had done this countless times, greeting a head of state or government official. The chief of staff looked down the receiving line which included the president's wife, Sharon, who would host the first lady of Argentina during her stay in the nation's capital. Next was Vice President Savage, followed by as many of the president's Cabinet as they could round up. The final part of the receiving line was comprised of assorted elected representatives and business associates who had ties to Argentina.

Madden smiled as he saw the guest at the end of the line. The familiar face had been an important part of these ceremonies in the past, but not recently. Not since Rosie had died. Madden felt a quiet sense of satisfaction that Ben Delstrotto had once again been invited to join them—as a respected international lawyer and government official as well as the widower of a vice president. In some small way, Delstrotto's presence spoke to Madden's hope that normalcy might return once again to the capital city, even though right now, under the surface, things were more abnormal in Washington than perhaps they had ever been.

"I bring you greetings from my country, Mr. President, and high hopes for our countries' relations," Galvez replied as they began the formal introductions of the guests in the receiving line.

The ceremony lasted maybe thirty minutes. For most of the time, the participants made the usual polite comments. That was, until President Galvez came to Ben Delstrotto. Madden thought he saw a look of surprise when Galvez first recognized the former vice president's husband, although after Madden thought about it, he was not so sure. In either case, after exchanging the usual pleasantries, Galvez moved on. When they were finished, Galvez and his party retired to their rooms to freshen up after the long trip from Buenos Aires.

. . .

Shortly after Galvez retreated to his suite, there was a knock on the door. A large burly man wearing the Argentine military uniform cracked the door, but just enough to check out the visitor. After a few hushed comments, the door opened and Gerald Lynn, Savage's aide, disappeared inside.

. . .

"I'll be glad when this day ends," President Winslet whispered as he made his way back up to his private quarters surrounded by the ever-present contingent of Secret Service agents and military operatives. Chad Madden nodded without saying a word, thinking the same thing. Every time a visit from a head of state interrupted his schedule, Winslet felt a little off balance, and now there was the added stress coming from within the White House. If Winslet had not made a prior commitment to Argentina's first lady when she requested to stay in the White House, he would have placed them in the penthouse suite at one of the hotels down the street. But he was a man of his word.

"We need to have Davenport get as much press as she can off this Argentine visit," the president muttered. "Keep the press vultures occupied. I'm sure they smell that something's going on. Fortunately we've been able to throw them off so far. It's only a matter of time before they dig up something suspicious if we don't get to the bottom of this soon." Winslet's eyes were sad, troubled.

Madden pushed himself to match the president's pace. "Let me put some things together for her and maybe arrange a few interviews," he said, slightly out of breath. "Unfortunately the media doesn't get too worked up about South America unless there's a revolt or one of their drug kingpins gets arrested. Even then they'd be more interested in a congressman tipping an Argentine stripper."

Winslet scanned every person they saw. With the presence of the Argentine contingent and the additional agents from the FBI and the Secret Service, the White House was filled with new faces. Any one of them potentially could bring harm to the president and his family. Winslet felt more vulnerable now than he had at any other time in his life. He did feel some reassurance, however, in knowing that the FBI had placed an agent on each of Vice President Savage's assistants, including Jason Clark. Their activities would be followed twenty-four hours a day until Winslet knew enough to take action.

"I think it's time we test the water," Winslet said under his breath. He looked over at Madden and stepped into a small alcove just off the hall so as not to be overheard. "Tomorrow, I'm going to drop you and Savage a top secret memo on a projected change in plans on the Mother Lode project." Winslet eased a little closer to his chief aide. "It won't be true, of course, but only you and I will know that."

Chad Madden eked out a smile and agreed to serve as the go-between for Winslet and the FBI. That way, Winslet hoped, this added security would not arouse too much suspicion. He was to receive around-the-clock briefings in case anything occurred that was even slightly suspicious. Madden also agreed to move into the White House until the siege was lifted or the conspirators struck.

. . .

Kenneth Trainer was waiting for the vice president when he arrived back at his office from the reception.

"Close the door!" Trainer ordered.

Savage had grown accustomed to his aide's outbursts. *Fortunately,* Savage thought, *before long Trainer will be gone.* He did not care how or where, as long as he would no longer have to deal with Trainer.

"What now?" Savage barked.

"I'll tell you what now," Trainer barked back. "They've put the FBI onto us."

Savage was shocked. He grabbed for the chair.

"Not now, old man." Trainer threw a look of disgust in Savage's direction. "Once you're president, you can call them off."

"How do you know they're on us?"

"I know because I recognized the agent who's following me. That's what I'm paid to do. He's not from the DC office, but I saw his picture in one of the files out on the West Coast."

"What do you think this means?"

"They've also placed agents on Peters, Lynn, and Clark," Trainer continued. "I recognized the one with Clark but not the other two. They must be new to the Bureau."

"Idiot. I told you not to involve that girl at the FBI!" Savage could barely keep from shouting. "You're going to get us all killed."

"Stop!" Trainer demanded, his manner abruptly calm. "Think about it."

"Think about what? My ass is just sitting out there if something goes wrong."

Trainer leaned forward, his gaze fixed on the vice president. "The president has nothing on you, only suspicions at most. We don't have to do anything," Trainer shot back, his voice now even. "We've done our part. For now, it's out of our hands until you take over."

Some of the redness faded from Savage's face as he took in Trainer's remarks. Trainer was right. In a very short time, the leadership would be his. They would have no other choice. And the FBI agents assigned to his advisers ... well, as far as he was concerned, they could all go to hell.

. . .

"So far, nothing suspicious," the FBI agent said in a low voice to Chad Madden as they huddled together behind the closed door of Madden's office. "Standard official duties for all of them."

Someone knocked on the door. "I'll be there in a minute," the chief of staff called out. "What about Trainer?"

"I've got my best man on him," the FBI agent answered. "But we can't follow these guys everywhere. He was in with the vice president for about ten minutes. We don't know what went on. But—"

"But what?" Madden interrupted.

"Well, when Trainer came out of the vice president's office, there was something different about his attitude," the agent continued. "It was almost as if he knew we were following him but didn't care." He shrugged. "You got me?"

"Keep me posted," Madden told him.

The agent started to open the door when Madden held up his hand, his eyes glaring. "You and the Secret Service are in this together. There is to be no competition about who does what. I want Winslet covered like a blanket. If anything happens, it's on your ass. Do you understand?"

. . .

Most of Winslet's regular duties had been put off because of the visit of the president of Argentina. Ordinarily the White House would not have gone to this much trouble for a South American head of state. But Argentina was different since Mario Galvez assumed power.

Galvez had turned his country around, making Argentina a player in the global economy after more than a decade of financial disaster. And he had not done it by exploiting oil and other natural resources; he had done it with technology, by converting his ample workforce from farmers and peasants into technicians. Galvez had learned from Taiwan and Japan how to direct the populace into organized manufacturing. He had learned from Columbia what happens when the workforce is underused and angry. Only time could judge the success of his efforts, but for the present he received high marks for rebuilding Argentina's infrastructure and repaying its vast debt.

The second official meeting of Galvez, Winslet, and their delegations was now entering its the third hour. Significant progress had been made in trade relations between the two nations when Winslet and his trade representatives called for a recess. Each delegation needed to caucus separately to see what they should do next as they struggled to make final the details of the agreement that would declare this visit a success.

"Mr. President, may I speak to you privately?" Galvez asked, his eyes darting from Winslet to his entourage of diplomats.

"Certainly," Winslet answered.

The president of Argentina appeared uncomfortable. "Alone, if you don't mind."

Surprised by Galvez's request, Winslet nodded. He motioned for Galvez to follow him out on the portico adjacent to the conference room that overlooked the White House lawn. Two of the Secret Service agents assigned to guard the president came rapidly beside the pair, but after a look from Winslet they withdrew a dozen paces. Once they were out of earshot from the rest of the group, Winslet waited for Galvez to speak.

"Mr. President," Galvez said, leaning up against one of the columns. "We have made great advances in my country over the last several years. But, as it is in your country, there is a constituency that does not want this progress."

The president listened intently. Argentina had changed. Unless turmoil from within brought an end to these advances, its future had never looked brighter. Where would this conversation lead?

Galvez continued. "The antigovernment forces have moved out of the countryside and into our corporate offices, so to speak. Because that's where the money is."

"How does that affect you?"

"In two areas," Galvez said. "Efficiency and reliability. Their graft has directly or indirectly decreased our final profit margin by about thirty percent."

"How can you be sure your problems are not just inequities that are common to expanding industrial systems?"

"Because." Galvez's speech slowed noticeably. "Mr. President, my people on the 'inside' have uncovered an organized effort working to make my country's progress fail."

"How have you tried to deal with them?"

"That's the problem. Unofficially, of course, we offered them their own area in which to operate, as our neighbors in Colombia have, but that was not enough. They want more. My troops were trained to fight rebel forces in the countryside, not in corporate offices."

"To a certain extent, those practices occur here. But instead of working to take down the company, the intent of such adversaries is usually to steal secrets that would enable them to put the competition out of business—the results are the same, but the process has a bit more sophistication. Welcome to the twenty-first century, President Galvez."

Galvez grimaced. Winslet continued anyway. "What does this have to do with me?"

"We need your help, Mr. President."

Every country in the world wanted America's help. The United States already allocated hundreds of millions dollars annually to support various projects in Argentina. Did Mario Galvez want more?

"Our country already gives Argentina a great deal of financial support. Isn't that enough?" Winslet realized that President Galvez had finally expressed the real reason for his visit. The three years Galvez spent serving in the military in his early twenties, fighting the drug cartels that tried to establish a foothold in his native country, had honed his killer instincts.

"That's not the type of help I was referring to," Galvez said. "We need *people,* agents who can infiltrate the rebel ranks and take them out from within."

"I'm sorry, but my country does not get involved in those kinds of activities," Winslet said immediately. "Our operations throughout the world are tightly focused in terms of American interests. You are asking me to support you against a cadre of corporate terrorists. That's not a commitment I'm willing to ask my country to take on."

Silence fell as the two leaders stared at each other. Winslet started to feel uncomfortable, but he was not going to back down from confrontation.

"I don't think you heard what I said, Mr. President." A look of anger crept over Galvez's face as he glared at the president. "I want your help in this matter. Maybe I should have said I expect your help!"

Now it was Winslet's turn to be angry, but he prided himself on never losing control. "Mr. President," Winslet said somewhat coldly. "My answer is no."

Galvez's voice was barely audible as he leaned forward and whispered a response in the president's ear. Winslet's eyes grew wide as he heard the one-word message. It felt as if a dagger had been thrust into his chest. He staggered back, bumping into the far wall of the portico.

"What are you saying?" Winslet stammered. "Are you trying to blackmail me?"

Galvez repeated the word. "Mother Lode!"

. . .

Accustomed to his routine, Jason Clark dreaded White House visits by heads of state. Today it was worse than usual. Not only was his schedule off, but he suspected someone was following him as well. He had noticed the man yesterday as he left the White House but did not think much of it. But this morning when he pulled out of his parking spot at his condo, he saw the man again, or at least he thought it was the same person. And not ten minutes ago he caught another glimpse of him, or someone who resembled him, here in the West Wing, just down the hall from his office. Presumably he was part of the massive White House security operation.

Clark ducked into the employees' coffee lounge and looked over his shoulder. He saw the now familiar face bent over an assistant's desk down the hall. This would be the real test, he thought. Quickly he backed out the rear entrance usually used by the catering staff and came out by the security station. "You OK, Mr. Clark?" the surprised guard asked at Clark's unexpected appearance.

"Yeah, sure, just hungry," Clark called back. After a few turns, he rounded the corner by his office and almost collided face to face with his suspected pursuer, who appeared out of nowhere. "What the hell?" he exclaimed.

"Excuse me, sir," the stranger said, his face flushed as he slipped on past Clark. Clark now felt his suspicions were correct. Immediately he went across the hall to Savage's office. The vice president's assistant had stepped out, probably for one of her frequent smoke breaks. He knocked on the vice president's door.

"Yes?" the answer came back.

Jason opened the door to see the vice president and Ken Trainer huddled over Savage's desk. He had the feeling he had caught them in some scheme they wanted to cover up, like two boys with their hands in the cookie jar.

"Yes, Jason," Savage stated blankly. "What can I do for you?"

Clark moved into the room, closed the door to the vice president's office behind him, and took a seat in front of the desk. "I think I'm being followed."

"What makes you think that?" Trainer interjected, rocking forward in his chair.

Clark told his story about the man who had nearly run over him in the hall. Clark could not quite put his finger on it, but something about Savage's and Trainer's responses did not seem right.

"Maybe it's just a coincidence," the vice president told him. "With all that goes on around here, after a while everyone looks familiar to me."

"I don't think so." Out of the corner of his eye, Clark caught a movement in the vice president's bathroom. He spun around and gasped as the familiar figure walked toward him. "Sir!"

"Jason," the older gentleman cut him off, extending his hand. "Since I was in the neighborhood, I thought it might be nice to look around again." He glanced over at Savage. "And the vice president was kind enough to accommodate me."

Suddenly Clark felt uncomfortable, as if he were intruding on the older gentleman's time. "Good to see you, sir," he said, as he remembered something he had wanted to share with Savage's guest.

"Now what were you saying about being followed?" Savage said sharply as if to rouse Clark back to the subject that had caused him to drop in.

"It's probably just my imagination, what with all the new faces," Clark answered as he reached for the door. "A lot of things are different around here, and it looks like I'm just going to have to get used to them. Good to see you, sir."

. . .

"I was just afraid that if we waited, it might be too late," Dan Russell said, sweeping his hair away from his face. He clutched the cell phone as he looked at the White House in the distance through the glass storefront of a coffee shop on Pennsylvania Avenue. "That hotel room was killing me," he chuckled. "You know me. I just can't let things go . . . that is, except for my job and girlfriend, apparently."

"And you're planning to do what, exactly, when you get there?" McCarty's voice was hesitant.

"Hell, try to see the president." Russell's tone turned somber. "I know it's not realistic, especially without an appointment, but if there's an epidemic and the CDC is covering it up, we've got to give that information to our commander in chief."

"Give me a call when you know something," McCarty muttered.

"Wait!" Russell barked out, trying to think through all the possibilities, even the most unlikely. "If you don't hear from me by nine o'clock, call every television station in town."

. . .

Trainer waited at least thirty seconds after Clark left the room, and then turned to the other two occupants. "He knows. I could see it in his eyes."

"No more killing in the White House." Savage held up his hand, his eyes moving from Trainer to the older gentleman. "We need at least a week, maybe two. Then Clark will have to go. Given time, he'll put it all together. He's a little dense, but now . . ."

Just then the door to Savage's office swung open as Clark walked back into the room. "I've been meaning to give you these, sir," he said, holding out a stack of papers to the older gentleman. "But with everything that's happened since Rosie's death, I've just not found the time to—"

Clark's voice cut off abruptly. Trainer had slipped out of his chair, come up behind Clark, wrapped his arm around his throat, and contracted his grip. Air gushed from Clark's mouth as his windpipe snapped. Only gurgling sounds could be heard as Clark tried in vain to release himself from Trainer's death grip. Vice President Savage and the older gentleman watched in disbelief as Clark's flailing limbs slowly grew limp as life drained from his body. His face went red, then purple, and he was still. His head lolled on his neck as Trainer released him.

The three stood in silence as Clark's lifeless bulk slumped to the floor. Then Savage lunged at Trainer, grabbing him by the jacket collar. "You crazy bastard!" the vice president screamed. "Now you've done it!"

Trainer looked startled, and then thrust the back of his right hand across Savage's unprotected jaw. A loud slap reverberated across the room as the blow sent the vice president reeling onto his desk. Trainer lunged toward the vice president, but the older gentleman stepped in the way.

"Stop!" he commanded.

Trainer paused. The vice president rolled off the desk; a small trickle of blood oozed down the side of his mouth.

"Clark had to go," Trainer spat out. "There was no other choice. I told you he knew."

"But here? Now?" Savage stuttered. He leaned over, picked up one of the spilled files that lay scattered around Clark's lifeless body, and opened it up. "Notes for Rosalyn Delstrotto's memoirs . . . he knew, but he really didn't." Savage glared at his chief aide.

"It's a problem," the older gentleman interrupted, unmoved. He turned to Trainer, who was straightening his jacket. "Take him in the bathroom until we can figure out a way to get him out of here."

Trainer obliged. He grabbed Clark's body under the shoulders and dragged him across the floor and into the vice president's bathroom. The older gentleman walked behind him, smoothing out the marks in the carpet left by Clark's lifeless shoes as they slid across the floor.

The older gentleman returned to Savage's desk and picked up the telephone. He dialed in a series of four numbers that connected him to Environmental Services. "Put Carmy on," he ordered.

"Yes," said the man with a Middle Eastern accent on the other end of the line. "What can I do for you?"

"We have a package in the bathroom of the vice president's office," the older gentleman said. "I hope you can help us dispose of it."

21

As the diplomats filed out of the room, Winslet turned to his chief of staff. "Meet me in the Oval Office as soon as you can."

Madden nodded in agreement, shocked at the urgent look of concern on Winslet's face. He quickly headed for his office first to see if anything new had turned up on the Leonard Palmer investigation. On his way out the door, his assistant stopped him.

"Have you seen Jason Clark?" she asked.

"No," Madden answered, feeling rushed. "Why?"

"Well, someone was looking for him. I think it was one of those new Secret Service agents who have been around here for the last couple of days."

Madden did not know where Clark was and did not like the fact that everyone was so aware of the extra security. He hurried to the Oval Office.

Winslet stood at the entrance of the hallway that lead to his private study. He signaled for Madden to follow him. As they entered, Winslet clicked on one of the televisions and raised the volume to loud. It was disconcerting to see the president take such precautions in his own private space.

"They know," the president said in a low voice. "About the Mother Lode project."

"Who?" Madden asked, surprised and confused. "The Argentines?"

The president nodded. Madden turned around and closed the door to the hall to assure them of a little more privacy. "How did you find out?"

"Galvez was trying to put the squeeze on me. He wants us to use the CIA to take out factions of rebel insurgents that have infiltrated many of Argentina's corporations. According to him, the insurgents are creating 'inefficiencies' that will keep his country from competing in the world market."

"What did you tell him?"

"I said no," Winslet replied. "Then he brought up the Mother Lode project and threatened to expose me to the world if I did not agree to his demands."

"Dirty bastard!" Madden exclaimed, clenching his fist. "It's blackmail."

The president squinted at his chief of staff, his look lost, bewildered. "The fake memo, Chad," Winslet whispered. "The one just you and Savage will get tomorrow. We have to wait to see what happens. I'm not sure what else to do."

Madden's chest tightened at the thought. "There's a leak so big around here, Mr. President, that if we don't plug it soon, it's going to suck us all down the drain."

. . .

His heart pounding, Bilkos pushed open the door that led to the state dining room. His eyes danced nervously across the hall as the Air Force Band, having arrived early, set up for the evening's event in the far corner. He scanned the place settings. The final count would probably be closer to one hundred and thirty.

He turned toward the head table, which was set for nine. The rest of the room was filled with sixteen tables, each set perfectly for eight guests. A flower arrangement sat on each table, adorned with two small flags, one for Argentina and one for the United States. A nice touch, he thought as he let go of the door and moved back into the kitchen. These Americans pretended to be so friendly.

Unnoticed, he moved through the orchestrated confusion of the White House kitchen. He knew these workers were considered some of the best, the anonymous people draped in white jackets and toques who scurried around him, completing their assigned duties. It was a pity that their dedication was to such selfish pleasures. The meal had an Argentine theme in honor of President Winslet's guests from the Southern Hemisphere. The highlight, however, was the prime sirloin steaks from south Texas, the ones Bilkos would help prepare. His mouth dry, he shuddered at the thought. His legs grew heavy as he approached his work station, but he continued to push on, knowing this was the culmination of his lifetime of sacrifice. He focused on the thought of the unspeakably beautiful reward awaiting him.

No one seemed to notice when Bilkos slipped on a second pair of gloves over his first. If someone had seen, he was prepared to tell them about a cut he had sustained the day before. He would say he just wanted the extra measure of protection.

Bilkos glanced at his watch. Dinner was to start at eight o'clock. With him and Barber working together, preparing and serving the whole main course should take about forty minutes. That would mean the dessert course should start at nine-fifteen, with remarks by the president and his honored guest given by nine-thirty. The event was scheduled to end by ten o'clock. But that was the most unpredictable part of the evening, since guests were always reluctant to leave such a glamorous event, and conversations usually dragged on forever. That was not his worry. Once the food was out, his job was done except for cleanup.

Beads of sweat broke across Bilkos's forehead as he began removing the plastic wrappers from the now-thawed beef. Stripped of their protection, the exposed pieces of red meat glistened beneath the overhead lights. He carefully laid each one on the large granite surface adjacent to the grill. A small amount of ruby fluid oozed onto the cold slab, forming a puddle at the edges of the pieces of beef. To the untrained eye, the difference would go unnoticed, but around the two pieces that Bilkos had received in the special package, there was a small layer of green liquid that had separated from the blood.

. . .

Chad Madden flicked on the LED of his iPhone; the private number to Jennifer Smitt's condominium flashed. He pulled out his cell phone and ducked into a small alcove just off the hall that led to the White House press room. She answered his return call. "I thought you were still under police protection," he said, concerned that she was vulnerable once more.

"I couldn't take being cooped up. Besides, what good am I in there if we have to clear up problems at the White House."

Madden cupped the telephone and stuck his head back out in the hall to see if anyone was listening. "You're no longer involved," he fired back quickly. "I've gotten you in enough trouble already. Besides—"

Jennifer cut him off. "I think Jason Clark is the key to uncovering the information you need," she interrupted. "He has better access to Savage and his boys than anyone else. I went back over to the Bureau and reviewed his file. Except for the six-month period when he took a sabbatical several years ago, his records are clean and don't appear to have been tampered with."

"From what he tells me," Madden answered, wondering if he should switch to a secure line on one of the White House telephones if they were to continue their conversation, "Savage's men let him in on only what they want him to know."

"Chad, if what we suspect is true, you only have to look at Rosalyn Delstrotto and Tate to see what will happen when Clark no longer fits in their plans. He could be in real danger."

Madden shook his head at the possibility. "Just what I needed," he muttered. He remembered that before he met with Winslet his assistant had told him they had not been able to locate Clark. "I'll try to track him down right now." Madden started to hang up, and then stopped. "Hey, Jen, take care of yourself. I just—" He wanted to say more, much more, but once again, he let the opportunity slip away. Jennifer's line went silent.

. . .

Madden dialed Jason Clark's back line but was answered only by his voice mail. He was equally unsuccessful with his cell number. Troubled by Clark's unexplained absence, he obtained through Padgett's assistant the number of the agent who had been assigned to follow Clark.

"The last I saw of him was when he went to the vice president's office," the agent told him, still stationed at his position just down the hall from Savage's office.

"Did you check to see if he was still in there?"

"Oh! No, sir!" the agent replied, static filtering through the line. "We were given strict orders not to intrude, just observe."

"When did he go in?" Madden demanded. "It's been a little over two hours, sir." "What about the vice president?"

There was a pause on the other end of the line. The agent said hesitantly, "The vice president and two other people left a long time ago."

"I'll be right down. Maybe your boss wouldn't mind if I go in to see." Madden's tone was sarcastic.

"That would be fine, sir." The agent now sounded alarmed.

Not five minutes had passed when Madden passed the guard at the entry point into the West Wing. Madden moved toward the agent, who waited for him anxiously outside Savage's office.

"The vice president, Mr. Trainer, and another man came out over an hour ago," the agent whispered, looking over his shoulder at Madden.

"And Clark?"

"I never saw him again after he went in." The agent turned and looked back down the deserted hall.

As they turned toward the vice president's office, the two men stopped dead in their tracks. From inside, they heard the muffled sound of the closing of a door.

"What do you think?" Madden whispered.

"I don't know," the agent said warily. "It's probably housekeeping. One of them went in there just after you called. He was pushing one of those large plastic drums on wheels they use to pick up the trash."

"It's too early," Madden sputtered. "They aren't supposed to be here until after ten."

The agent's eyes grew wide as he reached under his jacket and released the safety strap of his .38 Magnum revolver. Madden's breathing shortened as he wrestled with the possibilities that lay before him.

"Let me go in first," the agent said as he removed the revolver from his holster.

They were now just outside the door to the vice president's outer office. The door stood slightly ajar. Peering through the crack, Madden could see that the door to the back office was shut. Madden and the FBI agent moved quickly past the reception desk to the closed door.

The agent struck the door with his knuckles. First he gave a light tap. When there was no response, he made a fist and gave the door three swift blows. There was silence.

"Jason, this is Chad. Are you in there?" Madden called out.

There was still no response. The agent tried unsuccessfully to turn the knob.

"I have a key," Madden uttered softly, withdrawing a master key from his pocket that opened the door of every office in the West Wing, save one.

With his free hand, the agent inserted the key and gave it a turn. There was a click. The door was unlocked. He handed the key back to Madden and turned the knob. The door swung open.

At the far end of the room, Madden could see the large trash container the agent had mentioned. Otherwise Savage's office was empty. Nothing else seemed out of place as the two surveyed the vice president's private quarters.

"I guess housekeeping decided to come in early because of all the work they'll have to do later after the Argentina dinner," the agent said, his voice hesitant. "But why would he lock the door?"

Madden caught a reflection from the direction of the vice president's bathroom.

There was a small slit where the door was barely ajar.

"Look in there," the president's chief of staff murmured to the agent.

Without warning the door to the bathroom flew open and struck the surprised agent squarely across his unprotected face. His gun soared halfway across the room, and he fell back onto the floor.

Madden leaped back just as a bearded man with dark hair, dressed in the traditional uniform of White House Environmental Services, lunged for him. The man caught the chief of staff squarely around the chest and hurled him into the far wall.

Madden hit with a thud and lost his breath as the bearded man turned back toward the struggling agent. Madden watched in horror as the toe of the man's work boot crashed into the agent's right temple. The agent's unconscious body fell back against the vice president's desk as blood spurted from his right ear.

Madden struggled to catch his breath. In only seconds he would be next. Then he saw it, not five feet away: the agent's dislodged revolver resting under a chair. It was Madden's only hope. He dove for it.

The intruder lunged at Madden again and barely missed him as Madden scooted under the chair. The bearded man fell but was up again within an instant. Madden grabbed for the fallen firearm.

As the man reached for him, Chad squeezed the trigger and felt his fist jerk as a blast erupted from the borrowed revolver. The shot struck the bearded man squarely in the chest. He staggered back.

Two more shots rang out. Madden could not control his fear. The second shot missed, striking the far wall. The third shot found its mark. Madden saw a hole erupt in the intruder's forehead, just over his left eye.

Madden, still under the chair, gasped for breath as the bearded man's lifeless body slumped to the floor. The only sound came from the fallen FBI agent who lay gurgling in a pool of his own blood. The door to Savage's outer office flew open. Madden turned instinctively in the direction of the door, not knowing what to expect.

"Mr. Madden," a voice came from around the door. "Are you all right?"

"I don't know!" Madden barked back, still trying to catch his breath.

Two men clad in full black combat gear and carrying automatic rifles sprang into the room. They were part of the SWAT team that constantly guarded the outer perimeter of the White House. Standing behind them, several steps back, were the guards, their faces ashen with fear, whom Madden had passed earlier.

"It's all clear," one of the men in a black uniform shouted back.

Within seconds the vice president's office filled with security officers and additional SWAT team members. They went to Madden first, who was still trying to extricate himself from under the chair.

"You OK, Mr. Madden?" asked the security officer assigned to cover the Oval Office.

"I think so. Scared shitless though." Madden grasped his way into the chair, unable to gain the strength to stand up.

"Call the ambulance," one of the SWAT team members said. "This one is in really bad shape." They had rolled the FBI agent off his back so he would not drown in his own blood. "Get the medical team in here now, or it may be too late by the time the ambulance arrives!"

"Looks like you got him," the security chief remarked as he inspected the lifeless body of the bearded man.

"It was either him or me." Madden finally managed a sitting position and handed the FBI agent's revolver over to the officer.

"What happened?" the officer inquired.

"We saw this—" Madden started before he was cut off.

"Over here!" The call came from the direction of Savage's bathroom.

Madden, struggling to his feet, followed the officers as they crossed the office to the bathroom. The door now stood wide open. Propped up in the corner was Jason Clark's corpse. Madden reeled back at the sight, his vision blurring. Jason must have discovered what was going on.

Trainer! It had to be! Now Madden's only concern was to locate the president and make sure he was safe. "Get me Sterling Padgett," he shouted. "I don't care where he is. Get him, now!"

Madden stumbled back into the vice president's office. He looked around as more and more people began to file in. He grabbed the shoulder of one of the men in a black uniform. "Who's in charge?" Madden demanded.

"He is." The SWAT team member pointed to the man at the door to the outer office who was speaking into the walkie-talkie attached to his breast pocket.

Madden hurried over to him, stepping around the unconscious FBI agent. "Over here," Madden signaled to the officer as he went into Savage's outer office. The officer put up the speaker and followed Madden.

"Whoever did this is probably planning to do the same thing to the president," Madden said. "I can't explain now, but I think the vice president and his advisers are behind this." Madden knew he had to condemn Savage and Trainer before they had a chance to inflict more damage, but did he have enough evidence to make his accusations stick? And the uproar it would cause—he could not even begin to imagine.

"But . . ." the officer exclaimed, his face contorted in confusion.

"Winslet is probably at the dinner by now," Madden barked. "I don't care if you have to crowd every agent you've got under the dining tables, just make sure nothing happens to the president." The chief of staff stopped, his jaw fixed. "What I just said about the vice president and his aides . . . well, for now that's just between you and me."

. . .

Currently only a bystander at the occasion, the older gentleman pulled on his cummerbund. He marveled how the attention was always focused on those individuals who were in power. It had been months since he had worn his "penguin suit," as he called it. He hated the pomp and circumstance, but it was all part of the show. In a very short time, instead of playing a supporting role, he would be the one calling the shots.

He glanced at his watch as the evening's proceedings began. The Air Force Band started with Argentina's national anthem, followed immediately by that of the United States. There had been an unexplained ten-minute delay from the start time listed in the program, but except for the larger-than-expected security force hovering around the periphery of the crowd, he noticed nothing awry.

The two presidents stood side by side with their hands across their hearts. As the guests trickled through the receiving line, no one seen to take notice that Winslet and Galvez did not speak to each other. No one, that was, aside from the older gentleman. He grinned to himself, knowing that barely two hours before, one president had threatened to expose the other's secrets to the world if certain demands were not met.

. . .

"Be careful," Cleve Barber barked as he thrust his metal poker into the bed of red-hot coals. "If you let that grate fall, I could get hurt, and then where would we be?"

A lot better off than where you'll be soon, Jim Bilkos thought as he struggled with the heavy cast-iron grates that would serve as the cooking surface for the evening's main course. Barber was a tyrant, especially when the pressure was on, but he was also a great chef. Sweat rimmed Bilkos's collar as he held the grates higher so that head chef could distribute in just the right places the fired-up mesquite briquettes flown in from Texas for the night's event. After tonight, Barber's haranguing would no longer be his concern.

As he strained to carry out Barber's orders, Bilkos looked around. The White House kitchen was at full speed. The wait staff lined up to receive their final instructions. He noticed that two had been singled out to serve the nine participants at the head table. Barber had told him they were the best of the group. Bilkos later found out they were the two with the most seniority, both having years of experience serving the president and his guests.

When Bilkos had first started his job, he learned that in order to protect the president from foul play, his meals were supposed to be selected randomly from those fed to all the invitees of any given event. If, however, Winslet made a special request, his food was checked by an inspector from the FDA who was trained in poison detection. In most cases, the inspection was quite automatic, just a quick glance. If there was a question, he took a small taste from a clean spoon to detect any unexpected, odd flavor of a poison. Bilkos hoped that tonight would be no different.

"Now, if you will do me the honor of scraping these," Barber said, pointing to the large wire brush Bilkos was to use on the sizzling hot grates, "I will attend to the seasoning of steaks."

Bilkos seethed inside, furious that the pompous son of a bitch could not even trust him to sprinkle a little salt and pepper. But that was Barber's way—he was a prima donna whose oversize ego was matched only by his girth.

Bilkos kept a watchful eye on Barber as he performed his ritual. The assistant was careful never to lose sight of the two steaks he had added.

"Jim, my friend," Barber continued in his overbearing way, "seasoning is an art unto itself."

Bilkos nodded, grabbing the towel hanging from his apron to wipe the sweat from his brow. "I need some air," he called out and headed toward the swinging doors that led out to the main dining area.

"If you're going to be a chef, you gotta be able to take the heat, son," Barber half yelled behind him, smirking before turning back to seasoning his steaks.

Having more important things on his mind, Bilkos didn't respond. He pushed through the doors and looked across the massive room. He let out a slow sigh of relief as his eyes fell on a gray-haired man standing against the far wall. Bilkos tugged twice on his right ear. The older gentleman returned Bilkos's signal. The assistant chef's pulse quickened as he returned to the kitchen. There was no turning back.

. . .

"Here I am trying to trying to cover a state dinner, and Spurlock from the *Times* tells me they just took someone out the back in an ambulance. Do you mind telling me what in the hell is going on up there?" Marty Davenport's voice was clipped and to the point. Madden groaned into the cell phone. News was out already. "Am I always the last around here to know?"

Madden's mind raced as he tried to cover his growing tension. "I'll fill you in later. Just tell Spurlock and the others that one of the security guards on the second floor had a heart attack. That should keep them from trying to come up here for a while."

"I don't believe you," Davenport said.

"Then don't," Madden retorted. "But for everyone's safety, lie." He clicked off the phone.

"Mr. Madden," an aide called from the door to Madden's office. "There's a Doctor Dan Russell down at the West entrance, and he said he's not leaving until he sees the president."

Madden jerked around. "Don't bother me!"

The aide started to leave but then hesitated. "He said he was the one who came with Doctor McCarty to talk to the president about mad cow disease, and if he doesn't hear from either you or the president, he's going to the television stations."

Madden shuddered hard. Just what he didn't need: the doctor from Georgetown and that Texas cowboy—and more media crawling all over the White House when nothing was safe or certain. But maybe Russell knew something that could help. Maybe. "Send him to my office and have two guards with him at all times. No matter what, don't let him use the telephone until I get there."

. . .

The men's restroom just down the hall from the state dining room was temporarily blocked by two Secret Service agents; the vice president and Kenneth Trainer had it to themselves.

"Get yourself together, old man," Trainer spoke, his voice gruff, disrespectful.

The vice president leaned against the wall to hold himself upright. He was sweating hard. "I know, but you didn't have to kill—"

"The killing was necessary. And if you blow this, you won't have to worry about the authorities or what Central will do to you." His eyes bore through Savage. "I'll kill you myself with my bare hands. Am I making it clear enough for you?"

Savage lunged at Trainer, his disgust uncontrollable. "You bastard. I'm going to—"

Trainer's lighting fast fist caught Savage squarely in the chest and hurled his body into the far wall with a deafening thud. The vice president crumbled to his knees, gasping for air.

"Is everything all right in there?" one of the Secret Service agents stationed at door called.

"No problem," Trainer answered. "The vice president and I will be right there."

Savage spit out a wad of bloody saliva as he struggled to his feet. "Get away from me," he said forcefully. His eyes were glassy after the blow to his chest. His lips trembled. "When this is over, Trainer, I'm going to make it my top priority to see that you get your just reward." He would make sure of that. He grabbed a paper towel and blotted the blood from his lips, and then tossed the wadded paper in Trainer's direction. Trainer's face opened into a contemptuous grin.

22

CHAD MADDEN'S chest heaved as he fought to suck in more air. His quick dash to the State Dining Room, where the event was already in full swing, had temporarily robbed him of oxygen. Winslet and his Argentine guest of honor had already completed the reception line. The guests mingled among themselves at the far end of the room next to the bar.

Servers with trays of wine and cocktails moved in and out of the crowd. This time was used to become acquainted with new faces or to renew old ties before the formal activities began, and this atmosphere was heady with power and proximity to power.

Madden squinted, spotting Winslet and his First Lady holding court in the far corner of the ballroom. Madden pulled out his cell phone and punched in the top secret number. The president, his hands gesturing as he made a point, was mired in a deep conversation with Argentina's ambassador. Madden saw him reach in his pocket and pull out his ringing telephone.

"Just keep smiling, Mr. President." Madden whispered into his phone as he stepped back into the relative isolation of the hallway.

Winslet looked up, his eyes searching without direction. "What the . . . ?"

"Jason Clark has been killed," Madden continued in a low tone so that he would not be overheard. "We just found his body in Savage's office." Madden stepped back into the ballroom to see the president's response. His eyes locked on Winslet's.

"It appears, Mr. Madden, that I'm going to have to rely on your best judgment until I have concluded my obligations here."

Madden clicked off the phone and moved over to the door, where the head of the Secret Service contingent assigned to the president was stationed. "I want you to cover him like a suit."

"We're all over him, Mr. Madden," the agent interrupted. "I've got four agents within five feet of the president and eight more scattered throughout the room."

"I hope that does it," Madden muttered. The phone in his pocket rang. It was Sterling Padgett. Madden stepped out in the hall once again to take the call. "Have you heard?"

"I'm on the way over," Padgett replied. "Where are the vice president and Trainer?"

"I forgot to look." Madden felt embarrassed as he turned back toward the ballroom. "Hold on."

Madden walked back toward the noisy crowd, his eyes searching until he found Savage. He was by the bar, clinging to what appeared to be a very stiff drink. Savage met Madden's hard gaze but quickly looked away. Rafer Peters and Gerald Lynn were close by the vice president, having a conversation of their own. There was no sign of Trainer. Just as Madden was about to return to the hall to resume his call with Padgett, he felt a bump on his left shoulder.

"Excuse me," Madden muttered.

It was Kenneth Trainer. For an instant, neither man moved, their gazes locked in an icy stare only inches apart. A slight grin came over Trainer's face.

"It's OK," Trainer said, looking down at the cellular telephone in Madden's hand. "Can I help you find someone?"

"Ah . . . no!" the chief of staff said quickly. "Just doing the normal security checks."

"Well, keep up the good work," Trainer said, slipping back into the crowd. For a moment Madden did not move as he watched Trainer disappear in the direction of Savage and his cronies. Then he heard Padgett's voice, tinny in the phone.

"Sterling, are you still there?" Madden retreated to the quieter hallway.

"Yes!" Padgett answered.

"Meet me in my office as soon as you can get there."

The chief of staff approached one of the Secret Service contingent who was preoccupied surveying the crowd. "Put two of your best on Ken Trainer," Madden whispered. "Don't ask any questions. I'll explain later."

. . .

Madden found Sterling Padgett in the vice president's office. His agent had already been removed in the ambulance to Georgetown Medical Center. There was no report yet on his status. The whole crime scene had been cordoned off, and there was more security milling around the West Wing than Madden had ever seen before. Padgett was bent over, examining the intruder's lifeless body, when Madden entered the room.

"I thought I asked you to meet me in my office," Madden said sharply. Padgett stood up slowly, anger spreading across his face.

"Mr. Madden, I . . . well, let's go," Padgett replied, cutting off his fury.

Padgett signaled to the team of agents to continue their survey of the scene, and then the two headed off to the chief of staff's office.

"Padgett, it's only a feeling, but I think something is going down *right now*." Madden said urgently. The recent events were frightening. His president was in danger, and Madden felt he had lost control.

"We have the president covered. I just got off the telephone with the Secret Service and they are on full alert. My men are all over the place. For now, at least, I think he's safe—unless you want to abort the whole dinner and make the threat public."

"Which I don't want to do. But what if they use the same tactics on the president as they did with the vice president or Tate? From what I see, your people couldn't have protected them even if you had a hundred agents around them."

"I don't see how we can draw the shield any tighter." Padgett's voice turned harsh, authoritative. "Look, Madden. You seem to have forgotten who's in charge of the law enforcement around here."

Madden blinked, but he was not finished yet. "What about the larger picture? We both know it's not just Trainer and his boys. Now that they've thrown the White House in turmoil, why wouldn't they start making moves in other areas?" Madden's hands flailed as he started pacing around Padgett. "Have you checked with the CIA to see if there have been any abnormal activities in the Middle East? Hell, we can't rule out anything. September 11 ought to have taught us that."

"We've already thought of that. The CIA has put their agents on high alert. They will let us know if there is even a sniff of anything out of the ordinary." Padgett's response no longer projected his authority of just moments before. "Anything else, Mr. Madden?"

"See if you can reach Doctor Cornish."

Padgett looked at his watch. "No disrespect, but I think we need to concentrate on seeing the president through tonight's event. I'll have my people track down Doctor Cornish first thing in the morning."

"I don't think you heard me, Mr. Padgett," Madden fired back as he reached for the door. "I asked you to get him now!"

. . .

Padgett lagged behind and dialed the Bureau headquarters while Madden headed down the hall.

As Madden reached his outer office, the uniformed officer was standing in his door. "We have that doctor for you, sir. Doctor Russell."

Madden nodded and walked in, leaving Sterling Padgett in the hall to track down Cornish. "Doctor Russell," Madden said, his introduction abrupt. "I'll tell you up front that I don't like being threatened, especially about matters of national security. In fact, that kind of activity will land your ass in more hot water than you can imagine."

Russell swallowed hard but then stood, holding out his hand. "Thank you for—"

Madden cut him off. "You didn't leave me much choice, doctor. It was either see you or lock you up, because I'm sure as hell not going to let you go to the media with your trumped-up story about all these deaths being connected."

Russell picked up a trace of doubt in Madden's voice. "You and I both know these deaths are connected, Mr. Madden." Russell's voice grew more assured. "The problem I'm trying to figure out whether a person is killing these people off or if there's an epidemic and the cattle industry has paid somebody at the highest level to keep it all quiet."

Madden's eyes locked on his uninvited guest. He turned to the guard. "You can go," he said. "Doctor Russell and I can handle this from here."

Just as the guard started to leave, Madden held up his hand. "Tell Padgett to meet me in here as soon as he locates Cornish and . . ." Madden's eyes narrowed as he looked at the guard. "You didn't hear *anything* that was said just a moment ago."

. . .

"Doctor Cornish, this is an emergency," Madden said into the telephone he had taken from Padgett's outstretched hand. "What's the most likely way that the former vice president and Senator Tate contracted this kuru disease?"

"Ingestion of contaminated meat products," Cornish replied without hesitation. "Usually beef, but it could be any of the hoofed animals. I have my people looking into any other possible routes of contamination."

"Let me know if they are able to turn up anything other than tainted food." Madden handed the telephone back to Sterling Padgett. "Doctor Russell is the one who first alerted us that Rosie died of a variant of mad cow disease," Madden said, nodding at the doctor.

Russell moved over to Madden's desk. "Pull up the agenda for tonight's activities on the screen for me?" he asked and pointed to Madden's computer. Madden slipped into his chair and flicked on his terminal, typing in a series of commands. He moved away as the monitor responded to his request.

"Gentlemen, look here!" Russell exclaimed, pointing to the monitor illuminated before them. "The menu for tonight's dinner here at the White House."

Madden reached over Russell's shoulder and ran his finger up to the screen until it rested right next to the evening's entrée. "Texas Sirloin Beef," he whispered.

. . .

Under Cleve Barber's eye, Bilkos lay the glistening pieces of uncooked meat on the red-hot grill. He jerked away from time to time as the cold steaks hissed and spit when the flames licked at their raw surfaces. Barber had a system so that all the steaks would come out around the same time, which was vital in trying to feed one hundred thirty-five particular guests. What made things even more difficult was that they did not all want their steaks cooked the same way. The servers had taken their orders when the guests were first seated and relayed them back to Barber. The system worked well. Each course scheduled to go out at twenty-minute intervals.

Bilkos had already screened the room's layout and gone over the evening's program. The nine honored guests were seated at the head table, which was rectangular instead of round like the others. To Winslet's left would sit his wife, Sharon, then Vice President Savage, and then the Argentine ambassador with his wife. To his right were President Galvez and his wife, Selma, and then the American ambassador to Argentina and his spouse. As he watched the prized beef grow dark over the coals, Bilkos never lost sight of the two steaks he had inserted into the group—two ten-ounce pieces of beef that were about to change the course of history.

Almost enveloped by the oily smoke that swirled around his head, Bilkos wiped the beads of perspiration from his face. He coughed and sputtered.

"Do you need a break?" Barber asked.

"No!" Bilkos responded sharply. "No, thank you," he repeated in a more measured tone of voice. Bilkos knew he had to be in control of how the steaks were plated.

Barber nodded and turned to one of the servers. Even though Bilkos intended to serve the contaminated beef to the president only, he had an extra steak on hand in case the first one did not turn out right. With everything he and the others had gone through to reach this point, Bilkos knew Central would not want to let one overcooked piece of meat ruin their plans.

"Time for the main course," came the call from the head server, who had just stepped back from the main dining area. "The natives are getting restless."

Bilkos shuddered in the now-sweltering heat of the grill, knowing that his ultimate challenge was only moments away. He glanced back at Barber, who was still in deep conversation with the server, and then turned his gaze back to the grill. Although Bilkos had no loyalty to the American way, he had always admired how its citizens persevered during even the worst of times. He could learn from that. As Bilkos turned the steaks for one final blast of the flames, he whispered under his breath the famous statement from the near disaster of the ill-fated Apollo 13 mission: "Failure is not an option."

. . .

"Your husband does my country a great honor, Mrs. Winslet," President Galvez said, leaning forward in front of the president. "I feel confident that in the years ahead our two countries will find many places where we can come together for our mutual benefit."

Sharon Winslet nodded. She then moved back against her husband as the crowd noise rumbled across the massive room, making almost all but the most intimate conversations inaudible.

Winslet cleared his throat, the aftertaste of Galvez's threat still burning in his mouth. "I'm sure that day will come, Mr. President, but only when our relationship is held together by trust."

. . .

Bilkos's hand trembled as, one by one, he pulled the steaks off the grill. Stabbing his finger at the steaming meat, Barber grunted his final approval before each dish was covered. "The next plate is for the president," Barber said, his voice abrupt. "Pick a good one for him."

It had worked! His breathing shallow, Bilkos reached over to the far right corner of the grill and carefully lifted up the sizzling piece of death.

"This looks like the best of the bunch," Bilkos said, his smile forced. Barber nodded in agreement as the plate passed before him. Within twenty minutes, Jim Bilkos's job would be done. He would be a hero in his home country. Most important, thought Bilkos, his Allah would be pleased.

With the tray for the main table complete, each of the nine plates was covered and the name of the designee was scribbled on the top with a black magic marker. Barber quickly went through the same process with the other sixteen tables.

"They're ready," he called out.

The busboys filed by, lifting the trays to be taken out to the waiting guests. Bilkos could see small plumes of steam emanating through the vents of the covered plates. He let out a sigh of relief as the last of the trays exited the kitchen. The adrenalin rush that had propelled him through the last thirty minutes started to subside; Bilkos felt the strength drain from his legs. "I need a break," he barked to Barber, who was once again talking to one of the server.

Bilkos's pulse raced as he stumbled toward the small window on the kitchen-door exit that looked out over the crowd. He wanted to see the fruits of his labor; he wanted to see the president take the first bite of his steak. He knew that would be the beginning of the end—a rebirth where devotion to a higher cause would take precedence over the current American morass of self-gratification. Soon the likes of Jim Bilkos would be a hero just like the soldiers of World War I and World War II.

. . .

Puffing once again, Chad Madden appeared at the door of the State Dining Room. Sterling Padgett and Dan Russell were not far behind him. Was he too late? Were his suspicions getting the best of him? If he were wrong, there would be hell to pay.

Madden scanned the room. At most of the tables the servers had already started passing out the entrée plates. But the tray for the head table still sat untouched. Madden bolted in the direction of the president, almost knocking into one of the servers who was pouring wine at one of the back tables. Madden tried to brush him aside.

Suddenly Madden felt a tug on his arm. He spun around to see Ken Trainer behind him. Desperation began to well up in his chest. "Did you find what you were looking for?" Trainer asked, his tone almost sarcastic.

Trying to jerk his arm free of Trainer's grasp, Madden retorted, "I'm just about to."

"With all the Secret Service and the new FBI agents you've brought in, your boss should be fine," he said, tightening his grip on Madden's arm. "Why don't you just let him enjoy his dinner and we can take a few moments to get to know each other better. I have a bottle of eighteen-year-old—"

The man's grip was a vice. "I don't think so," Madden said, still unwilling to cause a scene. It was to no avail; Trainer wouldn't let go. Madden, his heart pounding, snapped around in the direction of the head table. The server was taking care of the Argentine guests first. Madden again tried to pull his arm free. Some of the nearby guests took notice of the commotion.

Madden looked over at Padgett, who stood near the door with his back to them, unaware of what was going on between him and Trainer. "Padgett!" Madden called out, his voice just below a scream as he pointed to Trainer. "Cuff him!"

"What?" A look of surprise crossed Padgett's face. "I said get him and hold him *now!*"

Sterling Padgett signaled to two Secret Service agents standing nearby. "You heard the man," Padgett said. "Put Mr. Trainer under arrest." The men dove forward.

Trainer loosened his grip on Madden as the agents approached. The vice president's aide scanned the room wildly, but there was nowhere to go. As guests in this quadrant of the room craned their necks to see what was happening, the agents cuffed Trainer's wrists behind his back and hustled him toward the large dining-room entrance. By that time Madden had made it to the head table with Russell following just two steps behind him, looking uncomfortable as he tried to keep up the pace.

The server had just picked up two more plates and was serving the ambassador to Argentina and his wife. There were two more plates remaining on the tray—one for the president and the one for the vice president.

Madden's mind raced. His throat was dry as he started to call out to his commander in chief, but he held back. Instead he reached to take the president's plate, an explanation to follow. Then it hit him. Madden smiled as he picked up two plate covers. When he set the lids back down, Madden did not replace them as he found them. He *switched* them. The vice president's name now covered the plate of the president's choice cut.

"I think we ought to let this play out, don't you?" he whispered to Russell, who finally stood beside him. Russell glanced at him, confused, and then went white when he realized what Madden intended.

Madden stepped back as the server approached.

"Good evening, Mr. Madden," the server said, not having seen what the president's chief of staff had just done.

"Good evening, Charles," a ruffled Madden answered. Sweat beaded his brow. Had he done the right thing? He wanted to blow the conspiracy open—but at what cost? "Are you taking good care of our president tonight?"

"I am," the server said proudly as he lifted the covers off the last two plates. "You know he always asks for me."

Madden nodded and then looked over at Russell. They watched Charles set the first plate down in front of the president.

"I hope this is just the way you like it, Mr. President."

"I'm sure it is, Charles," Winslet stated, barely looking up from his conversation.

Madden watched uneasily as Charles moved over to Vice President Savage, who had been preoccupied with the ambassador from Argentina. "Mr. Vice President," he said softly as he set the plate in front of Savage. "The chef picked this one out just for you."

. . .

Pushed and hustled toward the door, resisting and reasoning every step of the way, Kenneth Trainer had seen the switch. His eyes bulged in his crimson face as he wrestled to free himself from the two agents. "No!" he screamed out, no longer able to control himself as he watched the horror the events unfolding before him.

For an instant an awful silence fell over the diners as they looked in the direction of Trainer's scream. Within seconds he was completely surrounded by security agents from the FBI and the Secret Service, who forcibly carried him out of the ballroom as his arms flailed in all directions.

. . .

Savage's heart raced as he watched the president bite into his steak and then as he jerked his head toward the source of the yelling in the corner of the room. But his view of the commotion had been blocked already by the Secret Service agents. His stomach churned as he turned to the president's wife. "What was that?" Savage asked, worrying that some crazy person was about to destroy their plans.

"I don't know," Sharon Winslet answered, concern painted across her face.

Madden, in earshot of the vice president, stepped forward. Winslet turned toward his chief of staff, who returned his glance with a look of reassurance. "Everything is under control," he said to those seated around the president. "Mr. Trainer seems to have taken ill. You continue, and I'll go and check on him."

Savage reeled at the news but fought to keep control. "Come back and tell me how he is, Mr. Madden," he said, trying to keep his voice even.

As Madden moved away, Sharon Winslet looked over at Savage, whose forehead was now beaded with perspiration. "Jonathan, are you feeling OK?"

"Just concerned," he answered. "Mr. Trainer is one of my closest advisers." He cut into his steak reluctantly.

. . .

Like Trainer, Jim Bilkos had seen Madden switch the plates as he sneaked a look through the small window in the door to the State Dining Room. Unlike the vice president's aide, however, Bilkos did not lose control. His years of isolation and discipline in his native country had taught him that much. He stepped aside as one of the busboys came back into the kitchen carrying a tray full of empty plates. Bilkos had to act fast.

"Let me have your coat," Bilkos demanded.

"Why?" the busboy asked, awkwardly trying to balance the overloaded tray of dirty salad plates he had collected.

Bilkos did not hesitate. "I got one of the orders mixed up. You know how the vice president is when his steak is overdone."

The young man, in fact, did not know how the vice president would react if his steak was overdone, but that really did not matter; he seemed to buy the story, moving the tray from hand to hand as Bilkos stripped his jacket from his shoulders. Bilkos quickly put it on and tossed his chef's hat to the side. He grabbed another steak from the grill, threw it on a plate, and headed out the door to the ballroom.

Sidestepping several of the serving staff, Bilkos made his way over to the head table. By this time the Secret Service agents had dispersed to their preassigned positions. Bilkos looked down at the vice president's plate in horror, noticing his steak was already half gone. He quickly came around behind Savage, who was engrossed in a conversation with the Argentine ambassador. Bilkos tapped him on the shoulder, leaning over so he could be right next to the vice president's ear. "There's been a mix-up, sir," he managed, just above a whisper.

. . .

Savage shot up from his chair. His eyes were almost popping out of his head as he looked around desperately for the nearest exit. At first he walked slowly away from the table, but as panic took over, he broke into a run, exiting through the door into the kitchen, his throat now full of his undigested dinner. No longer able to control himself, his mouth sprang open as vomit sprayed out over a ten-foot area of the kitchen floor.

"I'm going to die!" Savage screamed out, froth still clinging to his lips. "How did you let this happen? You dumb bastard!" he ranted at Bilkos, who was right behind him.

. . .

Madden, Russell, and two Secret Service agents dashed after Savage. They entered the kitchen area just in time to see the vice president retching. The group pushed through the door just behind Bilkos.

Concerned that Savage might be in a dire situation, Dan Russell asked, "What seems to be the problem, Mr. Vice President? Can I help? I'm a physician."

Savage wheeled around in Russell's direction. "It's too late. No one . . ." He began to gag uncontrollably once again.

"I think he has food poisoning, sir," a small man in a waiter's jacket interjected.

He stood just to the right of Madden, Russell, and the agents.

Madden wrinkled his nose as he stepped gingerly to the side, trying to avoid the smelly, putrid mess scattered in front of the vice president.

Instinctively calling on his medical expertise, Russell moved toward Savage. "Here, let me see what I can do," he said, reaching around and loosening the man's collar. He grabbed one of Savage's wrists to check his pulse. "Any chest pain?"

Savage shook his head as his uncontrollable retching continued unabated.

"I can't tell from just this, but my guess is that the waiter is right," Russell said, keeping his hand against Savage's back as a form of weak support. "We really need to get him to where he can be properly evaluated."

Madden called out. "Get the paramedics up here, stat!"

Savage thrust out his hand in resistance. Although his eyes raced toward the exit, his wobbly legs were not prepared to follow suit. Madden stepped in, blocking the vice president's only path of retreat as the young server ducked his head and slipped away as if responding to Madden's command.

"We're ahead of you, sir." One of the Secret Service agents stepped forward. "The paramedics are on their way."

The vice president was no longer paying attention to what took place around him as he continued to retch. Russell pulled up a chair for him, but Savage refused to sit down. Madden turned to one of the Secret Service agents. "Be careful! I want you to impound the vice president's food," Madden barked. "Not just that." He gestured at the floor. "His meal back on the table too. The part he hasn't eaten." The chief of staff stopped and the color began to fade from his face. "While you're at it, you'd better get the president's too."

The agent's mouth dropped open. He dashed toward the door to the State Dining Room. Madden turned again to the other agent, who was fixated on the vice president. "Have Sterling Padgett meet me here, and get him to locate Doctor Joel Cornish, the head of the CDC. Tell him Doctor Russell and I have something we want analyzed."

Suddenly the retching sound that had filled the kitchen had stopped. Russell looked over at the vice president, who was grabbing at his throat as his fingernails tore into the skin of his neck. He was chocking! Russell lunged toward him.

"He's aspirated!" he called out, spinning the vice president around and grabbing him around the waist.

A sickening ashen color began to cover Savage's bloated face as his efforts to breathe faltered. Darkened blood oozed out of the scratch marks on his neck.

Russell locked his hands together and formed a tight knot around Savage's rotund waist. He jerked with his full force. Savage's head thrust back from the wrenching of Russell's blow, but it was to no avail. His knees buckled beneath him.

"Get me a small knife with a sharp point. I may need to do a tracheotomy," Russell yelled at Madden. "Breathe!" he barked out, pulling Savage's limp body into his with all the power he could muster.

Suddenly a thumbnail-size piece of undigested meat sprang out of Savage's open mouth and landed on the floor at Madden's feet. Russell gently let Savage go as the vice president, exhausted by the ordeal, sank to his knees.

Madden moved over, reached down and lifted Savage's head up by his chin. "Mr. Vice President," he muttered, his voice low so he could not be overheard by the Secret Service agent standing close by. "One of my best friends—and your former chief of staff—was found dead in your bathroom. Right now, I am not prepared to claim you had anything to do with it. But if you did, I will do everything in my power to make sure you never walk as a free man again."

. . .

His tiny cell phone cupped in his sweaty palm, Bilkos hovered in the far corner of the secluded pantry. Not twenty feet away, the paramedics strapped the resistant vice president on the gurney that would take him to Walter Reed for a more thorough evaluation. The cook's orders from the man in the Manhattan apartment were clear—get the vice president's plate before anyone one else could.

Tray in hand, he eased back through the doors to the State Dining Room and headed for the main table. Scattered throughout the room, the servers and busboys were busy cleaning off the main course plates in preparation for the desserts. Bilkos had made it to the table when he froze. Not ten feet in front of him, a gloved agent had just picked up the vice president's partially eaten steak. He placed the plate and its contents in a sealed container.

. . .

The older gentleman was seated at one of the back tables at the White House reception when the commotion surrounding Kenneth Trainer broke out. He was no more than ten feet away when the Secret Service forcibly ejected Trainer from the ballroom.

He also watched in disbelief as Chad Madden exchanged the vice president's plate with that of the president.

Ten minutes had passed since the vice president disappeared behind the kitchen doors. The president and Galvez were, once again, acting as if nothing had happened, appearing not to be alarmed by Savage's continued absence. The whole operation was unraveling around him. The older gentleman had to know more about what was happening. Trainer was a career professional; he would never talk, even if it meant his life. But Savage was different. He was a buffoon. The older gentleman knew he would spill his guts in a minute. He could not let that happen.

He left the table without an explanation. Exiting the ballroom, he headed off in the direction of the bathroom down the hall. Once he was safely inside one of the stalls, he pulled out his cellular telephone and punched in ten numbers.

Within seconds, he was connected to the tall, dark-haired man with the grotesque fingernails in the Manhattan apartment. "T. is out. From what I can tell, so is Number Two. Madden switched the cover on his entrée with Number One's," the older gentleman said, keeping his voice low and even.

At his console in New York City, as smoke swirled around his head, the man already had some answers. Bilkos had just called. "From what our man in the kitchen said, the vice president ejected the contaminated meat before he could be infected by it, but only time will tell," he said laconically. The laboratory—buried deep beneath a farmhouse in the Iranian countryside—had tested these prions on animals. The latest strain seemed the most virulent yet, with an incubation time that measured in days instead of weeks. For Savage, whatever the time was, it would be a wait in hell. "All we can do is cover our asses. I'm waiting on the command from Central to see what our next move should be."

. . .

From what Bilkos could tell, President Winslet wanted the agent to explain why his dinner was being confiscated. Bilkos had no other choice. They had the evidence. His only hope was to get as far away from the White House as he could, as quickly as he could. The investigation would be sure to implicate him. By that time he would have vanished just as silently as he had appeared.

Bilkos spun around and headed back into the kitchen. If he was lucky, he could be out of the employees' entrance within ninety seconds. He wasn't.

"What's going on?" he asked, catching one of the cooks by the sleeve after noticing that the Secret Service had taken up positions at the exit doors and was not allowing anybody to leave.

His hands loaded down with a dessert tray, the young pastry chef spun around. "The FBI has locked us in here until they find out what happened to the vice president. From what I heard, that even includes the guests."

Bilkos swallowed hard at the news. He decided to make himself as invisible as possible, melting into the shadows and waiting. For now, that appeared to be his only option.

. . .

Circumstances were otherwise for the older gentleman. Because he was so well known to the White House security team, he was one of the first to leave.

"I'm sorry for the inconvenience, sir," the familiar Secret Service agent said. "We're just following orders. You can go on through now."

Nodding, the older gentleman passed through the makeshift security checkpoint set up at the far end of the State Dining Room. But he would be back. He was in too far to turn back now.

23

MADDEN WHIRLED AROUND as Marty Davenport, her face blotchy with anger, stormed toward where he huddled with one of the agents in a far corner of the still chaotic State Dining Room. "Can't this wait until we get some of the guests out of here?" he said, knowing she was rightfully furious.

"Cut the crap," she threw back at him. "I'm out there busting my ass to make it look like everything's just cruising along, when the truth is we're on the *Titanic* ten minutes after the iceberg hit. First we had the unknown person taken out of the West Wing in the ambulance, and now the vice president himself has been hauled off. It looks like a Secret Service convention in here. The press sharks smell blood—because there is blood!"

Madden shot her a stern glance and looked toward the hallway to his left. "Follow me," he said, heading in the direction of the exit. "Let's find somewhere a little more private."

Davenport leaned against the wall of the small alcove just off the hall as tears flooded her eyes. Madden pulled out a wadded-up handkerchief from his pocket and handed it to her. "Listen, Marty, I'm not sure what's going on, but the president is in great danger."

Davenport looked up, her fury arrested.

"I don't care what cock-and-bull story you come up with until this crisis is resolved." He sighed. "After the vice president's episode in the kitchen, which at least all of the staff saw, maybe you could float the possibility there was an outbreak of food poisoning and say we're simply taking extra precautions for our guests' protection. Just keep the press off my ass!" Madden knew he was being rough and excluding her from the inner circle. But the less she knew, the less the media bloodhounds who roamed the White House could suck out of her, and the less her position would be compromised in the future—if there was a future.

"What about Trainer's outburst?" she asked, a look of doubt crossing her face. "People didn't quite absorb it at first, but I don't think you can blame that on an upset stomach."

Madden cut her a half smile. "Seriously, I think if you keep it vague, concern over possible food poisoning will float," he said, grabbing for the cell phone in his pocket. "Isn't that what press secretaries are supposed to do, be vague?"

"Press secretaries are supposed to know the facts first," she retorted. "It's really serious?" she asked.

"Yes. Life or death."

"Damn. I should have listened to my parents when they told me to take that job at ABC," she said, forcing a grin. "But then again, nobody would want my memoirs if I had." She moved back into the hall and disappeared into the sea of nameless faces that now clogged the White House.

Where was Padgett? Chad Madden charged off, almost knocking over Dan Russell, who appeared lost after coming out of the bathroom. "Why aren't you with Winslet?" he demanded of one of the Secret Service agents, who had been assigned to cover the president, coming out just behind Russell.

"I had to go," he stammered, and then started to head back into the dining room.

"Get the president and his wife up to their private quarters as soon as you can without making it look as if there's a problem," Madden ordered. "Have you seen Sterling Padgett, the assistant director of the FBI?"

"He's over in the West Wing," the agent said, pointing in the direction of Savage's office. "We took Trainer to the holding room. Then the boss wanted to go back to the crime scene. He said something about . . ."

Madden didn't wait for the agent to finish. He headed off in the direction of the West Wing as Dan Russell fell in right behind him.

. . .

Padgett glanced up just as Madden and Russell rounded the door. "Somehow Savage must have found out that he was given the president's plate," Madden said as he came up beside the assistant director of the FBI. "If it hadn't been for Doctor Russell here, the bastard probably would have choked to death and saved you guys in the Justice Department the trouble."

"It's possible the vice president might actually be sick," Padgett replied.

Madden's face flushed with anger. "Sick because he knows what's going to happen to him if we can prove he's part of a conspiracy plot to take out the president."

Sterling Padgett tensed up noticeably. "I've been in touch with Doctor Cornish. He and his staff are standing by to do anything we need."

"Tell them we're sending some food samples over tonight," Madden said. "He knows what we are looking for. But ask them to check for everything, including poisons, in case our murderous friends have changed their modus operandi."

Padgett turned back toward the pool of blood beside Savage's desk as Madden continued. "We need to pay Mr. Trainer a visit before your people at the FBI and the DC police cart him off."

"He's going to want to talk to his lawyer," Padgett answered warily, "before he says anything."

Madden dropped his hand to his side. "Mr. Padgett, Doctor Russell and I know that when it comes to matters of national security you guys in the FBI and CIA don't always play by the rules."

. . .

"They wouldn't let us go with him," Gerald Lynn fired into the receiver as his eyes crisscrossed his office in the far corner of the West Wing. Savage's aides had been separated from the vice president when he was taken by ambulance to Walter Reed.

"I don't care what it takes," the elderly gentleman barked into his cellular telephone. "You and Rafer Peters need to get to him. Am I making myself clear enough? Get him out of the hospital before he can talk, or, if all else fails . . ." He did not need to continue. They both knew Savage was their weakest link.

. . .

The lock to the holding room clicked as the surly guard pushed open the solid metal door. "You have some guests," he mumbled in the direction of Ken Trainer, who was seated at the metal table with his hands cuffed behind him.

Sterling Padgett pushed past the guard, followed by Madden and Russell. "Mr. Trainer, I thought you might want to spare us all a great deal of trouble and explain your erratic behavior tonight. We have reason to believe that you have information vital to the national security of this country, and I would—"

Trainer cut him off. "Listen, flatfoot, don't try to strong-arm me," he replied defiantly. "I was just doing my job, defending Savage."

Padgett stiffened visibly. A muted smile glistened on his lips. "From what, Mr. Trainer? Or maybe I should rephrase my question. From whom?"

The room fell silent as Madden, bursting with anger, stepped around Padgett. "Do you want to tell me what happened to Jason Clark?"

"I'm afraid I don't know what you're talking about. The last time I saw him he was—"

"Cut the shit!" Madden blurted, fighting to maintain control. "You either murdered him or had it done, just like that car salesman and the others."

Trainer's face paled in color. "Those are very serious accusations, Mr. Madden. I hope you're prepared to back them up." He wrestled with the handcuffs, repositioning himself in the chair. "You do realize I can account for where I have been at all times, and I have a very credible witness to back me up." He squinted, letting a slight smile break across his lips. "The vice president of the United States."

. . .

At Sterling Padgett's order, the Secret Service brought the all White House kitchen staff together before Madden's arrival. They had watched as the vice president left in the ambulance, but that was the extent of their knowledge. Muted grumbles permeated the room. Their mounting level of concern showed in their wary faces. They did not have a long wait. When Madden arrived, accompanied by Russell, he moved to the center of the room, holding up his hand to get everyone's attention.

"I'm sorry we have to detain you," Madden said, trying to sound calm. "But there's been a problem and we need your cooperation. You should be able to get back to work in just a few minutes."

Madden scanned the group, looking for the small man he had seen with the vice president. At first Madden couldn't locate him, since he was partially hidden by several larger chefs standing in front of him.

Suddenly their eyes met and Madden recognized him. Madden first recalled seeing the little chef when he said something to the vice president while Savage was having dinner. That was just before Savage exploded from the table. Madden next remembered sending the cook off to call the paramedics. There had to be a connection.

Madden picked him out of the crowd. "I believe you were the one who went to call the ambulance for us," Madden said, his eyes locked on the small-statured man. "What's your name?"

"Bil . . . Bilkos . . . Jim Bilkos," he forced out weakly as he shifted from foot to foot. "I'm sorry I couldn't do more to help. Is the vice president all right?" he said.

"Mr. Bilkos, the first report sounds encouraging from the hospital," Madden answered. "Would you mind if the FBI asks you a few questions?"

Bilkos stiffened. His eyes darted around the room as if he were a caged animal with nowhere to flee. Madden could sense the small man knew more than he let on.

Madden whirled around to Sterling Padgett. "I think you need to hold him for further questioning," the chief of staff said briskly as he reached for his cell phone. "I need to check on the president."

. . .

"Do you mind telling me what the hell is going on?" Winslet said, directing the two agents standing watch by the door of the president's study in his private quarters to leave.

Madden sighed, trying to catch his breath. "We think they were trying to kill you tonight by feeding you contaminated beef," he said. "At the last minute, I switched your plate with Savage's."

Winslet stumbled back. "Chad, you said *they* a moment ago." His voice grew weak. "Do we know for sure who *they* are yet?"

"Trainer for one," Madden answered. "He gave himself away tonight when he lost control. Savage and his other goons, probably." He stopped, almost overwhelmed by the events that were unfolding around him. "It's more than that, Mr. President. We're going to have to face the truth. If the interception on the Mother Lode project is true, and we have every reason to believe it is, then either the new administration or a faction of Saddam Hussein's old supporters in Baghdad, and probably in Iran, has not forgiven the United States for what we did to their country. Only this time, they've adopted a new approach—to take over your administration from within."

. . .

Dan Russell jumped in disbelief as Jim Bilkos sprang out of the group assembled in the kitchen and grabbed him around the neck. Russell tried to resist but stopped instantly when he caught the glimpse of a knife rising tight against his exposed throat.

"Make no mistake," Bilkos screamed, the vessels on his neck pulsating like a time clock. "I will cut him wide open if you . . ."

Panic blurred Russell's vision. He watched helplessly as Madden lunged toward him and then halted. Padgett and his agents, their weapons drawn, fell into a knee-lock position. The agents rose slowly and began to circle Bilkos and his captive.

"Put the knife down," Padgett said, his approach controlled from years as a field agent. "We won't let you leave. You have no choice but to surrender."

Russell choked for air as Bilkos half-dragged him toward the giant prep table at the far end of the kitchen. "I believe you're wrong," Bilkos said, barely above a whisper as he ducked behind the large counter, pulling Russell down with him.

The last thing Russell saw was Padgett's shocked look as he held up his hand to his agents, a signal not to open fire unless they must. Russell knew if that Bilkos was part of the operation, he was no good to them dead. They needed information, not more dead bodies. With his free hand, Bilkos's small, bony fingers suddenly reached up to the counter, where they grabbed a large carving knife left out after the night's activities. He glared at Russell, his eyes full of hate, as he brought the second knife down to his side.

"No sudden moves," Padgett was saying somewhere beyond Russell's vision. His pulse raced as he fought to keep from strangling. The small man's arm continued to compress his windpipe. His only chance seemed to be the officers he hoped were slowly moving up to take position and free him before this maniac put an end to his life.

"Mr. Bilkos," Padgett called out. "I am from the FBI. Put the knives back on the counter and let the doctor go. We only want to ask you some questions. You have not been charged with any crime."

Russell tried to look up to judge his captor's response. Bilkos's eyes, now fixed and glassy, stared off in the distance. It was almost as if he had gone into some type of trance. Without warning, Bilkos loosened his grasp on Russell, letting the small knife that had been held precariously close to Russell's neck fall to the floor. Since his legs were still entangled under Bilkos, Russell tried to roll to the side, but looked up to see the horrible picture of Bilkos raising the large carving knife over his head. He was trapped, paralyzed with fear, knowing that in just moments he would feel searing pain as Bilkos's knife pierced his body. He closed his eyes.

Russell's heart jumped as he heard the sickening sound of cutting meat. He tried to scream, but vomit filled his throat. A groan sounded in his ears as Bilkos's hot breath blew across Russell's face. Suddenly the full weight of Bilkos's writhing body collapsed hard upon him, followed by the thud of the cook's head striking the floor just to the side of where Russell lay pinned. A warm wetness trickled across his chest as the muted sound of raspy gurgling echoed beside him.

Russell's eyes sprang open to see four of the agents, guns drawn, standing over him. Sterling Padgett bolted around the end of the long prep counter. "You OK?" Padgett asked Russell as Madden, out of breath, came up behind them.

Russell could only nod, as the weight of Bilkos's now-still body lay across his chest. Padgett reached down and rolled the dead man off to the side, but then stopped. He gasped. Russell looked down. Blood covered his suit. Bilkos's blood. Russell turned his face toward Bilkos, seeing the large carving knife protruding from his bloodied abdomen—Bilkos's gnarled fingers were still wrapped tightly around the deadly weapon. Russell shivered, and then he spat the vomit from his mouth.

. . .

Madden, followed by Padgett and a still bloody and visibly shaken Russell, quickly moved past the large contingency of Secret Service and FBI agents who dotted the entrance to the First Family's quarters.

President Winslet stood at the door to his study. His eyes widened and he stepped back at sight of Russell's blood-stained suit. "Are you hurt?" he asked, his voice shaky.

"No," Russell replied. "It's the blood of the guy who cooked your steak. He's dead."

"Seems like he chose hara-kiri rather over telling us the truth." Padgett said, stepping forward. "For now, Mr. President, I would suggest that you and you wife stay in the private quarters or the Oval Office until we can figure this out."

. . .

Gerald Lynn breezed by the bevy of Secret Service agents who had taken up critical positions throughout the busy emergency room at Walter Reed Hospital and headed to the cubicle where the vice president was being evaluated.

"How're you doing, chief?" he asked, poking his head through the curtain. "The doctors say I'm going to live," the vice president, clad only in a hospital gown, said dully, his voice trembling. "They think I've got food poisoning. Hell, if they only knew, they'd be shitting in their pants. And they would know I'm going to die."

"What did you tell them?"

"Nothing," the vice president shot back, angered that his aide seemed more concerned about any secrets he might have divulged rather than his uncertain condition.

"OK." Lynn appeared to ignore Savage's dire comments and moved farther into the cramped area. "Let's get out of here."

"I don't think so. The doctors want to keep me here overnight for observation," Savage said, pulling the sheet up.

"Where are your clothes, Mr. Vice President?" Lynn interrupted as he searched the small cubicle.

"Listen, you asshole. I'm going to die," Savage moaned, wishing it was Lynn or Trainer who had gotten hold of the contaminated meal instead. "They switched . . ."

Gerald Lynn sprang forward, slapping his hand over the vice president's mouth.

Savage started to struggle but then calmed down, realizing Lynn was shutting him up, not killing him. Lynn leaned over and whispered in Savage's ear. "You're going to be all right. Our medical experts through Central tell me you got it out of your system before you could be infected."

"Really?" Savage brightened as a cautious smile crept across his face. "You talked to them about me?"

Lynn's eyes swept away as he continued his search for Savage's clothes. "We have to protect our number one asset, don't we?" He stopped and moved closer to the vice president, who felt a little better after Lynn's reassuring words. "They're holding Trainer. He'll have to take the fall for Jason Clark. That way you're still in the clear."

Savage's eyes widened. "What about my taking over the...?"

"Do you really think Central would have gone this far without a backup plan?" Lynn answered abruptly. "We have to get you out of here. Tonight! They want you back on line."

His pulse quickening, the vice president sat up on the stretcher. Reaching over, he pushed the emergency call button on the cord next to his pillow. Within thirty seconds the nurse at the front desk arrived. "Get me the doctor in charge, if you will," Savage ordered.

. . .

"Ladies and gentlemen," Marty Davenport began, shuffling though the notes scattered across the small podium. "During the otherwise successful state dinner for the president of Argentina, the vice president was taken to the hospital for what the physicians at Walter Reed have diagnosed as a mild case of gastroenteritis. We have been told that he is scheduled to stay in the hospital overnight for observation but appears to be doing well."

"Marty, what about the guard who supposedly left here earlier with a heart attack? And now we've heard rumors of a stabbing in the kitchen," a familiar voice piped up from the back of the crowded room. "Is there more going on around here than we're being told?"

The White House press secretary gazed directly at the White House correspondent from CNN, her shaking hands hidden behind the podium. "John," she answered, trying to suppress the catch in her throat. "Have you ever known us to do that before?"

"Let's just say, Madam Secretary," the correspondent continued to press, "there appear to have been times when your selective recall has been used to the administration's advantage."

A suppressed laughter rustled the room and then died down. For the present, the press corps seemed satisfied with her explanation. They turned their attention to the other rumors.

After fielding a few more questions, Davenport brought the briefing to a close. "It's getting late. We've all had a long day. First thing in the morning, the staff will arrange private meetings with representatives from the delegation from Argentina for any of you who are interested." Story or not, at least for the time being, they would be off her ass.

. . .

It was almost midnight by the time Savage and his aides arrived at the vice president's residence, located on the northeast grounds of the Naval Observatory. The ride back from the medical center had been uneventful. The vice president signed himself out of the hospital against medical advice and agreed to return if anything untoward arose. The Secret Service was alarmed, but the vice president went and they had to follow.

Not until Savage and his accomplices were back in the security of his quarters did they feel safe discussing the earlier events of the evening. An unexpected guest had arrived at the residence about thirty minutes earlier. Since he was familiar to the security forces assigned to the vice president, his entry was no problem. The older gentleman, still in the tuxedo from the White House dinner that had gone so wrong, was waiting in the den when Savage and his party entered.

"That bastard, Madden, tried to kill me tonight!" Savage blurted out when he first saw the elderly gentleman.

"Maybe," the elderly gentleman replied. "Or maybe he was just trying to force our hand."

Savage was puzzled. Peters closed the door to the den and flipped on the television with the remote control. They huddled together around the large, overstuffed sofa near the middle of the room.

"Madden and this Sterling Padgett from the FBI are on to something, but so far they don't know what," the older gentleman continued. "If luck is on our side, Kenneth Trainer will take the fall, and you, Mr. Vice President, will still be in the clear. Trainer is a good soldier. He has been well trained for this very contingency and will be rewarded for his dedication to the cause."

Because of his relationship with Trainer, which was tortuous at best, Savage was surprised his former aide would sacrifice his own life for his, but then again it would be for the cause and not for Savage himself. Although he was relieved, Savage wasn't sure whether the elderly gentleman meant Trainer would get his reward here or in another life. In either case, as far as Savage was concerned, as long as Trainer did not implicate him then vice president was better off without him.

"Central is working on a new plan. I cannot be more specific except to say that Bilkos was not the only individual on our side who has a trusted position in the White House," the older gentleman said softly to Savage. "As long as you are the vice president, we are still only a heartbeat away, as they say." He smiled and patted Savage's hand.

Chad Madden sat on the edge of his desk looking out over the room. He had dropped a still-shaken Dan Russell at his hotel about an hour earlier. It was after one o'clock in the morning. He was exhausted by the evening's events, but still not ready to call it a day. He had been able to convince Russell that the CDC was not the enemy. If there was an impending epidemic of mad cow disease infiltrating the country's food supply, all his contacts in Washington were still in the dark about it too. Who the real enemy was (and how Bilkos fit into the scheme, since he was not involved with the deaths of Rosie, Tate, and Jason Clark) was the underlying concern that kept Madden's mind racing with possibilities. He needed to check with Jennifer Smitt now that she had volunteered her services once again.

The FBI had halted their investigation of the crime scene for the night, but they were prepared to begin again first thing in the morning. The West Wing was deserted except for security guards stationed outside the Oval Office and at the door of Vice President Savage's office.

Trainer's outburst and loss of control did not make sense unless he knew the president's food was tainted. But Madden couldn't prove anything. And it could not be that simple, he thought. Trainer would not have been able to do this all alone. He had to have had inside help, and not just the crazy cook and the bearded man from housekeeping who had nearly ended Madden's life. These people were professionals, but they were more than that as well. That was the part that troubled Madden the most—their apparent disregard for their own lives. Madden shuddered, feeling a haunting connection to the September 11 attacks that continued to trouble them all.

Madden was not sure why he sensed a similarity, but discovering the person who leaked the Mother Lode project was central to finding the answer. He reached over to his desk and unlocked the lower drawer on the left side of his desk. Inside was the large stack of papers. Below, the infamous files.

Suddenly one of Madden's many thoughts jelled. He flashed back to the sight of the vice president standing behind this very desk. Even though Savage was second-in-command at the White House, he was not supposed to be in Chad's office. Much of the information in that drawer was confidential information relating to presidential business—all but Madden's files on the proposed vice-presidential candidates. Madden remembered Savage's comments about looking for the Mother Lode project papers. Why do it then, in the middle of the night?

Madden started to close the drawer when the answer struck him. Savage was not looking for the Mother Lode papers. He was looking for the candidates' files. And the only reason he would have wanted to see them was because he knew they had been altered.

His suspicions were confirmed. Savage had to be part of the plot. Madden still was not sure what the plot was, or who beyond Savage and Trainer might have been behind it, but if the steak intended for Winslet came back positive for kuru disease, the plan was obvious.

Madden needed proof. As long as the vice president was still in office, then Winslet's life, and probably his own, were in grave danger. Madden opened the drawer again and started to reach to the bottom of the pile for the files, but then drew back.

Fingerprints, the chief of staff thought to himself. It was a reach. But if Vice President Savage had gone through the files before Madden interrupted him, that would be proof enough, maybe not for the FBI to bring an indictment, but it was convincing enough for Madden.

. . .

Although there could have been jurisdictional questions, the FBI won out on who would be responsible for the investigation, since the White House was on federal property.

Sterling Padgett's two top assistants kept Trainer up all night. But true to the older gentleman's prediction, he had not broken.

Padgett had wanted to charge Trainer with Jason Clark's death, but the evidence was all circumstantial. Despite Madden's vehement protests to the contrary, he had to let Trainer go. Since the bearded gentleman from Environmental Services had been caught red-handed at the scene of the crime and was no longer able to testify in his own behalf, Trainer's attorney would argue that his client was not the most likely suspect. Unless the prosecution could come up with hard evidence, there was no chance that he could get a conviction against Trainer.

. . .

"Central has decided Trainer has become a liability. He knows too much." The man in the high-rise Manhattan apartment blew a large plume of smoke out the side of his mouth and then snuffed out his cigarette. "We can't just let him run loose out there without the risk that he might reveal our hand. Regrettably, this seems to leave us no other choice."

"I will make the connection," the voice on the other end of the line replied before the line went dead.

The course of Trainer's future was no longer in doubt. He would be forced to make the ultimate sacrifice.

. . .

When the FBI's investigative team arrived at the White House around seven-thirty that morning, Chad Madden was waiting for them. By the time he finally made it back to his condominium the night before, it had been almost time to return again. A brief message Jennifer Smitt left on his answering machine revealed no new information but told him that she would be back at FBI headquarters first thing in the morning. A short nap, a shave, and a shower, and he was back on the job. After telling Marty Davenport to leak to the press corps that Savage turned out to have a mild case of intestinal flu and was resting comfortably at his residence, Madden headed for Savage's office.

"Who's in charge here?" Madden questioned. One of the investigators pointed to the agent huddled over the pool of blood beside Savage's desk. Madden signaled for the agent in charge to follow him to his office.

"I need a favor," Madden demanded, making it clear that it was no favor at all as he headed down the hall and into his own back office. "Dust these two envelopes and their contents for fingerprints," Madden said, pointing to the two large manila envelopes at the bottom of the pile in his open desk drawer. "This may be related to your investigation down the hall."

"May I ask how?" the agent inquired. His confusion was apparent in his voice.

He kept looking toward the door that led back down the hall to the vice president's office. "Nothing new at headquarters, so I thought maybe you could use some help over here," Jennifer Smitt interrupted, poking her head around the door. "It's just the FBI agent in me."

Madden hoped it was more, but right now all he could do was smile at her, gratefully and tiredly. "Padgett is going to have your butt if he finds you over here."

"What's going on?" she asked, ignoring Madden's remonstrance.

"I was just asking special agent . . . Myers," Madden hesitated until he came up with the name, "to check these envelopes for fingerprints. If my suspicions are confirmed, it will go a long way toward solving the problems in the vice president's office."

"I'll get my people down here as soon as I can free somebody up," the agent said, flicking his eyes in Madden's direction as he edged out of the room. "But with all the other things we're trying to cover, it may be a while."

Jennifer interrupted. "Agent Myers, back when I was out in the field, fingerprinting was one of my specialties. If I can use your equipment, maybe I could help out."

The agent stopped and turned back around. "If that's all right with Mr. Madden," he said, clearly eager to turn the task over to someone else.

"What about Padgett?" he asked, feeling now he was being caught in the middle.

"Chad, I'm a big girl." A slow smile broke out across her lips. "I think I can take care of this myself."

. . .

"Hell, I'm scared to eat anything," Winslet muttered under his breath in Madden's ear as they waited for the president of Argentina to arrive for the breakfast conference. "I even wondered about using bottled water to brush my teeth this morning."

Madden nodded, his own uncertainties about to get the best of him. "We need to talk," he said. "Alone."

With all that was going on at the White House, it was almost impossible for President Winslet to keep up the appearance that all was routine, but he had to try. Madden had agreed to brief the president hourly on events as they unfolded. For the present, there were two agents outside the door of the Oval Office and two other agents who accompanied the president everywhere he went in the West Wing. Additionally all presidential appearances outside the White House had been cancelled until the situation was stabilized. Davenport would float the story that the president had a milder case of the same bug that affected Savage and that the president's doctors advised him to cut back on his activities for a couple of days.

Winslet set aside thirty minutes for one final meeting with the president of Argentina. There was still some unfinished business Winslet wanted resolved. The president had asked for the meeting to be private, so only President Galvez, his top aide, and Madden were invited to the Oval Office. There was no need for interpreters, since Galvez spoke fluent English and the president understood some Spanish.

"Mario," Winslet said. "I want to get right to the point."

Unlike the day before, President Galvez now seemed uncomfortable, shifting nervously in his chair. Winslet stood up from behind his desk and walked around it to sit on the edge, not two feet from the president of Argentina. "I'm going to forget about some of your comments yesterday, because I respect what you have done to bring your country into the twenty-first century. But, I am *NOT*—" Winslet's voice thundered across the short span between them. "*Not* going to be intimidated into doing your dirty work."

Galvez arched his back at Winslet's outburst. "Mr. President, my information could create quite an uproar in your press if you are caught diverting funds from—"

Knowing that US monies could be given to Galvez's opposition, Winslet cut him off. "If you follow through with your threat, I'm sure those you consider to be a danger to your country will be more than willing to share some of the millions of dollars in foreign aid that our country gives to yours each year. And what about that so-called 'secret' bank account you have set up for your family in the Cayman Islands? I'm sure your fellow countrymen would have something to say about that."

Galvez's eyes grew wide as he listened to Winslet's continuing tongue-lashing. He held up his hand as he tried to respond, but Winslet wouldn't let him. "Do I make myself perfectly clear, President Galvez?"

Mario Galvez nodded, his eyes glassy from shock. Madden knew there was nothing else the man could say to the most powerful political figure in the world.

. . .

It was close to nine o'clock by the time President Winslet had a few minutes alone with his chief of staff. "Mr. President, let's go out into the Rose Garden," Madden said as he headed for the portico. The president followed, knowing the garden area was one of the few places their conversation would be muted completely from Savage and his cronies' listening ears. Yet even then he was not totally sure.

"My guess is that your steak was infected with the same organism that killed Rosie and Tate."

"How do you know?"

"I don't . . . yet." Madden answered. "Evidently it takes a while to positively identify these organisms. We should have some answers by sometime tomorrow. The people at the CDC took your plate, which maybe I should call the vice president's plate, for analysis last night, along with the one you actually ate."

Now the president was totally confused. He asked, "Why Savage's plate?"

"Because it was meant for you, but I switched them at the last minute. You should have seen his face when he found out. He almost puked his guts out."

"How did you know?" the president asked.

"We'll never know for sure, since the cook—the one who talked to Savage just before he jumped up from the table—killed himself last night. According to the kitchen staff, the guy was one of the two chefs who helped prepare the steaks, so he must have been in on the plot, assuming the results come back positive for the organism."

"What about the rest of the White House kitchen staff?" Winslet demanded.

"They're all under suspicion until we get some information back from the CDC tomorrow. If they find something, the kitchen staff will all be brought in again for questioning until we get an answer."

The idea that a member or members of his own staff had attempted to poison him made Winslet's blood run cold. If the president of the United States could no longer trust his own security system, then he was no better off than a caged animal. He would have to rely on guts and cunning and suspect everyone.

"What about Clark's death?"

"He must have gotten too close to the truth. The dead man from Environmental Services who nearly killed me is the obvious suspect," Madden replied. "But my guess is he was just there to clean up someone else's mess, probably Trainer's."

"And Trainer?" Winslet asked, his fists wrenched in a ball.

"Padgett sequestered him for questioning but had to let him go," Madden answered. "I tried to get them to hold him for no cause, on grounds that he poses a threat to national security."

"It scares the hell out of me that he's still out there." Winslet tightened noticeably. "At least I can ban him from the White House."

Madden nodded. "I saw the look in the eyes of the guy from Environmental Services who wanted to take my head off. And I saw the bloodied cook with the knife buried in his belly. If Trainer is in with them, I'll bet my money he'll go to his grave with his secrets."

Winslet looked over at Madden and realized that the ordeal was far from over. Who was behind it? Suddenly the cell phone in Madden's pocket chirped to life. Their time alone was finished.

"Stay with your security at all times," Madden said. "The same goes for Sharon. I have arranged to have all your food brought in for now."

"What about you?" the president asked.

"I have a job to do," Madden said. He shrugged. "We can't just sit back and let things happen. Look at Rosie, Tate, and now Jason. I'm convinced that Savage and Trainer aren't acting alone, but are players in a much larger arena. I just haven't figured out who's pulling their strings. The answer is out there. It is probably closer than we think. There is some other information I'm waiting for. If it comes back positive, I'm going to try to force their hand."

"I'm not sure you have that authority," Winslet answered, the hairs on the back of his neck bristling against his collar. "You should leave those kinds of things to the Padgett and his people."

"Respectfully, Mr. President, as your chief of staff, they don't have the intro I do. The less you're involved the better." Madden broke eye contact with the president as he looked back toward the portico. "Let's just say I'm about to put your running mate to the test."

24

"Regarding Jason Clark's death, we don't have much, I'm sorry to say," Padgett told Madden. "He died of asphyxiation. That's a fancy name coroners use for being choked to death. My people did notice several fresh bruises around his neck, which usually means he didn't go by his own choosing."

"Any leads?" Madden asked.

Padgett hesitated. "Unless my people turn up DNA evidence or something, there's not much chance we're going to able to hang this on our leading suspect and make it stick. The guy from Environmental Services will take the fall. Trainer's lawyers will see to that. You did what you had to do, Madden, to save your life. But it took out our only witness."

Was Padgett's remark meant to be taken as a compliment or criticism? "Did your agent tell you that I had them dust my desk drawer and the envelopes?"

"Yes," Padgett said, "I was just about to get to that." He pursed his lips. Madden could tell he was miffed about

Jennifer Smitt's surprising involvement in the case. But if the conspiracy was going to lead to the second most powerful leader of the Executive Branch, Madden needed hard evidence. Not circumstantial, but direct. And whether Padgett liked it or not, Jennifer's experience could be of help.

"We got the prints. Or maybe I should say Agent Smitt, who is involved with the case now, took a set of partial prints off your two envelopes and your desk drawer. We were lucky—it didn't look like many people had touched them."

"Whose prints did you find?"

"Yours, mine, Jennifer Smitt's, the president's, Congressman Rolands' . . ." Padgett replied, saving the best for last. "And Vice President Savage's."

"Bingo!" Madden shot back.

"It gets even better. The vice president's prints were on every drawer of your desk, including the one with the envelopes."

"You have made my day, Sterling."

"Not so fast," Padgett replied. "Savage's smudged prints were also on the top of each of the files in one of the envelopes. The clearest prints were on your file."

Madden gulped. "What are you trying to say?" he asked. "We already knew that, didn't we?"

"In a sense, yes." Padgett answered. "But with your file included in the group, if Savage is smart, it could tell him that you might have been on the list as well."

The thought made Madden gasp. Madden had never considered himself to be in the line of fire. But now he also was a target of whatever murderous plot Trainer and the others had instigated. He wondered whether he too had been poisoned.

"Maybe we should assign somebody to you until this situation is resolved," Padgett suggested.

Madden thought about Padgett's offer for a moment. "No, there's enough security around this place already." He hesitated and shot a glance in Padgett's direction, hoping it would not seem too obvious. "But you might want to keep a close eye on Ms. Smitt."

. . .

"I just wanted to thank you for—"

Jennifer interrupted him. She was worried and she felt helpless. "I couldn't stand by and let you guys try to take this on alone," she told Madden over the telephone. "It looks like Savage was all over your desk. That alone may not be enough to convict him, but it's good enough to move him to the top of the FBI's list. It was worth doing, even if Padgett hates me forever."

"He won't hate you forever," Madden said. "You were only acting on the cause of justice, and to protect your country."

"I don't think the bureaucrats will see it that way. When this is finished—assuming we're not all dead—I'm going to ask for a transfer to the West Coast office, maybe even get out of the Bureau altogether. Anything for a fresh start."

She could hear Madden gasp through the receiver. "I guess I was hoping that if we survive whatever comes next, that you and I could—"

Unsure of what she should say, Jennifer clicked off her phone without answering, leaving him unsure whether her abrupt response was meant as a yes or no.

. . .

The Secret Service agent rang into Savage's bedroom over the intercom in the vice presidential residence at Number One Observatory Circle. "Mr. Vice President," he announced, "the president's chief of staff is here to see you."

Savage felt instantly even more ill. Over twelve hours had passed since the fiasco at the Argentine dinner, and he was still not feeling quite right. He hoped Central was correct in saying that he had removed the agent from his system before he could become infected. Madden had never come to his residence before. Why now?

"Did he say what he wanted?" Savage asked the agent.

"I didn't ask him, sir. I didn't think it was any of my business."

Savage knew the agent was right, but his fingers fidgeted, grabbing at the cord wrapped around the telephone on his nightstand. He could not give things away now. He had to continue to hold himself together until he knew more about Central's new plan.

Maybe Madden was just checking on him since he had been so sick the night before. But probably not. Savage knew his behavior at the dinner was hugely suspicious. How much had he given away? He told the agent to wait a minute and then pulled out his portable telephone and punched in the ten-digit number. Within seconds he heard a querying voice on the other end.

"Tell Central that Chad Madden is downstairs to see me," Savage said in a muffled tone, his eyes wandering aimlessly around the room. "What should I do?"

"Nothing!" Gerald Lynn answered abruptly. "He may suspect, but he has no proof. You're still in the clear. I'll send Peters over, but that may take thirty minutes. Someone has to stay at the White House, just in case."

"Just in case what?" Savage demanded anxiously.

"Forget it," Lynn replied. "We're about to put the back-up plan into action. You just worry about yourself. Let Madden do all the talking."

"OK," Savage replied meekly.

"Remember this, Savage: You are still the vice president. If Madden gets out of hand, let the Secret Service do the dirty work for you. After all, they would only be doing their job by protecting the second most powerful political figure in the country. Don't let him get at you."

The vice president punched off his cell phone. Then, his fingers trembling, he picked up the receiver. *How much further must the killing go?* Savage thought. Back on the intercom, his courage renewed, he said, "Tell Mr. Madden to make himself comfortable. I just have to put on some clothes, and then I'll be right down."

. . .

The White House guard tipped back his hat and looked over at Dan Russell, his hand cupped over the telephone receiver. "Mr. Madden's assistant says he's not there," he barked.

Disappointed, Russell looked out the barred window of the West Entrance guard house. He'd saved the vice president from choking to death and almost lost his own life in the process, but he was still no closer to the truth. Although still unsure of the CDC's role, he was now convinced the deaths of Delstrotto, the senator, and Dr. Thomas were all linked to the same source and that Savage and his thugs were involved.

"Ask Madden's assistant if I can come up and wait for him to return," Russell said. Even though he knew he had been valuable to Madden, Russell knew he was still considered an outsider—an amateur in a sea of professionals. As if that made any difference in a catastrophe of this magnitude.

The guard muttered a few inaudible words in the telephone and turned back to Russell. "She said it's up to you. But she doesn't know when he'll be back."

He had come this far. Russell had no intention of going back to Texas without an answer. He knew he was out of his element. But if he wanted to make amends for his mother's bloody, mangled body cradled in his arms on that rain-swept night so many years ago . . .He stood up and headed toward the door.

"Tell her I'm coming up."

. . .

"I hope you're feeling better, Mr. Vice President."

"Thank you, Chad," Savage answered, trying to control the edge in his voice. "They told me at the Medical Center it was probably only a mild case of gastroenteritis. My guess is that was their medical jargon for a bad case of food poisoning. I'm better now, but the doctors said I should take it easy for the next couple of days." He chuckled deliberately. "I'm certainly sorry to have made a scene, but I'm afraid it couldn't be helped. Please convey my apology to the president. And what brings you over here?"

"Well, the president and I are glad it was nothing serious," Madden continued, his eyes shifting around the room.

Savage could tell the chief of staff had some agenda, probably unpleasant, possibly dangerous. He needed to draw him out as long as possible until Peters could get there. "Can I get you some coffee?" Savage asked.

Madden's eyes shifted back to the vice president. Had he been looking for something? "Ah . . . that would be fine, sir."

Savage led Madden into his study where he always kept a pot of coffee warming over a portable brewer. Even though he was racked with anxiety, the vice president was determined not to let it show. By the wall, pouring coffee, Savage opened up a conversation about how the president was holding up. "I know it must be rough on Winslet—the shooting of the guy from Colorado in the holding room, and now Clark getting killed in my office by someone from Environmental Services, and—"

Madden interrupted firmly. "Mr. Vice President, let me get right to the point."

Savage spun around, knowing his delaying tactics were over. He glanced past Madden, who had now taken up a seat on the sofa across from him. Fortunately for Savage, the door to the hallway was still open. In the distance by the front door, Savage could see the back of one of the Secret Service agents who had been assigned to guard him. He did not remember everything about last night, but the vivid image of Madden standing over him and the chief of staff's threatening comments as he lay sprawled on the floor of the White House kitchen made him shudder.

"Go . . . go on, Mr. Madden," Savage said, struggling to keep his voice firm, his courage bolstered by the presence of his security officer out in the hall.

"I want to know why you went through the president's personal files."

Keep steady. Let yourself be shocked. Stay calm. "What makes you think that I did?" Savage asked, trying to act surprised.

"The FBI lifted your fingerprints off the candidate files in my desk. You had no right to go through them."

"I'm sorry, Mr. Madden, but I'm not sure what you mean." Savage knew exactly what was meant, and he knew Madden knew he did.

"The night I found you at my desk?" the chief of staff fired back.

The vice president was ready. "Oh, that night. I told you I was looking for the files on the Mother Lode project. I'm sorry if it appeared to be more than that." He smiled.

Madden's face hardened further. "If that were so, why did you take out the files?" Madden shifted on the sofa. "Once you opened the envelope, you could see immediately they weren't what you were looking for."

Savage felt his neck and forehead erupt into sweat.

"Or were they indeed what you were looking for, Mr. Vice President?" Madden had Savage where he wanted him. Alone. Almost. "You wanted to see what the president and I knew about how you—and whoever else you're involved with—

doctored the background on the vice presidential candidates, didn't you?"

Savage did not try to answer the chief of staff's allegations. Instead he groped for the cup of coffee on the table in front of him. They knew. Fear raced through his body, and his hand started to shake uncontrollably, knocking the cup of steaming hot liquid all over the carpet. He looked up at Madden, who was now only a blur. Panicked, he blinked, trying to focus on his hand. He couldn't. He remembered what Trainer had told him the first symptoms would be, back when Rosalyn Delstrotto was infected. Central was wrong. He had not gotten the dreaded agent out of his system soon enough. Savage knew the awful truth. He had the disease.

"No!" Savage yelled, jumping up from the sofa, almost falling over the coffee table in front of him. A wave of nausea welled up in his throat as he staggered past Madden in the direction of his desk at the far side of the room.

. . .

Chad Madden sat frozen on the sofa, his mind keenly focused on what Savage's next response might be. He had pushed the vice president past the breaking point. He had no idea what to expect. A clatter from the hall broke behind him. Madden snapped his head around as he heard the door to the hallway close. His eyes grew wide as he recognized Rafer Peters moving into the room.

Peters quickly reached under his breast pocket and pulled out a revolver. Madden was paralyzed with fear.

"What in the hell are you doing?" Peters screamed as he looked across the room at the vice president stumbling around.

"I have it, you idiot!" Savage cried. "I have the disease. I'm going to die!"

"Just shut up," Peters ordered, moving over to a spot directly behind Madden.

"We'll get to that later. What does Madden know?"

"Everything," the vice president snapped back, saliva now dripping from his lower lip.

Peters looked down at Madden, who still had not found the courage to move. "I'm afraid we have a problem, Mr. Madden. If you make a sound, I will kill you right now."

Madden knew not to respond. He fought to stay in control of himself as he watched Rafer Peters take his cellular telephone from his jacket pocket. Holding his weapon in one hand, Peters punched in a telephone number. From what Madden could tell, the call was answered immediately.

"Savage says Madden knows everything," Peters said into the phone. He waited for a response. "Yes, sir, just as you say."

Peters punched off his phone and put it back in his jacket pocket. He looked down at Madden and then up at the vice president. "He's on the way over." Peters's voice was void of emotion. Madden swallowed hard when Peters reached inside his coat and pulled out a four-inch stainless steel cylinder. Panic set in when he recognized it was a silencer that Peters was screwing onto the barrel of his handgun.

Madden knew if he was going to save his own life, he was had to act fast. He thrust out his hand in Peter's direction.

"Wait!" he called out to Savage, who had by now reached his desk. "You'll never get away with this, Mr. Vice President. Winslet knows I came here to confront you. Before it's too late, you have a chance to—"

"Shut up!" Peters barked in a muted tone, leveling the barrel of his .44 Magnum to just inches away from Madden's forehead. Madden closed his eyes, waiting for the end to come.

The sudden crack sounded as the shell exploded in the chamber, propelling its projectile forward. The sound rocked

Madden in blinding fear. He felt a sharp sting on the back of his head. His senses shot out, trying to survey the damage. To his shock, he was still alive.

Madden quickly opened his eyes. He saw Rafer Peters's head tilted backwards as blood streamed out of the hole in his chest and soaked the front of his jacket. A look of disbelief was etched on Peters's face as he slumped to the floor. Madden looked around for Savage and saw him through a cloud of the gun's smoke.

Within seconds the door to the hallway flew open as the Secret Service agent jumped into action, his gun drawn as he scanned the room. He looked down at the body of Rafer Peters, whose jacket was now completely covered in blood. Then he saw Madden, and followed his gaze to the vice president, who was standing by his desk on the far side of the room. The agent did not appear to see the gun in the vice president's hand, which hung at his side. The agent raised his weapon in Madden's direction.

"Wait!" Madden screamed out. "Don't shoot!"

The vice president remained silent, his eyes glassy and fixed. He slumped into the chair behind his desk.

The agent looked at Savage and then saw that Madden was not armed. He lowered his weapon. "I need an explanation, now, sir!"

They both looked at Savage as the vice president, his face contorted in a look of confusion, laid his weapon, the same gun he had just used to shoot Peters, onto his desk.

"I have to phone the president," Madden said. "He has to know what's going on."

The agent nodded as Madden pushed himself up from the sofa. At first he could barely stand, still weak from the ordeal he had undergone. He looked around the room for a telephone, since he had inadvertently left his cell phone in the front seat of the car.

There was only one phone in the room. It was on the vice president's desk, right next to Savage's revolver.

As Madden cautiously moved in the vice president's direction, Savage recoiled. A bewildered look shot out of his eyes as he jumped up from his chair, grasped his gun, and thrust it into his jacket pocket.

"Put that down, Mr. Vice President," the agent called out.

Savage rushed into the bathroom. The agent stopped and pulled out his walkie-talkie. "Get in here!" He yelled to whoever had the other walkie-talkie. "And get an ambulance over here stat! The vice president just shot one of his own aides."

Madden grabbed the receiver of the telephone sitting on Savage's desk. He dialed the president's private line, the number that went to the red telephone in the top left-hand drawer of the desk in the Oval Office. Madden's call was answered on the third ring. "Mr. President," Madden said.

"Who's calling?"

Madden felt his heart jump in his chest when he realized the person who answered the telephone was not Winslet. For a brief moment he could only hope he had dialed the wrong number, but then the sickening feeling of reality overwhelmed him. He recognized the voice on the other end of the line. It was Gerald Lynn. The vice president's trusted aide—the only one of Savage's inner circle who was not accounted for.

"Mr. Madden," Lynn said with unnerving coolness. "Is that you?"

"Yes, yes," Madden answered with shallow, short breaths. What was Savage's aide doing in the Oval Office, answering the president's phone?

"It's funny you should call at this time," Lynn continued. "The president and I were just talking about you."

"Put the president on," Madden ordered, knowing somehow he had to warn Winslet and find out what was going on in the Oval Office.

"I'm sorry, but that's not possible," Lynn remarked as if nothing out of the ordinary had occurred. "Put Savage on the telephone, if you will, Mr. Madden."

"He's in the bathroom," Madden snapped back. He looked around the room, searching the blank face of the Secret Service agent for answers.

Suddenly Lynn yelled into the telephone. "Get Savage out and on the telephone now! Or there won't be enough left of your president to bury!"

Madden was horrified and almost dropped the receiver as he moved around the desk. "What?" Madden barked into the receiver. "What are you saying?" He beckoned to the Secret Service agent, who was now heading in the direction of the bathroom, where the vice president was still holed up.

By then, two other Secret Service agents had come running in. Madden looked up as the first agent, in urgent whispers, began to fill the others in on what had happened.

"Give me the president," Madden demanded, stalling for time. His eyes searched Savage's desk. He reached down, fumbling at the top drawer before he finally pulled it open. Madden grasped for a piece of paper and picked up a pen.

"Mr. Madden," Gerald Lynn said. "I have four pounds of plastic explosives strapped around my waist. Don't ask me how I managed it, but I can assure you I'm telling the truth."

Madden reeled back in disbelief. He had no choice but to believe Lynn. If Savage's aide had made it into the Oval Office, the rest had to be true. Madden scribbled down a note and handed it to one of the agents.

Lynn continued. "If you do not do exactly as I say, the president and this precious Oval Office will evaporate."

"What do you want?" Madden asked. If he could only get a sense of why Lynn was holding Winslet hostage, then maybe . . .

"Not so fast," Lynn shot back. "I want to speak to Savage first. Then we can talk."

The agent squinted as he strained to read Madden's note before handing it off to the other two agents.

G. Lynn has president in Oval Office. Lynn wired with plastic explosives. What demands, don't know yet. Call S. Padgett. Take Lynn out! NOW!

"I'll call back in five minutes," Lynn continued. "This time, you'd better make sure the vice president is available." The telephone went dead before Madden could respond.

. . .

The president huddled at the far end of the sofa as Gerald Lynn stood hunched over his desk, barking his demands into the telephone. He had not believed Lynn when he first slipped past the security outside and locked the door to the Oval Office after him. But when Lynn flashed the tiny remote detonating device and unbuttoned his shirt, revealing the packages of explosives strapped to his waist, the president knew he had become a hostage. Other than knowing that Trainer and probably Savage were involved, Winslet was still in the dark.

Winslet had attempted to hit the panic button under his desk, but it was too late. Lynn's powerful blow to his chest knocked the president back and away from his desk. Now all that the most powerful political figure in the world could do was wait, rely on others, and pray.

. . .

One of the Secret Service agents was already on his cell phone when Madden hung up the receiver.

"Yes, sir," the Secret Service agent told his supervisor on the other end of the line. He turned to the others. "Lynn is holding the president hostage, but he won't tell us what he wants until he hears from the vice president." There was a pause as the agent listened to his earpiece. The agent turned to Madden. "Did Lynn say anything else?"

"He said he would call us in five minutes and that Savage had better be available."

The agent repeated Madden's message over his phone.

"That's it!" Madden blurted out as all heads in the room turned in his direction. "He wants to make sure Savage is *available.*" The color faded from Madden's cheeks as he turned to face the agent. "Lynn doesn't want anything in exchange for the president."

"Sir?"

Madden now realized the awful truth: Lynn was preparing to do his job. As soon as he knew Savage was all right, he was going to kill the president. "He'll take the president with him like the kamikaze pilots of 9-11."

An odd quiet fell across the room. *This can't be,* thought Madden, still holding the receiver. His arms hung at his side. He was helpless to change the course of events that were rapidly unfolding around him. In a few minutes, the man in the bathroom, the man who was at least partially responsible for the deaths of six people, maybe more, would by law become the next president of the United States. And when it happened Madden would be able to prove nothing.

The agent standing over by the door called out to Madden. "We can't let this—" A single shot exploded from the direction of the vice president's bathroom.

. . .

Ready to take over his new role that would change the world's power structure, the older gentleman pulled up to the security gate of the vice president's residence. He was not surprised to see the ambulance and a collection of security vehicles out front. There were even two DC patrol cars parked on the grass.

"What's going on?" he asked the security guard, fully expecting to hear that the president's chief of staff had been killed when he tried to assault the vice president.

"I'm not at liberty to say," the security officer answered initially, but he appeared to change his mind when he recognized the familiar figure. "But since it's you, sir: The vice president has been shot."

"Who did you say?" Tempering his shock at the alarming news, the older gentleman asked again, his knuckles white in anticipation.

"The vice president!" the distraught officer blurted out.

Ben Delstrotto backed his car onto the street and headed off into the night. Where to, he wasn't sure . . .

. . .

Seated in a chair against the far wall of Madden's outer office, Dan Russell leafed through the pages of the *Washington Post* when a man dressed in black combat gear appeared at the door. Startled, the assistant jumped up from her desk, a look of shock across her face. Russell jumped up too.

Transferring his automatic weapon to the other arm, the man put his finger to his lips. "You'll have to get out of here," he said, his nostrils flaring. "One of the guards will take you down the back way."

"What's going on?" Russell asked, still continuing to hold on to his open copy of the paper. "I'm waiting for the chief of staff."

The man half-pushed the frightened assistant through the door to the hall. "Come on," he ordered Russell.

"Wait!" Russell said. He had to project assurance and keep himself in the action because he was still the outsider. "I'm a doctor in emergency medicine. Maybe I can help."

"Listen, *Doc*," the man in black answered, his tone harsher. "Nobody stays. The president is in—" He stopped.

"In what? Danger?" Russell demanded, his heart pounding in his chest. He was now more sure than ever. He had to stay. "I don't know what's going on, but think about it for just a minute. I might be the one person around here who can help you if there are any injuries—and you're sending me out of here?"

The man in black held up his hand as he reached for the portable receiver attached to Velcro on his shoulder. "What's your name?"

"Russell," he answered. "Doctor Dan Russell."

Within thirty seconds, the answer came back through his earpiece. "The boss said everybody out," the man in black spouted. "Now let's go."

"Call Madden," Russell sat back down forcefully. "Otherwise, you'll have to carry me out."

"Or shoot you," the man in black retorted. He made a move toward Russell but then halted, grabbing the small receiver once again. "This guy Russell won't leave unless he talks to Madden," he spit into the mouthpiece.

Within seconds the telephone on Madden's assistant's desk lit up. The man in black picked it up, listened momentarily, and then thrust it in Russell's direction.

Russell's heart pounded as he reached for the telephone. "It's something I have to do," he said into the receiver, the force in his voice masking the fear that coursed through his body.

"You're crazy, but . . . OK," Madden told him. "They have the president held hostage in the Oval Office. I need you as my eyes. Ever killed a terrorist before?"

"No. It'll be my first time."

"Give me back to the SWAT guy."

Dan handed the telephone back. "Madden wants to talk to you."

"Yes, sir," the man in black answered as he cradled the telephone receiver. "Madden said you could stay. He says you're one of the few around here he could trust." He slung his rifle strap over his shoulder. "But first I have to get you a flak jacket and a protective headpiece."

. . .

The man in the Manhattan apartment fixed his eyes on the monitor as his tobacco-stained fingers typed out the message on the keyboard in front of him. He was brief and to the point: *As soon as our man can verify number two is in position, he will pull the plug.*

He leaned back in the chair and tapped out his last cigarette, and then tossed the wadded-up pack in the direction of the wastebasket. It had been a harrowing several hours after the mix-up at the state dinner, but now Central's back-up plan was ready to be implemented. With Winslet out of the way, there would be nothing to stop Savage and Delstrotto. Lighting the cigarette tip with his butane lighter, he sucked in a well-deserved drag, letting the smoke leak from his nose as the jolt of nicotine coursed through his veins.

His concentration broken by the familiar chime, he reached for his cellular telephone. Waiting for the second ring, he recognized Delstrotto's number as it flashed before him on the LED. "Yes," he slipped out, a smile breaking across his lips.

When he heard what Delstrotto told him, he fell forward in his chair, his mouth open in disbelief. His freshly lit cigarette tumbled to the carpeted floor below, the red-hot embers burning into the unprotected pile. A small plume of smoke began to drift upward. In his haste, he did not notice it, because he only stopped long enough to snare his crumpled jacket off the back of the chair before leaving the Manhattan apartment for the last time.

. . .

After exactly five minutes the telephone on the vice president's desk began to ring. Chad Madden picked it up on the first ring.

The paramedics had arrived seconds before. They began resuscitation procedures on the vice president's lifeless body but saw it was useless. He had shot himself in the mouth. Spattered blood and fragments of Savage's brain coated the bathroom wall like graffiti. They covered Rafer Peters with a sheet until the initial examination by the FBI could be completed.

"The vice president is still in the bathroom," Madden told the man on the phone, looking over at Savage's lifeless body that was now being loaded on the gurney. "He said something about a bad headache, poor vision, and dizzy spells. He told me to tell you to hold tight and he would call you back."

"You're lying," Lynn said.

"He's too sick, he says. He's retching. Believe me, I want him to talk to you." The chief of staff could not control much about this situation, but the one thing he could was access of information. Lynn had no way of checking if Madden were telling the truth.

And remembering Senator Tate's symptoms from when he visited him in the hospital, Madden could only hope Gerald Lynn did too, since Lynn was probably one of those who was responsible for Tate's death. He would have reason to believe Savage was deathly ill—but still alive.

"This is ridiculous. I am going to kill the president if . . ." Lynn paused. "When will he call?"

"Do you want me to ask him?" Madden said, trying to put Lynn off a little longer.

"No!" Lynn's answer came back abruptly. "Just have him call me as soon as he comes out. Tell him he's got two minutes. I don't care if he throws up into the phone."

Lynn's response made Madden chill to the bone. One of the agents thrust a note in front of Madden. "Let me talk to the president!" Madden said forcibly after reading the message.

"No!" the vice president's former aide shot back. "You're not going to trick me."

"Calm down," Madden said, his tension mounting. "We just want to make sure he's still all right. If you've already killed him there's no point in talking."

There was a long silence as Madden listened to the muffled tones on the other end of the line.

"Chad, is that you?" Winslet asked in a hoarse voice.

Madden felt a wave of relief. At least he was alive and seemingly unhurt. Madden nodded to the agents who were standing over him and then again glanced down at the note the agent had given him.

"Mr. President, are you all right?" Madden asked. "We're doing everything possible at our end to resolve your situation."

"Thank you, Chad," Winslet replied, falteringly. "It's pretty scary. I think Lynn means what he says."

"President Winslet." Madden always addressed the commander in chief with that title when he meant for the president to really listen. It had been their code ever since the two first became a team. "My mother always said, cover your ears and get down on the ground if you're ever in danger."

"That's enough!" Lynn blared in Madden's ear. "Get Savage on the telephone. I'm running out of patience."

There was a click on the line as the telephone went dead.

"Do you think he understood what you were trying to tell him?" one of the agents asked.

"I hope so," Madden answered back, looking over the note once again: *We're going in with a stun grenade. Get the president to cover his ears and get down.*

A Secret Service agent entered the room from the hall. He walked over to Madden, who was still seated at Savage's desk. "Sterling Padgett is on the line, waiting for you."

Madden picked up the receiver. Padgett told him that his officers would take over at the vice president's residence, while the Secret Service would be in charge of the White House situation for now.

"The SWAT team has confirmed that Lynn and the president are in the Oval Office. What they can't substantiate is the part about the explosives. So we have to assume he's telling the truth."

"He may not be of much help, but I gave clearance for Doctor Russell to be with the SWAT team when they go in," Madden interjected.

"Why in the hell did you do that?" Padgett shot back. "These guys have trained for years to hone their skills. Russell is an amateur. He could endanger the whole operation."

Madden was in no mood to argue; he had an additional concern. "Padgett, there's an established line of succession to the presidency. Right now, every Secret Service agent in the city is tied up either here or at the White House. I need for you to put your men all over Congressman Jim Rolands, Speaker of the House. Within the next few minutes, he may well become the next president of the United States."

After Madden hung up, the agent picked up the other telephone on Savage's desk and punched in the number. The call was answered immediately.

"The president has been given the instructions," the agent told someone. "We don't know on this end whether he understood. The rest is up to you."

. . .

Russell watched as the SWAT team leader nodded the go-ahead signal to his elite team of ex–Special Forces graduates who gathered just down the hall from the Oval Office, ready to put their lives on the line to save the president. If he was going to be part of the operation, he had to make that same commitment. Russell overheard the leader tell the group that the ultrasound scanning machine brought in by the FBI revealed there were only two occupants of the Oval Office.

"It appears one is sitting on the sofa, presumably the president, and one keeps pacing around the room," he said in a low voice. "That's as close as we can get to an ID." The leader, dressed in full combat gear, pointed to each individual on the team as he moved down the hall, breaking them apart. "Your side will take down Lynn. Keep him from activating his firing mechanism. The stun grenade should give you twenty to thirty seconds. Lynn should not be able to hear you coming because both eardrums will have been perforated."

He then turned to the second group, who had lined up on the other side of the hallway. "You'll cover the president like a blanket. Then I want Doctor Russell trailing in right behind in case the president needs CPR. Remember, if the Doc gets hurt, he's no good to our mission."

Russell grimaced at the SWAT team leader's apparent single-mindedness. His heart raced. He knew that if Lynn was able to detonate his explosives, none of this preparation would matter.

"The main concern is the firing mechanism to Lynn's explosives," the team leader continued, his tone somber but ordered. "If it works by activation trigger, that means Lynn has to push it. That gives us a fifty-fifty chance to rescue the president." He stopped, a look of sadness clouding his eyes. "On the other hand, if the trigger works by a release mechanism, that means all Lynn had to do is let go, and then the stun grenade will be the beginning of the end. Gentlemen, let's take a moment before we . . ." His voice dropped off as they all stood in silence.

. . .

"They're stalling," Gerald Lynn muttered repeatedly as he paced back and forth. "But it won't work. I'll blow the top off this place and then they'll know that we are everywhere." He stopped and spun around, his eyes glaring at Winslet. "No one is beyond our reach, even you. Isn't that right, Mr. President?"

Winslet shuddered. "You must be reasonable," he answered, his suit soaked with sweat. "What will killing both of us and blowing up this office accomplish?"

"You just don't get it, do you?" Lynn shook his head. "The world is about to change. We are at the dawning that historians will write about for centuries to come." He stopped and gestured with the hand that was holding the detonation device. "Unfortunately we won't be around to see it happen. But what a beautiful legacy I will leave!"

. . .

"Ready," the SWAT team leader whispered. The group moved down the corridor to the Oval Office.

Swathed in his flak jacket, helmet, infrared goggles, and armored ear protection, Russell felt like a Star Wars figure, but his weakened knees were barely able to propel him forward. The pneumatic battering ram, which had been brought in from police headquarters downtown, was quietly put in position. Russell had been told that when it was fired it would deliver almost a thousand pounds of pressure against the locking mechanism of the door to the president's office, instantly tearing it from its molding. The only thing keeping the door from flying into the room and injuring the occupants would be the three hinges on the other side.

The group leader and his counterpart on the other team took up their positions on either side of the door. Through his goggles, Russell squinted to see that both of them were holding a stun grenade whose detonation time, according to the SWAT team leader, had been shortened to three seconds. The usual eight seconds would be too long, allowing Lynn time to detonate his device.

The muscles in Russell's chest went taut when the team leader held up his hand signaling they were ready. "Now!" the team leader blurted under his breath as he thrust his hand down.

The blast of the pneumatic battering ram and the cracking sounds of the door disintegrating under the sudden force sent shock waves coursing through Russell's body. Reflexively he jerked back as the door to the Oval Office flew open. Almost instantly came the flash of the two stun grenades as they exploded somewhere inside the Oval Office.

"Stay with me," hissed the SWAT team member just in front of him as the group poured into the smoke-filled room. Not accustomed to operating under the ghostly images of infrared lighting, Russell stumbled into the murky darkness, seeing only the silhouette of the flak jacket in front of him. Lost in the sea of floating images, Russell fought to orient himself when, unexpectedly, he tripped over a pair of outstretched legs lying motionless in the darkness. Choking against the smoke, he pushed away only to feel a sudden tug throwing him sideways. "Over there," the angry voice of the SWAT team leader barked, pointing off to the right.

It was then Russell realized he had mistakenly found Gerald Lynn, whose limp body lay partially propped up against the far wall. He recoiled at the sight of the man, his arms hanging limply at his side, blood streaming out of his nose and both ears. Russell started to turn when the call went out. "He moved!"

Instantly the team assigned to Lynn swarmed over his semiconscious body, grabbing desperately at his flailing extremities. Russell stood paralyzed in horror, watching helplessly as Lynn's left hand grappled weakly at the firing mechanism he held.

He knew Lynn was trying to activate the explosives and blow them all to hell. It would now be only a matter of seconds.

Russell jumped back, almost falling over his own feet as three quick blasts shattered through the smoky darkness. He looked up to see the officer in charge standing silently over Gerald Lynn's bloodied body. A plume of smoke came from the barrel of his still-smoldering AK47.

"I'm not getting a pulse on the president." The shrill voice off to his right shook Russell back to reality. He dove in the direction of the call. Within seconds, he was able to locate the president lying motionless on his stomach on the floor, his hands still clasped tightly against his ears.

"Roll him over," Russell barked as he joined the team assigned to cover the president. He ripped off his goggles and protective ear covers as his fingers groped the fallen president's neck, searching for a pulse. Feeling nothing, Russell ripped open Winslet's shirt and put his ear against Winslet's exposed chest, trying to hear a heartbeat, though the recent blasts had rendered him temporarily deaf. He arched back, raised his tightened fist over his head, and then sent it crashing down, striking the president directly over his sternum. Immediately he leaned forward, grabbed the president by the chin and nose, placed his mouth over Winslet's, and gave two quick breaths.

"Get the paramedics in here," he barked as he started to pump repeatedly on the president's chest. Suddenly Russell drew back as muted groans floated up from the president's mouth.

"What the . . . ?" Winslet mumbled, his slitted eyes searching for the truth.

"You're going to be all right, Mr. President," Russell said, leaning over close to his ear. He rolled away from the fallen president as exhaustion eclipsed the relief he was felt now that the ordeal was over.

A faint smile broke across the president's lips as he looked over at Russell, who now lay eye to eye beside him. "You saved my life."

Russell's heart jumped at the president's words. The recurring image of his mother's anguished face flashed before him. He had been waiting for those words since that tragic late afternoon many years ago. Maybe now his nightmares would be over.

EPILOGUE

IT HAD BEEN ALMOST A WEEK since the horrible chapter in American history had come to a close. President Winslet was evacuated by helicopter to Walter Reed National Military Medical Center immediately after the explosion. Except for a mild concussion and one perforated eardrum, the president had survived the event unscathed. It would be three months until a final determination was made about any permanent hearing loss. For a multitude of reasons, some related to the continuing concern over his security, the presidential stay in the hospital was extended several extra days.

Since there was no conclusive proof of Savage's involvement in the attempted conspiracy, Winslet decided to let the public think the vice president was a hero. According to the official White House press release citing the Secret Service agent on the scene, Savage, trying to defend the president's chief of staff, took a bullet to the skull before the agent had a chance to put an end to Rafer Peter's rampage. The vice president was given credit for saving Chad Madden's life, and the entire administration attended his funeral at the National Cathedral and burial in Arlington National Cemetery.

Although Kenneth Trainer had been charged with the death of Jason Clark, according to the authorities his chances of conviction were considered slim to none. Strangely enough, he disappeared almost immediately after his release. Even his lawyer claimed he did not know where his client had gone. If Trainer did not appear in another forty-eight hours, the $200,000 in bond money—put up by an unknown benefactor to assure his release—would be forfeited.

The news of the attempted assassination of the president and Savage's abrupt death spread over the nation, obliterating all other stories. Unfortunately "Central" had done its job well, wiping out all traces of any connection between the three vice presidential aides and any outside party. The whole matter was dumped into the lap of the FBI. But with two of the three leading suspects dead and the other missing, the investigation was at an impasse. Even the press, unrelenting in its efforts to get at the real truth, was stymied. So as with such stories, even one of this magnitude, they began to move on, leaving only the conspiracy theorists to fan the flames of public interest.

. . .

"You weren't serious about that transfer, were you?" Madden could hear the uncertainty in his voice as he poured Jennifer a second glass of wine.

Jennifer looked up into Madden's face. His features were muted in the dim light of the restaurant. "I've got nothing to keep me here." Her finger rimmed the glass of freshly poured Cabernet. "Maybe I should say no one."

"I've worked out a deal with Winslet, if he still wants me to stay on for the remainder of his second term," he said, reaching over and resting his hand on hers. "As soon as he's back in the Oval Office, there're going to be times when he has to run this presidency without me. I want to step back and just advise. Somebody else can run things day to day."

Jennifer's expression softened. "And what exactly do you plan to do with your free time?"

"I guess that's up to you."

. . .

"I thought I might find you here," Carver Whipple said as he pushed open the door to the trauma room where Vice President Rosalyn Delstrotto had fought her losing battle for life. "Don't like parties?"

Dan Russell nodded and looked back at the table, bathed in the gentle glow of background light, where he had tried to resuscitate the nation's second-highest-ranking elected official. "Something like that." As had happened often in the last days, his mind wandered back to an earlier time, recalling that rain-swept highway where he sat with his dying mother in his arms.

"Me neither," Whipple returned. "But the staff wanted to do something to show you their appreciation." He shook his head. "Hell, you're a bona fide hero. Even your girlfriend seems to have forgiven you for running off to Washington and leaving her here."

Russell grinned. "I'm afraid I have a little more making up to do before that's true."

"Let me ask you something." Whipple fingered the handle on the door. "Why did you do it?" he asked. "Put all this on the line—your job, your girlfriend—for what?"

Russell squinted in the semi-lit room and turned toward his colleague. "I hoped it would help me sleep better at night."

. . .

The president sent for his chief of staff from his hospital suite at Walter Reed. It was close to 7:30 p.m. by the time Chad Madden finally arrived at the president's suite. Madden, trying to get by on five hours of sleep a night, looked ten years older than he was. In spite of his promise to Jennifer the night before, he had been up since four o'clock that morning.

"You look a little drawn, Chad," Winslet said, noticing Madden's growing fatigue. "Give me a couple more weeks to let things even out around here. Then you need to take a long vacation. Think you can hold out?"

Madden squinted and slumped down in the chair beside Winslet's bed. "I've managed it for the last four years, Mr. President. I should be able to handle a few more weeks."

The president nodded, barely acknowledging Madden's last remark. "Chad, I need to pick a vice president. The last time we didn't do a very good job. I've been running over a list of possibilities," he continued, forcing a smile. "No FBI files yet, though. Rolands was here yesterday to check on me. I asked him if he would accept the position, but he wants to stay where he is. I can't say I blame him. The Speaker of the House is a very powerful position."

"Do you want me to reactivate the old list, Mr. President?"

"No, Chad," the president answered, his tone somber. "Lying here in this hospital bed has given me a lot of time to think. We need someone the public can trust. Someone who doesn't have any skeletons in the closet—and with no burning personal agenda other than supporting this administration."

"You mean like Rosie?"

The president turned to his chief of staff. Madden could see the answer in his face. "Chad, could you give Ben Delstrotto a call? He's probably still at Number One Observatory Circle. See if he can come over for a visit?"

CHARACTERS

Raymond Winslet	President of the United States
Sharon Winslet	President's wife
Rosalyn "Rosie" Delstrotto	Vice President of the United States
Benjamin Delstrotto	Vice President's husband
Jonathan Savage	Senator from Maryland, vice president upon death of Rosie Delstrotto
Dan Russell, MD	Emergency-room physician at Irving Central
Cindy French	Dan Russell's girlfriend
Carver Whipple, MD	Dan Russell's boss
Britt Barkley	Irving Central's chief executive officer
Chad Madden	Chief of staff to the president
Jason Clark	Vice president's chief of staff

Insurrection at 1600 Pennsylvania Ave.

Letha Sims	Administrative assistant to President Winslet
Kenneth Bradford Trainer	Aide to Vice President Savage, code name T.
Rafer Peters	Aide to Vice President Savage
Gerald Lynn	Aide to Vice President Savage
Andrea Levin	Assistant to Senator Savage
Marty Davenport	White House press secretary
Godfrey Thornhill	Secretary of State
James L. Rolands	Congressman from North Dakota, Speaker of the House of Representatives (next in line for the presidency after the president and vice president)
Harrison Tate	Senator from Colorado, majority leader of the Senate
Howard Lee	Senator from California, conservative Republican
Derek Stanton	Chairman, governing board of party
Sterling B. Padgett	Assistant director of the FBI

Jennifer Smitt	Employee at the FBI, former girlfriend of Chad Madden
General Clayton Spivy	Commander of Andrews Air Force Base
John Arnold	Secretary of the Army
General Laura Briggs, MD	Chief executive officer, Walter Reed National Military Medical Center
Clayton Thomas, MD	Pathologist at Georgetown Medical Center
Lt. Colonel Weldon West, MD	Pathologist at Walter Reed National Military Medical Center
Sam Gunn	Pathology technician at Walter Reed National Military Medical Center
Lowell D. McCarty, MD	Vice chairman, Department of Internal Medicine, Georgetown University
Jed Willerson, MD	Toxicology Department at Georgetown Medical School
Joel Cornish, MD	Director of the Centers for Disease Control and Prevention

Insurrection at 1600 Pennsylvania Ave.

Leonard Palmer	Friend of Senator Tate from Colorado
Stanford Melton	Acquaintance of Leonard Palmer
Ambassador Rasheed	Ambassador to the United States from Kuwait
Mario Galvez	President of Argentina
Selma Galvez	Wife of the president of Argentina
Lucky Brown	Aging White House security guard
Buttons	White House chief of security
Jim Bilkos (aka Alkos Parum)	White House cook
Cleve Barber	White House head chef

ABOUT THE AUTHOR

Photograph by: J. L. Hutchins

Rob Tenery, MD, is an ophthalmologist who first began his writing career when he authored commentaries dealing with current events that were impacting the health care profession. His expertise acquired from representing medical organizations on the local, state, and national levels led him to become a monthly contributor to the nationally distributed periodical *American Medical News* from 1990–1998.

It was toward the end of his tenure that he decided to put to paper a more comprehensive look at the evolution of his chosen profession, resulting in the publication of his first book, *Dr. Mayo's Boy: A Century of American Medicine*. He then followed with his second and third books, *In Search of Medicine's Moral Compass* and *Bedside Manners*. Both chronicle the delivery of health care in this country from its inception and the increasingly complex evolution of those who deliver care as they act as advocates for their patients.

Marrying his high school sweetheart, Janet, was the impetus for his fourth book, *Chasing the Ponytail*—a coming-of-age love story set in the 1950s and early 1960s as they grew up together in Waxahachie, Texas, and were in a relationship through their college years.

Having a keen interest in the uncertainty on the world stage, Dr. Tenery's latest novel, *Insurrection at 1600 Pennsylvania Avenue*, combines his experience in medicine with political intrigue, resulting in a scenario this country could face in the near future.

Rob and Janet have two children and four grandchildren. He continues to practice ophthalmology while writing weekly posts for his blog, *Diagnosis for Democracy: Insights into the State of Our Union,* and is working on his next novel.